Reviews for Patricia Perry

"Two and a half centuries have passed since the explosive events brought to life in Patricia Perry's hugely enjoyable first novel *Quest for the Source of Darkness* took place. Now her much-anticipated novel and sequel, *The Fortress of Darkness*, draws the reader back into the magical realm of her imagination. Lock your doors, light the candles and lose yourself in the world of Patricia Perry."

Brian R. Hill—author of *The Shintae*

"Pat Perry's *The Fortress of Darkness* is a fantasy novel with heart. Perry writes a world that begs to be explored, one page at a time."

Steven Manchester—author of *Pressed Pennies*

The Fortress of Darkness

By Patricia Perry

PublishAmerica
Baltimore

© 2007 by Patricia Perry.
All rights reserved. No part of this book may be reproduced, stored in a retrieval system or transmitted in any form or by any means without the prior written permission of the publishers, except by a reviewer who may quote brief passages in a review to be printed in a newspaper, magazine or journal.

First printing

All characters appearing in this work are fictitious. Any resemblance to real persons, living or dead, is purely coincidental.

At the specific preference of the author, PublishAmerica allowed this work to remain exactly as the author intended, verbatim, without editorial input.

Cover art by Lynnette Torres
torris@rcn.com

Back cover photo by Pamela

Visit the author's web site: www.questforthesourceofdarkness.com

ISBN: 1-4241-8097-X
PUBLISHED BY PUBLISHAMERICA, LLLP
www.publishamerica.com
Baltimore

Printed in the United States of America

*This book is dedicated to Stephen Langley
and Danielle Soares, two special souls taken too soon.*

Special thanks go to Patty Ellis, Jerine Watson, Darcie Roy and Ann Souza for all their invaluable help, technical support, patience and guidance.

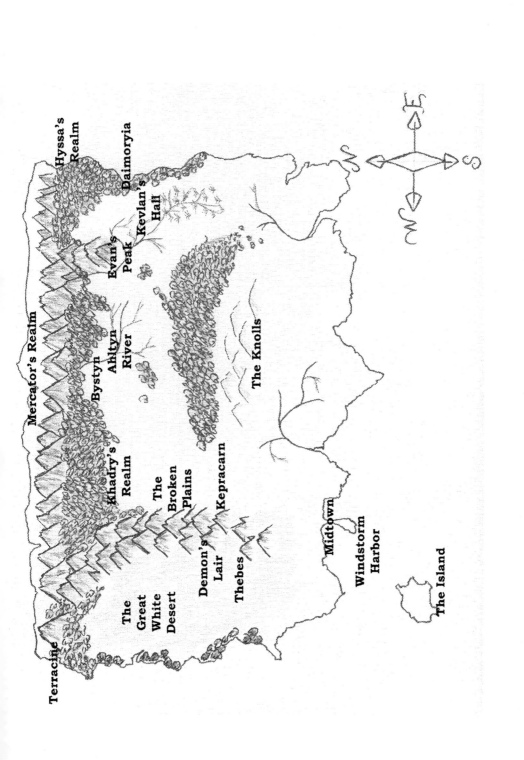

Prologue

The Lady of the Sands stood upon a dune facing east, her diaphanous gown gently swirling in the soft breeze. Her pale skin was tight around her mouth and dark eyes. The scent of ozone filled her nostrils as she sensed the ominous approach of a storm in the growing cloudbank on the horizon. She had dreaded this moment.

More than two hundred and fifty years had passed since the elf Prince Danyl had vanquished the demon Mahn in front of Bystyn's walls, but remnants of Mahn's evil power still existed, like the remembered undertow of a deadly tide.

The Vox who now occupied Allad's body collected every shred of Mahn's dark magic, combining it with its own brand of malevolence to forge a new variety of power. This Vox' name was Emhella. His plan to rule the land differed from the one Mahn had conceived. Emhella had decided to assemble the magic in the land by himself and not by leading an unwieldy and unpredictable army of mortals. However, he had to wait for the bearers of the Green Might and the Source of Darkness to die before he could take those powers. The magic had extended their lives but they were still mortal.

Danyl and Ramira had settled in a small cabin near the city where they had one son named Tarat. Danyl passed away first, his body brought back and interred in the family crypt beneath the castle in the city. Emhella could not penetrate Ramira's magic to take the Green Might because the Source served as a buffer against any evil power. He did manage to capture the Source of Darkness upon her death, but the Green Might had already vanished by that time.

The Races had retained their alliances for nearly a hundred years after the great battle but the ties that bound them finally loosened, unraveled, and then broke. Styph ruled the elves for more than a dozen years before dying of an infection. His sister, Alyssa, took the throne becoming the first of many queens to rule the elves. She continued to distrust King Cooper and soon ceased sending emissaries to Kepracarn, officially severing that link. Seven and Clare regrettably had no children, thus the kingship passed on to various dwarves who ruled poorly and made many unwise decisions. The worst choice concerned the Rock Lords who launched numerous attacks against the dwarves at Evan's Peak. Some of the Forest Elves integrated with the city elves while the rest returned to their woods and subsequently disappeared without a trace. The Herkahs retreated back into the Great White Desert where Zada gave birth to a son conceived the last night she and Allad had shared together. She stayed with the Tribe for a year before venturing forth to search for Allad and release him from his terrible imprisonment by the Vox. She died never having been able to fulfill her promise.

King Cooper did honor his vow to avoid killing any more Herkahs. He shifted his focus to the southwest and began to trade actively with the people living on the peninsula and the island. His fortunes and influence grew until he was involved in everything in the southwest region. Cooper's relationship with his brother Mason and sister Sophie remained cool and not even their deaths could bring him back to Bystyn.

The terrible lessons of the past were lost on the living but they would be the ones to pay the price.

-1-

    The milling crowd began to swell, drawn by the drama-taking place in the middle of the street. The scowls, sneers and cruel words were flung at the elves along with the rotting fruits and vegetables they picked out of refuse bins. A ring of men, sticks and whips in their hands, surrounded two battered and bruised elves. The elves raised their bloodied arms to ward off the missiles but there was nothing they could do to block out the callous insults. One of the men at the edge of the circle held three leashes in his hand, the large dogs at the ends growling as they strained to reach the elves. The mongrels pulled the man forward, his smirk revealing blunt, crooked teeth the color of mud. He spat on the ground, the spittle slowly sinking into the hard dirt.

    "I oughta let these rascals loose on you!" he yelled, the late morning sun casting his shadow across the prone elf.

    "Hey!" One of the man's companions walked over to the elf kneeling on the ground. He had one lacerated hand on his thigh with the other spread out on the ground. The welt around his right eye distorted his features but it could not extinguish the fear on his face. The man kicked him in the side and laughed as the elf fell forward with a painful thud. The heckler slammed his stick across the elf's back then stepped to the side as another man flicked a whip at his leg.

    "Get up and run or I'll unleash these curs," he hissed at the elf, grabbing him by the front of his filthy tunic and yanking him to his feet.

* * *

August sauntered along the wooden sidewalk fronting the shops for many blocks along the avenue, the sloping tin roofs providing some shelter from the blazing sun. August peered into the nearest store, the dust from the street drifting in and settling on sacks of flour and sugar stacked near the door. Light filtered in through the dingy window facing the avenue. A defiant rat scurried beneath a row of shelves lured by a slowly growing pile of corn meal. He stuck his hand into his sagging pouch, pursed his lips and walked on. He ran his fingers through his black hair, his ebony eyes scrutinizing the crowd of people jammed together along the main street. It was difficult to see anything. He peeked between the shoulders and heads of those lining the street and immediately regretted doing so. He struggled to retain a stoic expression but what the men were doing to the elves was appalling. He cringed as they beat the poor victim, the desire to rush over and slice them open nearly overwhelming him. The bile began to rise in his throat, collecting in his mouth until he spit the feeling of powerlessness and disgust onto the worn walkway.

The elf glanced warily around then looked over at his friend. The taller elf stared back then subtly nodded in agreement. The throng cheered and waved their arms, encouraging the release of the dogs, and then let out a deafening roar of approval the moment the elf sprinted away. He began to run as fast as his exhausted body could go, the surge of adrenaline bringing him toward a line of trees and brush about a quarter of a mile ahead. He sprinted into the thicket, ignoring the branches and thorns tearing at his skin and clothing. The sweat pouring down his face aggravated the scrapes, but he had no time to worry about them. He had to run. He had to get away and report what had happened. The barking and shouting echoed behind him in the woods. The crashing sounds increased, as did the dog's howling. He glanced over his shoulder and saw the shadowy forms closing the distance between them, his own strangled cry of fear barely audible in his own ears.

August watched the long-legged elf flee. He knew the being's short-lived spurt of energy wouldn't take him very far, leaving him vulnerable to what these men had in mind. The elf headed for the trees and the second he disappeared into them, the men released the dogs, mounted their horses and dashed after him. August clenched his jaw, the muscles bulging against his tanned skin. It took a great deal of willpower to keep the hatred off his face. He held his breath as the minutes ticked by, then closed his eyes as the screams of a dying man reverberated back to the town. The grisly sound elicited shouts of approval from the throng that had gathered to watch the offensive spectacle. He glanced over at the remaining elf, who stood immobile, his gaze riveted to the place where his companion had run. August scanned the crowd for anyone who showed the slightest inclination to help the elf. He saw women wearing faded gingham dresses raise their hands up to shield their eyes, women whose cloying perfumes failed to mask their unpleasant body odor. Men clothed in sleeveless woolen tunics and homespun trousers exchanged handfuls of coins. Children sat on the walkway laughing and swinging their legs back and forth. August took a deep breath then exhaled slowly as the men turned their attention to the remaining elf. He discerned the growing bloodlust in the crowd.

The elf scrutinized the crowd, pausing briefly on August's strong figure. The elf noticed the man with the dark hair and even darker expression. *Perhaps there will be a witness after all*, he thought.

"Run!" shouted one of the antagonists flicking his whip near the elf's head.

August couldn't understand why the elf took off on a dead run toward the same trees where his friend had been killed. Didn't he realize the men and dogs were already there? What was he trying to do? August couldn't believe what he was seeing. The elf bolted into the woods, heedless of the death awaiting him. He had had enough and walked back the way he had come before this travesty began. The crowd became restless then bored as the sound they longed to hear never traveled to their ears. August crossed the dusty street, ignoring the horsemen racing back to the town as he headed for the city on the peninsula to the south.

* * *

Windstorm Harbor was bustling with activity when August stepped onto the quay less than an hour later. Several boats laden with merchandise were tied up alongside the passenger schooner on the main wharf. Buyers poked through crates filled with goods; families came to pick up their loved ones and workers arrived in droves.

August crossed his arms and leaned against a barrel of rum at the end of the pier. He watched five burly men grab the lines and tie them to the stanchions before shoving the gangplank into place. The voyagers streamed off the boat even before the platform was secure and received more than one crass comment from the workmen for their impatience. The travelers meandered around crates of wares, carts of edibles and casks of oil and wine, waving at friends and family waiting for them. August pushed a section of his hair away from his forehead, his black eyes searching the crowd for his friend, Clay.

A flock of gulls circled overhead, their beady eyes taking inventory of whatever lay exposed on the docks. They swooped defiantly over the boxes of fish and other edibles, stealing at will while ignoring the brooms wielded by the angry vendors. They fought each other for every scrap, the loser squawking loudly at the winner. August ducked under a pile of lumber when a gang of children chased the scavengers away. He spotted a broadly smiling Clay in the middle of the throng. August shook his head and grinned back at his friend: his peace and quiet was now gone.

Clay strode confidently toward August, his faded green cap tilted jauntily on top of his light brown hair. His green eyes examined everything in sight. He picked his way through the crowd, his lean frame weaving along without ever touching anyone or anything. He stopped in front of August, dropped his satchel and slapped his friend on the back.

"Augie! I've missed you!"

"I've longed for you, too," August muttered good-naturedly. "How was your trip?"

"Good. You should come with me next time."

August eyed the creaking vessel and wrinkled his nose at the odors emanating from it and from some of the passengers tramping by. Not far away, he could hear a mother shushing her screaming children as their father yelled at her to control them. He glanced out beyond the harbor, absently rubbing his stomach at the waves breaking violently against the breakwater.

"Not for all the riches in the land."

"You don't know what you're missing, Augie. You don't like the water, do you?"

"I like it in a glass."

Clay grinned at his friend and picked up his pack. They walked along the well-worn cobble-stoned street up the hill into the heart of the city where markets jammed every available spot. They squeezed past carts laden with fish, vegetables, cookware, herbs and hundreds of other items from the mainland and the island. Women haggled with vendors over prices and traders argued loudly with buyers. It was chaotic bedlam but everyone enjoyed the custom of bargaining. The friends sidestepped two drunks swaying unsteadily on their feet as they left a tavern, then August shooed away a group of children looking for handouts. Clay and August watched the little thieves pick the pockets of the inebriated men who were too intoxicated to give chase.

They walked a few more blocks then turned down a narrow alley and entered the White Sails Tavern. The place was dingy and filled with smoke, the food was the best in town. The serving wenches wore low cut bodices and were more than willing to bend over for the customer who tossed an extra coin their way. They searched for a place to sit through the smoke and shifting bodies. Clay and August found a table at the rear of the tavern and Clay placed his sack between his feet then leaned forward on his elbows.

"Fish stew, sausages and potatoes, or boiled bacon?" asked the server. She placed two mugs of ale in front of them and waited for their reply.

"Two stews," replied Clay looking around to see who else was in port as the serving wench walked away, swinging her plump hips provocatively.

"Thumbless Tom disappeared a few nights ago," said August, lifting up his tankard of ale. "I guess he won't be borrowing any more silver from anybody."

"I'm surprised he stayed alive as long as he did." Clay looked over at August, whose grave expression puzzled him. "What?"

"The Midtowners used a couple of elves for sport. They chased them with dogs into the woods."

"When?"

"About two, maybe three hours ago."

Clay's face took on an ashen cast. He sipped his ale in silence, his gaze fixed on August. The saucy young woman brought a tray of food, placing bowls of stew in front of them and a platter of bread and cheese in the middle of the table. She winked at Clay before heading over to a nearby table filled with empty plates and overturned bowls. Clay picked up his spoon, scraped the dried residue off with a fingernail and began to eat.

August spoke in low tones, careful no one in the pub could overhear him. "Something has spooked the locals and now they are paying more attention to every stranger in town." He raised his eyebrows as he lifted a spoonful of the spicy stew to his lips.

"You and I are not 'strangers', Augie."

"Aren't we?"

The locals were a mish mash of individuals, some highly educated and rich and others with very little schooling and indigent. They all, however, shared an uncanny ability to remember faces. Failure to do so left them open to being cheated more than once by the same person. Many had seen Clay and August over the years but few knew their names. Clay finished his meal and waved the serving wench over to refill their mugs, then looked out the windows as the afternoon shadows lengthened. August knew they had to leave as soon as possible. It wasn't safe to travel the main road off the peninsula during the night and, even if they left right away, they would only make it a third of the way out by nightfall.

Clay swigged down the last of his ale. "Are the horses at Calla's?"

August nodded. "We'll go there and stay the night."

They paid for their meal and departed the tavern, winding their way up to the main road and heading west toward the outskirts of town. They reached a collection of barns surrounding an old house as the sun's dying rays stained the land and sea in brilliant shades of vermilion. Clay knocked on the door. A heavy woman with shrewd features opened the door and smiled.

"Well, well, well. Look what the southern winds blew in!"

"Evening, Calla," Clay greeted the woman, carefully lifting the brim of his cap.

"You boys gonna sleep here tonight?"

"If you don't mind."

"Not at all. A couple of spare coins should suffice. I didn't know if you wanted silk or linen sheets so I took the liberty of covering the mattresses with my own, personal finest bedding." She jerked her head toward the back of the house, grabbing Clay's tunic as he walked by with one hand and holding her other out to him. He fished around in his pockets and dropped some change into her palm. She smiled revealing a mouth full of blunt teeth and released his shirt.

"Sleep tight, boys."

They walked to the end of the short hall and entered the room on the left. August lit the lamps while Clay started a fire in the blackened stove in the corner. The days were warm but the ocean's damp chill made even the hardiest soul shiver. They looked at the miserable room and shook their heads in disgust. The discolored mattresses were rolled up at the foot of the beds, exposing the bed's rusting springs. Clay pulled out pieces of straw and dingy bits of fluff from the numerous tears in the mattresses and held them up for August to see.

August ran his hand over the sheets that had been tossed with little regard onto the springs.

"What does she use to wash these things in? They feel like a barnacle-covered rock!"

"She washes them?"

"That is not something I want to think about as I curl up for the night," August mumbled.

"The bedding is the least of your worries," replied Clay stepping on a multi-legged insect trying to scurry away.

"I hope the bedbugs aren't as big."

"That *was* a bedbug."

They pushed chairs closer to the stove to escape the raw air seeping into the room. Burlap bags stamped with faded black letters hung awkwardly from rusty nails across the top of the windows. The draft moved the heavy material back and forth. Clay accepted the flask August took out of his pouch, swallowed a mouthful of the amber liquid and shuddered, his lips pulling back as he noisily inhaled through his teeth. He took another swig and handed the bottle back.

"Where did you get that?"

"I traded for it a few weeks back," replied August. "Good, huh?"

Clay wiped the tears from his cheeks and stared into the fire. He had been traveling with August ever since they were children. There had been plenty of adventures but never a place to go home to. August seemed to be content living in the desert when they were apart but Clay felt restless no matter where he went. Clay removed his cap and hung it on the arm of the chair then ran his fingers through his hair until it was completely disheveled. He smoothed it down as best as he could then tucked it behind his ears.

"Those are going to get you into trouble some day," said August, glancing at Clay's elegantly pointed ears.

"So are you."

"Clay, why don't you just go there and find out about your family?" he stated, the pensive look on his friends' face one he knew all too well.

"It's too far away."

"So is the island, yet you make many trips there."

"That's different…"

"You aren't going to find the answers you need on the island."

"I hate it when you're right," Clay said after a long silence, blowing out the lamps before resuming his place in front of the fire.

They propped their feet up on stools, preferring the uncomfortable chairs to the musty bed teeming with vermin. They ignored the tiny scuffing sounds across the worn wooden floor and drifted off to sleep, but ever alert for noises made by those who walked on two feet.

* * *

They awoke at dawn; the drab light flowing in the window proof it was going to stay foggy until at least noon. Clay arranged his hair over his ears then put the cap on his head, glancing out the window one last time. The road north would be enshrouded for many miles before they escaped the ocean's hold over the weather. Bandits loved hiding in the fog. They slung their packs over their shoulders and walked into the small eating area of the cottage. Small loaves of still steaming bread, hard-boiled eggs, sliced ham and mugs of tea awaited them at one of the tables near the front window. Calla couldn't clean to save her life but her cooking was legendary. She stood in front of the table wiping her hands on her soiled apron and smiled, the sight of her teeth threatening to steal their appetites.

"Morning boys! Up for some breakfast?" Her outstretched palm was inches from Clay's chest. She inclined her head in thanks and closed her fingers over the pieces of silver.

Clay and August filled their stomachs then stashed the rest of the food into their satchels, which already held provisions they had purchased in the city. They had enough supplies for at least a week. Clay looked questioningly at August, who shrugged and nodded his head.

"Calla! We'd like to say good-bye to your palm, if you don't mind. Calla?"

"That's not like her, Clay. She moves pretty quickly when it comes to..."

Clay peered through the tattered curtains, a curious August pulling back the corner of the drape beside him. Calla was talking to a group of men, occasionally pointing toward the house. They exchanged a few more words then the strangers mounted their horses and sped away. Clay and August pretended to take stock of their equipment as Calla came back inside. She smoothed her grubby apron with nervous fingers and offered them a weak smile.

"Bounty boys...hunting for those pointy-eared fiends. Just the thought of those devils running around here makes me nervous. Now, you owe me..."

Clay took her hand and dropped the money into her palm, touched the brim of his cap and walked out into the misty morning right behind August. Neither one spoke a word as they headed for the barn but both were tense and watchful for any signs of danger. They saddled up their sleek black horses and led them out of the stable, jumping on their backs in one fluid motion. August glanced toward the house just in time to see the drape falling back into place.

"I think Calla has traded us in for some new friends." He spurred his mount into a gentle trot to the main road.

"Let's go." Clay egged his steed on, moving it into a graceful lope, the moisture in the air dampening the flopping manes. The scent of pine and cedar was redolent in the early morning air.

They rode in comfortable but wary silence, unmolested for several miles, grateful the sun was finally burning away the fog. They remained vigilant, especially near the section of the road marking the boundary at the top of the headland. The area here was very narrow, no more than a mile or so across, and the only way through was to pass by way of an outpost just to the south of Midtown. It blocked the route and no one passed without paying a duty, even if you had no goods to declare. There was no way to avoid it for giant boulders stretched from each side of the gate to the water and guards patrolled the complex. There were two lines waiting to get through the gate: the one on the right for wagonloads of goods and the one on the left for travelers without merchandise. Clay and August were relieved their waiting time was short.

"Ten silver each," said the guard, writing down the amount in his ledger. The sentry glanced briefly at the two men while they counted out the coins. Another guard standing several feet away narrowed his eyes at the pair then mumbled something into the sentry's ear after he had taken the money and waved them on.

Clay and August rode nonchalantly into Midtown, making their way through the settlement. The rhythmic striking of a hammer on an anvil rang out and the smell of well-seasoned meats emanated from the kitchens of many inns. Stores proffered everything from nails to livestock. From a second floor balcony, scantily clad young women beckoned seductively. August shook his head at Clay who grinned broadly as one of the women blew him a kiss. A commotion growing steadily louder behind them got their attention. As they twisted around in their saddles, they saw dozens of men galloping up the road, weapons drawn and ignoring the people dodging out of their way. Clay's stomach began to sink.

"Augie, you don't think they're after us, do you?"

"Head north to the desert!"

The two of them leaned low against their steeds' muscular necks, daring to glance backward at their pursuers for seconds at a time. Their swift horses increased their lead, their lengthy strides bringing them closer and closer to the edge of the town. Shops and storefronts blurred together as they sped by; people stared, some shouted encouragement to the men chasing them. A few blocks separated them from the open plains and freedom. A movement in between the alleyways caught August's attention. He focused on the next side street as they rode by it then cursed under his breath.

"Clay! They're going to try and cut us off up ahead!"

"Keep riding!"

They let go of the reins and pulled out their weapons; their knees gripping their mounts. The well-trained horses acknowledged their masters' shifting in the saddle, lowering their heads even more and increasing their speed. They approached the last of the buildings and saw the two bands of men converge on them. The leading riders attempted to stop the fleeing pair and immediately regretted their decision. August swung at his attackers with the razor sharp blades of his swords, slicing through flesh and bone with minimal effort. Clay checked a blow from a third assailant with a pair of daggers then stabbed the man's shoulder. Blood gushed from the deep wound and the attacker fell from his horse onto the rocky ground. Clay and August spurred their horses onward, rushing out onto the plains and toward the Great White Desert shimmering brightly on the horizon.

They reined in their steeds about an hour later, after having put many miles between themselves and the outpost. They sought shelter from the afternoon heat beneath a clump of broad-leafed trees, a cool stream winding near their roots. They rubbed down the horses then let them graze freely on the thick grasses. The friends sat down close to the edge of the copse, keeping an eye out for any signs of danger. Clay studied his lifelong friend, noting the lines of uneasiness visible on his face. The blatant killing of elves and Calla's willingness to turn them in made both of them even more apprehensive.

"What happened while I was gone?" Clay rested his arms on one knee, his brow furrowed in concentration.

"Several unpleasant situations," August replied, plucking blades of grass from the ground.

"Tell me."

"Four elves have been found in this area and all of them have been slain. No one knows why they have ventured to this part of the land but then again no one bothered to ask them, either. I've seen the Dark Clan in the desert riding at night on top of the dunes. And…" He hesitated.

"And what?" Clay gently urged him, wiping away the perspiration on his forehead. The Dark Clan kept to themselves, yet he did not doubt that August had seen something in the darkness.

"I've seen a hooded and cloaked figure standing motionless near the edge of the desert. I remember one very quiet night in particular. The full moon illuminated the shape and I watched as it fell to its knees and dropped its head to its chest. I could have sworn I heard it…weep."

"A woman?"

"Perhaps, it was hard to tell."

Clay thought about the dream infiltrating his sleep of late, the vague image confusing no matter how many times he saw it. He dreamt of a cottage surrounded by trees, brush and thorns; the porch sagged, the steps splintered and rotten. Branches had broken through the windows; the once white paint had peeled away revealing weather beaten gray planks. Something indistinguishable moved within the decaying cabin, taunting him with its obscurity.

"What do you suggest we do, Augie?"

"We can't go back to the harbor and it'll only be a matter of time before Kepracarn hears about us. Now might be a good time to look into your roots."

"What makes you think the elves will welcome us?"

"Your pretty ears?"

"Very funny," he replied throwing a clump of dirt at his friend.

"What's the worst that can happen? They slam the door in our faces?"

"I guess we could get close enough to check things out."

"It's settled, then. We'll journey north of Kepracarn then follow the forest eastward."

They mounted up and headed north, careful to avoid the clusters of farms bordering Kepracarn to the west. Their path brought them to the edge of the desert, the setting sun transforming the sands from white into yellows then reds. The wind began to blow across the dunes, sending gyrating columns of sand into the deepening night sky. The hues took on shades of purples and blues the darker it became then, as the last of the light retreated, left a sea of silver in its wake. The swollen moon hung so low on the horizon Clay thought he could reach up and touch it.

Clay and August removed the saddles and bridles and let the horses loose. The animals never ventured far. Clay stared at the majestic pair, recalling the first time he had seen them. He and August had been walking not too far from their present location when they had spotted the pair of horses off in the distance. They had thought about trying to capture them then laughed at themselves for even thinking about attempting such a daunting task. They walked on and noticed the animals were paralleling their course, moving closer and closer toward them. Intrigued by their strange action, the friends stopped and watched the horses shake their heads and nuzzle each other as if in conversation. They were transfixed, unable to move as the animals trotted over to them, each horse seeming to choose one of the men. The mare grabbed Clay's cap and cantered off a few paces, daring him to chase her. He called her 'Essa' after the blue-black, velvety flowers on the island. August named the stallion 'Tauth' simply because, after calling him several other names, the horse responded to that one. Thieves and strangers had tried to steal the animals, quickly realizing their error in judgment. The horses lashed out at the robbers, biting and kicking them furiously. He had no idea where the horses had come from but appreciated their loyalty and their company.

"Here," August handed Clay a bowl of broth and a slab of bread. He poured some of the golden, steaming soup into a bowl for himself and hung the small pot back over the glowing coal.

"You had a good idea, Augie. We've spent so much time wandering in the southwest we forgot about any opportunities that might exist elsewhere."

"Maybe Calla did us a favor."

"Perhaps," he admitted then finished the rest of his meal.

Clay leaned back on his blanket, resting his head against his saddle and staring up at the star-encrusted sky. He noticed the moon's pockmarked features had diminished somewhat but it still dominated the heavens. He watched August smother the ember with the remainder of the broth then place the charred lump on top of the overturned pot to dry.

August flopped back onto his blankets, sighing with contentment as his body made contact with the sand. It had been a long day for them both.

"Sleep well, Clay."

"You, too." Clay pulled his cap down over his eyes.

August rested his head in the cradle of his interlaced fingers and looked up into the night. His thoughts went back over the years he had known Clay. The two of them had been friends their whole lives. They had both been dropped off on a farm just to the east of the Broken Plains as infants. They knew nothing of their families or who had taken them there. The homesteader and his wife, who already had five children of their own, gave them food and shelter. The oldest two, a tall, brown-haired boy covered in freckles named Max and a redheaded girl with big feet named Hally, were very jealous of the two of them. The siblings blamed Clay and August for everything, including their own misdeeds and laziness. Max and Hally plotted the worst offense in their parents' eyes. Hally sneaked into the boys' shared bed and Max 'discovered' the unforgivable transgression. He yelled out and the farmer came running, then hit the boys with a switch as they desperately tried to explain what they could not understand. The man worked them harder than ever afterward, much to the fiendish delight of Max and Hally. August couldn't help but grin, for as much as Max and Hally hated them, they loathed having to work even more. Well, they ended up with their own chores plus they had to share in the ones he and Clay left behind. He and Clay departed the farm when they reached adolescence, seeking their fortunes in the southwestern corner of the land. Clay had discovered

Windstorm Harbor and the island; August gravitated toward the desert. That was nearly ten years ago.

Augusts' lids slowly drooped then closed, the events of the past few days stealing away the last of his conscious energy.

* * *

The elf brought his arms up too late. He felt his cap being jerked off his head and Essa's impatient hoof pounding the dirt. He opened his eyes and stared at the animal nickering in his face, his hat dangling from her teeth. Clay patted the mare's nose but she would not relinquish his cap until he stood up.

August was already awake and packed, sitting with his elbows resting on his knees grinning broadly at him. "You sleep as long as the rich folks in Windstorm." He handed Clay a cup of tea.

Clay sipped his tea, stretching out the kinks in his muscles as he surveyed the land around him. He liked the way the pre-dawn light bathed the desert with a peculiar pink shade, which reminded him of the salmon-colored shells found along the island's beaches. He had learned the flat shells had sharp edges the natives used as knives and weapons.

Clay drained his cup, shook the droplets out onto the sand, and stashed it in his pack. "How far do you think the city is?"

"I'm not sure." August mounted his horse. "All I know is it lies somewhere south of those mountains."

He pointed toward a white and gray smudge running horizontally in the north.

"What do you think? A two or three week ride?"

"About that, maybe even longer if we stay here and talk about it some more."

"We'll cross the Plains and then swing east. With any luck we'll run into some elves once we cross onto their lands."

"And with any luck they won't kill us."

"That, too."

They journeyed north along the edge of the desert, their goal the line of spiky mountains running in a southward direction. They prevented the desert from encroaching any further to the east and blocked the lush landscape from penetrating to the west. Both climates met and sometimes clashed beyond the last line of hills. The desert would invade the fertile soil during the dry spells and the grasses and trees would take back what it had won during the rainy seasons. Clay could see the bright green and brown hues pushing toward them even from this distance. The low line of clouds gradually forming in the southwest promised rain, which would soon fall and help the greenery claim a little bit more land from the desert.

The two friends kept an eye out for any unwanted visitors. They had no idea how determined the group from Midtown was in tracking them down and they weren't about to wait and find out. Man avoided the desolate sands and that suited the two of them just fine. Thunder pealed in the distance, rolling sluggishly across the miles toward them. Storms in these parts were rare but powerful. Those which managed to hold together while crossing the hot and humid expanse from the sea became stronger as they collided with the cooler air at the end of the range. Clay and August urged their horses on, hoping to reach the rugged bluffs before the tempest erupted.

They reached the foothills in the early afternoon, galloping east then north once more, ignoring the plains that stretched away from the eastern face of the range. Scrubby trees and undersized brush grew out of the brick-colored soil, their tenacity equaled only by the tufts of pale yellow grasses sprouting up beside them.

Clay followed August as they rode parallel to the mountains. A cool wind blew in from the west, quickly followed by thick clouds that looked like old piles of dirty wool. They drifted overhead, blotting out the sun and the entire western horizon. The air felt heavy and oppressive, the bolts of lightning flashing dangerously nearby and the thunderclaps reverberating loudly in the riders' ears. Raindrops the size of their thumbnails began to fall sporadically from the sodden mass overhead. It would be only a matter of time before the skies opened up and drowned them. August pulled on his reins, jumping off Tauth's back before he came to a complete stop. He led his mount into one of the many clefts in the side of the mountain. Clay scanned the area one last time then dismounted and led his horse in behind him.

August squatted down and dug out a small hollow in the soft ground with his knife then deposited a shiny black lump into it. He lit it, placed a makeshift spit over the glowing ember then handed the empty pot to Clay. The elf placed it on the ground outside the recess, retrieving the full pan a few moments later. A warm mug of tea was what they both needed to chase away the chill in the air. They ate the last of the eggs and slices of ham, the thunder finally abating for a short time.

"We might have to spend the night here and hope that the sun hardens the ground before…Clay? Is something wrong?"

Clay cocked his head to the side straining to hear the peculiar sounds echoing faintly in his ears. He thought he heard faint cries and rocks bouncing down the side of the mountain but nothing crashed to the ground in front of the opening. He shook his head and the ghostly noises disappeared, carried away on a rumbling vibration running through the very core of his being.

"Hmm? No, nothing's wrong. Just tired, I guess."

"Well, get some rest. We have a long way to go."

-2-

    The four men dressed in ragged clothing scrutinized the winding trail disappearing into the pines a hundred yards ahead. The leader of the brigands rubbed his callused hand over his pockmarked face, his gaze traveling over the treetops and focusing on the mountain sticking up into the blue sky. A cloud blotted out the sun exposing a row of uniform slits along the face of the rocky crag. One of his companions lifted the patch covering his right eye and splashed some water on the still-healing wound. Someone with an unsteady hand had sewed his lid to the flesh below his eye. A third man repeatedly flicked his thumb over the edge of his sword, his greasy black hair combed straight back from his face. The fourth thief angrily slapped at the huge green flies biting him, his scrawny arms flailing wildly at the voracious insects. Perspiration dripped down their faces and bodies. The man with one eye pulled his sodden tunic away from his barrel-shaped chest, cursing the heat.

    The leader jerked his head and the ragtag group moved cautiously up the path. They walked beneath the cool shade of the overhead canopy, picking their way over rocks and roots. Scraggly shrubs sporting purple berries poked up from the path and branches stretched across above it. The footpath wound its way upward steeply, the band puffing as they leaned forward, grabbing at anything they could reach to keep from falling backward. Bugs launched themselves at the saturated men, gnawing mercilessly on their exposed skin. Red bumps erupted between the scratches all over their bodies. They clawed at the itchy swellings, drawing more blood and flies. The one-eyed man scowled and gripped the pommel of his sword's hilt more tightly. The leader stumbled on the path and began to fall rearward frantically clutching at anything to stop his downward plunge. He slid to a halt inches from the one-eyed man.

"Clumsy oaf," the one-eyed man snarled as he stepped on the other's back. "This had better be worth all this trouble."

The leader grabbed the one-eyed man's boot and yanked him to the ground, his fists connecting with the man's face before he toppled on top of him. The other two watched for a moment, the corners of their mouths curled in amusement before they pulled the two apart.

"That's enough! We'll all take turns flogging him if there's no riches up there," the man with the oily hair promised.

The ascent began again, the way up starting to level off. They could hear water roaring into a pool and see mist in between the leafy branches of the trees to the right of the trail. The robbers meandered through oaks, pines and maples then stopped at the edge of a cliff. The waterfall flowed into a deep tarn from several hundred feet up, the small lake emptying out into a swift stream rushing back down the mountain. A rickety bridge with ropes as handholds spanned the gorge, the missing planks making even the hardy thieves pause. The leader stepped onto the trestle, hesitating as it creaked and swayed beneath him. He waited until the movement subsided then slowly walked forward. His men followed one at a time. They reached the other side and looked warily back the way they had come. The one-eyed man wiped his mouth with the back of his hand; the thin bandit scratched his groin. The leader stood with his hands on his hips at the base of the path, and stared up at the mountain. He glanced at the sentry post. The small hut's roof had toppled into the building and the doors and windows lay jumbled where they had fallen long ago. Vines wound their way around the splintering posts and weeds poked through the rotting floorboards. He took a swig from his water skin then hiked up to Terracine's door.

***

Master Felix descended the well-worn stone steps, clutching several scrolls against his brown woolen vestment. His graying hair hung in a thin braid down the middle of his back; his receding hairline promising there would be less to plait in the future. The Master's black eyes were permanently bloodshot from decades of reading by lamp and candlelight. His footsteps echoed within the vast chamber carved out of the mountain as he walked toward the front of the immense library. He placed the scrolls into one of hundreds of carved out niches along the walls of the chamber, jumping backward as a fist-sized spider crawled from out of the darkness.

"How many times do I have to tell you not to scare me like that, May?"

The spider lifted her rust-colored abdomen up into the air in response. Felix recovered from his fright and held his finger out to her, smiling as May grabbed onto it with her front legs. The bands of black, cream and rust around them were beautiful to behold. She playfully nibbled on the tip of his finger with her needle-like mandibles, careful not to break the skin.

Felix sighed and turned around and faced the empty chamber. The engraved oak tables used to be piled high with books and the chairs filled with children and young adults from every corner of the land. Kings and commoners alike would sit beside one another and learn from the Masters. The students had tended to the gardens, kitchen and their own sleeping quarters on the second floor. The entire place had hummed with a quiet energy.

Felix strolled over to one of the tables. There were burn marks on the surface; bits of candle wax forever sealed into the wood and some areas were worn smooth by elbows and, in some cases, foreheads. Felix grinned at the memory of his apprentices studying well into the night and falling asleep on the table. His smile faded. He hadn't had a single pupil in more than ten years. A low growling sound pulled him out of his reverie.

"What is it, Charla?"

The little fox' ears were flat against her head, the reddish fur standing straight up on her back. She and her brothers had been found years ago, the hunter who had killed their mother having left them to die. Her brothers had returned to the forest surrounding Terracine as soon as they were old enough but Charla had chosen to stay with him. He was eternally grateful for her company. Felix looked over at the entrance and cocked his head.

The leader and his men stood in a single line in front of the massive double doors. The one-eyed man squeezed the sweat out of his patch then readjusted it over his socket. He spat on the ground and drew his weapon, his comrades following suit. The leader surged forward and placed his hand on the handle, smirking broadly as the door opened immediately.

Felix rushed ahead to close and lock the door but the daylight streamed into the dimly lit hall before he could cover half the distance to it. He shielded his eyes from the sunlight, squinting as the intruders charged in. Charla growled from somewhere behind him, her hostility retreating into the shadows as one of the men chased her away. The cold feel of metal against his neck stilled any thought of fighting back.

"Where's the gold?" the leader demanded, his face nearly touching the Master's cheek.

Felix grimaced with disgust as the man's foul body odors enveloped him and lice moved in his filthy hair. His comrades were in no better shape.

"There is no gold here," stammered Master Felix, beads of perspiration popping out on his forehead.

"I'm only going to ask once more...*where is it?*"

"You'd be wise to move on. I'll be more than happy to give you food and..."

"Shut up, old man! You and that mangy beast aren't going to do a thing to us!"

"No, but..."

A terrible shriek echoed throughout the mountain, freezing the remaining three men into place. They glanced around, licking their dry lips and looking into every dark recess. Something moved from out of the shadows and slowly padded into the light of the open door. Charla sat down, her brown eyes fixed firmly on the aggressors, her muzzle pointing toward the floor. The leader looked into Felix' eyes and saw not fear but pity.

"Who's here with you?"

The leader's hair stood on end. He turned Felix around, keeping the knife against his neck and forcing him to back up toward the door. His companions were on each side of him for a moment only. A black silhouette bolted out of the mountain's darkness and grabbed the one-eyed man, whose blood-curdling scream pierced the others' ears. The other man met with the same fate. Felix closed his eyes; he could feel the rapid breathing of the leader against the back of his neck.

"I'll kill him! I swear I'll do it if you come near me!" The man's guttural voice was strident with fear.

"*Too late.*"

The leader stopped breathing and froze as the whispered words registered in his mind. He pushed Felix away and spun about to meet the threat but found no one standing nearby. He glanced over at Felix who had squatted beside the fox then picked the frightened animal up and held her in his arms.

It's scared but isn't running away? The man's instincts finally kicked in and he forced himself to turn around to face whatever had slain his comrades. The mighty warrior he had expected to face was not standing behind him. He stared at the pale features of a slender young woman with silver eyes and short, unruly black hair.

"You?" the leader chortled.

"Me," was the raspy reply. She hissed at the man, exposing rows of gleaming white teeth as sharp as any well-honed sword.

His predicament was suddenly no longer humorous. He brought his dagger up but the air in front of him was empty. He began slashing at the place where the woman had stood a moment before, his panicky strokes getting slower. He blinked several times to shed the beads of sweat dripping into his eyes. This was all wrong! That slight girl couldn't have killed his men!

A movement to his right urged him to lift his sword in defense but he was a second too slow. He swung his knife up to prevent the black blade from slicing into his throat but his dagger suddenly felt alien in his weakening grasp. The clattering of metal bouncing upon the stone floor filled the vast chamber. It reverberated forever throughout the hollowed out mountain.

The last thing the leader saw were a pair of black daggers slicing up into his chest, the blades so sharp they cut through his bones. The woman caught the back of his collar as he fell and dragged him over to the door with one hand.

"Thank you, Sara."

"I'll clean up the mess, Master Felix."

Felix placed Charla on the floor and took a deep breath. He watched Sara haul the bodies out the door, then fetch a pail and a mop; she swabbed the blood off the stone floor without ever glancing up at the Master. Felix turned and went up the stairs to his room overlooking the garden and pulled the curtain aside.

Sara took the bucket outside when she was through and emptied its contents into the dirt alongside the mountain trail. She flipped the pail upside down and sat on it gazing at the sunlight falling through the leaves. Delicately winged insects flew in lazy circles through the yellow luminescence, which made everything appear warm and inviting. She stood up and strolled into the late afternoon light, pausing in the center of the glade. She sat on the thick grass, and then stretched out on her back, her hands behind her head, absorbing the vibrant colors all around her. She heard Charla's high-pitched whimper and smiled as the fox sprawled out beside her and place her smooth head on Sara's stomach. She scratched Charla behind her ears, as the fox slowly drifted off to sleep.

Felix let the drape fall back into place. He, a man born on the island far to the southwest, was the keeper of the all the Race's histories. His only companions were a fox, a spider and a demon, the latter's kin having tried to annihilate the Races long ago. Those who cared the least in the past were now responsible for the future. Why should they care if Terracine stands at all? Man was too busy getting rich and expanding his borders. The elves hadn't taken a single step off their lands for a long, long time. No one knew what happened to the dwarves. The Herkahs had retreated far into the Great White Desert. The Islanders were perfectly content to trade with Kepracarn. The people in the south had pushed eastward leaving a wide section of land uninhabited.

"Why bother?" he muttered aloud.

The only visitors they had were thieves, hunters, or people who had gotten lost in the dense forest surrounding Terracine. The robbers fared poorly here and the hunters had learned not too pursue their prey too closely to the mountain. The hapless soul who managed to survive and depart never came back. Felix presumed that they might have encountered the marauders lurking in the woods.

The Master sat down in his overstuffed chair wondering who would take over for him when he passed on. Sara was quite bright and enjoyed delving into the histories but he somehow doubted that's why she came to the mountain. Felix thought back to that day nearly a year ago when, on a warm summer morning, the demon girl came to Terracine.

Felix finally allowed the hard truth of the Races indifference toward Terracine into the forefront of his mind. He was alone and that situation was not about to change any time soon. He stashed his sputtering hopes in one of the niches then spent the better part of a month closing up the unused dormitory rooms on the second floor. He began the rather sad task of storing the manuals and writing implements in the library when the large iron ring banged against the sturdy oaken door. The sharp sound had startled him. He walked over to the entrance and peeked out the slit to see who was knocking but could only see a mop of wild black hair. All of a sudden, a face came into view as the figure popped up on tiptoes to glance in. Luminous silver eyes gazed innocently at him from a pale yet flawless face. He could not fathom how this child ended up on the mountain.

"May I help you?"

"I'm looking for lodging and to learn."

"Really? Who sent you?"

"I came on my own."

Felix had shrugged his shoulders and let her in, mindful of her peculiar appearance. She was a quiet girl who, without being asked, took care of the everyday chores during the day and studied all night. It wasn't until several weeks later when a pair of robbers broke into Terracine that he discovered her talents and true identity. Their fate was similar to the last party she had dispatched and her ferocity in killing them stunned the Master. The demon had initially frightened him, the facts and lore sometimes indistinguishable. It had been difficult to gaze upon her precious features and not remember the savagery that distorted them when she slew the raiders.

Sara's dark side, however, only emerged when threatened. She had tended to him when he had fallen ill over the winter; a certain death sentence had she not been there to look after him. He shook his head back and forth. A demon, loathed and feared by all those composed of flesh and blood, cared more for him than his own kind.

* * *

Sara ascended the spiral staircase into the very top of the mountain. She began to perspire more heavily the farther she went up, coughing as the heat and dust settled into her lungs. She held on to the lamp, the glow illuminating the irregular walls of the mountain and the intricately designed wrought iron staircase winding upward. Her legs began to cramp prompting her to sit and rest for a few moments. She glanced overhead. A faint breeze touched her heated face and the subtle moaning of the wind echoed in her ears. She was close. She continued her climb, brushing up against the sides of the mountain as it came to a near point at the apex. Sara took a deep breath, blew out the lamp and stepped onto the ledge.

The stars glittered in the inky sky. She scrutinized the land to the south as she had done for every night since she arrived at Terracine. The hours ticked by yet she remained on the shelf, her gaze moving over the dark land. It frequently focused on an unseen place to the west and about a hundred miles south of where she now sat. She closed her eyes and let the image materialize within her mind.

The stone cabin, its dark wooden frame and thick panes of glass blended in with the supple birches, tall grasses and clusters of boulders. The house hugged the riverbank, the steady waters turning the creaky wheel beneath the dwelling. Herbs and vegetables grew in plots along the southeastern side of the building; chickens pecked for seed in front of the coop. Neatly stacked piles of wood occupied the eastern section of the house, the overhang and half walls protecting them from the elements. Snow-capped mountains loomed to the north; the desert spread out on the other side of the hills to the south and the ocean's cobalt-hued waters dominated the west…

A brief pulse of energy broke through her reverie. Was it another false alarm? Perhaps she had imagined it? Maybe… The night suddenly lost all of its warmth. She could barely see through the cloud escaping from her mouth every time she exhaled and her skin rippled with gooseflesh. Sara closed her mind and grabbed the sides of her trousers to still her trembling hands. The moment she had been dreading was about to unfold before her. She backed up until her body was flat against the mountain, her hands grasping the rocky protuberances. The air fluctuated and the closer the ripple came the more difficult it became to breathe. Fear gnawed at her but determination kept her from fleeing the ridge. She swallowed hard just before the wave slammed into her nearly knocking her from her perch. The vile gust slammed into her like a board of spikes steeped in acid. She could feel the points slice through her and nail her into the rock at her back. *Stay calm…don't panic…* The surge lasted for many long minutes, pummeling her with an intensity threatening to tear her apart. She clung to the mountain long after the crest subsided. She slid down onto the ledge and pulled her knees up to her chest trying to purge the disturbing sensations still lingering within. He was now strong enough to achieve his ambition. It was time to go. Sara lingered until the rim of the sun reached over the horizon then entered the mountain.

* * *

The glass urn stood upon a craggy stalagmite, its base coated with the dust of time. The tar-like seal around its mouth smelled of decay and dripped down along the sides like candle wax. A molten pool surrounded the cone-shaped formation. It gurgled and sizzled with energy, flinging bits of lava up into the pungent air. Its orange and red glow barely penetrated the gloom. The jagged enclosure shifted every time the thick, soupy tarn belched up another sticky bubble releasing a short-lived fire.

THE FORTRESS OF DARKNESS

The flames reflected dully off the grime-coated vessel then sank back down into the blistering liquid.

Twisted creatures scurried amongst the black rocks, their humps and bony protrusions casting bizarre shadows against the walls. They snarled and whimpered as they reached for the receptacle. It was too far away but they could not deny its summons. They fought with each other, slashing and biting to keep the others at bay; their responses irrational considering none would be able to obtain the urn. One of the distorted beasts lashed out against its brethren, toppling it into the fiery river. It burned to a crisp before it even hit the surface, its brief shriek of pain reverberating throughout the cavern. The sound excited the rest, the cacophonous screeches and howls echoing harshly within the subterranean hollow. The demons skittered over the bare rocks, their claws shaving dust and splinters off the exteriors.

The things suddenly froze and went silent; their misshapen heads cocked to one side for a moment before they scattered into the darkness. Rounded pus-colored eyes peeked from out of the gloom toward the arched blackness looming on the other side of the chamber. Boots crunched down upon the gravel and lumpy soil, yet never wavered over the uneven ground. They became louder until a hooded and cloaked shape even darker than the opening entered the cave. It stood motionless for a moment then walked over to the edge of the flaming lake and stared at the fragile vessel in its midst. A hand lifted out from within the mantle and pushed the cowl back exposing the features. The black eyes glittered coldly as they viewed the stranded receptacle then blazed with fury at a demon crawling at his feet. He kicked the creature into the scalding morass and smiled glacially as the other beasts ran for their lives. He raised his hand, pointed a finger at the urn and creased his brows. The vessel began to quiver and shake sending the amethyst sparkles into motion.

Mine, he thought.

He left the urn alone and abruptly headed back up the corridor, following the rocky trail upward. The demons shrank against the uneven wall, cowering as he passed them by. Stalactites and stalagmites linked together throughout the vast underground complex. The misshapen things scurried behind them or clambered up into the gloom, the scraping of their claws sounding shrill in the confined network. A yellowish fog began to roil low to the ground the nearer he came to the surface. It reeked of decay, its icy touch freezing the flesh on contact. He moved through it without feeling any of its effects and climbed the last few steps up into the land.

Bizarre lights without any apparent source illuminated the swirling mist and the distorted objects stranded in this dismal place. He walked on a path barely visible in the murky light. The dense haze seemed to go on forever. He kept to his bearing, crossing through it and halting beneath a star-encrusted heaven. He opened his mind, sending wave after wave of energy out into the blackness. He detected a faint blip, subtly nodded and proceeded east.

* * *

Sara stood at the doorway looking up at Felix. The Master sighed heavily as he gazed at the satchel hanging to one side and the blanket roll suspended from her shoulder. She had been here for a year yet it seemed as if it had been a lifetime. He reached into his robe pocket, pulled out a small leather pouch, and handed it to her, the jingling sound within loud in the vast and now even emptier mountain. He glanced down at Charla, the little fox sitting beside him with sad brown eyes and laid-back ears. Sara squatted in front of her and hugged her, smiling as the fox licked her face.

"Will we ever meet again, child?" He asked, touching her silky cheek while fighting the loneliness already creeping into his heart. Her abrupt decision to leave Terracine was not unexpected. She had arrived in the blink of an eye and would depart in the same manner. He had always known that deep down inside, but that did not make it any easier.

"I would wish that more than anything, Master Felix."

An odd swishing sound prompted them to look overhead. At first, they could see nothing in the semi-darkness, and then a shape slowly emerged from the dimness above. It descended until the light filtering in from the open door illuminated the spider dangling over Sara's shoulder. May dropped onto the rolled up blanket and scuttled about a couple of times until she found a comfortable position. She held out one of her pincers to Felix. The Master ran his finger over the top of May's head and down her abdomen that she lifted in the air for him. It was surprisingly smooth, almost velvety to the touch and unusually warm for a spider.

Sara kissed Felix on the cheek, stroked Charla's silky fur and walked out the doorway. She stopped and turned around, offering the Master an encouraging smile before heading down the well-worn path. He watched as she descended the steps leading from the mountain, every one she took taking her farther from his sight. Her knees disappeared into the ground then her waist, shoulders and finally her mop of black hair. He stared at the point where she had vanished for a long time with Charla's head pressed against his leg.

Sara hiked down the mountain with ease. She reached the other side and continued to move downward until she reached the disintegrating sentry post. She looked up toward the mountain but saw only mighty oaks, maples and pine trees interspersed with huge outcroppings of blue-gray rocks. Shadows fell across Terracine's summit concealing the openings. She moved on, the mist rising from the waterfall capturing a rainbow that arched gracefully over the lake. She stepped onto the span, the weathered boards barely creaking beneath her slight frame. Cool air washed over her as she carefully leaned over the edge of the wobbly bridge. May nervously plucked at her hair, urging her to cross the dangerous gorge as quickly as possible. The young girl grinned at the spider and heeded her persistent demand to move on.

She made it to the other side then sat down on a fallen log and sipped from her canteen, her gaze tentatively moving toward the southwest. He was somewhere in the land and she would need help in stopping him. Where was she supposed to look? Who would believe her even if she found someone who wasn't afraid of her? She certainly could not undertake this responsibility by herself. She replaced the top of her flask and hung it across her shoulder, mindful of a sprawled out May.

"Where shall I look, May?"

Sara decided to take a chance even though she would be vulnerable to anyone who was capable of crossing over the current flowing between the mortal world and the beyond. She feared this place and of slipping into its icy embrace; the thought of bobbing endlessly within those dreadful waters making her blood run cold. Sara had no choice, though, and closed her eyes. She began to relax. The bird and insect noises started to diminish then grew silent. The tree she sat on no longer felt hard against her backside. She no longer felt the slight breeze blowing across her skin. Her heartbeat became almost nonexistent and she no longer filled her lungs with air.

...She stood in the pitch-black darkness and waited. Odors erupted all around her. The peppery smells made her eyes water while the moldy ones turned her stomach. The stench of decay was everywhere. She shivered with dismay and cold, the flow becoming distinct in front of her. A wide ribbon of haze and water meandered for as far as she could see, its progress impeded by shadowy forms poking upward from the smoky surface. The river circumvented them, splashing angrily against the protrusions in its way, the spray hissing menacingly as the droplets fell back into the waters.

Tiny flickers of light began to discharge in the river, almost all of them red, the color of demon existence. The rare silver sparkles were absent. This place did not hold the answer to her questions. She began to withdraw then stopped as a faint, out-of-place scent washed over her. It was fresh and clean, reminding her of the waterfall located on the mountain. She slowly spun around seeking its origin before it diminished, then cursed under her breath as the last vestiges evaporated before she could identify it...

Sara brought her hand up to shield her eyes from the bright sunlight. When they had adjusted, she removed her hand and stared in the direction she was facing when she returned to the mortal world. Her bearing did not offer her any encouragement: heading south would leave her vulnerable to her vile kin. If caught she would either have to descend into that noxious chasm or be killed.

She remained immobile for a long time, debating her next course of action. To go there or try her luck elsewhere? What should she do? A subtle breeze originating from the south touched her face and carried with it an earthy aroma. The redolence could easily have been attributable to the forest surrounding her. She took a deep breath then looked down at May waiting for her on the toppled oak. Sara held her hand out for the spider then raised May up to her face.

"I hope I'm not making a big mistake."

The spider rubbed its two front legs together as if in anticipation.

Sara paralleled the craggy mountains running south, marking her progress by the changing landscape around her. She had left the dense woods surrounding Terracine a few days ago and now walked along the grasslands scattered with clumps of small trees and brush. She could see that these, too, were thinning out and her cover would soon be gone altogether. She glanced toward the cliffs and crags, the occasional fissure the only place of concealment left to her. Sara looked up at the sun and, as much as she enjoyed feeling its warm rays, realized it would not be her friend during this part of her journey. It would broadcast her presence until it sank on the other side of the range.

The demon girl knew that Kepracarn and its outlying villages were only a few days march more to the south. The Man city, so she heard, was not friendly toward anyone not of their Race. A demon would surely garner a great deal of dubious responses. If whomever she sought were there, she'd be hard pressed to find him or her. She could try to disguise herself but rubbing plant dye on her skin but that would not detract anyone's attention from her eyes. Sara mulled over her choices and the problems that would evolve with each one. She was so focused on the 'what ifs' she failed to see a group of riders to the south. May did and tugged on Sara's hair. Sara slipped into the nearest crevice, hoping she hadn't been spotted and watched as the band gradually angled toward her. The spider scrambled after something that had caught her attention deep in the cleft, leaving Sara to observe the horsemen alone.

The closer they came the further she pressed herself against the jagged rocks. They rode on with a purpose, and for a moment, Sara thought they had detected her and were on their way to apprehend her. They scanned the exterior of the mountain as they continued north, halting every so often as one of the men dismounted and disappeared into an opening. *This is not good, Sara.* A quarter mile separated them from her and she glanced around to see if she could worm her way into a niche. The pounding of hooves and the communications between the men grew louder every second. Sara wasn't afraid of a dozen burly men on horseback but the fewer people who knew of her presence in the land the better. The shadows distorted the gap making flat surfaces appear like rents. She bumped against solid rock on several occasions before finally finding one she could squeeze into, if she stooped over. Not a moment too soon for one of the men got off his horse to investigate the fissure. She squatted in the small breach watching the man's shadow worm his way toward her hiding place. He couldn't fit his brawny shape through the last break but that didn't stop him from dropping onto his stomach and groping through the space.

Sara tried to press herself against the back of the gap but the unyielding mountain refused to grant her even an inch more. The man's hand stopped grabbling about a foot away from her boot: he had reached his limit. Sara slowly exhaled with relief as his arm retreated, her stare never leaving the spot where it had just been. *He's given up!* Her premature feeling of luck was immediately replaced with alarm. The man's hand reappeared armed with a sword. He poked and thrust the weapon at her, missing her feet by inches. His aim was getting better and she desperately grabbed onto a rock, putting it in front of her boot just before the tip of the sword rammed into it. Sweat began to pour down her face and her cramped muscles began to protest her position. He was going to find her. Sara unsheathed her black daggers and waited for the man's hand to come within striking distance. *A little bit more…come on…another few…* The man suddenly stopped jabbing and screamed out in fear. He scrabbled away from her, the mountain beating him up as he bumped into it in his rush to get away. His shouting soon faded.

Sara gaped at the opening then relaxed as May sauntered in. She repeatedly hit the ground with her front legs then walked away. Sara struggled to exit her hiding place, her stiff body unwilling to bend in any direction. She massaged the pins and needles from her muscles when she finally emerged from the cleft. Sara peeked around the corners of the fissure and watched as the men rode full gallop back the way they had come.

"That was too close. Thank you, May."

The spider cleaned bits and pieces of green and black off its body, fastidiously removing every scrap. She repeated the same procedure on her knifelike mandibles. Sara ate some food and slept for a short while. There would be enough distance between her and the men when they started out again.

THE FORTRESS OF DARKNESS

Sara stood and stretched, scanning the area around her for any signs of danger. She looked up at the sky and shook her head. Compressed gray clouds blotted out the sun; a curtain of rain at their forefront appeared like a smudge of charcoal. Lightning flashed persistently within the billowing mass and she could hear the thunder even from here. She thought it prudent to wait out the storm here and withdrew back into the fissure beneath the vaulted stone.

The first raindrops smacked into the earth with a force strong enough to send the finer dust up into the air. They did not remain suspended for very long as the shower beat them back onto the ground. Sara unrolled her blanket and hung it over her shoulders to ward off the chill, the rain obscuring everything beyond the entranceway. The downpour took on a steady beat, its tempo and the dreary afternoon lulling her to sleep...

The stream meandered past the stone and timber cabin, which was nestled within a ring of birch and aspen trees. Eviscerated fish dried on screens. Bright yellow leaves stood out starkly against the brilliant blue sky. Sara looked down at the wild apples in her basket, their golden-green skin mottled by patches of red. She ran toward the house, the apples bouncing wildly in the container. She tripped over a rock and landed with a painful thud on the ground, the fruit spilling out onto the grass. She sat up and stared at her pint-sized knees, the abrasions welling up with little beads of blood. The front door creaked open, her tears blurring the figure emerging into the daylight...

Sara slowly opened her eyes and took a deep breath.

The tempest lasted into the early evening hours. The rain began to abate then stopped altogether but the muddy land made travel nearly impossible. Sara glanced at the exposed rock at the base of the mountains, their sloping base free of the sticky soil. She collected her things and stepped out into the crisp night air.

The demon girl cautiously followed the range's curves until the full moon reached its apex. A faint haze encircled it. Time was growing short. She had passed by numerous crevices along the way, each beckoning her to climb inside and rest. She ignored them, continuing her foolhardy search for help. A series of vague bends where the wet earth lapped up against the dark stone halted her progress. Dawn's watery hues stained the sky to her left. She placed her hands on her hips contemplating what she should do when an odd sound caught her attention. She cocked her head and listened intently. May clambered up on top of Sara's head and bobbed up and down. The girl moved forward, mindful of what might come out of the darkened recess. May jumped onto a thin ledge and disappeared into the pitch-black niche, ignoring the indistinct sound of hooves kicking pebbles.

Sara slid her weapons out and eased her way into the breach, the glow given off by the embers of a campfire just enough to make out the shapes within the space. Two black horses stared unconcernedly at her from the rear; two bodies slept soundly near the coals. She noticed a movement in the gloom up above and held her breath as May came to a halt in between the two figures. She dangled on her thread trying to decide which one would have a rude awakening first. Sara attempted to wave the spider off but May ignored her and opted for the one on the left.

-3-

Something moved along Clay's chest. *That damn horse!* He sleepily brought his hand up to shoo away the animal but instead of finding a velvety nose his fingers brushed against a stick. No, several twigs. Twigs that moved? Clay hesitantly reached out once more and felt something large bump against his palm. He slowly opened his eyes, blinked many times then held his breath in fear. The biggest spider he had ever seen sat on his stomach, razor sharp mandibles gnashing back and forth. He leaned ever so slightly to his left immediately freezing as the spider mimicked his movement. He swallowed hard, his eyes nearly bursting from their sockets as he tilted the other way. The creature swayed menacingly at him. *Sweet mercy!*

"Augie?" Clay's voice was nothing more than a nebulous memory. Had he spoken aloud? He dared to glance over at his sleeping friend. *Augie? Please wake up!*

"Augie!"

"What?" August rubbed at the sleep in his eyes and gazed over at Clay. His companion rested on his elbows staring with fright at him. August squinted in the semi-darkness, wondering what was wrong. The horses were calm but Clay was anything but.

"Big...spider...on me..."

"You woke me up because of a bug?"

"*Look!*"

August gave Clay a skeptical glance then sat up to get a better view. He half-heartedly scrutinized Clay's blanket but saw nothing, including the motionless form standing off to the side near their feet.

"You must have been dreaming…" The huge spider crawled onto Clay's lap and stared at August who inched away from the insect, disregarding Clay's pleas for help.

"Come on, Augie!"

"Oh, for heaven's sake."

They gaped at the slight woman detaching herself from the shadows and sliding her hand underneath the spider's abdomen. She deposited the spider on her shoulder, crossed her arms in front of her and waited for the two friends to regain their composure. August stopped scooting backward and Clay started to breathe normally again though neither one looked away from the young woman.

"Who are you? What do you want?" demanded Clay, watching the spider settle down as if it were a dog. It turned around a few times then lay still, legs curled up underneath.

"I'm Sara and this is May. We didn't mean to startle you."

"The spider has a name?" asked August, taking a step backward as May half rose from Sara's shoulder.

"Do you two?"

"I'm August and that's Clay."

"The two of you wouldn't have upset anyone, would you?" She inquired after a long pause.

"What do you mean?" asked Clay.

"A group of men were scouring this area late yesterday afternoon." She watched them exchange worried looks, and then stare at her with open suspicion.

"Are you in league with them?"

"Hardly, Clay. I barely escaped being taken by them."

"What are you doing in these parts?"

Sara studied Clay. He was lean; his angular features accentuated by eyebrows gracefully arching upward. He pretended to massage his temples but in actuality strove to rearrange his brows. Those were easier to manipulate than the pointed tips of his ears pushing through his hair.

She glanced over at August, smiling unknowingly. *What an interesting threesome we are, she thought. A Herkah, an elf and a demon could make someone very rich.* She smirked at them and shook her head back and forth, the elusive aroma of the forest lingering faintly within the cave.

"What's so funny?" Clay inquired. The morning light was beginning to seep into the crevasse and her features were becoming more visible. The slim girl with the light gray eyes and short black hair looked anything but dangerous.

"Your heads would make me a very wealthy woman."

"Are you planning on doing just that?" August pulled out his knives and took one step in front of Clay. May rose to her legs in response and hissed threateningly at him.

"I'm hardly in a position to do so even if I wanted to."

"Why?" demanded the elf, narrowing his eyes at an approaching Sara.

"Look closely and see for yourself."

Sara turned and faced the morning sun as it flooded in. August and Clay hesitated for one moment before walking close enough to study her face, mindful of May hovering protectively over her shoulder. Her eyes weren't light gray but the same as molten silver; her brows slightly feathered upward along the top as they curved toward her temples. Her skin glowed warmly reminding them of pearls just scooped out of the water. Her compressed nails curved to an understated point but, they were sure, could rip out a man's throat with little effort.

"A demon?"

"There's no such thing, Augie."

"You can argue all you want but I can assure you I am not the only one in the land."

"Are the others as…friendly as you are?" Clay glanced over at May who was making her way down Sara's side. The spider dropped onto the ground with a barely audible thud and skittered over to him. He bit his lower lip as she crawled up his leg, his eyes beseeching Sara to retrieve her.

"Not likely." She watched May grab his tunic then launch herself upward onto his shoulder. The elf cringed, fighting the urge to flick the spider off in fear of enraging her. Her pincers and mandibles, mere inches from his flesh, were far too imposing.

"I think May likes you, Clay!"

"Yes, that's very nice. We have to go now so would you be kind enough to take her back?"

"Where are you heading?"

"Opposite from wherever you are," replied Clay. "The spider? Please?"

Sara did not budge. She stood there with her arms crossed and head tilted to the side. The minutes ticked by and no one moved. The elf closed his eyes and sighed heavily.

"North then east. Would you like to come along?" he said in a resigned voice.

"Yes." Sara walked up to Clay and coaxed May onto her hand then deposited the spider onto her pack.

"Oh…wonderful! It's not enough your pointy ears are going to get me into trouble now I have to contend with…her. At least she's more pleasant to look at than you."

Clay and August saddled up their horses, all of them eager to get on with their trek. Sara rode behind August, his powerful steed not even noticing her slight frame. They galloped north where Sara had begun her journey south. What had taken her a week to cover on foot was completed in two days on horseback. They reined in along the outskirts of the forest clustered at the foot of Terracine, the mountain not visible from their vantage point.

Sara gazed up in that direction anyway, wondering how Master Felix was faring. She didn't like leaving him alone. Her choices, however, had been few. She dismounted and placed May in a maple tree then helped rub the horses down.

August prepared the meal while the elf checked out the area, walking in a large circle around their camp. She joined August who offered her a little smile.

"Clay is on his way to try and meet up with his family."

Sara could see the elf in between the branches and brush. He stopped and looked toward the east for the longest time then lowered his head. August kept his attention on the pot of stew simmering over the campfire, the barely hidden look of worry surfacing every now and then. She touched his arm and smiled at him.

"I was under the impression he already traveled with his kinfolk."

"He's never seen another elf…" his voice trailed off, chased away by the horrible memory of the beaten elf in Windstorm. He was grateful Clay had not yet disembarked to witness that terrible scene. Had the locals known he was from the desert he would have suffered the same fate. He stopped stirring the stew and gazed at Sara. She waited patiently for him to tell her what was on his mind or not to. Clay's return prompted him to remain silent. August handed them full bowls then fixed one for himself.

"Your cooking abilities are quite praiseworthy, August."

"He sews, too," added Clay around a mouthful of food.

"You'll make someone a fine catch someday," she teased.

"Unlike him," August pointed his spoon at the elf.

The sun descended into the west igniting the sky in brilliant shades of red, orange, gold and blue. The few thin clouds lingering in the sky shimmered with a warm, melon hue. August watched Sara close her eyes and hold her face up. Her pale skin absorbed the beautiful sunset tints giving it a polished bronze hue. She opened her eyes and, for a split second, they reflected the lavender that pulsed in the sky. She stared wistfully into her clasped hands.

"What *are* you doing out here, Sara?"

"Looking for someone, Clay."

"Who?"

"I'm not quite sure yet."

"Sounds a bit foolish, doesn't it? Searching for someone you don't know?"

Sara shrugged her shoulders ignoring his suspicions, which floated in the warm night air in her direction.

Clay jumped as May lumbered past him, her abdomen dragging on the soft grass. He grimaced with disgust and handed August his empty plate as the spider crawled into Sara's lap. Clay could have sworn the huge insect burped.

"We should be within the patrols range in another day or so," August's voice cut through the awkwardness.

Clay suddenly became very withdrawn. He picked at the grass then muttered a good night before wrapping himself up in his blanket. August stared at his friend for a moment then resumed packing up their gear.

Sara looked from one to the other, observing them closely. The elf kept to his journey because he had to and August followed by virtue of their friendship. Their destination was driving a wedge between them and even she, an outsider, could see what was happening. The thought saddened her deeply. She scooted over to sit next to August.

May waddled over and crawled up onto Clays' stomach, too full to do anything more than sprawl over it. The elf did not move.

"You should get some rest." Sara watched August's hands as they rapidly knotted the leather laces of the knapsacks.

"I'll keep watch first, Sara, and then you can take a turn."

"I don't sleep much…especially at night."

"Demons don't rest?"

"Never at night."

"Why not?" he asked tentatively.

"Sleep well," she replied quietly after a few moments, afraid her answer would repulse him and remind her of the heritage she sought to forget.

August tried to read her face but she kept her feelings carefully concealed. He nodded and retired, falling asleep almost immediately.

Sara kept vigil over them, listening more for the bandits that roamed this part of the land than for any demons. The latter never ventured far from the noisome pit on the other side of the range. She gazed into the shadowy forest, which fluctuated then disappeared, replaced by a moment from her past.

Dawn was still hours away when she heard the kettle whistle. She pushed away the down comforter, braving the cold as she hurriedly got dressed and ran downstairs into the kitchen. She grinned at the man standing beside the fireplace, the deep creases in his face spreading outward like ripples on a lake. His wiry form seemed lost beneath his woolen shirt; his large and knobby hands looked like they belonged to a man twice his size. She ran into his waiting embrace, giggling as he picked her up and hugged her.

Eppe, I want to go with you!

Sweet Sara.

He kissed her on the forehead and closed his soulful brown eyes.

Please? I want to see the pretty horses again!
Do you remember what happened the last time you went with me?
She stared at his fraying collar then began to pluck at the loose threads.
Sara?
I bit the pony.
That's right, Sara, you bit the pony.
Eppe's gentle tone of voice drew her attention away from his neckline.
I won't do that again, I promise...I promise...I promise...

She glanced over at Augusts' unprotected throat, the steady beating of his heart making the arteries spring back and forth against his skin. She shuddered with revulsion, the bile rising into her craw.

* * *

Clay awoke before August and set fresh coals into place in the depression. Clay handed August a mug of tea just as he sat up, the bread and cheese cut and waiting. August playfully rubbed at his eyes.

"Clay? Is that you? No, no, it can't be! Up before the sun *and* serving breakfast?"

"Eat and shut up," grumbled the elf, unable to keep the smirk off his face.

They finished their meal then mounted up, paralleling the dense woods eastward. They rode in silence, keeping an eye on the brown and green expanse to their left. All around the travelers was silence, other than the birds and small, furry creatures scurrying beneath the verdant boughs. They could see the tops of the colossal mountain range to the north, their washed out sheer cliffs so high it seemed like the sky rested on their crests. The open grasslands to their right were warm and dry but the air seeping through the trees was cool and refreshing.

They stopped at midday, sharing sips of water and handfuls of dried fruits and nuts.

Sara wanted to tell them why she chose to ride with them but Clay's personal mission stilled her tongue. She wasn't even sure if Clay and August were the ones who were supposed to help her.

"Riders," said Clay rising up from the ground.

August and Sara joined him, looking east gradually discerning the dozen or so riders heading their way. The closer they came the more details the traveling companions were able to observe. They were elves and sat their mounts well. Their horses were stockier than Essa and Tauth yet no less supple. Their braided bridles and saddles glowed warmly, the leather well worked with oils. The dark green blankets ended in golden tassels. The elves wore sleeveless buckskin jerkins and brown trousers, longbows and swords at the ready. Clay was so mesmerized by the elves he neglected to notice the unfriendly expressions on their faces. August and Sara had and retreated beneath the trees' shadows. The group halted a short distance away, conferring with each other before one of the riders approached Clay. He spurred his horse into a slow walk until he was close enough to be heard speaking.

"You are trespassers and must leave these lands immediately," he commanded, scrutinizing first Clay then August and Sara. His eyes narrowed with distrust at their odd appearance, and something else. His gaze traveled back to Clay and focused on his green eyes. Their unusual color seemed to be the trigger that befuddled him.

"We mean no harm, good sir," Clay stated. "I'm trying to reach my kin in Bystyn."

"You were born there?"

"I'm not sure."

"Then you have no kinfolk living in the city."

"You don't understand, I..."

"*You* don't understand. Only elves born in Bystyn are granted access to it. You have one hour to get off elven lands."

Clay stared hard at the elf suppressing the feeling to knock him off his horse. He belonged to the elven Race but was to be denied passage because he didn't know where he was born? Were there renegade elven communities out there that weren't welcome in Bystyn? He glanced down at his feet and took several deep breaths before looking up at the elf.

"You're being unreasonable."

"One hour," was the terse reply. The elf locked eyes with Clay for a moment longer then reined his horse around and rejoined his group.

"Captain Ansar?"

"We'll wait until they leave," Ansar stated, trying not to appear too interested in the threesome.

Clay glared at him, the heat rising up into his face. He didn't know if he were embarrassed or angry at having been brushed off. He ignored Sara and August standing beside him.

"Where to?" asked August.

"Anyplace but here," Clay grumbled and headed for the horses.

They rode west, stopping when the patrol ceased shadowing them and made camp for the night. They ate in silence, August and Sara respecting the sting in Clay's heart. His downcast demeanor began to change as the evening wore on and he joined in their conversation.

"What's Terracine like?" asked August.

"It's a hollowed out mountain filled with books, maps and anything that you can write on. Years ago it was filled with students from all over the land but not any more."

"Why not?" Clay sat cross-legged, listening to her speak.

"Master Felix, the keeper of the mountain, told me people were content to learn only about that which concerns them. They stopped caring about interacting with other Races and abandoned Terracine."

"That's ridiculous. Why don't we go there?" suggested Clay.

"We can't."

Clay and August looked at Sara with puzzled expressions. She brought her knees to her chest and wrapped her arms around them, shivering ever so slightly even though the night was warm. Her silver eyes took on a tarnished cast.

"Did something bad happen there, Sara?" asked August.

"No, not there, not yet anyway."

August thought about the suspicions growing in the land, not just in the south. An undercurrent of unease hovered across the land, one that people felt but could not identify. It didn't interfere with their daily lives though they paid more attention to what was transpiring around them. Calla had sensed it and she turned them in to the authorities not out of logic but out of fear. Man blamed the elves and pretended to thwart their anxieties by slaying them. The Herkahs, too, discerned that something was out of place, and left for the safety of the desert. The elven patrol that had denied Clay entrance into Bystyn radiated distrust, too.

"What's going on, Sara?" asked August in subdued tones.

"I went to Terracine a year ago to watch for the signs foretelling the return of Emhella. He was the Herkah called Allad who was taken by the evil Mahn hundreds of years ago. Danyl of Bystyn used the Elven Might to destroy Mahn, but the evil's black magic was scattered all over the land. Vox/Allad spent all of his time gathering it up and piecing it back together. The Vox' own brand of corruption altered Mahn's weakened power and changed it to conform to the Vox' will. The Vox that had invaded Allad's soul metamorphosed into the evil spirit Emhella. The nimbus around the moon is one auspice. The other happened a week ago. The morass on the edge of the Great White Desert opened up. Emhella is back in the land."

"Why are you telling us this?" Clay inquired in a low voice.

"Because I want you to help me."

"To do what?"

"Defeat Emhella."

* * *

Balyd trudged into the expansive library on the first floor, depositing his armful of papers on the top of the immaculate desk carved out of oak before dropping into the chair, exhausted. He rubbed his haggard face then ran his bony fingers through his thinning hair. He had been First Advisor to this queen for five years and the queen before her for thirty years, each hastening his aging in their own way. The previous queen, Tryssa, had spent all of her time trying to avoid any outside contact. She was under the impression the elves had everything they needed. Tryssa was convinced any outside interaction would lead to discord. The elves were doing well but the loss of communication with the other Races left them isolated and detached from events in the land. The First Advisor understood remaining disconnected from the other Races left the elves open to sudden and unfortunate predicaments. He had defied Tryssa, secretly sending out chosen elves to explore and report what was occurring in the land around them.

The current queen, Aryanda, was Tryssa's niece and inherited the throne from her childless aunt. Aryanda's youth and receptiveness to the world around her had initially given Balyd hope of rejoining the other people. His optimism was short-lived. Her curiosity about the land around her started out innocently enough. The more information she gathered the less she focused on communicating with them and the more she concentrated on identifying something specific to their Races. Balyd remembered the last time he saw Aryanda. She was tall and slender, her hazel eyes never wandering far from the large mirror in her chambers. Her long blonde hair had been painstakingly plaited and wrapped into a complex ponytail in the back of her head held there by bejeweled combs. Her silk gown swished as she moved, the sound reminding Balyd of the inconsequential whisperings among adolescent girls. She had not bothered to conceal the arrogance radiating from her finely chiseled features. Aryanda was both intelligent and vain, a combination that greatly disturbed him.

He walked over to the open window and stared out at the garden. The last news he had had from his scouts mentioned nothing out of the ordinary. Kepracarn thrived and continued to expand into the south and east; the dwarves were still missing and the other Races remained absent from everyone's view. Aryanda wasn't interested in trade, contact, or even of locating the dwarves but sought something else.

"Lord Balyd?"

The First Advisor jumped and self-consciously grabbed at his chest, turning around to see the startled look on the young elf's face. The elf tentatively handed him a book then bowed before heading for the door. Balyd glanced at the title then at the elf.

"Wait. What's your name?"

"Taman, sir."

Balyd scrutinized the elf from head to toe. Taman's stocky frame, straight dark brown hair pulled back into a short braid and gray eyes were at odds with the book he had just returned. The First Advisor had never seen Taman before and wondered what someone not on the households' staff was doing borrowing books from the library. He wasn't a thief or he wouldn't have returned it. Balyd had been so preoccupied with his thoughts Taman could simply have left it on his desk and sneaked back out without the First Advisor being any wiser. The elf, however, had made it a point to get his attention. He gazed at the title once more then crossed his arms cradling the book against his chest. This youngster had to have read other books before this one.

"How many times have you been in here?"

"A few, sir. Actually, I've long ago lost count."

Balyd spent a great deal of his time in this chamber, and other than the terrace, there was only one entrance. He thought he knew every nook and cranny in the library yet this young elf came, took whatever reading material caught his fancy and left without ever being seen.

"How do you get in?"

"I didn't mean to cause any problems, Lord Balyd, I simply wanted to learn…"

"How?"

Taman stared at the First Advisor, noting keen interest and not hostility flickered in his eyes. Balyd did not act pretentiously like the other lords and ladies who would have had him immediately arrested and not bothered to talk with him.

"There's an unused passageway…I accidentally leaned up against a portion of the paneling and it opened. I'll show you."

Taman led Balyd to the back of the library past rows of shelves and a set of heavy oaken doors housing the precious artifacts collected over the centuries. He stopped in front of a nondescript section of the wall and ran his fingers along the middle of the right side. The segment slid open silently revealing the darkness beyond the library. Taman looked at Balyd, the First Advisor's face frozen in complete astonishment as he gazed at the spider webs stirring lazily from the top of the doorway. His eyes narrowed as he sought to make out any shapes in the inky breach.

"There's one step down then the hall runs straight until it reaches the end of the building. There's a false door leading out into the garden."

Balyd followed Taman into the darkness, grabbing onto the back of his tunic for fear of becoming lost, tucking the book into one of the large pockets of his robe. The young elf moved forward without hesitation but Balyd was compelled to place one hand along the wall to maintain his bearings. His fingers touched one too many unseen insects, their feelers and multiple legs sending shivers of revulsion up his spine. He quickly dropped his arm back to his side. The air was stale here although he could feel slight puffs of air against his skin now and then. He felt Taman slow then stop, his finger scratching at the wall sounding loud in the First Advisor's ears. He heard a distinctive clicking noise then closed his eyes as daylight flooded in from the opening.

His eyes adjusted to the light but he did not recognize this corner of the garden. Weeds and scraggly brush crowded around a stone bench stained a greenish hue, the flagstones leading to the seat barely discernible beneath thick clumps of overgrown plants. A long neglected rose bush grew behind the bench. Its thorny canes sported a few haggard leaves and a single bud that appeared brown and ragged looking. Balyd felt pity for the bush and wished someone would put it out of its misery. A thick curtain of vines choked off this spot from the rest of the garden and Balyd doubted anyone even knew this place existed. He looked up and espied bits of blue in between the gray-green spiky leaves on both sides of the wall separating the structure from the city, then over to the corner of the castle. The gray mortar crumbled beneath the vines' tenacious offshoots, the residue accumulating at the base of the wall in little piles.

"And?"

"I climb in and out over there." He pointed where the wall met the building, the branches in the trees forming a natural ladder.

"Why this book?"

"*Harbingers of Evil*? Have you read it?"

"Yes, but I'm interested in hearing what you have to say about it."

"The book speaks of an event that has been gradually taking place over the past two centuries and, when complete, marks the return of an unspeakable evil."

"I've read that myth."

"You don't believe it?"

"No."

"Do you doubt the war took place on the plains beyond the gates?

Perhaps the Elven Might and the Source of Darkness were nothing more than figments of the author's imagination?"

"That was over two hundred years ago, Taman! The Green Might defeated the Evil and sent it to the bowels of Hell where it belonged!"

"Did it?"

"Of course, you daft boy!" Balyd lost his bluster as Taman began to read from the book.

" 'The Vox was seen gathering the vestiges of what Mahn once wielded; the Evils' power having settled like ashes over the land. It would be no easy task to find the scattered fragments but the immortal fiend had all the time in the world to do so. The Vox will have amassed all the bits of black power when three halos surround the full red moon'. When was the last time you gazed up at the night sky, Lord Balyd?"

The First Advisor took a long, deep breath letting it out slowly as he stared at Taman. Balyd did not believe in magic nor did he place much faith in fables, even those steeped in truth. This young elf was convinced what he read was true. Balyd looked into Taman's features searching for doubt or deceit. He saw a pair of world-weary eyes watching from within a young man's face. He noticed he couldn't see the pupils in Taman's gray eyes; it was if the charcoal hue had absorbed them. He shook his head, concentrating on the unusual elf sitting cross-legged before him.

"Why does all of this intrigue you, Taman?"

"Have a glass of wine near midnight on your balcony, Lord Balyd."

The First Advisor was unable to open his mouth fast enough to call to Taman as the elf effortlessly vaulted up the branches and over the wall. He remained seated for a long time then picked up the book. He stood and studied the intertwined mass of green and brown vegetation in front of him then glanced over to the now-hidden doorway. The third exit was out of the question. He wormed his through the thicket, cursing under his breath at the sound of tearing cloth.

* * *

Balyd sat at his desk running his finger over the edge of his half-empty glass, the book neatly placed by his side. He had read and reread the chapter on the Vox; the words burned into his mind and Taman's caution echoing repeatedly. What could that boy know anyway? The celestial sequence was specific, too exact for him. He drained his goblet and walked out onto the balcony. He kept his gaze focused on the flat stones and only the reddish cast on them induced him to look upward. Balyd swallowed hard at what he saw.

The stars and a bulging full moon the color of wet bricks filled the indigo sky. He sighed with relief then felt the hairs on his arm rise. A blurry yet unmistakable corona encircled the moon. No, the words contained in the book were nothing more than myths. The crimson orb would not foretell the coming of the Vox. Taman, whoever he was, had been misled and was doing the same thing to him. Balyd went back inside, closing the door firmly behind him.

The book filled the First Advisor's vision, its leather cover embossed with modest letters that belied its contents. He sat down and pulled the volume closer, his fingers reaching for then moving away from the cover. He pushed it aside and grabbed a pile of reports, reading the pages without heeding one word on them. He was about to reach for it again when a knock on the door broke the spell the tome had on him.

"Enter."

"Lord Balyd, Queen Aryanda wishes to see you," stated the attendant, bowing deeply to the First Advisor.

Balyd entered the queen's reception chamber and waited for her. She sauntered in minutes later, her hand resting intimately upon Caladan's arm, wearing a pale blue silk nightgown. Her undone hair fell below the small of her back. Aryanda's alabaster skin was a testament for her hatred of the sunlight and glowed luminously against her dressing gown. Her eyes, however, glittered more like diamonds as she surveyed her servant standing before her. She stepped away from her escort and waited, holding head haughtily to one side.

Balyd bowed impassively to the queen, ignoring Caladan's churlish smirk. *Mangy fop*, he thought.

"You summoned me, my Queen?"

"What news have you about the city's affairs?"

"Nothing that could not have waited until tomorrow, my Lady."

"I am asking for an update, Lord Balyd, not some strenuous activity on your part."

"The reports are on my desk…"

"Then may I suggest that you fetch them."

"I don't need to 'fetch' them to tell you there are no changes to be passed on to you, my Queen."

"Insolence does not become you, Balyd."

"I apologize, my Queen, but it is late and I…"

"Lord Caladan has shown some remarkable promise and I would like you to enlighten him with your duties."

Caladan? That bootlicker? Tall, handsome and charming without a trace of intelligence, Caladan had managed to seduce Aryanda into considering him for the second most important position in the kingdom. The elf's conceit and lust for power would undermine everything Balyd had secretly worked to sustain. *She would be better off if she had ordered me to train an earthworm. I am not about to turn over my position to this pompous fool who would ignore the needs of the elves.*

"Would my Queen allow me some time to gather together information to help Lord Caladan's transition?"

"You have a week."

"It will take longer than that, my Queen."

"Eight days, then. You are dismissed."

Balyd nodded and walked out the door, stopping to peek in before it closed completely. He took a deep breath as Aryanda slipped into Caladan's arms. The First Advisor rubbed at his throbbing temples but he could not erase the embrace from his mind.

* * *

Balyd went to the library early the next morning, Aryanda's order crowding out everything in his mind. She was a danger to Bystyn and he was the only one who could see the truth of that. Unfortunately, there was no one he could turn to for help. He dared not seek help from anyone within the castle. He sipped from his mug and stared out into the garden, contemplating his next course of action.

THE FORTRESS OF DARKNESS

The image of the moon pulled the corners of his mouth down. If Taman was correct, then Aryanda and Caladan were the least of his worries. The lack of cohesion amongst the Races did not bode well if this Vox was lurking in the land. Aryanda would certainly dismiss the Vox altogether or state that it would never dare enter elven lands.

What in the Four Corners was he thinking? Vox? Magic? That daft boy was doing nothing more than distracting him from his duties. He had more important and urgent things to focus on. He drained his cup and placed it on his desk. A shadowy figure moving between the bushes and trees in the garden caught his attention. He cocked his head expecting Taman to appear but the shape was too tall and thin to belong to the elf. Balyd watched until the figure came into full view then gasped as the elf fell in exhaustion against the window. Dried blood covered his forehead and the scrapes along his knuckles. His clothes were filthy and torn; his cloak embedded with bits of grass and grime. He struggled to remain erect but slid down into a heap at the bottom, his eyes staring, wide and unblinking. It was Garadan, one of the elves Balyd had sent in search of information in the land.

-4-

Whistler carried hoes, rakes and shovels on his shoulders, his mind conjuring up ways of using each one against the Rock Lords. He wanted nothing more than to bury an axe into Kevlan's skull. The chieftain's merciless practices had resulted in the deaths of twenty dwarves so far this season. The Rock Lords forced Whistler and his kin to march by the decaying bodies every day, reminders of what happened to those who were too frail or obstinate to toil for Kevlan. It took a week for the carrion and insects to reduce the corpses to bones. Their skeletons, scattered by the scavengers, still littered the path to the fields. He kept his eyes averted from Kevlan's ruthless practices.

Whistler's rust brown hair was plastered to his forehead; the sweltering sun continued to bake his skin. The overseer snapped his whip, the lashing tip cutting into Whistler's back eliciting nothing more than a silent snarl. The dwarf's bright gray eyes focused on the foreman and bored into him with such hatred that the Rock Lord's face blanched. He raised his hand to inflict more pain in Whistler's direction then thought better of it. He shouted numerous insults but kept the whip lowered. Whistler threw the gardening implements on the ground and glared at the rock towers in the northwest. The sun glinted off the river flowing around the base of the mountain where his ancestors had ruled for countless centuries.

"*Get to work, maggot!*"

Whistler turned his head sideways, listening for the distinctive popping sound of the cruel horsewhip. He picked up the broad headed hoe and slammed the metal blade into the ground. He buried it up to the haft into the dusty earth, tugging hard to dislodge it from the unwilling soil. His gaze traveled from the white bones strewn across the ground, up to the craggy spires then over to the dwarves laboring beneath the watchful glare of their foremen.

Hard labor had chiseled Whistler's muscles as strong as tempered steel; his resolve transformed into focused power. He wore the countless lash marks on his back as badges of honor, refusing to yield beneath their relentless insistence.

Whistler smashed out a furrow and moved over to start another row, heedless of the following dwarf trying to smooth out the groove and keep up with his furious pace. He brought the hoe down again and again, imagining the dirt-encrusted blade biting into one of his captors. Two rows then three and four were completed. The sun beat mercilessly down on him then reflected back up from the ground. Dust rose upward, invading his eyes and mouth and sticking to his sweat soaked skin. He despised the dwarves' predicament and himself even more for being unable to help them. He began to gasp, becoming short-winded, his muscles protesting, his essence refusing to quit. He fought off the arms that attempted to stop him, recklessly pushing aside both dwarf and Rock Lord. He became wild and unruly, striking out at anything that touched him, unable to differentiate even between languages. A blow to the back of the head stunned him and he finally collapsed to the hard earth.

* * *

Whistler slowly opened his eyes, aware of the cool compress on his forehead but his blurry vision was unable to focus on whomever was being kind enough to care for him. The faint hint of lemon grass and rosemary wafted into his nose, eliciting a slight smile on his face. He closed his eyes and relaxed, knowing it was Elena chiding him while tending to his throbbing head.

"You grow more foolish by the day! The Overseer might not be as gentle the next time and he'll crack that thick skull of yours wide open!

Stop flinching or I'll administer a thump on your noggin you'll never forget." Her kind expression belied her stern words.

"Are you done?" he whispered through cracked lips.

"Hardly! The other dwarves think you're crazy—a sentiment I'm beginning to share—and prefer the whip to working with you out in the fields. Poor Harald is still gasping for air after trying to keep up with you!"

"Now are you done?"

"No. This is the third time in as many weeks that this has happened and…"

"What time is it?" Whistler struggled to rise even as the blinding pain in his head and the queasiness in his stomach urged him to lie down. He ignored them both and sat up on the edge of his bunk.

"Suppertime. Do you want something to eat?"

"Not right now."

Elena tied her blonde hair into a ponytail, her crisp blue eyes studying Whistler intently. The Rock Lords would normally have slain such a troublesome captive yet they allowed him to live. Kevlan initially enjoyed torturing him then took bets on how long it would take to break Whistler's spirit. The Rock Lord ceased wagering several years ago. Elena saw that far away look in his eyes again and sighed, resigned to link her fate with his.

"So what's your plan?"

"What?"

"Your mind races even when we are intimate, Whistler."

"The less you know the better."

"Oh really? And what shall I…no, *we* dwarves do, when the time comes to break the shackles that bind us? Stand by and applaud while you…"

Whistler placed his hand over her mouth and pushed her down on the bed, ignoring the defiance blazing forth from her eyes. Her body was taut and ready to spring at him like a cat on a bird and one wrong word was going to set her off. *When I have all of the details, I'll share them with you. No, wrong thing to say, he thought. If the Rock Lords suspect you know anything they'll torture you into telling them the plan. No, that would make her very angry.*

"I'm so mad and frustrated right now all I want to do is break each and every one of their necks with my bare hands."

He stared intently into her stormy gaze, the seconds ticking by like hours while he waited for her to relax. She began to loosen up, removing his hand from her mouth then pushing him off. She leaned up on her elbow, continuing to look deeply into his unyielding eyes.

Hold on, Whistler, just a few more moments!

"This conversation is far from over, Whistler."

"I'm well aware of that, my sweet. Now, would you please let me sleep for a while?"

Whistler lay back, ignoring the slats digging into his back through the thin mattress. He closed his eyes, listening to Elena quietly moving about in the Spartan shack. He could picture every detail of it in his mind. Drafty windows flanked the crooked door. The worn and faded rug was unraveling along its edges. The rough-hewn table and chairs were nearly indistinguishable from the crude walls. Elena cooked over a pot-bellied stove; the pot, pan and ladle hanging to one side and a few dishes neatly stacked in a freestanding cupboard on the other. The sideboard also held dried food and spices.

Elena tended to the herb garden and was permitted to take a few plant clippings home. She dried them over the stove then tied them into strips of cloth for future use. She worked for the Healer and paid careful attention to his techniques, especially the ones for cuts, scrapes and fevers. The dwarves suffered from those ailments the most. They shared the hard bed and their clothing fit into a small nightstand.

Whistler's mind conjured up the compound. There were about a thousand dwarves living here, a half-day's walk from Kevlan's Hall, the current Rock Lord leader. The Rock Lords' city name changed with every new ruler. The new Lord customarily erased his predecessor's name and replaced it with his own.

There were a hundred huts for the dwarves clustered in the center of the camp, more than half of which housed only males. Work shacks and fields surrounded them. There were no fences. Guards patrolled the perimeter walking wolf-dog hybrids, kept hungry in case a dwarf decided to run away in the middle of the night. The dwarves called these crossbreeds Dribbies; the mangy animals were constantly drooling and foaming at the mouth.

Situated to the east was the Hall; the complex was located near an open plain with little, if any cover. Hundreds of rivers and streams crisscrossed the plain, the largest and deepest originating from high in the mountains and ending about ten miles northwest from the compound near Evan's Peak. The dwarves' ancestral home was both a beacon and a taunt as it rose high into the sky. Whistler tried to imagine what it looked like. He gave up and determined he would find out himself some day. But first he had to get away.

A spontaneous sprint to safety was out of the question. The Rock Lords would chase him by horse and with Dribbies. The horses were fully secured and every wagon, whether being driven by a Rock Lord or dwarf, was thoroughly searched before it went beyond the camp. It was regrettable the dwarf was a full third shorter than the Rock Lords or he could have disguised himself in their garments and simply ridden away. *A pair of wings would make life a tad easier, he thought. Or perhaps the elves charging in to the camp on horseback, swords and bows drawn to liberate his people. I have a better chance of sprouting wings.*

The scent of lemon grass and rosemary became stronger. Elena was coming to bed. She snuggled up against him, positioning her arm over his chest and snoring softly moments later. He kissed the top of her head, grateful he had such a wonderful mate. He couldn't imagine life without her. He heard Dribbies barking and growling in the night not too far away, then the high-pitched screech of some hapless animal that had wandered into the compound. Probably one of those annoying water rats. The stupid thing should have stayed in the stream. Dribbies hated water, avoiding even shallow puddles. Whistler's eyes snapped open and his heart began to beat a little bit faster.

Most of the streams around the camp were no more than waist deep and could be ridden through or jumped by a horse. They meandered in disarray from the river flowing out of the mountains near Evan's Peak. He knew them and the plain well, having spent most of his time breaking up the hard soil just to the south of the waterways. If he could mask his scent enough to confuse the Dribbies, there was a possibility of being successful in getting away. Elena shifted in his embrace, which reminded him of what could happen to her if he did manage to escape. The Rock Lords would torture her remorselessly to find out how he had disappeared. She wouldn't tell them even if she knew, no matter what they did to her. Whistler refused to leave her behind to face the Rock Lords. She was strong and would be able to survive such a harrowing flight.

* * *

Whistler smiled inwardly. The Rock Lords had brought them to work near the densest collection of waterways for the past week giving Whistler plenty of time to study them. The dwarf whittled his options down to two: fewer rills and more running room or more streams with less open ground. Wading through the water would eat up precious time but would protect them from the Dribbies. He would have to decide today. There would be no work over the next two days due to the celebrations marking Kevlan's tenth year reign. It would be the dwarves' first respite in a year. It was also the most opportune time to withdraw from the camp.

Whistler exhaled slowly, grabbing the wheelbarrow handles and pushing it back for another load of dirt. Kevlan planned to erect barracks here in anticipation of expanding his borders. The sentry quarters, once completed, would block any future escape attempts. Whistler intended to be long gone before buildings of any kind stood upon the plain.

Sweat glistened off Whistler's deeply tanned torso, his muscles rippling beneath his scarred skin. He was strangely indebted to the Rock Lords for making him this strong. He would need every ounce of strength to break their shackles and flee. He saw the Overseer approaching out of a corner of his eye, leading a leashed Dribbie. The beast's coarse black fur hung in matted clumps along its sides, the drool hanging in yellowish strands from its jaws. The Overseer stopped, keeping the Dribbie a mere foot away from Whistler and stared at him. The creature reeked of garbage, upon which Dribbies preferred to sleep. The animal shook its head splattering the dwarf with slobber then proceeded to lick himself.

"I can't tell the difference between his spit and your sweat."

Whistler glared at him but said nothing. He rubbed off some of the perspiration and saliva and flicked it at the Dribbie. It growled and snapped at him, taking advantage of the extra leash the Overseer had loosened. The Dribbie drooled all over the dwarf's boot. The urge to throttle them both flared briefly in Whistler's eyes and the Overseer bristled. He sneered malevolently and moved on, careful to keep the dwarf in his sight.

The day finally ended and the dwarves packed up their gear. The sun was low on the horizon when they entered the compound. Whistler's companions were thinking only about the rest they were going to enjoy but Whistler had other ideas. He entered his shack and winked at Elena cooking dinner before washing up.

"I'm going to help Mary tomorrow," she said putting the plates and silverware on the table. The cups tilted to one side on the warped surface, the tea almost dribbling over the cup's rim.

"That's nice." Whistler scanned the hut, taking inventory of what they would be taking with them. It wouldn't be much.

"I might be gone all day."

"Uh-huh."

Elena stopped stirring the pot and eyed him suspiciously. He was none too fond of Mary and to spend so much time away from him would normally have incited quite a discussion between them.

"She asked me to sleep with her mate."

"That's fine."

Elena marched over to him and stuck her face in front of his. He blinked several times and smiled at her.

"What are you up to, Whistler?"

"Later."

"No, now!"

"*Later!*"

They ate, cleaned up the dishes then carried their tea out onto the porch. They sat on the steps, chatting with neighbors and enjoying the balmy early evening air. The dwarves relished their short-lived time away from toiling for the Rock Lords. The shack across the way erupted into music and song, the musicians and singers spilling out onto the street.

THE FORTRESS OF DARKNESS

They tapped their toes to the joyful notes of the flutes, drums and stringed instruments. The happy sounds smoothed away the lines of worry on the dwarves' faces leaving them appearing years younger. Laughter echoed off the stark wooden buildings for the first time in a long time. Whistler held Elena's hand, momentarily forgetting they were enslaved. The enthusiasm was contagious. The couple watched the musicians sauntering up and down the narrow streets followed by dozens of dwarves.

Whistler sighed and looked up at the stars and full moon, the sky appearing peaceful. He did not relish leaving this place, feeling as if he were abandoning his kin. They had looked up to him as their leader. Whether or not they were successful was secondary to the feeling of betrayal they would surely feel. He couldn't help them if he were stuck here. He nudged Elena and the two of them went back into the house.

Whistler carried the chairs into the far corner of the room and sat down, Elena following suit a moment later. She tried to read what was on his mind but he refused to open his thoughts to her. He took her hands in his and spoke in low tones.

"Listen carefully, my love. We are going to leave this place tomorrow night. I need you to make a poultice that will dull the Dribbies' sense of smell. Make up two packs with food, medicine and little else. The only other things we'll need to carry are blankets. Go help Mary tomorrow and do whatever else needs to be done."

Elena grabbed the front of his tunic tugging him toward her until their noses touched. Her blue eyes blazed with fire and a flush rose up into her cheeks. She pressed her lips into a thin line when he raised his brow at her.

"*You had best not leave without me or I'll hunt you down, Whistler.*"

"I wouldn't dare, my love."

The day passed agonizingly slow. Elena went to Mary's house and Whistler played cards with some friends. She cleaned the hut later that afternoon and hung out their washing. Whistler fixed a loose floorboard on the porch. Their neighbors also caught up on chores that had been set aside. Whistler and Elena delighted in the merriment continuing from the previous evening, then retired to share their love for each other. They were optimistic about their chances but realistic at the same time. Anything could happen.

* * *

Elena tied the pouches up tightly then checked the straps on the blankets. She glanced over at Whistler who stowed away a sharpened hoe blade. He had found a rusted one while digging in the dirt and exchanged it for the new one he broke off the tool he was using. It wasn't quite a sword but it was better than nothing. She went to the cupboard and took out the plaster. She applied it to their exposed skin, their trousers and boots. Whistler inhaled and grinned broadly: river mud, thyme and a hint of garlic. He went over to the window and cautiously pulled a corner of the curtain back. The dried out remnants of a bush tumbled unhindered down the quiet street past darkened windows. It was time. Whistler embraced Elena and kissed her passionately on the lips. He mouthed *I love you* and touched her cheek when she repeated it. They took deep breaths then sneaked out the door.

They kept to the shadows, moving soundlessly through the compound toward the northwest. They halted at the last cabin, their backs pressed against the uneven boards waiting for the sounds of pursuit. Everything was quiet. He grabbed her hand and towed her into the murkiness. She clung to it with all her might trusting him with every fiber of her being. They sprinted noiselessly in the direction of the open plain, their hearts beating loudly in their ears. Their breaths sounded raspy in the utter stillness as they raced across the flat ground. Many dwarves had probably taken this same route only to be found and torn apart by the Dribbies. They pushed that thought from their minds and sped on, not willing to become part of that unsuccessful group. Whistler slowed their pace then stopped, listening for any sound of pursuit. Crickets chirped all around them and a light breeze blew past them from the south. A night bird screeched in the gloom startling them both but the distraction was welcome.

They continued on, their leg muscles and lungs beginning to burn with the exertion. They had a long way to go. They finally reached the first stream and carefully entered it. The water was cold, refreshing their heated bodies. They held their packs overhead crossing as quickly as the unseen terrain allowed. Whistler climbed out of the water first and hauled Elena up after him, the water seeping from their clothes dripping on the ground.

"Rest?" he whispered into her ear.

"No, not yet."

They were near the framed pattern of the new barracks' foundation, the rectangular imprint lost in a murky puddle. He headed in a more northerly direction using the shadowy mountain as his guide. Adrenaline kept them moving at a quick pace and they prayed it would circulate through their bodies long enough to put a few more miles between themselves and the camp. The moon dipped lower on the horizon and each step became more laborious.

Whistler decided to stop for a brief rest. They drank from their canteens, sharing the tangy leaves Elena plucked out of her pocket. They chewed on the pulpy bits, the juice being quickly absorbed into their bloodstream. It eased the throbbing in their bodies, replacing it with a burst of energy. The sudden far-off barking carried across the empty plain. Whistler grabbed Elena and the pair was off once more.

Sweat dried on their faces as quickly as it formed except along the backs of their necks. They swung their shoulders back and forth to increase their pace, their soggy collars gradually abrading the skin along the base of their skulls. They pulled the sodden neckbands away from their skin to no avail. The yelping grew steadily louder, carried toward them by the wind drifting from the south. They had to assume they were being followed or risk making a huge mistake.

Whistler guided Elena slightly eastward toward the next waterway. Their initial plunge into the previous stream would only buy them a few minutes. Once they crossed the next one they would have to reapply the salve. The black ribbon was just ahead. They sucked in their breaths as the even colder water soaked their bodies, now creeping up to their armpits. Whistler knew the next one would probably drench them all the way up to their necks. The flow was swifter this time and it took more effort to pull themselves out on the other side. He almost lost his grip on Elena's hand, panicking as the current tried to take her away. He hauled her out and fell in an exhausted heap beside her.

"It's going to get worse," he murmured to her.

"We've come too far to worry about that."

They smeared on more of the dressing and proceeded at a brisk walk. Evan's Peak loomed directly ahead instead of to their left. The faint pounding of hooves accompanied the barking off in the distance. Either the Rock Lords were making an unexpected bed check or someone saw them go. They increased their pace, steering for the smudged line of trees still too far away. Their feet hit the ground in unison, the rhythmic beat carrying them far into the night. They had been on the run for hours and noticed the first faint stains of light in the eastern sky. Time was slipping away from them. They began to jog, not yet willing to expend too much of their stamina in case they were forced to flee from the Rock Lords. Whistler heard the rapids gurgling up ahead and halted. The milky light of the pre-dawn hours illuminated groups of slender trees and thigh high brush hugging the embankment of the river. They ran toward it, the sounds of pursuit still drifting in their direction.

* * *

The Rock Lords walked silently down the streets, the Dribbies pulling on their leashes as they snuffled at everything. One Dribbie would scrabble to a porch and urinate on it inducing the other one to cover its scent. Their favorite watering ground was a few houses down. The Rock Lords stopped in front of Whistler's shack and let the Dribbies void to their hearts content. They knew the hybrids hated this dwarf and often fought each other to be the last one to leave their mark. The dwarves would awaken and Whistler would open his door to toss a pan full of water at the mongrels. The sentinels belched loudly then waved their hands in front of their faces to dissipate the stench of onions, ale and boiled meat. The Dribbies snapped and bit at each other, pulling against their tethers in an attempt to fight. One of the sentries glared at the closed door waiting for the dwarf to come outside.

"He's probably rolling the wench," smirked his comrade, a lecherous look contorting his gaunt features.

"Hey! Maggot! The boys are here paying their respects!" The guard frowned. This was his game and Whistler wasn't playing according to his rules. He paused another moment then stomped up the steps and banged on the door. Silence. He cocked his head, pulled out his sword and tried the handle. It clicked open. The door creaked noisily in the early dawn hours; the dull thud as it hit the wall making them jump. He glanced down at the Dribbie. It cautiously sniffed at the gloomy interior then sat down, tongue flopping over one side of its jaws, and drool out the other side. They surged into the shack and looked about, the curtain in front of the bed getting plenty of attention. The sentries moved forward, yanking it down and sticking the points of their weapons against the sleeping figures. They pushed harder and harder but no one budged. The guard grabbed the corner of the blanket and wrenched it back exposing the carefully positioned pillows.

* * *

"How far do you think we've come?" asked Elena, massaging her aching calves.

"Not far enough."

The sun would be up in less than an hour and their haven loomed darkly a few miles ahead. Whistler knew the sentry's tactics and surmised they would have found their empty bed by now. Pursuit would be inevitable and the horses would cover the ground quickly, led by the Dribbies. He accepted another leaf; slathered on the last of the poultice then helped Elena to her feet. He stared into the shadows before them and wondered who or what they were going to encounter. He had no idea where the Elven city was located or what changes had occurred in the land since the dwarves' enslavement by the Rock Lords. He felt a hand on his arm and looked at Elena. There was just enough light to illuminate the hope and trust shining from her eyes. He offered her an encouraging smile, took her hand and they resumed their journey to freedom.

The sun's first rays broke over the horizon, slowly spreading across the flat plain. It chased away the gloom of night, and their cover. It washed against the eastern side of Evan's Peak looming directly in front of them, the granite face appearing soft and pinkish. The mighty river running south then meandering around the mountain became visible; the rushing water sounded threatening. They approached it and gazed into the swiftly flowing waters. Elena knelt beside the bank and stuck her hand into the river, immediately removing it as its icy touch chilled her to the bone. She looked up at Whistler then cautiously rose to her feet and gazed in the same direction as her mate. The movement along the southeast horizon was still distant, the dark shapes barely discernible in the dusky light. She took a long breath then slowly exhaled.

Whistler scanned the river toward Evan's Peak hoping he'd find something to help them cross more safely. If they attempted to traverse it here they would be swept around and end up near where the riders were heading. They walked along the river, looking for anything that would suffice. Whistler stopped and stared at the entrance to the mountain. Tendrils of mist seeped out of the damp interior, oozing down the broken steps carved out of the mountain, stirring the weeds poking out between the cracks. It continued to advance until it drifted into the sunlight where the bright rays withered the fog. A shaft of light traveled toward them and fell upon a collection of branches and flat rocks. Whistler walked over to the debris and smiled. It was the remnants of a bridge.

The weathered and splintered beams had survived the ravages of time and neglect even though the planking had not. The posts were evenly spaced except in the middle of the river where the supports disappeared. He scratched the back of his head, surveying every detail in front of him. Were they there but so far beneath the water he couldn't see them?

"Whistler, we have to go."

The dwarf glanced toward the now fully visible riders. He nodded and descended the steep embankment, clutching at the wiry grasses to steady himself. He sucked in air as his feet then his legs and waist disappeared into the frigid waters. He began to shiver as he helped Elena down into the river, careful to keep a firm grip on the post. She grabbed the strap on his pack with one hand and the shaft with the other. They worked their way toward the center of the river, the ice-cold flow constantly trying to tug them into its black depths.

They reached the middle and stopped, the freezing waters sapping their strength but not their resolve to persevere. Whistler groped with his foot and found the fractured beam with his knee. They would have to submerse themselves if they wanted to use it. Where was the next one? Deeper still? Gone altogether? He looked over at Elena and frowned. Her face was pale, her lips were turning blue, and she was shivering uncontrollably. He brought his hand up to motion her downward, his ashen skin and purplish nails appearing garish in the early light. They plunged toward the pylon, the icy water feeling like daggers being thrust into their heads. Whistler grabbed the wood and tried to see where the next one was located. It was down another two feet ahead of them. He towed Elena forward and clutched the beam with his weakened fingers. The next support was above the water but the cold was draining his ability to think and feel. He pushed on, seizing the remaining pillars with urgency bordering on panic. He propelled himself toward the opposite riverbank, grasping at whatever held his weight. He turned to help Elena out of the water but her frozen flesh and bones couldn't keep the contact any longer.

She slipped away from him and began the dangerous journey toward the Rock Lords now less than a couple of miles downstream. Whistler scrambled onto the flat ground on the other side and followed her as she bobbed along then disappeared beneath the water. She was too exhausted and cold to do more than stare at him. He shouted words of encouragement to her, praying an opportunity would allow him to reach out and grab her. He glanced up ahead at the bend in the river where a tree had fallen down the embankment. The current was heading in that direction. He forced his benumbed legs to hasten, sliding to a halt and lunging on top of the unsteady log seconds before she drifted by. He reached out, clutched the back of her tunic, and fought the river for her life.

He pulled her out, the cold emitted by her frozen form seeping into his overheated body. He vigorously rubbed her face, legs and arms and called out her name. She sluggishly returned to consciousness and smiled weakly up at him.

"We have to keep moving, Elena."

"I know…help me up," she replied in a weak voice. Elena tried to take a step and collapsed to the ground. "I can't feel my feet, Whistler!" Her wide eyes implored him for help.

"Just keep putting one foot in front of the other, Elena," he put his arm around her, "they'll warm up in no time."

The sun's warmth slowly dried their clothing except for the spot on their backs where the sodden packs rested. Their blankets, once light, now felt like boulders. They slammed against their bodies and threatened to topple them backward as they hiked up the hill overlooking the river. They made it to the top and concealed themselves within the trees and brush, then glanced back the way they had come. Evan's Peak towered into the cloudless blue sky, the ancient fortification seemingly calling out to them to enter it and reestablish its glory.

The Rock Lords, however, were the ones answering its silent plea. They reined in a quarter mile south of where the dwarves had entered the river and scanned the area. The couple ducked further into the vegetation and watched their pursuers. The Dribbies snuffled about trying to pick up a scent, and then began to fight each other. The Rock Lords dismounted and beat them apart before snapping the leashes around their mangy necks. One of the guards pointed southwest and, after a brief but animated conversation, the others followed him.

They remained motionless for a long time watching the riders getting smaller and smaller. They feared the Rock Lords would head far enough south then find a way across and capture them in the coming hours or days. They walked westward keeping to the safety of the fragrant pines, the dappled sunlight beginning to thaw their chilled bodies. They rested briefly, eating soggy food and kneading their aching muscles. The color was slowly seeping back into their faces as the sun looped in front of them. They came upon an open area and decided to stop for a while. They unrolled their blankets and hung them to dry on the low hanging branches. Whistler and Elena stripped off everything except their loose undergarments and suspended them, too. It took Whistler a long time to make a fire. They had decided it would be less noticeable during the daylight and would help them warm up before it got cold in the nighttime.

Elena filled the pot with water from a nearby stream and placed it over the flames then spread out everything else to dry.

Whistler lay back on the ground and gazed up into the cloudless sky. A hawk floated effortlessly in lazy circles; its wings never flapping as it rode the thermals high in the air. Once their wings dried out they, too would fly away. He began to doze off, the sun's heat relaxing him as it seeped into his flesh and muscles. They had succeeded in escaping the Rock Lords but it remained to be seen if they could find help to liberate his folk. Where were they to find the elves? None of the dwarves could remember anyone who had contact with them. Whistler had no idea where Bystyn was located or if they would be welcomed if they did find the Elven city. What was he supposed to do if they chose to ignore him? A chill rippled through his body, stealing away his momentary tranquility. He opened his eyes and sat up, his fatigue replaced with anxiety.

Elena ran her hand over some of the clothing, taking down what had dried and readjusting what now hung in the shade. He saw the bruises and cuts marring her limbs and side. He glanced down at his own body and absently rubbed at the discolored welts and jagged scratches. They were fortunate neither had any broken bones or internal injuries. Whistler smiled with pride at her. The strength running through her originated in her soul and radiated outward to him. He doubted he could have prevailed had she not been by his side. He was determined to keep her safe at all costs.

* * *

They awoke at dawn, their bodies sore from their exertions. They collected their things and headed west paralleling the sheer mountains to the north. They stared at the trees and bushes with wonder. The clusters of hardwoods out on the plain were thin, their leaves tiny; the thicker stands only vague outlines on the horizon. Elena reached out, plucked a beech leaf from a branch, and stroked it against her cheek. She glanced over at Whistler who remained vigilant for any signs of danger. She sighed and reluctantly let the leaf drift to the ground.

They made steady progress, heading farther and farther away from their slave masters yet did not meet up with anyone during their journey west. It had been more than a week since they stepped onto the land on the other side of the river. Food was plentiful. What Whistler didn't trap Elena was able to pick from bushes heavy with berries. They started with optimism every morning but it was a growing skepticism that lay down beside them at night. Their relief was slowly turning into impatience.

The rumble of thunder off in the distance urged them to seek shelter earlier than usual. They spotted an overhanging rock and ducked beneath it. The thunder grew louder and the rain began to pour from the skies. The dwarf couple brought their knees to their chests to keep their feet from getting wet. They peered out at the shimmering curtain of water drenching the earth; the soft pattering sound was not enough to soothe their nervous spirits. Elena began to hum a song, her melodious notes calming Whistler's anxiety. The shower began to diminish; the sun chased away the clouds leaving a glistening mist in its wake. They emerged from their refuge and looked up. The sky was blue once more and the last vestiges of the clouds dissipated beneath the bright orbs' glare. The trees sparkled with the droplets as they trickled onto the emerald grasses. The air smelled cleaner and the pair inhaled deeply.

"We still have several hours of daylight left, Elena, perhaps we should take a more southerly route?"

"Let's stay the course for the rest of this day then change direction tomorrow."

"I wish we knew where we were."

"Save your wishes for when we really need them, Whistler."

They walked on, their distorted shadows growing longer behind them as the afternoon wore on. Their shoulders began to slump, their eyes focusing on the ground in front of them. They were beginning to think they were the only people in the land. They followed a vague trail, the setting sun bathing them in a warm, soft light. Whistler halted and stared ahead. The trees were becoming smaller and there were wider swatches of open area. Bushes and grasses were more numerous and they could see a broad plain through their thinning branches. Whistler glanced toward the ribbon of trees continuing on north and west then turned back to the plain. Elena looked back the way they had come, then at her mate.

They headed for the last line of undergrowth, squatting down to remain unseen as they scanned the vast plain to the south. They gazed eastward and saw the undulating line of the forest they hid within. Whistler narrowed his eyes as he studied a dark blur directly south of them. The gathering darkness spread eastward and the indistinct shape was soon lost in the shadows.

Whistler was about to speak when the sound of muffled hooves broke the silence. He pushed Elena deeper into the brush and took out the hoe blade. The riders came from the west but he could not ignore the fear the Rock Lords had somehow circumvented them. He listened then smiled: there were no snarling and growling noises. He waited quietly, the outsiders emerging into view. Two horses and five people halted before him. He glanced over at Elena who nodded encouragingly at him. Whistler stepped out from their place of concealment when the riders were close enough to see him clearly. They reined in immediately, the opposing travelers staring at each other with a combination of confusion and suspicion.

-5-

"You're crazy!" shouted Clay. "What makes you think the three of us could destroy this Emhella even if he did exist?"

August studied Sara's features. There were lines of worry pulling at her skin. She exhaled slowly, her dainty hand pushing aside a section of black hair from her forehead.

"Why is he here?" asked August.

"You actually believe this drivel? Come on, Augie! He isn't real!"

"He wants to finish what Mahn started."

"And that is?"

"Destroy the land."

"Who's Mahn? Why are you paying any attention to her tale, Augie?" Clay's sarcasm sliced through the air. He walked away, glancing briefly in the direction the elves had gone.

August had never heard of Mahn, Vox, or what had transpired years ago until Sara told them the story. He did not doubt demons existed because her presence proved that. How far-fetched would it seem if there were malevolent creatures skulking around? The land was ripe for upheaval and none of the Races cared what went on beyond their borders. Many, like himself and Clay, were nothing more than vagabonds trekking wherever their hearts desired, with no loyalty to anyone but themselves. Their boredom and hunger for adventure had brought them to this point.

"Why us, Sara?"

"Because there is no one else," she replied in a small voice.

He reached over and took her hands into his, his fingers trying to massage warmth into her cool flesh. She flinched and sought to break the contact, a faint red tinge coloring her cheeks.

"That won't help, August, but thank you anyway."

"What do you want us to do?" He reluctantly released his grip, his fingertips grazing against hers eliciting the smallest of smiles on his face.

"I doubt that Clay will..."

"He will, trust me. He needs to wash away the bitterness of being rebuffed and this is the perfect solution."

"I'll let you know *if* and *when* Clay consents."

The evening breeze flowed unobstructed across the open plain and stirred their clothing and hair. It carried with it earthy aromas and the chirping of insects hiding in the grasses. The first stars glittered overhead, their twinkling becoming more pronounced as the sky faded to black. August cooked and kept an eye on Clay. The elf sat with hunched shoulders on a little rise, a dejected silhouette blocking out the dark shapes beyond.

Sara accepted the plate of vegetables and meat and the mug of tea. August fixed a second dish and carried it over to Clay. He squatted down beside his friend for a few moments, patted his shoulder then rejoined Sara. They ate in silence, gazing toward the elf now and then. After they finished their meal, they cleaned and stowed the gear.

Sara and August sat in front of the embers mesmerized by the moths fluttering erratically over the orange glow. The gentle radiance softened August's strong features yet accentuated his almost meditative countenance. A relieved smile touched his lips. Sara followed his gaze and nodded faintly as Clay emerged from the shadows. August handed him a small flask before the elf flopped down on the grass. He uncorked it, took a long swig and passed it over to Sara. She sniffed it and shuddered, took a small sip, her eyes watering as the liquid trickled into her mouth.

"This Emhella...what exactly is he?" Clay finally asked.

"Emhella is...was a Vox, one of the highest forms of demons." Her companions' blank stares caused her to pause for a moment. "There were three types of demons in the land before Prince Danyl of Bystyn slew

Mahn outside the gates of the Elven city. The lowest form is the Kreetch, which still exist. You also have the Radir and the Vox. The Radir and the Vox are capable of possessing a human but only the Vox can manipulate their hosts. Emhella, the strongest and most ruthless of the Vox, seized Allad's body. The Herkah was the greatest fighter in the land and Emhella put Allad's tremendous attributes to good use. He used Allad's combat skills to exterminate the Radir and the Vox, leaving him unopposed in carrying out his plan."

"What does he look like?"

"He's a larger, brawnier and meaner version of August."

"That wasn't a compliment, was it?" August was listening intently as his friends discussed him as if he weren't there.

"Augie isn't a Herkah, Sara. Just because he feels most at home along the desert doesn't mean he's a nomad."

"I've seen enough Herkahs, Clay. Trust me…August is one of them."

August opened his mouth to protest, the mere idea that he was related to the Dark Clan the most preposterous thing he had ever heard. He was nothing more than an orphan, drifting across the land like a dandelion seed that never lands long enough to take root. To associate him with the legendary Herkahs was ludicrous.

"And this demon's agenda is what?"

"He wants to accumulate all of the magic he can find then use the combination to open up the underbelly of the land."

"What does that mean, Sara?" asked August, his head tilted to one side, his heart starting to beat a little bit faster.

"The land below is sterile. It is nothing more than rock, molten lava and sulfurous vapors. It would smother the living and allow all the demons to inhabit the land."

"Does he have any of the powers yet?"

"Yes, Clay. He has the Source of Darkness. The Source," she explained as they listened intently, "was the magic Mahn sought. A demon named Ramira housed that power and she used it to trap Mahn deep within her spirit where Danyl battled and defeated him. Danyl and Ramira were destined to be with each other not just because of what fate had in store for them but also because of the love that bound them together. We must find the heir that bears the Green Might and we must find him or her before Emhella does."

"If what you say is true then we must get into Bystyn and find the bearer." August spoke firmly with conviction.

"They won't let me in, Augie. What makes you think they'll believe this story?"

"We'll just have to find someone who will listen to us."

"How? Try and convince the next patrol to escort us in?" Clay snorted.

"The wielder of the Elven magic is not in Bystyn," Sara interrupted them.

"How do you know that?"

"I am a demon, Clay, and am bound to my origins. I can venture to a place where the river of the netherworld and all its peculiarities flow and with them the fragments of all magic. The Green Might is lost within this current."

August and Clay exchanged uneasy glances. Sara's words sent shivers up and down their spines yet Clay remained unconvinced. He spotted May sitting on his pack, the spider's front legs supporting her head. Was this insect actually paying attention to human conversation? Her head swiveled toward him and, for a moment, he thought he saw her nod. He blinked several times then peered at her again.

"Can't you use your abilities to pinpoint the bearer?"

Sara took a deep breath and closed her eyes. She shuddered with fear and revulsion every time she thought about that transcendental space. It peeled away your beliefs and everything you ever learned. It stripped you of your emotions, dreams and self-made delusions. It revealed the truth about who you were and made you live by that reality. A brief image of August's exposed throat pulsed in her mind and though she immediately cast it out, her mouth watered nonetheless.

"It is not a place I would want to venture into very often," she replied, her stomach churning at the fading vision.

"Perhaps we can head east and try knocking on Bystyn's door from a different direction. Maybe we'll happen upon a patrol that's a bit more sympathetic," suggested August, the long silence and indecision as to what to do pressing down on them.

They spoke no more, choosing instead to get as much rest as they could. Clay glanced over at August's obscure shape. *So, you're a Herkah, my friend. At least now you know your heritage. I can't even get my own kin to let me into the city so I can do the same.*

August stared up into the star-filled heavens, the pulse of the far off desert pounding in his veins. He had always wanted to believe he was a child of the sands. The desert dwellers had migrated into the far reaches of the desert a long time ago yet they continued to live and breathe in his dreams. He expected the same 'welcome' from them that Clay received from the elves. Outsiders in any Race found it difficult to become part of the whole. He noticed Sara's shape in the near darkness. She stood watch over them as she had since the moment they left the mountain. What lived within her that allowed her to distance herself from her heritage? Sara filled his vision, her delicate beauty whispering to him from out of the dimness. August rose from his bedroll and sat beside her, her luminous eyes welcoming.

"What compels you to undertake this task?"

"I've been down in that frightful lair, August," she murmured, trembling at the memory.

"But that isn't the only reason, is it?"

"No. None of us can change what we are but we can decide who we want to be. I like the sunlight on my face and watching the leaves change color. I miss Master Felix and Charla and am grateful for your company."

"You're more human than you give yourself credit for, Sara."

"That means a great deal to me, August." Her eyes filled with tears as she struggled to maintain her composure. She almost succeeded until August's arm wrapped protectively around her shoulders. The teardrops trickled unheeded down her face and onto his tunic.

* * *

August studied the forest running parallel with the massive mountains to the north. The craggy peaks seemed to loom directly overhead, the dull gray rocks appearing imposing even though they were awash with the sun's soft golden light. He bit his bottom lip in thought as he attempted to gauge what lay between the woods and the base of the range. He glanced to the east then back to the north.

"What are you mulling over?" asked Clay as he adjusted Essa's bridle.

"The elves will be extra vigilant now but they can't confront us if they can't find us."

Clay followed August's line of sight. "You want to go in there?"

"Why not?"

"We don't know what's on the other side."

"We know what's waiting for us on *this* side."

"August's right, Clay, we may be safer there."

Clay shook his head and jumped up into his saddle, waving August and Sara by. The trio entered the outer perimeter, the saplings and bushes allowing some light to penetrate. Essa and Tauth carefully picked their way over rotting trunks and around partially buried boulders. The daylight behind them began to diminish; the only sounds came from the creaking leather of their saddles and the occasional snapping of twigs. They could see sections of the cliff in between the treetops as they rode through the murky silence, its drab bulk looking as if it were about to fall down on top of them.

Sara noted the pines. The coarse bark curling away from the caramel colored trunks exposed an underlying layer of pale gold. The deep green bristly needles were as thick as spikes. A pair of deer moved through a stand of hardwoods to their right, the buck's proud head crowned with an impressive rack. Chipmunks darted from one rotted out log to another, their high-pitched squeaks muffled within the mossy undergrowth. The sun shone down from directly overhead. Dust particles shimmered within the bright shafts of light. They rode into a clearing and stopped, noticing overgrown pathways, partially filled in fire pits and lichen covered hatchet marks on the trunks.

August glanced upward, his brows knitted together as he espied a platform tilting dangerously from a massive bough. A pile of splintering lumber lay in a jumble at the bottom. He saw May jump up onto Sara's head and slowly turn around, the spider's curiosity as keen as his own.

"I wonder who lived here."

"Whoever it was has been gone for a long time, August," Sara said in quiet tones, her gaze falling on a clay pitcher, its unadorned surface riddled with fractures.

They pushed on, hoping to reach the other side of the woods before nightfall. The sun's rays began to angle into the forest then faded from view, the peculiar half-light making everything appear blurred and closer than they actually were. A peculiar silvery glow began to penetrate the trees in front of them, its source revealed about an hour later.

The companions halted at the edge of the woodland, gaping at the vast wall of granite rising up into the heavens a half mile before them. A cold wind ruffled their hair and clothes, prompting them to put on their cloaks. May clambered into Sara's hood and pulled as much material over her as she could.

The boulder-strewn passage ran for miles in either direction, the desolation it exuded silently shared amongst the trio. They stared upward into the fog-enshrouded peaks, the mist surging down then retreating to the summit. The horses snorted nervously and jerked their heads.

"Let's go," Clay's voice broke the spell the mountains had on them.

The companions followed the range as it ran in a nearly straight line east. They were surprised yet relieved there were no patrols in this area. The days wore on and they continued without meeting anyone along the way. They had been traveling for five days when they spotted farmlands and villages miles to the south through gaps between the trees. People worked the fields and drove wagons all under the watchful eye of guards. A vast structure rose up from the plain to the southeast, the light reflecting off the gray walls and towers. Clusters of shapes moved along the flat land all around it; some entering while others exited the city.

"It's remarkable," breathed Clay, his eyes wide with amazement.

"Very impressive," agreed August.

Sara studied the city. It was indeed grand yet it exuded a sense of being imposing as well. It appeared prosperous so why then deny Clay access to it? She could understand them being suspicious of herself and August but not of the elf. *We were fortunate not to have needed any aid.*

They hid themselves in the shadows of the trees, watching the goings on around Bystyn until the sun disappeared behind the mountains in the west. Clay was so preoccupied that he failed to notice May sitting beside him. She tugged on his tunic demanding his attention, skittering away a few inches when his unfocused eyes finally turned to her. She no longer made him jump out of his skin but he did instinctively try to brush her aside when she simply appeared by his side. August and Sara watched them from a few yards away, fascinated by May's attraction to the elf.

Clay caught a moth fluttering by and hesitantly held it out to the spider. May ignored the insect, her attention never wavering from the elf. Clay let it free then lay down on his side, cradling his head in his hand and holding out his other palm toward her. She crawled demurely over to it and gently nibbled on the tip of his forefinger. She slowly crept onto his hand and curled up. Clay's brows knotted first in surprise then in confusion. He had expected to feel a scaly, cold body but May's smooth abdomen radiated warmth and her imposing legs tickled his skin. He held her up closer to his face, his keen ears picking up the faintest of purring even though his mind told him that spiders didn't make sounds.

"Why is May so different from others of her kind?" he asked Sara.

"I suppose for the same reason we are all distinct from our own," replied Sara.

"She sure likes you though," added August.

"Yes, she does, doesn't she? I wonder why?"

The evening breeze stirred the leaves, the peaceful rustling sound blending perfectly with the crickets and night birds chirping in the gathering darkness. Sara inhaled the clean, fresh scent of the land and closed her eyes. She sensed the dampness in the air and anticipated the reviving sensation rain would bring once it cleansed the land of summer's heat. Nearly imperceptible flecks of bright green lights danced momentarily across her closed lids, their soothing presence easing the burdens of her journey. She opened her eyes, the slight smile on her face fading away as she beheld Clay's features. He seemed frozen as he stared intently and with a touch of uncertainty at her. She glanced at May, and the spider's attention firmly focused onto her. August joined Clay and May and mirrored their unexpected responses.

"What's...what's wrong?"

"Your eyes, Sara..."

"They're shining more brightly than the finest emerald," August finished Clay's statement. The seconds ticked by as the verdant hue in her eyes ebbed then disappeared.

"Now they're silver again."

Sara took a deep breath, her gaze never leaving Clay as she shifted her weight onto her knees and one arm, trembling as she reached for his cheek. Clay sat motionless; August licked his dry lips, his gaze darting between the elf and the demon. May cowered in Clay's palm as Sara's cool fingers touched the elf's heated skin.

For a brief moment, nothing happened. Sara's body began to relax and Clay began to breathe again when complete darkness surrounded them. They could not see anything, not even each other; only the contact between their flesh existed in this fearful place. The air they inhaled and exhaled threatened to freeze their lungs; their bodies shivered in the frigid void. This was not the place Sara dreaded but that did not diminish her anxiety. They could hear each other breathe and feel the condensed droplets on their skin. The wait seemed interminable.

They could hear the rush of air heading for them but neither could move. They began to breathe more rapidly, their hearts racing with a nervous panic. The outer bands of the invisible wind wrapped around them then the howling and screaming began. The madly spinning vortex suddenly exploded, bathing them in silver and green, the sheer force of the power making them tremble. Tears streaked down their cheeks as the pressure squeezed at them from every direction, then everything became still in a hazy half-light.

Sara clasped Clay's hand tightly, afraid of losing her only connection to life if she let go. She could feel his fingers interlacing with hers, the sensation giving them both some measure of security. The fog began to close in on them then the icy blackness took over once more.

August hastened backward away from Clay and Sara, their opaque shapes fluctuating within a peculiar light. He welcomed May's contact, the spider clinging to his skin and tunic as she watched the unfolding drama with him. His emotions revealed in his expression ranged from surprise to shock to confusion. He was anxious for his friends' well-being, more with every passing second, yet he could not move a muscle to try to yank them out of their trance. He dared not blink or breathe. *Come back…come back from wherever you have gone! Please!* He noticed Sara's fingers laced tightly with Clay's and Clay's hand tightened on hers. Finally, his friends slowly returned to the present. Sara toppled over, the Herkah saving her from falling face down into the ground as he lunged toward her. Clay landed on a thick patch of grass.

The elf came to first, rubbing at his face and head. He tried to focus his gaze, complaining of double vision. He looked over at two Augusts holding onto two Sara's, the 'girls' dangling limply in his arms. He tried to clear his head by shaking it and crawled over to them. He stroked Sara's face then placed a damp cloth on her forehead.

"What in the Four Corners happened?" demanded August.

"I'm not sure, Augie," replied Clay in a subdued voice. "It was the strangest thing I've ever experienced."

* * *

Balyd tended to Garadan's injuries, which were thankfully superficial. He gave him water and food, patiently waiting for the elf to collect himself before asking him any questions. He studied Garadan's face and felt his stomach turn. Disbelief tempered with fear and anger filled his loyal servant's brown eyes. They were wide with a pain not solely due to his wounds. Balyd dabbed at the man's scraped knuckles and cuts, keeping his eyes averted as Garadan spoke in a dry, choked voice.

"We headed south, Lord Balyd, just as you suggested, ending up on the outskirts of Kepracarn. We were careful, avoiding any contact with the men living in that area, managing to observe without being seen. Things went well for us until a group of men caught Dardan out in the open. They chased him and the three of us were forced to intervene. We managed to hold our own for a while then Dardan was slain. The men overwhelmed us and we were taken prisoner."

Balyd pushed Garadan's sleeves up and flinched. The rope burns around the thin wrists were raw and he could feel the heat they gave off. He gently plucked out bits of fiber sticking out from the open sores then cleaned and bound the injuries. He helped the elf slip his tunic off and winced at the whip marks striping his gaunt torso. What hadn't been lashed pulsed with ugly bruises. The elf hadn't just been taken prisoner; he had been deliberately tortured.

Garadan sipped water to moisten his throat but the cool liquid did nothing to refresh his parched soul. He thought to himself that he would probably remain thirsty even if he drank the Ahltyn River dry.

"The men made us walk to the peninsula in the far southwestern corner of the land. People spit at us; threw rotten food in our faces and called us names we didn't understand but we grasped the hatred and fear in their tones. They beat one of my men to death in the square then let the other one go. They laughed and jeered at him as he ran across the open expanse back up toward the land. They drank from several skins of ale while they waited, then set out after him with drawn swords and hunting dogs. They returned a short time later holding his head up in the air, the frozen expression of horror on his dead face forever imprinted on my mind.

"Then it was my turn. They yanked my tunic up over my shoulders and began to whip me. When that bored them, they told me to run. I headed for the nearest cover, the dogs snarling at my heels. The lead dog lunged for me and I was fortunate enough to grab it and snap its neck and toss it to the others. They smelled blood and stopped chasing me to tear the animal to pieces. I could hear my pursuers cursing at the hounds but only one man continued to follow me. I climbed into a tree and waited for him, shoving him off his horse and taking his place in the saddle.

"I scrounged for food wherever I could and lost the horse two days out. It broke a leg when it stepped into a burrow and I had no choice but to put it out of its misery. I had to hide from the sentries, resting during the day and running at night. I didn't think I'd make it back, Lord Balyd."

"Why all that hatred toward the elves, Garadan?"

"I don't know, my Lord."

Lord Balyd heard the echoes of Taman's voice in his head. Had the elf been correct about the Vox? Perhaps Man had just become less civilized during the years since the elves last had contact with them. No. They were climbing up the ladder of success and would have no need to revert to barbarous actions—that was reserved for desperate people struggling to survive. Balyd needed more answers and the only one he could trust to find them would need several days to rest and recover from his plight. His own days in the company of the queen were dwindling. He would not be allowed to participate in the meetings concerning the city affairs when his influence was no longer desired.

"Something other than my news troubles you, doesn't it Lord Balyd?"

"I'm going to be replaced by Caladan soon."

"You must be joking!"

"No, son, I'm afraid not."

"But there is the threat of real danger out in the land and Caladan would only distract the queen more!" Garadan sat up, the cloth falling unheeded from his forehead. He grabbed Balyd's arm.

"I must seek out someone that can help us!"

"You need to rest then…"

"I'll be ready to travel in the morning."

"And where will you go, my friend?"

Garadan stared at the braided rug under their feet, the once bright blues and greens faded with time and use. The lazy circular weave appeared more oval than round and he could see the gray stone between the torn stitching. He imagined the city might well be like the rug: well worn, warm and useful but fraying nonetheless. He knew Lord Balyd had done everything he could to mend it back together but it was too much for one person. He also knew the queen did everything she could, albeit unwittingly, to pull apart the stitches. *What we need was a ruler who…no! That was treasonous thinking!* He prayed silently Balyd could not read his mind.

He chanced a furtive glance at Balyd. For a fleeting moment, Garadan thought he saw fear in the older elf's expression.

"I'll go wherever you think help can be found. There's something else, isn't there?"

"Yes. I have learned our self-indulgent complacency is not our worst enemy."

Balyd told Garadan about the Vox and the omens that Taman had reported to him. He had expected the young elf to scoff but Garadan chewed his lower lip and seemed to believe every word Balyd spoke.

"That might explain why the Kepracarnians reacted the way they did.

They already sense something isn't quite right and our presence might have made them think we're the reason for it."

"You…"

A rustling in the rear of the library stilled the conversation. Garadan instinctively reached for his sword and stood up, swaying unsteadily on his feet. Balyd slipped his hands under his wide sleeves until he grasped a pair of knives strapped to his forearms. A shadow emerged from the dim back section of the chamber and Balyd sighed with relief as Taman walked over to them. The stocky elf studied Garadan with narrowed eyes.

"Sheathe your weapon, Garadan. This is Taman, my little library mouse."

"What happened to you?" asked Taman after carefully shaking the elf's injured hand.

Balyd decided to trust Taman and proceeded to tell him about Garadan's missions. Both elves knew the information they passed onto Taman could cost them their heads, but Balyd was convinced Taman had no intention of sharing it with anyone outside this room. Taman crossed his arms and listened intently, especially to the reactions of the people that had killed Garadan's men. He nodded in sympathy toward Garadan and shook his head in dismay when Balyd revealed his successor.

"This is going from bad to worse," Taman stated quietly.

"Do you have any ideas, son?"

"My thoughts could get me killed, Lord Balyd."

"We'll debate that later on."

"We have to find the bearer of the Green Might and hope he or she is able to kill the Vox."

"The Elven magic hasn't been needed in a very long time, Taman, and I haven't seen anyone in the castle worthy enough to harbor it in themselves."

"I'm hoping it isn't in the queen," muttered Garadan.

"Prince Danyl was the last elf to wield it and he didn't know it dwelled within him until it was nearly time to use it against Mahn. It would have been passed down through his bloodline."

Balyd was lost in thought as his mind traced back Aryanda's lineage to Danyl's time. Prince Styph, Danyl's older brother and crown prince, succeeded their father, Alyxandyr. Styph ruled for about a dozen years, dying before producing any heirs. Prince Nyk, also an older brother, had perished during the battle. Princess Alyssa, their sister, became queen and it was through her line that Aryanda now governed. Danyl and Ramira had left the castle and taken up residence out on the plains, removed from the affairs of the city. They had one child; a boy named Tarat who they sent to Terracine when the boy was eight or nine years old. Tarat returned to Bystyn a man but didn't stay for very long. He left after less than a year and was never heard from again.

"Danyl's line ended after only one generation," Balyd said.

"Danyl's line *disappeared* after only one generation. That does not mean it ceased to exist altogether."

"What are you saying, Taman?"

Both Balyd and Garadan leaned forward, their eyes unblinking and their expressions gravely serious.

"Danyl and Ramira chose to remain outside the city's walls, content to live a quiet and unobtrusive life together. They instilled this into Tarat who decided the anonymity of Terracine was preferable over the too formal atmosphere within the castle."

"So Terracine would have any records concerning his offspring?" asked Garadan.

"Perhaps."

"How long would it take to reach the mountain hall?"

"We wouldn't have time for that even if the archives reveal all of Tarat's descendants, Garadan. The Vox' presence would already have disturbed the Elven Might and it would have compelled the bearer into action."

"How do you know that?"

"I'm a library mouse, remember?" was the vague response. "Most of what I've told you is conjecture based upon what I've read."

"So all we have to do then is find the bearer and convince him or her to fight this Vox?"

"That's what I believe, Garadan."

"Do you know how vast this land is? Have you ever been outside this library?"

"Yes, to both questions but if we don't try it won't matter who is handed Balyd's power or who reigns, now will it?"

Garadan and Balyd were silent for a long time trying to make sense of what they had just learned. Garadan would be unable to make any journey until he recuperated; Balyd was a few days away from losing his position and the bearer, if he or she even existed, could be anywhere in the land. Balyd glanced at Taman. The elf held his gaze, his gray eyes never wavering for one moment.

"Who are you?" Balyd asked in hushed tones.

"I am simply an elf who does not wish to be thrust into the lightless world of the Vox."

"Suppose you do venture out and attempt to find this heir," mused Garadan.

"How will you know that he or she is the one?"

"You must rely on your gut instinct to tell you, Garadan."

"Do you have a plan?"

"Yes, Lord Balyd. The bearer's power will be responding to the Vox and should be somewhere between here and the Broken Plains. If we sneak out and head south then turn west we should…"

"Most of the elven patrols are in that section of the land, Taman."

"Then we ride north and follow the corridor between the forest and mountains instead."

"'We'? 'We' are you and I, Taman. No one else can be trusted."

Taman glanced over at Balyd who shrugged his shoulders in response. Taman hadn't been looking for an army to pursue the wielder but he had hoped for more than just one other companion, an injured and exhausted one to boot. The late afternoon shadows filtering into the silent library grew longer with every passing minute. Demons and magic hovered invisibly in the air between the believer, the doubter and the worrier.

"Could you be ready before sunrise?" asked the skeptic quietly.

"I'm ready now," replied the convinced.

Balyd led them to the storage chamber in the rear of the chamber where no one ever went anymore. He gave them blankets and food and hoped they would rest before their unusual journey began.

"I'll gather enough supplies for you both," the First Advisor stated, the gloominess accentuating his haggard features.

"We'll be gone before you awaken, Lord Balyd."

"I usually sleep in the library, Garadan. Taman can attest to that."

Garadan nodded then turned the lamp down low, watching the closing door cast a huge silhouette against the wall. He lay down on top of an elongated box just wide enough to support his wiry frame and exhaled, his body starting to relax. He glanced over at Taman sitting cross-legged on three flat chests he had pushed together. His hands rested on his knees and his back was ramrod straight. His eyes were closed and beads of perspiration glistened above his upper lip and on his forehead. Garadan leaned up on his elbow fascinated by Taman's odd behavior. The elf's lids gradually opened. Garadan could see the other's eyes clearly even in the dimness of the chamber. He felt the hair rising on his arms and the back of his neck as the whites of his eyes appeared filled with large black shapes. *Sweet mercy! What in the Four Corners of the land is going on?* Taman blinked and his eyes returned to normal. His gaze traveled over to Garadan.

"Is something wrong?"

"Your eyes…"

"They react to the displacement of any magic in the land, good or evil."

"And what kind of wizardry did you just sense?" asked Garadan, still mesmerized by what he had seen.

"It wasn't clear."

Garadan lay back down and placed his arm over his eyes but Taman's bizarre expression would not go away. He did not frighten easily, even when the men and their dogs had pursued him. Something abstract and eerie inhabited Taman's body and soul, something that could not be confronted with sword or fist. His exhausted body slowly shut down his mind and, as much as he wanted to remain awake and contemplate what he had seen and heard, he fell asleep.

Taman shook him awake, ignoring Garadan's startled response when he saw Taman standing over him. Balyd handed them steaming plates of food and mugs of tea then double-checked the contents of their gear.

They did not speak while they ate nor when Balyd administered to Garadan's injuries one last time. They left the room and headed toward the hidden door, stopping just long enough to shake hands and silently wish each other well.

Balyd watched the darkness swallow them up then closed the door, shutting his eyes and visualizing the elves scurrying down the pitch-black corridor through the garden to the exit near the dying rosebush. He could imagine them scaling the wall using the tree, then disappearing over the enclosure. He took a deep breath and resumed his duties.

Taman led Garadan through the rarely used alleyways behind the courtyard, moving silently through the darkness. Garadan had lived in Bystyn all his life yet had never known these side streets even existed. Taman proceeded without hesitation making right and left turns with such frequency Garadan soon lost his bearings. He followed the brown elf until Taman suddenly stopped. There were four gates into and out of the city: the largest one the main entrance in the southern section and three smaller entries in the east, west and northern portions. Garadan studied the black void behind the gated entry, the two sentries standing guard over the northern entrance leaning casually against the wall. He and Taman waited patiently for nearly a half-hour when they heard voices approaching from the right. The sentries walked away from their post to greet another pair of guards. Taman tugged on Garadan's sleeve and the two of them slipped through the murkiness using buildings as cover. They pressed their backs against the bulwark and used their shadows as they worked their way to the black alcove. The guards were preoccupied with each other, talking and laughing in subdued tones as the two elves slipped into the recess. Taman tied part of a rope around the wood and made a slipknot before he and Garadan lifted the bar off the brackets. They opened the portal just enough to squeeze through then Taman lowered the wooden brace back into place. He yanked on the knot a couple of times then grinned as the end slithered through the other side.

The elves headed due north keeping an eye on the rising sun. The companions hastened toward the line of trees and brush up ahead. There were fewer patrols in the northern section but they kept an eye on everything from the city to the woods. Their pants' legs picked up the dew clinging to the grasses; faint rustling sounds were the only noise they made. They reached the low growing bushes and the first slender birches as the sun peeked over the horizon. The pines and oaks engulfed them as they watched daylight illuminating the gray walls of Bystyn. They paused briefly then resumed their trek.

Taman kept the pace slow for Garadan's sake, checking on the taller elf's condition as they continued toward the mountains. They stopped around noontime, resting in the shade of a maple tree.

"How are you feeling?"

"Better than I thought I would, Taman."

"We should reach the gap late this afternoon."

"And then which way?"

"East."

"Is that what you...*saw* last night?"

"Yes."

"Good magic or evil?"

Taman watched insects as they flitted in the light and listened to birds chirping in the branches overhead. It was peaceful here and for a brief instant Taman almost changed his mind. The serene locale took on a gray cast and he attributed the cold seeping into his bones to the closeness of the mountains.

"We'll find out soon enough."

They turned east, the sun warming their faces as they followed a barely discernible trail on the ground. Deer frequenting these woods had traced a path to the orchards a few miles to the south, the lure of apples and other fruit hard to resist. The forest line undulated here, the leading edge of the woods invading the plains one moment then receding toward the mountains the next. They could see wide swaths of open land, orchards and fields of wheat through the sparse thickets. Taman and Garadan noticed two black shapes in between the bushes up ahead and ducked down behind a fallen tree. They worked their way forward but could only see horses. Shapes moved near them but it was impossible to determine who they were. They had to get closer.

Garadan and Taman had swung halfway around when the animals froze in place, their noses wide and their great black necks held upright.

The movement on the other side of the undergrowth ceased. They were so intent on not moving a muscle they never noticed a shape dropping down from the branch over their heads until it dangled inches from their faces. They instinctively scurried backward snapping twigs and disturbing bushes in their haste to escape from the huge spider. Garadan recovered first and took out his sword, swinging the flat part backward, ready to smack the creature as far away as possible.

"I wouldn't do that."

"What? Who are you?" demanded Garadan pointing his weapon at this new threat. He watched the stranger approach grimacing as the oncoming elf held up his hand and allowed the spider to scrabble up onto his shoulder.

"You first."

Garadan looked at the newcomers and scratched his chin. There was nothing unusual about the elf. His dark companion did nothing to hide his rounded ears or the undertones of danger flowing through his strong frame. The slight girl was a mystery to him. Her silver eyes and pale skin made her appear fragile; her downcast gaze gave her an air of daintiness. He glanced at her hands and stared at her curved nails. He could feel Taman shift beside him as he, too, studied the strangers.

Taman's attention drifted between all three of the strangers. Why were they sneaking past the city? Where were they going? Didn't they know there was very little farther to the east? Where was the girl from? She was both lovely and peculiar at the same time. *Think, Taman, think!* The brown elf tried to recall anything he had read that could answer his questions. He thought harder but came up with the same blank results.

The three companions stared at Garadan's bruises and cuts noticing his battered knuckles. He was a head taller than his traveling partner who stood unscathed beside him. The bigger elf had dark circles under his eyes and a slight stoop in his shoulders while the other one seemed to be in good shape. These two had walked different roads. Why then were they marching on the same one now?

Clay took a deep breath as he looked upon his elven kin. Questions demanding to be answered popped into his head. What was the city like? What were your customs? Do you know anyone who misplaced a baby years ago? These two weren't as unfriendly as the guards they had met on the plains but their faces still radiated distrust. Curiosity and something else flickered in their eyes. Clay couldn't quite identify it and he didn't know how to ask them about it.

"I am Taman and this is Garadan." Taman was aware Garadan glanced sideways at him but he didn't take his eyes off the others, especially the spider. It scrambled down the elf's side and up the girl's body.

"I'm Clay and these are August, Sara and May," he pointed his forefinger at the spider, smiling as she gently nibbled the tip.

"You realize you're trespassing on elven lands, don't you?" asked Garadan.

"Are you going to escort us off as well?"

"When and where were you told to leave?" Garadan scrutinized the strangers. These outsiders had already been confronted once yet had chosen to ignore the order and continued on. He looked over at the horses then toward the south facing cliffs in the north. He had used that disregarded route on more than one occasion without ever meeting another soul. Had the elven patrols finally begun to monitor it?

"How do we know you aren't going to take us captive?" Clay saw the uneasiness melt from Garadan's face. He glanced over at Taman.

The elf had stopped chewing his bottom lip in thought and opened his mouth to speak. "We aren't guards...well, he is but we aren't here to apprehend anyone."

"Then you're sneaking around just as we are," August stated wryly.

"You didn't answer my question, Clay."

"We were challenged along the western edges of the plains. The leader of the patrol was adamant about our departing your land."

"What made you decide to follow the corridor?" Garadan inclined his head toward the mountain range.

"We took a chance." Clay shrugged his shoulders.

"Why are the elves so resolute in keeping strangers out of the city?" Sara finally spoke up.

Garadan and Taman remained quiet for a long time, the small band of companions saying nothing to break the silence. Garadan contemplated the task set upon him by Lord Balyd and Taman thought about the need to seek help from those outside the city's gates.

"They have chosen isolation and regard anyone not born within the city as an outsider. The queen…"

"The queen," Taman finished for Garadan, "Has lost sight of her purpose and prefers to indulge herself on things that are better left alone."

"Those are words teetering on the verge of treason, Taman," Clay stated in low tones.

"Call them what you wish."

"Are your injuries the result of your point of view?" Sara inquired.

"No." Garadan closed his eyes, immediately opening them again as the memory of the beatings and flight for his life filled his mind. They needed to rest and perhaps share a meal so that he and Taman could gauge the newcomers. He didn't feel threatened by them and secretly hoped they could somehow help with their quest.

"There's a place about a half mile east where we can talk and eat," he suggested then walked off without looking back to see if they accompanied him.

Taman watched him move off then glanced over at the strangers. He took a quick breath then caught up to Garadan. The three companions hesitated for a moment then decided to take a chance with them. Garadan led them up a slight hill then over a small stream winding through grasses and delicate saplings. The spongy moss growing along the rivulet was a pleasure to tread upon and the horses found it quite tasty. The animals ignored their riders and grazed on the deep green carpet. Garadan halted beneath a broad oak tree, its ancient trunk large enough to conceal three people standing shoulder to shoulder. Its roots snaked out all around its base and they had to be careful not to trip over them. August squatted down and started digging out a depression for the charcoal to cook something.

"No! No fire!"

"Relax Taman; there will be no flame or smoke from this."

The Herkah completed his task and soon everyone was eating soup and absorbing the heat. Penetrating fingers of cold drifted down from the mountains and the warmth emitted by the small briquette was more than welcome. May burrowed into Sara's cloak, turning around until all anyone could see was her head.

"What befell you, Garadan?" Sara's soft voice reached out to him.

She and her friends winced as he recounted how he had acquired the wounds. His tone of voice was laced with remembered pain and bitterness. No one spoke when he was through; no one could imagine another human inflicting such horrors upon another.

"I saw them." August finally confessed. "I was there when they set you on your way, Garadan. I should have done something."

"That would have spelled your own doom, August." The vague recollection of that one person within the crowd not participating in the frenzy flickered briefly in his mind. The chances of meeting up with that bystander weeks later were too coincidental to ignore.

Clay looked at his lifelong friend remembering when the Herkah had reluctantly revealed the injustices done to the elves. August hadn't gone into any detail then but Garadan's words recalled that terrible day too vividly.

"You traveled from the harbor all the way to this point? Why?"

"We are simply seeking adventure, Taman."

"All of the excitement is found in and around Windstorm Harbor," Garadan reminded Clay.

"Demon!" Taman nearly shouted, the endless forays into the recesses of his brain finally paying off.

"Where?" demanded Clay, August and Sara in unison as they rose to their feet and drew their weapons.

Garadan looked over at Taman, the strangers' reaction a mixture of expectation and an odd resolve. They slowly sheathed their arms and resumed their places around the ember glowing hotly between them. They studied each other, searching for signs of treachery but found only an unspoken urgency flowing amongst them.

"I meant...you...no insult intended," Taman felt the flush rise in his cheeks.

"No offense taken," Sara replied.

"You three traveling the land together is not something you come across every day."

"No, you don't," agreed August, choosing not to reveal the truth behind his own assumed heritage.

"Perhaps we should exchange our reasons for being here," suggested Garadan, the peculiarities mounting with each passing second.

"You wouldn't believe us," said Clay.

"Try me."

"All right then. A terrible demon intends to unleash the contents of the underworld upon the land and exterminate all living creatures. The three of us would like to prevent his scheme from becoming a reality."

Taman's jaw dropped in amazement. *This couldn't be! This was an awful joke…no it was a trap! Someone must have found out about their mission and was preparing to take them prisoner. They were going to be brought back to the city where they would be severely punished for disregarding the queen's order then there would be no one left to fend off the evil!*

"Does this devil have a name?" Garadan crossed his arms and stared at the others.

"Emhella."

"Would this *Emhella* happen to be a Vox, Clay?"

"He would. How do you know about Vox, Garadan?"

"Wouldn't Sara be under his influence?"

"Not likely. What about the Vox?"

"We seem to be sharing the same assignment. My little bookworm friend here says that books and a configuration in the heavens have announced Emhella's arrival. I must confess I wasn't fully convinced until now."

"What else did the tomes tell you, Taman?" asked Sara.

"That the Races of old would band together and try to defeat him."

"They are scattered, unconcerned, or absent," stated Garadan. "It would be impossible to unite them into an army to annihilate the demon."

"Magic, not soldiers is the only thing that can precipitate his downfall," Sara explained.

Taman stood and walked over to the stream where he hunkered down and drank from the cold water. He could feel the chilly liquid as it collected in his stomach. Magic. It was as plentiful as the stars in the sky and just as elusive, too. He remembered the first and only time he attempted to capture the whirling haze as it seeped into his soul. It had sizzled then flared to life scorching the enclosure around his spirit. The pain had been sharp like the time when he was a child and fell onto a pile of broken glass. His lot was to discern the powers, not to wield them. He heard someone approach but he did not rise and turn to see who it was. He didn't need to. The darkness she had been born in reached out and encircled him with a faint mist. It reminded him of coal dust.

"Are we supposed to seize the forces and use them against the Vox, Sara?"

"All I know is that we have to do everything we can to keep them out of his grasp. What burden do you bear, Taman? What do you know about the Might flowing through the land?"

"I feel it, Sara. It progresses through my body yet it will not allow me to handle it. It...it punishes me if I challenge it."

"Magic has a purpose for everyone it touches, Taman."

"So you don't think I'm crazy then?"

"Hardly."

"It's so difficult to trust anyone nowadays, Sara. Even now I am tempted to grab Garadan and propel ourselves away from you."

"We won't stop you if that's your decision."

He placed his hand on her back and gently guided her back to the others. If the three companions meant to do them any harm, they would already have done so. They needed help and the strangers seemed to fulfill that requirement. He would have been more skeptical had the magic not steered them in this direction. Fate, he surmised, worked her own brand of wizardry and who was he to gainsay her?

The air grew colder as the sun took its warmth into the west. The group decided to camp here for the night. Sara volunteered to keep watch.

"I'm not sure I feel comfortable with a demon guarding us," Garadan's skepticism was met head on with an icy stare from August.

"Don't worry, Garadan, there isn't enough meat on your bones to sate me anyway," countered Sara.

Garadan's cheeks reddened as the others, including Taman began to laugh. He mumbled an apology then rolled himself up in his blanket.

Sara smiled as the companions followed Garadan's actions. Soon several dark cocoons snored quietly beneath the boughs. Her gaze traveled over to Clay who shifted restlessly in his sleep.

Clay wandered the island, hiking up steep hills as he hacked at the broad leaves blocking his path and view. He heard water falling from a great height to his left and the ocean waves pounding the rocky coast to his right. Sweat dripped into his eyes forcing him to squint. His clothes clung to his body hindering his movements. The machete grew heavier in his hand and each stroke felt as if he were lifting an anvil. The water sounds became louder and resonated closer together until they became one. He tripped on a root and toppled forward, panic exploding in his gut as he plunged head first down a waterfall gushing into an endless sea. Black, barb-tipped fins circled below him and bloodstained snouts poked out of the water to watch his descent. They flopped onto their sides and opened their mouths forcing him to bring up his hands and shield his eyes from the sun reflecting off their razor sharp teeth. The merciless orb burned into his skin causing it to crack and bleed. He grimaced as his blood spattered onto the sea, which further excited the ravenous beasts awaiting his flesh and bones. His arms and legs flailed desperately trying to halt his downward motion but it was all for naught. The impact knocked the breath out of him. The water sucked him down for a long time. He could feel his lungs begging for air as his downward progression finally slowed then stopped. He frantically swam upward toward the light clawing at the ocean determined to keep him as her own. He saw the dark silhouettes racing in his direction. They grew larger and more distinct then swam together to become one enormous brute. Its dorsal fin loomed like a mountain then it finally reached him. It bumped against his chest, its coarse nose abrading the skin away. Clay tried to beat the monster off with his fists but they became raw then bled attracting it even more. He stared into its dead eyes; eyes that never blinked. His lungs could take no more and he instinctively gasped for air. Water rushed into his lungs and he began to retch and heave in the briny eternity he was trapped in. The last thing he saw was a huge tail fin snapping toward him. It smacked him alongside his head and then everything went black…

"Clay? Clay!"

The elf opened his eyes, his aching body screaming in protest. Green, brown and black hues fused together then spun in nauseating circles. His hands gripped the earth under his body, his fingers disappearing into the rich, dark soil and grass. A cup of water was pressed against his lips, the liquid sending ripples of hysteria into his very soul. He reached out and pushed it away with a vengeance, then sluggishly returned to the glade north of Bystyn.

"Bad dream," he managed to say through a constricted throat and punctuated by the frenzied look in his eyes. He remained silent, while his companions determined which direction they should take.

"We have to go west to confront the Vox," said Taman.

"That won't do us any good," retorted Sara.

"We can't stay here!" Garadan chimed in.

"Let's keep calm and make an intelligent decision," added August.

Clay rubbed his temples, the back of his neck and his shoulders. The discussion was growing louder and aggravated the pounding in his head. The lingering effects of the nightmare were anything but pleasant. He glanced up and noticed May several feet away. The spider's attention was firmly fixated on something in the east. Clay struggled to focus his senses in that direction but he could detect nothing except what transpired around him. May turned her head and looked back at him. She held his gaze for a second then began to scramble toward the east.

Her conviction fascinated him and before he realized what he was doing, he found himself walking beside her. He paid no attention to the others. He strode after the spider, the growth of the forest around them absorbing the others' shouts. May stopped up ahead and waited for him. He shook his head and grinned as she clambered up onto his shoulder.

"Tired already?" She tugged on his collar urging him on. His companions finally caught up to them and the clamoring started all over again.

"Where are you going?" August inquired.

"There's nothing out this way, Clay," Garadan chimed in.

"If May wants to head in this direction then that's where we'll go," stated the elf.

"You're listening to the spider?" Taman was incredulous.

Taman and the others decided to humor Clay for a while, considering they had no idea which way to travel. The morning wore on. They could see Bystyn through the breaks in the trees far to the southwest. When they paused to rest near late morning the city was nothing more than a dark smudge on the plains. They resumed their trek, keeping the mountains to their left and heading due east. They circumvented a series of large boulders, their gray surfaces absorbing the sun's warm rays.

A cluster of tall bushes behind them obstructed their view and for a brief moment, Clay was reliving his nightmare. He silently chastised himself as he marched around them, halting so abruptly August bumped into him.

-6-

Emhella waited in the shadows beneath the trees studying the city a few miles to the north. His hawk-like features were devoid of emotion as his piercing black eyes scanned the area. No bird or cricket song broke the silence around him; nothing scurried on the ground or in the trees near him. The grass beneath his boots and the leaves within his reach wilted and hung limply from the branches. He never once had to raise his hand to shoo away the mosquitoes flitting hungrily just beyond his invisible barrier. He stood for hours watching everyone enter and exit Bystyn. The afternoon turned to dusk and still he remained in place. Scattered clouds obscured the moon rising in the inky sky. Emhella adjusted his hood and stepped out of his concealment and onto the plains surrounding Bystyn. His long, unhurried strides brought him to the gate shortly before midnight.

He relied on his host's memories, entering the city unseen and choosing the dimly lit alleyways to make his way toward the castle. The air within the dark side streets was stale with a faint scent of garbage. A rat squealed in the gloom up ahead, its cry stifled by the low growling of a cat. He kept to the shadows and continued to walk in a northerly direction until he came upon the series of homes and buildings belonging to the lords and ladies of the court. He stopped and studied them from his position.

Alyxandyr, the king during Allad's time, had chosen to sequester all but the most essential members of the court to this part of the city. He wanted to avoid the scheming and gossiping within his own house. It also sent a strong message about favoritism to the members of his royal household. His decision had worked well enough.

He could see guards patrolling the streets in between the buildings housing the upper segments of the court. One pair emerged from the darkness across the street from him and another appeared halfway down the block to his right. They meandered up and down the avenues, met in the middle, and then repeated their vigil going the other way. Emhella let them pass then slipped to the other side as soon as the guards disappeared. He picked up his pace and passed through the nobles' quarters before the patrol looped back.

The demon proceeded through the park in front of the castle and then melted into the gloominess beside the citadel. He scanned the building, his gaze resting on an open window on the second floor and the thick vine of English ivy leading up to it.

* * *

Aryanda's slim form rested beneath silken sheets, her braided hair coiled over her shoulder like a pale snake ready to strike. A slight breeze stirred the curtains and drifted over her. She shivered and groped for her blanket, pulling it over her body and the blue stone pendant resting on her chest. She shuddered and furrowed her brows then a low moan escaped her partially open lips. She shifted her legs and arms and turned her head to the other side. She opened her eyes and the first thing she saw was the vase of flowers on her bedside table. The once fragrant blossoms drooped and smelled of rot. She blinked several times yet the image remained. *They were fresh when I went to bed!* She rolled up onto her elbow and reached out to touch them when a silhouette detached itself and rapidly approached her.

A scream built up inside her throat but she could not set it free. Fear turned her muscles to pulp. She plopped back onto the bed, tears of fright running down her face. She began to gasp for air and finally managed to lift her arm up to ward off the hand reaching for her neck. It clamped down on her flesh and began to squeeze the life out of her. Another hand yanked back the blanket and jerked the necklace free. The intruder held one end of the chain up letting the stone slide off and fall onto the bed. He scooped it up and deposited it in his pocket. Aryanda convulsed then lay still. Blood trickled out of her mouth and nose staining her flawless skin. Emhella stared at the dead queen while the last of her warmth evaporated in the chilly room then left the same way he had come in.

Emhella dissolved into the early morning light and headed out of the city. The Lady of the Sand had been careless in allowing these weak mortals to safeguard the stone. It would have been safer in a nest of sparrows. He would take it back to the desert and follow the magic as it drifted back to her lair. He grinned at the prospect of wresting her magic away and adding it to his own. He would let her live, of course, and chain her to the very walls of hell. He disappeared into the leading edge of the forest to the west of Bystyn keeping to the shadows. He hesitated, and then turned, sniffing the air around him. He lowered his head, his black gaze darting in every direction. It was imperceptible but something was there nonetheless, just on top of the wind. He looked toward the west, his hand clutching the stone then glanced back the way he had come. He pulled his hood up, placed the ornament in his pocket and faced the first faint rays of the rising sun.

* * *

Lord Balyd trudged toward his library, his dour features discouraging anyone from speaking to him. He was supposed to turn over his documents to Caladan today and that task left a bitter taste in his mouth. *What in the Four Corners is wrong with that woman? Why can't she see that Caladan will do nothing for the elves?* He moved past the staircase leading to the royal quarters when an ear-piercing shriek reverberated throughout the castle. It grabbed and crushed his innards and froze the guards at the main entrance to the castle. Balyd finally gained control of his body dropping his papers to run up the stairs. The queen's handmaiden was at the door, her hand to her mouth and her face contorted in horror. He brushed past her and entered the room.

Fright leached across Aryanda's arrogant features, the dried blood and terrible bruises around her neck standing out starkly against her pallid skin. He saw the chain nestled amid the blanket folds but the stone was missing. He glanced over at her dressing table, the bejeweled hairpins and adornments reflecting the sunlight that flooded the room. He turned his attention back to the corpse and noticed the flowers out of the corner of his eye. Aryanda demanded fresh blooms be placed by her bedside every night and woe to the servant who forgot to do so.

"Lord Balyd? What are we going to do?" asked Hardan, the captain of the queen's guard as he skidded to a halt beside the First Advisor. His weathered face contorted with shock as he gazed upon Aryanda's lifeless body.

"Call an emergency meeting and make sure *everyone* is in attendance. Lady Tam," he addressed Aryanda's maidservant, "Take care of the queen."

"Shouldn't we search for the murderer?" suggested Hardan.

"Yes, but don't frighten the city with the news of Queen Aryanda's death just yet, Hardan."

Balyd headed for the council chamber. Whoever had killed the queen didn't want the exposed treasures scattered throughout her room—all he coveted was that damned stone. He could have taken it from her without resorting to taking her life. One well-placed blow to her head and she would have been unconscious. What was it? Aryanda never took it off. She seemed obsessed by it and now someone had taken the bauble. Why would someone kill the queen for a gem?

The stone had been passed down through the generations ever since the Green Might had been used to defeat Mahn. A young girl...Cricket, yes, Cricket was her name, brought it to the city. Balyd thought hard trying to remember anything else about the gem but no one had given it much consideration then either. Balyd stopped in mid-stride, uneasiness running up his spine like a multi-legged insect. Someone wasn't disregarding it now...someone who knew its real value. He quickly walked back to the queen's chamber paying no attention to the questioning looks of the servants. Balyd glanced from the open window to the dead blossoms then over to the shroud-covered queen. He walked over to the window and looked down. The foliage clinging to the gray stone building appeared brown and wilted, especially in the center portion of the leafy vine. Balyd took a step back, the blood draining from his face. He struggled to contain his emotions…and the growing fear gnawing at his insides. The queen and the bouquet had succumbed to something evil and corrupt. There was only one thing he knew of that fit that description and it had the audacity to sneak into the castle and take the stone. It wouldn't steal the gem if it weren't useful for its evil purposes. *Please let me be wrong!*

* * *

All the members of the court were waiting for him when he entered the chamber. They mingled in the gallery, the various families' banners with their coats-of-arms hanging overhead. Many wore shocked looks on their faces; others blanched at the thought that their benefactress was dead. Aryanda had been an only child and had left no heir. There were a few kin living within the city but their ties to the queen were too distant and the elves didn't think very much of them.

Balyd would be the logical choice to rule the city until they could find a suitable replacement or, if possible, a legitimate member of the royal family. The queen had, however, already informed the court about her decision to replace him with Caladan. Her death would interrupt that process and allow him to retain his position for a while longer. His expertise would be vital to whomever took control of Bystyn. The lords and ladies of the city glanced sideways at him. Hardan approached him and handed him several sheets of paper. Balyd scanned the report, the messy handwriting smudged here and there. He looked up and frowned. Caladan worked his way through the groups stopping to speak a few words into their ears or just patting them reassuringly on their backs. He needed their support, plying them with charm and encouragement. He locked eyes with Balyd then comforted one of the women.

"I'd like to bring this emergency session to order," stated Balyd as he took his seat.

The elves drifted over to their places and sat down. He waited a few more moments for them to collect themselves then he began to speak. Sniffles punctuated his words but he would not allow them to distract him.

"A terrible tragedy has befallen this kingdom. The horrible and abrupt murder of our queen has left us bereft of a leader. We must band together and choose someone to replace her and to find who committed such an atrocity. We are all aware of Queen Aryanda's familial ties and must make a choice before any outsider learns of this calamity. If we are perceived as vulnerable we might be open to attack."

"Who would you like to see on the throne during this critical time, Balyd?"

"Someone who has Bystyn's interest at heart, Lord Caladan. Lady Wyntyn is more than qualified to take the reins." *And certainly not an idiot like you.* "Does anyone take exception to Lady Wyntyn?" The chamber was silent.

"You honor me, Lord Balyd. I will, of course, do my best to help during this transition period but I will not sit on the throne."

Balyd nodded graciously and felt some relief coursing through his mind. Lady Wyntyn's neutrality should appease both sides and her no-nonsense approach to her duties should keep the court in check. She was one of the oldest members of the court and even Aryanda respected her commitment to the city. The petite, graying Lady walked over to the queen's chair but did not sit in it. She respectfully pulled it away from the counsel table and remained standing. *Now for problem number two.*

"The counsel will decide whether or not Lord Caladan shall take up my duties as Queen Aryanda had ordered. Lady Wyntyn?"

"Those in favor of Lord Caladan's advancement please rise."

Some of the members of the court exchanged looks and hesitantly rose to their feet while others stood without a second thought. Everyone within the chamber counted those standing. Half of the counsel wanted Caladan to replace Balyd. It would be up to Lady Wyntyn to break the tie. The iron lady took a deep breath.

"I propose that Lord Balyd remain at his post until Queen Aryanda's successor has been chosen and that individual shall be the one to decide who shall be First Advisor. If anyone wishes to speak against my decision let them do so now." The room was quiet. "Very well then. We will convene again in a week's time and will then select our new ruler. We all have our own obligations to attend to in the meantime. This meeting is now adjourned."

The court dispersed, bowing to Lady Wyntyn on their way out of the chamber. Balyd was one of the last to leave, the uncertainty in his eyes not lost on Lady Wyntyn. Balyd was not one to be worried over his position. She too had little conviction in Caladan but she knew Balyd well enough to know something else disturbed him. It would not be prudent to huddle with him at this moment. She needed to maintain that air of neutrality if she, and through her, the city were to remain effective.

Lady Wyntyn and Lord Hardan entered the library after knocking several times. They found Lord Balyd staring out into the darkness beyond the windows, a half-empty cup of tea dangling precipitously from his forefinger. The lines on his face made him appear older than he was.

"Lord Balyd?" Hardan's voice brought him back from wherever his mind had gone.

"I'm sorry, I didn't hear you come in. Please sit down."

"I want to know what's going on," Lady Wyntyn stated in her straightforward manner.

Balyd took a deep breath reliving everything that had occurred since Taman opened his eyes to the evil in the west. Would they believe him? He could trust them both but they, like he had tried to do, would renounce the truth. He had no choice. He told them about Taman and confessed his role in sending out a handful of elves to gather information about the goings on in the land. He revealed what had befallen Garadan and his comrades and how Garadan and Taman went in search of the wielder of the elven magic and to find out what they could about the demon. Hardan's brow remained arched in doubt and Wyntyn stared evenly at him the entire time he spoke. He took a deep breath then told them about Aryanda's death.

"I think this Emhella knew that some sort of magic existed in the blue stone she always wore, because nothing else had been touched. The chain it hung from was worth more than half the jewels in her room, yet it was cast aside. The flowers by her bedside and the vines outside her window were wilted…dead…killed by something no one could explain. Thieves might have damaged the ivy but not destroyed the freshly picked flowers."

"You willingly violated Queen Aryanda's orders to remain on elven lands and you coerced others to do so as well," Hardan sternly reminded him.

"I take full responsibility for everything."

"Your status in the court would be completely wiped away if they knew about that."

"Then turn me in, Hardan! I did not proceed with that dangerous task to increase my status within the court: I did so to protect Bystyn!"

"What do Taman and Garadan hope to accomplish against this demon…if it exists?" Lady Wyntyn cut in and effectively stifled the argument.

"I truly do not know, Lady Wyntyn," replied Balyd tiredly.

"What *do* you know?" demanded Hardan.

"That we are all doomed if they fail to accomplish anything."

* * *

"Why did you stop?" August asked stepping around his friend to get a better look.

A short man with rust-colored hair and bright gray eyes stood in front of them. His marked torso rippled with muscles and no one doubted he wouldn't use the hoe blade in his brawny hand. *We've met enough strangers to fill up half a city!*

"Dwarves…" muttered Taman, his charcoal eyes wide with astonishment.

"Elves?" asked the dwarf tentatively.

"Yes, amongst others," replied Clay.

"I am Whistler and this is my mate, Elena."

Elena abandoned her shelter and joined Whistler. She gaped at them, afraid that if she blinked they would disappear. Did fate smile down upon them? Had they really succeeded? She reached over and grasped Whistler's arm, her vise-like grip making his tanned skin turn white beneath her fingers. She gaped from one to the other. They were all so different, especially the young girl with the nearly white skin: there was something almost feral about her. The tallest of the men sported bruises and cuts on his lean face and she could see more on his arms. None of the others had any injuries that she could detect. The dryness in her throat urged her to drink some water but she could not move to lift the canteen hanging from her shoulder.

Garadan studied the pair. He had no idea where the dwarves lived but he did know there were no communities of any kind within a week's ride of Bystyn. He noticed the tears in their worn clothing and the grass and soil stains on their blankets. Their exposed flesh had a dull cast and their hair hung flatly down their heads. Their eyes radiated desperation and her nervous fingers moved restlessly across his forearm. Garadan knew that look all too well.

"We need help," Whistler stated.

"We can see as much. What do you require? Food? Medicine?" asked Clay.

"An army to liberate my people."

"You…what?"

Whistler licked his chapped lower lip. His rumbling stomach broke the silence. He glanced over at Elena. Her wide eyes, strained features and subtle nod gave him the courage to speak.

"The Rock Lords, a barbarous race living in the east, began to seriously attack my people more than a hundred years ago. My ancestors were initially able to keep them at bay. They continued to pound away at Evan's Peak until it finally became necessary to send for help from the elves. Support never arrived. The dwarves were unable to plant crops and soon used up whatever food they had stored. Weakened by hunger, our warriors were incapable of fending off the aggressive Rock Lords. Evan's Peak fell and the dwarves became their slaves.

"My forebears were marched south and east where they were forced to work the land for the Rock Lords. They imprisoned us in a compound and beat us at will. They encouraged the Dribbies…hybrid dog creatures…to hound and attack those dwarves who refused to comply with their orders. These," he brushed his hand against the scars marring his body, "are compliments of their cruelty. Elena and I finally did the unthinkable. We escaped. We gambled on the fact that the elves might have pity on us and fight to free my people."

Garadan and August stared at the ground. The Rock Lords' brand of savagery was not a situation limited to the dwarves. May crawled out from Sara's hood, drawing a gasp from Elena as the spider rubbed its head against the girl's pale cheek. Clay took a deep breath and exhaled slowly.

"We can't help you, Whistler," Taman confessed in quiet tones.

"Why in Hades not?"

"Because the elves are currently being ruled by a callous queen who refuses to acknowledge anyone beyond her borders. She spurns any person not born in the city."

"Besides there are more sinister things happening in the land," added Sara.

"What could possibly be more terrible than an entire race of people being mercilessly oppressed?" Whistler nearly shouted.

"*All* the Races being eradicated from the land," replied Taman.

Whistler narrowed his eyes at the strangers. They were not being unsympathetic to his plight yet showed no inclination to aid them. His only duty was to secure help for his people. He didn't care about the business this odd collection of individuals might be involved in. He stared at Taman who began to speak once more.

"There is a powerful demon loose in the land, Whistler, and his only purpose is to secure all of the magic and turn the land into eternal darkness. If he succeeds then you won't need to free your people…they'll all be dead."

"Are you looking for him?" Elena finally spoke up.

"Yes."

"What will you do once you find him?" asked Whistler, unconvinced that magic even existed.

"We're not quite sure yet."

"Let's go, Elena, I've heard just about enough foolishness for one day. I wish you well."

"Where will you go?" demanded Garadan. "You'll be turned away if you try to go to Bystyn."

THE FORTRESS OF DARKNESS

"Then we'll look elsewhere!"

"Man will only kill you and the desert dwellers are weeks away by horse," August informed him.

"Then we'll keep going until someone listens to us!"

The companions watched the dwarves walk away, Elena talking to him and pulling on his arm. Whistler suddenly halted and faced her, his animated features and wildly gesturing hands having no effect on her. She crossed her arms, cocked her head and said nothing as he ranted and raved at her. He stopped to take a breath and Elena stuck her finger in his chest and quietly spoke to him. He turned his head when she was through and stomped back to the group. His face was bright red and the veins and tendons along his neck nearly stretched out of his skin. Elena joined him a moment later.

"Please do not misinterpret our impatience with rudeness," stated Elena, "We're just exhausted and fearful for our kin."

"That's understandable, Elena. We would gladly take on your cause but not until we are through with our own task," replied Clay.

"Oh...oh," breathed Garadan watching Taman's eyes become smeared and unsettled. The horses danced about nervously, their ears laid back and the whites of their eyes showing. They pulled on their reins and ran away from the group. No amount of coaxing could bring them back. August ran after them, returning a few minutes later. He shrugged at Clay and pointed toward the southeast.

"What's going on, Garadan?" Clay demanded.

Sara gaped at Taman then shuddered as invisible ghostly fingers brushed against her skin. Panic rushed up from her stomach squeezing her lungs and dulling her bright eyes. She spun around then stopped and began to back away from some unseen thing to the west. Beads of perspiration erupted on her skin and soaked the hair around her forehead.

"Sara?" August called out to her.

"This isn't good, is it?" asked Whistler taking Elena's hand tightly in his own.

"We have to go...*now!*" Sara yelled and ran in the direction of the mountains, May clinging desperately to her hood. The spider bounced up and down as she struggled to climb into the safety of Sara's clothing. The others followed her more slowly, constantly checking over their shoulders for their invisible pursuer. The dwarves kept pace with them, their duty to their people shelved for the time being. Garadan grabbed Taman, the trance leaving the elf docile.

They ran north, spurred on by the malignancy slowly manifesting itself in those not gifted with being able to sense the darkness. The warm afternoon and brilliant blue sky dissolved into chaos. A chill wound its way into their overheated bodies sending shivers of fear up and down their spines. Their feet churned up chunks of sod as they sped away from their hidden pursuer. They yanked at their clothing whenever it became entangled on branches. They slapped away low hanging boughs forcing whomever was right behind to duck or brace themselves for the stinging hit. The dwarves nearly choked on the myriad of questions rushing to their lips but they prudently followed the elves through the trees and over rocks and roots. The group fled on, passing through the last line of pines and oaks before skidding to a halt. A half mile of open ground separated them from the imposing mountain range. They scanned the areas to their right and left, then snapped around to face the direction they had just come from.

It suddenly grew very quiet. No bird song. No small animals chattering. The breeze stopped. No one breathed. They gawked at the shape calmly walking through the forest, black hood and cloak hiding their pursuer but not the evil emanating in waves toward them. Clouds began to obscure the sky veiling the sun as if it did not want to witness what was about to happen. The figure emerged and stood just beyond the last line of trees.

Garadan and Clay half-heartedly reached for their weapons and Whistler gripped the hoe blade in his hand. Sara began to breathe heavily never noticing August held her limp hand in his. Her eyes were wide with terror as they beheld her worst nightmare. When he spoke she nearly collapsed to the ground.

"You are a long way from home, Sara. Come," he held out his gloved hand toward her, "let me take you back." His tone was quiet, almost fatherly.

August pulled her closer but no amount of support could stop her from trembling. Emhella was her master no matter how much she wished it to be otherwise. She began to inch forward like a child who has done wrong. August tightened his grip on her, his eyes filled with defiance. Emhella let out a low, disdainful chuckle.

"She is demon-seed and will betray you."

"You can't have her," August managed to speak even though he could barely breathe.

"She will abandon this ridiculous pretense of being human and revert to her true self," he whispered almost seductively. "How long before you or one of your companions wakes up with a ripped-open throat?"

"No..." moaned Sara.

Emhella suddenly ignored her sensing the faint pulse amongst them and the hunger stroked his tainted essence once more. He would return to his fiery lair with two powers this time. It would be an easy thing to do. He grew tired of the situation and rushed them. He flew at them like black lightning intent on incinerating the puny mortals with one fell swoop. He was halfway to his stone-still quarry when an icy blast of air poured down over them from the mountains.

Gooseflesh erupted on the mortals and their breath partially obscured the black death that had unexpectedly halted in mid-motion. The comrades instinctively crowded together unsure of what this new threat was. The cold mist surrounded them, the ice crystals pressing into their flesh feeling like the fingers of the dead. They could hear Emhella fuming beyond the frigid haze. The soupy mixture, as unpleasant as it was, kept him away from them. The fog slipped under their feet and lifted them up into the air. They could do nothing more than silently gasp and feebly clutch at each other's hands as the cloud raised them higher and higher. They were helpless and prayed that whatever elevated them upward would not change its mind and drop them back to earth.

They watched the world below them become smaller. The trees became blots on the blurry ground and the near vertical mountains filled up most of their sight. Then something else came into view. It was indistinct at first then took on an astonishing form. The companions would have rubbed their eyes if they could have moved their hands. All they could do, however, was stare.

Sara gaped at the ethereal face inches from her own. The woman's stern features framed by shoulder length hair that began to twist into horns around her head until nearly a dozen spikes curved away into the mist. Sara felt the wraith's long fingers around her waist, the nails digging into her sides. She shivered as the blood trickling from the punctures froze to her skin. That sensation paled when the apparition's hostile gaze bored into her mind. The wraith opened her mouth revealing rows upon rows of sharp teeth. She lunged forward and all Sara could do was cringe as the cavern of blades filled up her entire vision. She was back in that hated lair once more gagging on the fumes and reeling from the screeches exploding all around her. She lingered in the dark recesses, waiting for the right moment to flee this appalling place...

Taman shuddered as the magic flooded through him. The blackness had been replaced with a dizzying palette of bizarre colors that blended together with a frightening speed. He felt his stomach turn and his mind blister as the hues shrank then exploded in front of his eyes. He gulped in huge draughts of air to steady himself even though the frozen crystals seared his lungs. He began to choke on the ice clogging up his windpipe...

Clay stared transfixed at the face inches from his own. It scrutinized him with an intensity he had never before encountered. The wraith exuded an almost noble quality demanding the elf's attention. Clay could do nothing but give it to him. The elf held his breath as the phantom reached up with his other hand and placed it on Clay's chest. It took every ounce of willpower not to scream in pain as the hand disappeared into his breast and reached down into his soul. It fondled then probed his spirit with a rudeness that wilted his self-respect and left him feeling completely meaningless. An image formed in his mind. Clay staggered about in a field of wheat, the rotting heads sending powdery bits of dust up his nose and into his eyes. He choked on the foul particles and tried to rub the grit from his eyes. He could see the topmost lookout towers over the brittle grasses but the gray shapes receded with every step he took toward them...

A milky haze without form or substance enveloped Garadan. There was no up or down only the pushing, shoving and manhandling of something lurking within. It taunted him with its nearness then faded away as he swung at it with his fists. It poked at his healing wounds evoking the terrible memories of watching his men die then fleeing from the crazed tormentors. He should have stayed and died with them. His cowardly behavior mocked him as a leader. They perished before him once again, one at a time, and all he could do was witness their executions over and over again…

The ghostly faces of dwarves he did not recognize surrounded Whistler. They glared at him in anger and disappointment, silently deriding him for his inability to save his people. He strove to wave them away with his hands but they refused to vanish. Their voiceless thoughts penetrated into his skull like awls. *Charlatan. Betrayer. Pretender.* The vision merged becoming a lonely mountain on the edge of the plains. Vermin scurried out of the dismal openings and faint lamentations floated upon tendrils of yellowish smog oozing toward the frigid river. He stared into the icy blackness and saw himself wearing a crown of blood-encrusted bones…

A line of Herkahs proudly sitting atop their magnificent horses rode past August. He had always secretly believed he was descended from these noble people. They glowered down at him and, as he hung his head in shame noticed the ill-fitting Herkah garb hanging loosely from his body. They were too big for him…no…he was too small, too insignificant to wear such revered garb…

Emhella roared with fury at the receding cloud of wraiths. The ancient spirits of the mountains guarded their realm with a passion keeping both mortal and demon from setting foot in their domain. They despised both equally and were merciless toward anyone daring to scale these ranges. They were born when the land was young and were composed of the remnants of water and air. They had fed on the energy of the earth and it was this magic that flowed through their essences. It was a wild and raw might, too much for even him to try to secure. He could not destroy them but he blasted the wraiths with his anger nonetheless. The retreating mist split in half as his dark magic sped impotently toward it then poured over the peak and disappeared from view. All Emhella could do was hunker down and glare at the apex.

***

Elena knelt beside Taman and shook him awake just in time to roll him over and hold him while he retched upon the tan outcropping they had landed upon. She held his loose and sweaty hand in hers and brushed back a lock of his hair. She helped him sit up and stared into his eyes. The whites were slowly pushing the gray swirls back into place but he had a difficult time focusing on her. It took several long minutes for him to be able to stand on his feet without swaying.

"Feeling better?"

"I…where are we?"

"On the other side of the mountains, I guess," she replied scanning the surreal landscape around them.

The orange sky was devoid of clouds and sun and cast a peach-colored hue over everything. They were in an immense crater ringed in by cliffs so sheer and high they seemed to poke into the heavens. Massive vertical rents marked their surfaces and extended from the peaks down into the valley's ground. Clusters of black trees draped with long strands of moss sprouted up amongst chest high grasses topped with fuzzy tufts. There was a peculiar sheen to them that was indeterminate from their vantage point. A steady breeze stirred the grasses and moss and the unmistakable sound of tinkling glass reached their ears. It was a soft and melodious tone reminiscent of wind chimes on a warm summer's night. This place did anything but lull them into a state of somnolence.

"Where are the others?" asked Taman.

"We must have gotten separated from Sara, Clay and Whistler…they could be anywhere in here," replied August.

"That fog…" stated Elena quietly peering around for the eerie mist while rubbing her arms for warmth.

"Ancient spirits…rescued us from…him," replied Taman.

"Certainly not friendly," muttered Garadan remembering the jabs and disturbing images.

"I agree," said August.

Elena studied them with concern. The only thing she had experienced within the haze was being cold and the unsettling feeling of being hoisted up into the air. She noticed the dark circles under their eyes and the distraught stooping of their shoulders. They looked as if they had awakened from unpleasant nightmares. *Where were the others? Were they hurt? Had that demon somehow managed to keep them from getting over the mountain?* She peered into the very center of the valley where shards of black glass reached up out of the grasses. They gleamed like broken spear tips even from this distance. Elena shivered at their menacing appearance then glanced around for Whistler and the others.

"We have to find them," she whispered more to herself, the need for Whistler's touch never so urgent.

"What do you propose we do, Elena? Meander through that stuff until we bump into them?"

"Easy Garadan," August placed his hand on the elf's arm. "Do you think those wraiths will come back and lift us out of here once Emhella is gone?"

"I don't think so," said Taman concentrating on the black spikes in the center of the valley.

"You're not suggesting we go there, are you?" asked Garadan.

"If we can see it so can the others," replied Taman. "How much food and water do we have?"

"Enough for a few days if we ration it," answered August after taking a quick inventory.

Taman nodded subtly then jumped off the rock. The others hesitated for a moment then followed him. Their boots kicked up little puffs of dust as they walked; knots of stubby grasses were scattered here and there. They grew larger and more numerous the closer they hiked to the sea of grass. Garadan stepped on a lump of grass, the crunching sound making them all look down. They stared at the shattered green remnants then at each other. He squatted and ran his fingertip over the pieces flinching at the shard sticking out of his forefinger. A drop of blood rolled lazily from the puncture wound after he plucked the glass out.

"That explains the sound," he stated.

"And the gloss," added Elena.

They moved gingerly forward, careful not to tread on the fragile yet dangerous grass. It reached their shins then their waists and finally swallowed them up completely. They made sure they stepped on the exposed ground as they wound their way toward the black monolith. They cautiously pushed aside the smooth stalks blocking their way. They were cool to the touch and they were mindful of keeping the needle-like shafts away from their faces. Garadan could barely see over their tops the further they moved into the sedges and stood on his tiptoes to mark their progress. It soon became necessary for him to hoist Elena onto his shoulders to make sure they were still heading in the right direction.

"Let's stop here and rest," August said, the frustration of getting nowhere fast noticeable in his voice.

"How tall do these things grow?"

"They aren't, Taman, the land is sloping downward," corrected August. A few more yards and they'd all have to stand on each other's shoulders to see over the grass. He heard something and turned toward the sound just in time to see shadows passing through the grasses off to his right. He squinted and thought he saw riders silently moving by. He blinked but they did not disappear.

"What do you see?" asked Garadan.

"There," he pointed at the specters.

"I don't see anything."

"You don't see the horsemen?"

"No, August. Are you feeling well?"

"Yes…" his voice trailed off as the phantoms evaporated right before his eyes. He had seen them earlier when he was within the wraiths hardhearted embrace. They didn't like those whom they had saved yet had done so anyway. Why? To torment them at will on this side of the mountains?

"Are we still heading in the right direction?" asked Elena nervously.

Garadan glanced down at the rocky ground. The dirt and gravel path continued on far into the forest of grasses. He scratched the side of his head and looked back the way they had come. A wall of shiny green blocked the pathway. He frowned at his distorted image barely visible in the melon colored light.

"Oh…oh. Look," he pointed at the barrier forming before their very eyes then down at the gradually fading path.

"Well, it seems as though we're supposed to proceed in this direction," Taman stated dryly.

The air grew cooler during their descent into the hollow and the grasses soon blotted out the sky. The sedges lost their greenish hue and gradually took on a dull gray shade instead. They no longer swayed, becoming more rigid the further they descended into the crater.

"I guess this is what a flea sees on the back of a dog," said Taman more to himself than for his companions' ears.

"It reminds me of when I was a boy and crawled through the corn fields," added Garadan.

"Is this place getting bigger or are we shrinking?" asked Elena.

They all halted at the same time and stared at the dwarf then at the bizarre landscape around them. It had appeared flat when they had first surveyed it from the outcropping but the grasses could easily have veiled the sloping ground. The idea of their becoming smaller was ridiculous at best. At this rate, they would be tripping over the grains of sand before they reached the peculiar ruins in the center of the depression.

"You look the same size to me, Elena," stated Taman.

"It's not us," muttered Garadan checking each of his companions' appearance.

"What do you think we'll find once we reach that strange set of peaks?"

"With any luck our other friends and a way out, Elena," answered Taman.

They moved on and August saw the faint specters paralleling their course. He said nothing to his companions and tried to ignore them but they stayed near enough for him to see them. They dispassionately watched him from atop their horses, the thick forest of stalks never impeding their way. August concentrated on Garadan's back but his attention kept drifting over to the riders. Were they coming closer or were his eyes playing tricks on him?

Garadan stayed on the gravel trail, listening to his friends' breathing, the tense silence eerily reminiscent of the seconds before a thunderstorm unleashes its fury. He looked over to his left and bumped into one of the beefy stems. He cursed his lack of alertness and focused on the way ahead, carefully keeping to the middle of the path. He felt a hand on his shoulder and turned around expecting to see August but found himself alone instead. Had he lost his companions? He called out to them then exhaled with relief as three shadows extricated themselves from the surrounding grasses. His ease was short-lived as the ghosts of his men materialized in front of him. Their eyes radiated anger and betrayal; their bodies were rife with horrible wounds. They had been his responsibility and he had failed them. He had led them to their deaths and was now doing the same for these people. What right did he have to guide them through this peculiar territory? Was he leading them to their deaths, too? He cringed as one of his men moved toward him and raised his battered hand…

"Garadan! What's come over you? *Garadan!*"

Garadan fought to control himself, grateful that Taman shook him out of his terrible nightmare. He drank from his canteen with shaking hands afraid of revealing what he had just seen. He could not muster the courage to share his darkest hours with them.

"I'm fine," he managed to say then jerked his head at Taman to take the lead.

Taman nodded then moved into the forefront. The landscape did not change for a long time and the monotony soon began to dull his concentration. The stalks became blurs and the sound of his boots on the ground took on a methodical *thud-thud* tone. *How far away were they, for heaven's sake! The hollow hadn't appeared that distant from the edge!* The minutes became hours and still they trekked through this mundane place. Taman was about to suggest they rest for a bit when the forest around him began to change. Tiny prisms of light began to form and danced at the edge of his sight. He rubbed his eyes but the vibrating energy remained.

He watched with fascination as it flickered and elongated until it formed a continuous line in front of him. It sluggishly extended upward obscuring the grasses behind it until it disappeared beyond his vision. It transformed from red to green and finally into a deep blue. It shifted like water, inviting him in to wash away the burden of his quest.

"What's he looking at?" whispered August.

"I don't know…there's nothing there," replied Elena in hushed tones.

"Well...there might be," Garadan remembered Taman's confession in the castle. "He has the ability to sense magic, or so he told me."

"Is that a fact?" she murmured. "If that's true then I hope it's the good kind."

"Maybe we're near the ruins," stated August, the whinnying of horses echoing in his mind.

"I hope so, too," agreed Garadan trying to shut out the shadows lurking in the stalks.

Taman took a deep breath and opened his mind allowing the sapphire waters to flow into it. He shivered as the cold poured into his soul but he did not flinch. To his and his companions' complete surprise a huge wave burst over them and lifted them off the ground. They swirled and bobbed in the icy waters daring not to breathe but feeling their lungs begin to burn. They were drowning in a forest of grasses. They collided into one another; the painful impacts reassuring for it meant they were still together. The sensation of rushing toward where they first began their journey suddenly ceased and reversed itself. They were being sucked back into the direction of the hollow with such velocity that it felt as if their skin was being peeled off their frames. Then in one swift motion, they were unceremoniously deposited on dry land. They coughed and gagged on the water they had swallowed and inhaled gratefully, then slowly looked around. They were on a wide strip of dirt; their clothing dripping water onto the reddish surface as they stared at the menacing ruins a short walk away.

-7-

Harald collapsed onto the porch steps, dirt and dust caked into his hair and skin. His stomach growled and his ragged tunic hung limply off his shoulders. He turned his throbbing palms over, glaring at the broken blisters and abraded skin. Pus oozed from one of the cuts near his thumb. He watched a group of dwarves pass by, their hunched shoulders and downcast eyes a testament to their lives since Whistler and Elena had escaped. The women were now kept separate from the men. Food rations had been cut in half and the dwarves no longer had one day to rest.

Harald rose painfully to his feet grabbing onto the post for support as he trudged into his cabin. He grimaced at the stench greeting him as soon as he opened the door, eyeing the chamber pot in the corner. He wouldn't be allowed to dump it into the waste channel for another two days. He remembered the horrible fate that had befallen his friend Jan. Jan couldn't stand the horrible smell anymore and carried his pot toward the pit behind the compound against the Rock Lords' orders. The guards had unleashed the Dribbies and they tore Jan apart. What was left of his corpse was pushed into the cesspool. Jan's death had been terrible indeed but at least he no longer suffered under the Rock Lords.

The dwarf took a swig of water. The lukewarm liquid did nothing to slake his thirst and the hard bread he picked up nearly crumbled to dust in his fingers. Harald licked the scraps off his hands then plucked the bits off his filthy shirt. He glanced hungrily at the netting hanging from the rafters. There were three apples left…no, two for the third one had become brown and mushy and strained through the mesh. He reached up and pulled out all three, discarding the rotten one and eating the remaining two. His stomach barely acknowledged the sparse meal.

Harald retreated to the porch to escape the stifling heat and stink. He sat down on the riser and watched the sun bathe the land in soft orange and golden hues. He had always loved this time of day and not just for its beauty. It used to mean there would be plenty of food and pleasantries with his friends and neighbors. The Rock Lords had allowed them some relaxation, a trade-off for stronger and less resentful slaves. Whistler had never accepted that, though. He had considered one minute of subjugation an affront without equal. Whistler. He almost begged to be whipped and was always obliged by the Rock Lords. Why Kevlan had never killed him was a mystery. Now he and Elena were gone and Harald was sure Kevlan regretted not having done so. Whistler had been the unspoken leader of the dwarves and there was no one who could replace him.

Harald looked down the street and sighed with relief as Mary and a few other women brought the men's rations. It wouldn't be much, he knew. She walked up to the porches and handed small bundles to the dwarves. A pair of guards leading Dribbies trailed her to make sure she did not distribute more than what was approved. She did not look at any of the faces keeping her gaze on the weathered basket hanging from her shoulders. Mary stopped in front of Harald's shack. Her face appeared gaunt and her skin sallow. Mary had been a stout woman but no longer. She seemed lost in her clothing and her arms, once hefty, were spindly and pale. She delivered his provisions and turned to go.

"Thank you, Mary," Harald said in a raspy voice.

Mary stopped and looked over her shoulder at him, the haunted glaze in her eyes melting for just an instant, replaced with a hardness that surprised even Harald. He glanced over at the other women with her and saw the same tenacity briefly flare in their eyes.

"Move along you worthless wenches!"

Harald scowled at the guard as he roughly pushed the women on with his staff. He suddenly forgot his hunger and exhaustion. His shaking fingers separated and assumed a claw-like position before curling up into tight fists at his side. Whistler and Elena were no longer here but their spirit to survive permeated the compound. They had not abandoned the dwarves but sought help to free them from these appalling bonds. Harald didn't care how long it took them to return. He would do everything in his power to keep the embers of hope burning until they did come back.

* * *

Lord Kevlan sat on the throne carved out of fragrant cedar wood and covered with furs: two bear hides complete with claws and three wolf pelts. He absently picked at the claws draped over the armrests; his dark eyes focused on the huge antler light fixture suspended in the center of the room. Bright light filtered into the chamber through the open doorways but failed to chase away the dingy shadows clinging to the dull plaster on the walls. The furniture was rough-hewn and stained dark, a sharp contrast to the rich textiles the Rock Lords had stolen from the villages in the east. Kevlan especially valued the deep blue and vibrant green blankets and rugs. The former hung over the chairs and the latter strewn before the throne. No one, however, was allowed to sit or step on them except for him. Gold was plentiful within the room and came in all shapes and sizes. There were elaborately crafted candlesticks, the arms in the shapes of animals, their open mouths holding the candles. A wooden box, its lid resting against the plastered wall, held a variety of miscellaneous items including a curious flattened bottle. It subtly tapered out from its mouth to the base, the body partially encased in tarnished silver. The metal had been skillfully forged into a forest scene: the treetops connected along the top and the roots intertwined along the bottom. The deep, rich emerald hue of the glass shone from behind the metalwork. Cups, plates and bowls were neatly stacked on the table against the wall. A golden sword and shield hung on the wall to the right of the dais and a chest of gold coins sat atop a table to the left. Blood, some dried onto the slabs of stone some fresh, was spattered in front of the table.

A Rock Lord with a bloody bandage on his right hand knelt beside the table wearing nothing but a loincloth. His knees were turning white, his body quivering with exhaustion. He lurched forward a ways. Kevlan reached beside the throne, pulled out a sword and smacked the man with the flat of the blade sending him flying off the dais. He struggled to stand but could only grovel for mercy at Kevlan's feet.

"Forgive me…father."

"Get him out of my sight," growled the Lord.

His face radiated disgust as the guards dragged his son out of the room. Kevlan inwardly hoped that his only other son wasn't as greedy…or as stupid. He glanced over at Tarz, his highest-ranking commander. Tarz' indifference brought a slight smile to Kevlan's face. He jerked his head and called the messenger forward ripping the papers out of his hand before the courier had a chance to bow to him. Kevlan scanned the reports. Everything was running smoothly but the one piece of information he sought was not in any of them. He looked up and grabbed the messenger by the front of his shirt jerking him within an inch of his nose. The carrier didn't need to be asked the question—he already knew what it was.

"We have not found them, my Lord Kevlan."

Kevlan shoved the man aside and glowered at everyone in the room. No one dared to meet his gaze. The stale air reeked of sweat, ale and old food. He had to get out. He walked past his men and out into the warm sunshine calling for his horse, castigating the stable hand when it was not immediately brought to him.

He jumped on its back and galloped away from the failure and frustration contained within his hall. He rode past the dwarves' compound and beyond the foundations of the sentry post. He ignored his bodyguards who kept a respectful distance away from him. He finally stopped resting his hands on the pommel while staring at the old dwarven stronghold to the north. He imagined Whistler looking back at him, daring him to come and get him. Kevlan spit on the ground. *You should have killed him when you had a chance.*

Kevlan wondered where they would have gone. He knew they would seek help but the only people close enough to do so were the elves. They had been solid allies for years but that had changed once the dwarves became enslaved. Could Whistler resurrect that alliance? Kevlan imagined the elves pouring onto the flatland Whistler and Elena in the forefront. The Rock Lord was no fool and although he doubted Whistler could succeed he wasn't about to discount that possibility either.

He would stake every dwarf to the ground between here and the compound. Over a thousand bodies placed haphazardly would impede both horse and soldier. Whistler would certainly not jeopardize the very lives he wanted to save. Channels and traps could be dug along the far reaches of the land and his men would ride between the bodies and the pitfalls. The Rock Lords would try to force the elves toward the bound dwarves and wait for them to back off in fear of harming them. They would abandon Whistler and Elena and ride back to their city. Kevlan grinned. He pictured the dwarf pair standing dejectedly side-by-side waiting for Kevlan to approach them. They'd drop to their knees and appeal to his humanity. *I'd let you two live. You, Whistler, will be chained to the wall behind my throne and Elena will be the recipient of my lust.* Kevlan's smirk broadened then began to fade as his imagination took an unusual turn. *What if they did manage to muster up an army and succeed in overrunning my lands?*

The image of the defeated dwarves wavered then took on a menacing appearance. The elves rode hard at Kevlan and his men swords hacking at the Rock Lords as their horses somehow managed to avoid harming the victims tethered to the ground. Arrows whistled past his ears. Whistler, his eyes blazing with fire grew larger and larger as he sped toward him. The howl escaping the dwarves' throat slammed into him even at this distance nearly knocking him to the ground. Kevlan's horse dropped beneath him the arrow buried deep in its great neck. He couldn't pull out his blade to protect himself as Whistler clung to the pommel with one hand and buried the sword into his chest with the other.

Kevlan flinched as the imaginary edge sliced through his breast. The 'battle' faded away but it did not take his apprehensions with it. Whistler's resourcefulness had kept him alive all this time and he would certainly revert to it to fulfill his obligation. He was a danger within the compound and an even greater one outside it. He had to insure that anyone Whistler might turn to for help would disregard him.

"Tarz," he called the guard over to him. "Send someone to get enough supplies to last for at least two weeks then tell them to meet up with you by the river."

"What are my orders, Lord Kevlan?"

"To warn the elves of two very sick dwarves."

* * *

Tarz and two others rode due west the white flag with the blue circle in the center fluttering on the pole stuck in the saddle behind him. They had been on the road for nearly a week and had yet to cross paths with any elves. Tarz' dark eyes were devoid of mercy and the muscles on his upper body distorted the flat green tattoos. His longevity in Kevlan's personal guard was rooted in his extraordinary ability to carry out the Lord's orders. The blood of Easterners, dwarves and even other Rock Lords stained his sword and perhaps he could add a drop or two of elven blood to the unsympathetic mix. That wasn't his task this time but there always could be another time. Tarz' mouth stretched into a fiendish grin. If the elven patrol chose to fight instead of listening then he would be more than happy to oblige them. His status would be elevated in the Hall…perhaps even on par with the present Lord. Kevlan had made so many enemies in the Hall—especially his own flesh and blood—that they would be more than willing to join up with him to seek revenge upon the Lord. Levor, the son who knelt beside the open chest of gold, would be the first to volunteer. He would have the edge.

The dwarves had their place in the scheme of things but the Easterners had all the wealth. They had control of the lush forests, orchards and rich farmlands not like the stubborn earth and sparse vegetation the Rock Lords owned. They had access to the ocean where goods from the islands filled their larders and coffers. They had women so beautiful they made men stop in their tracks. The Rock Lords raided their outlying villages and towns stealing the inferior goods found there. Daimoryia, the Easterners main city, held the real treasures. He had seen the city himself a few years back. The blocky buildings had thick walls forming a horseshoe shape around the northern, western and southern sections of the city. The Easterners lined gigantic blocks of stone from the ends all the way to the edge of the sea, effectively cutting off any access to the city via land. The only way into Daimoryia was through one of dozens of gates scattered along the outer walls. The eastern portion was exposed to the ocean but anyone deciding to attack from there would be forced to traverse the gauntlet to get to the city. The Easterners had used the land around them very well but he was sure he could find a way in if given enough time.

Tarz reached into his pouch and extracted a cluster of *phel*. He stared at the pale purple fruit then bit into one of them. It was like biting into a sack of spit. He shoved the rest back into his pack the faint image of the city shimmering before his eyes like a mirage. He glanced over his shoulder at the glimmering heat rising up on the plains behind him. Scrubby trees. Coarse grasses. Tasteless crops. Dry heat and dust. His gaze traveled over to the low, deep green line far off on the horizon. Cool shade. Clean water. Access to nearly unlimited riches. All that and a ruler too weak to grasp them. Kevlan was more interested in shoring up his pride by catching and torturing two dwarves. Tarz didn't care if they lived or died. Their presence or absence changed nothing in his life. The blurry line continued to shimmer in the distance. Tarz turned his attention back to the task at hand. They would be close to elven lands by noon tomorrow and, with any luck, wouldn't have to travel too far to meet up with a patrol. Tarz didn't care if they were perceived as aggressors and chased away; in fact, he hoped that would be the case.

The softly glowing sun warmed their faces as it sank in the sky. Tarz scanned the area for a place to spend the night and decided upon a huge willow elegantly bending over a stream. The horses could graze on the thick grass and they could escape beneath the cool canopy of leaves. They ate jerky and small squares of hard bread, washing them down with water from the rill. One of Tarz' men squinted at a nearby bush. He walked over to it and fumbled beneath the broad leaves extracting several bright red spheres. He brought those to his companions and went back to the bush twice more. The sweet yet tart berries were an unexpected treat. The Rock Lords discarded the phel clusters, which barely drew the attention of the flies.

Tarz assigned the guard duties then lay back on the spongy green carpet. He leaned against his saddle and sipped from his canteen. He thought about Whistler. Kevlan had kept him alive because he wanted to break the dwarf's indomitable spirit but Whistler's will was much stronger than Kevlan's. The dwarf became a challenge then an obstacle and finally morphed into a danger. Kevlan's stubbornness had created the weapon of his own downfall and it was now loose in the land. The Rock Lord feared the dwarf would succeed or Kevlan would never have sent him on this mission. Kevlan's rule now hinged on Whistler's death or capture.

He glanced at the sleeping Rock Lord a few feet away then over at the vague silhouette standing guard beneath the shadow of the trees to his left. Tarz took a deep breath and exhaled slowly. He moved without disturbing a single blade of grass, placing his hand over the man's mouth while slicing open his throat. He rose to his feet and casually approached the sentinel who quickly met the same fate. He collected his things and his dead companions' horses and headed north leaving the corpses for the scavengers attracted by the smell of blood.

* * *

Clay, Sara and Whistler turned away from the broad expanse of oily water lapping up against the sheer cliffs. The greasy water was taking forever to dry as it rolled down their bodies and clothes in slow motion. The way out was impossible leaving them no choice but to survey the tidal flat they stood upon for another route. The channels were straight but crossed each other at a hundred different points and not one ran uninterrupted toward the island in the center. Sharp, obsidian points extended upward from the bracken that seemed to choke the plot of land sitting in the middle of nowhere. The warm light of dusk bathed everything in ginger hues except for the strange formation on the island.

Whistler moved a few steps and grimaced at the squishing sound under his feet. He could feel himself gradually sinking into the soft ground and smell the salty tang of the water seeping into his boots. He moved over a few feet and shook his head.

"Can you see the others?"

"No…nothing is moving on the marshland," replied Clay as he, too took a few steps forward.

"We have to go there," stated Sara grateful for the eight legs clinging to her neck. She had thought May was lost when they had crashed into the viscous swamp and barely managed to crawl to the surface. They could not wait to escape its syrupy confines and had to labor to pull themselves and each other from its dense embrace. Sara had frantically searched through her cloak and hood for her, panicking when she found it empty. They scrutinized every square inch of the soggy ground they stood on but did not find her. Clay saw one of her legs sticking up out of the surface and dove in to save her. The two of them had been nearly lost in the oily muck. May tucked her head under Sara's chin and it would take a disaster of epic proportions to dislodge her this time.

"I think we should head for the cliffs and see where the others are," stated Whistler.

"We can't," said Clay his tone bordering on defeated.

"Why in Hades not?"

"Look for yourself."

Whistler turned around and furrowed his brows in disappointment. A dense, grayish smoke rose from the far edges of the water and quickly obscured the cliffs behind it. It silently glided in their direction stirring the metallic liquid as it passed over it. Numerous ripples erupted at its forefront but the concentrated water could not outrun the mist.

"Wonderful. *Elena! Elena!*"

"Stop, Whistler!"

The dwarf glanced annoyingly over at Clay then followed his gaze. The haze shivered and retreated a few feet before moving forward at a slightly brisker pace. He moved to stand beside Clay and Sara ignoring the slurping sound his feet made when he walked.

"Let's go," he whispered.

They slogged across the first spongy hump and reached the channel dividing it from the next series of mounds. The waterways were not wide and Clay tugged on the marsh grasses dangling over the muddy prominence: their deep roots would not relinquish their hold. *It would be a simple thing to jump over them and grab onto the grass for support...whoa! What's this?* Clay pushed aside several blades and grinned. Dozens of tiny crabs scurried out of the light and retreated into holes in the muddy side. One

THE FORTRESS OF DARKNESS

wayward crustacean tried to scramble into an opening and was promptly shoved out by the owner. It met the same results several more times then used its claw to coat itself with mud to protect itself from the light. The silt ran off its body leaving it vulnerable to the elements. It stood there and clicked its little claw, staring at him with its stalk eyes. Clay could have sworn he heard it sigh with dejection and felt a pang of sympathy for it. He dropped the fronds and suppressed the emptiness rising from his soul.

Clay vaulted onto the next mound and squirted water everywhere when he landed. He wiped his eyes and face then waited for Sara to leap over to him. She alit without displacing a drop of water. Whistler tumbled more than bounded over the channel and rolled to a stop several feet away from them. He stood and scowled at the sodden clothing sticking to his body.

They walked for hours yet the island never seemed to get any closer. The strange mist, however, did. Whistler fine-tuned his ability to hop over the waterways and every victory made him less irritable. They stopped to rest and share a quick meal, careful not to eat too much for they had no idea how long they would be stuck in this odd place.

"What do you think they want us to find here?" asked Whistler.

"I don't know. Sara? Any ideas?"

Sara tilted her head until her cheek rested on May. The spider nuzzled her back then gently nibbled on her skin. The wraiths had been most unkind in handling her, their cruelty flaring to life once more as she stared at the island...

She walked through the noxious mist barely acknowledging the icy droplets clinging to her skin. She passed by the contorted frames of ill-fated trees and misshapen shadows, her goal a ghostly depression just beginning to take shape in front of her. Sara swallowed hard, her fascination and repulsion increasing with every step she took. A black silhouette blocked her way: the opening. She slowly moved beneath the bramble-encrusted entranceway careful to avoid the finger length thorns sticking out in every direction. Their points glittered even in the ashen half-light.

She descended into the pit, wary of what thrived in the harsh red-orange glow flickering up from within. She reached the bottom and, after hesitating for a moment entered the cavern. She wiped the sweat from her forehead as she looked around, gaping at the dozens of pairs of yellow eyes staring unblinkingly at her from behind rocks and pillars. Other than a few plaintive whimpers, there was silence. The air felt oppressive, the pungent odors settling into her eyes and lungs like sand…

Reality invaded her memory and shoved aside the image leaving her gazing into the canal. She could bleed, cry, laugh, sing with little impunity but love came with a high price. The demon part of her abhorred that emotion and punished her for trying to embrace it.

She loved Master Felix and that emotion forced to funnel the added demon hatred onto those wandering too closely to Terracine. The bandits were the recipients of her retribution when they had rushed into the mountain. She had experienced a primal gratification while tearing them apart and had been powerless to stop herself. She had lost that precious connection to her human lineage, the very bond that made her existence tolerable. Sara remembered how badly she had wanted to respond to August's gentleness and subtle affection. She couldn't, of course, because to do that meant someone else would have to bear the brunt of her demon half. The deeper the emotion the more savage the response became. Her reflection changed sending a shiver of revulsion up her spine. Gone were her dainty features and the soulful expression in her silver eyes. A blood-smeared face and a malignant glare that frightened her replaced them.

"Sara?" Clay's concerned voice cut through to her.

"What?"

"Why are we being coerced into journeying to that island?"

"We'll find out once we get there."

They finally noticed the island getting larger and took a small measure of comfort in their progress. Time no longer made any sense and they no longer abided by it. It could have been ten minutes or ten years since the wraiths transported them over the cliffs. It no longer mattered. They were here and would not be able to leave until they reached their destination. They had not seen anyone and began to wonder if their friends even made it over the mountain. They each had lost someone they cared deeply about and could only hope their loved ones had somehow survived.

Clay appreciated Sara and Whistler's presence but missed August dearly. The elf felt a sudden twinge of sadness. August would undoubtedly pursue his Herkah heritage once this dangerous journey ended. Clay wasn't welcomed in Bystyn and he fervently hoped that

August would be more successful with the Herkahs' acceptance. Moreover, what would he do if August remained with the nomads? Well, he'd hop a schooner and head back to the island. There were plenty of opportunities there. And loneliness. Clay shook his head free of those dark thoughts concentrating instead on the hill looming in front of them.

Whistler thought about Elena and everything they had been through from the moment they met at the camp until now. They first saw each other as children. He had mercilessly teased her and she had, one day, had enough and punched him square in the nose. She had stood over him, bottom lip stuck out in defiance and hands on her hips daring him to get up. He did but very cautiously and keeping one hand raised while he got to his feet. He held out his hand in reconciliation and she took it. He remembered how hard she squeezed letting him know she would never take any more of his bullying ever again.

Their relationship grew slowly over the years until he could not recall them ever being apart. The Rock Lords did not allow the dwarves to marry but he and Elena exchanged their vows in a way that no master could ever break apart. Her indomitable spirit humbled him and her bottomless faith sustained him. He could think of nothing bad about her. If it hadn't been for Elena, he would never have accepted the heavy cloak of leadership. His hatred and bitterness were unwelcome characteristics in a leader but they had kept him focused all these years. He beat his mind with them as effectively as the Rock Lords whipped his body. He was a troublemaker not a savior.

Whistler sighed remembering the images the mountain wraiths had shown him. They summarized his failures perfectly. Unless something dramatic occurred, he would certainly not be in the forefront of an army riding in to save his people. *My kin probably think Elena and I will nevermore return to the compound. They'll probably think we deserted them.* Whistler's gaze dropped down onto the ground as the flush of ineptitude crept into his cheeks.

They continued on their course for a long time. They jumped over channels and soggy humps so often that the effort became second nature to them. Run-hop-land-walk. That became their entire world and their goal grew agonizingly slowly in front of them. They leapt over yet another of the countless waterlogged sections of land and stopped in their tracks. What had taunted them from afar suddenly towered over them. They stood and stared at it, hands on their hips and necks craning upward.

The obsidian structures shone like crow feathers; their haphazard angles all combining to form perfect points far above their heads. They could just make out a jagged entryway in the middle beckoning them into its black maw. Small round rocks lay strewn around the opening and the companions became awestruck as they moved closer. Some of the stones were broken in half revealing brilliant silver, green, blue and red crystals. They glittered even in the plain light. Sara knelt down, picked one up, and turned it in her hand. She stared at the sparkling points until they filled her entire vision. She heard the vague echoes of a waterfall and felt its gentle spray cool her face. Her hand became cold. She placed the rock back on the ground and picked up a red one. She immediately dropped it and blew on the blister forming on her fingertips. Sara looked over at Clay who held a green stone.

"What do you sense, Clay?"

"The smell of dirt and the feel of grass."

Whistler stood in front of the entranceway studying the passageway as it curved away toward the right. He could see a faint light reflecting off the smooth walls. His companions joined him and the three of them entered the corridor together. They walked around the outcropping and found themselves at the edge of the bowl-shaped amphitheater. They could see their indistinct images on the opposite wall staring back at them. They gaped in awe at the mosaic floor.

In the center was a compass with four swords pointing into the proper directions. A sleek dragon, intertwined within their elaborately designed hilts, gazed unwaveringly into the northeast quadrant over a pit of fire. They stared at the flames, their imperceptible flickering stoking the apprehension growing in their stomachs. Foam tipped azure waters filled the southeast area hissing ever so faintly where it abutted the fire. They shivered and glanced down upon the pure white border beneath their boots. They stepped onto the black outline and felt the chill leave their feet.

THE FORTRESS OF DARKNESS

* * *

Taman picked up a silver rock and closed his eyes. A gentle breeze stirred his hair. Tendrils of silver, blue, green and red rose from their respective stones and twisted together to form a solid braid of light. It vaulted upward and pulsed with a vibrancy that could have split the very mountains in half. The energy swirling in front of him summoned a response from deep within his own body. His spirit paid homage to the power gyrating before him compelling Taman to his knees. He exhaled scattering the radiant column as if it were nothing more than dust.

"What are they?" asked Garadan quietly his gaze firmly fixed on Taman's humbled features.

"They are the essences of the land and the very reason you exist, Garadan."

"We should go inside," stated the elf careful not to step on any of the stones.

Garadan led them into the peculiar structure cautiously moving around the section of rock blocking the light. Elena, Taman and August were a step behind him. They were within the edifice much more quickly than they had anticipated and gaped down at the image on the floor. Elena placed her hand on August's shoulder and Taman leaned against Garadan for support as they absorbed the beautiful depictions.

The elegant dragon stared away from them, its clawed wings and talons gripping intricately forged hafts. The northwest section was filled with billowing clouds, the breeze subtly stirring the group's hair and clothing. Grasses and trees sprouted in the southwest enclosure, its neighbor to the north ruffling the leaves and blades. They too vacated the white strip encircling the entire floor.

Taman's grip tightened as the colors began to swirl together. He became dizzy and his empty stomach began to push the bile up into his throat. The hues formed a broad eddy grabbing at him as it gyrated inward. The blue sky turned dark then as black as the walls around them. This place was rife with magic and it sought recognition. Taman tried to speak but the whirlpool sucked the breath right out of his lungs. He watched the teal hued dragon, still clutching the swords, rise from the center of the mosaic. It glared at him with crimson eyes as tiny bits of flame escaped through razor sharp fangs. He felt compelled to bow down before it but his knees wouldn't comply. The world stopped shifting and his nausea slowly subsided.

The nebulous column on which it perched began to solidify becoming a befogged mirror. They shuffled around the pillar looking at the uneasy faces looking back at them. They were careful not to walk on the sea of tiles and the burning fires. The companions had marched completely around and halted where they had started.

* * *

Clay, Whistler and Sara marveled at the greenery and clouds as they, too sauntered around the dragon-topped stele of mist. The undertones of power resonated sharply within the amphitheater and originated from the column in the center. An image began to form within it, one that elicited a sharp intake of breath from Sara.

Ruins rose eerily up from the shattered ground, a bloated full moon surrounded by three halos hung low in a bluish green sky. Bits of the ghostly heavens glimmered through sections of its broken walls. Mist clung to the foundation and curled lazily upward. A humped shape appeared briefly on the ramparts, its bulky form indistinct beneath the haunted half-light. It grasped the edge of the rampart, its covered head looking down upon the indistinct figures gaping upward at it. The ghoulish silhouette straightened and hissed with satisfaction then disappeared from view leaving the group alone. They were spellbound and unable to move. Clay looked over at Whistler. They were standing so close their shoulders touched yet he could not see the dwarf in the reflective surface of the pillar. The dwarf's confounded expression and partially open mouth prompted him to gaze at Sara. Her eyes were wide and her hand pressed against her throat.

August and Garadan braced a slumping Taman, watching the remnants of the citadel fade away. Elena felt a sickening knot grow in her stomach. She heard Garadan exhale and August shift nervously beside her but could not see them in the mysterious exterior of the column.

Taman leaned less and less against the elf and rubbed his face with shaking hands. He swayed a bit on his feet then regained control of his legs. The pilaster dropped back into position the moment he did so. The blue sky chased away the darkness. They blinked hard at what they saw standing directly across from them. Was this a trick by the wraiths or of whatever existed here? They had made a complete circuit of the arena and should have seen them then.

"Whistler?"

"Elena? August? Are you real?" the dwarf's raspy voice carried clearly across the tiles.

Both groups rushed toward one another carefully avoiding the dragon now back in its appropriate place on the floor. They exchanged hugs and handshakes then both groups revealed how they had come to this location after the wraiths had brought them over the mountain. None of them, however, spoke of their personal nightmares along the way.

"Did you see the ruins?" asked Garadan.

"We did," replied Clay then looked over at Sara. Her downcast eyes and tight jaw spoke volumes about what they had seen. "Sara? Do you know that place?" he gently prodded.

"It is called 'Varek-Tor'—the Fortress of Darkness."

"I hate to even ask but…what is it?" asked Whistler pulling Elena closer.

"It is Emhella's tower," she whispered hoarsely. "It will rise from the land once Emhella has all of the magic in his possession."

Clay looked down while Garadan and Whistler traded glances. They were stuck on this side of the range with their way out through the tall grasses or over the marsh. Neither passage was desirable.

"You all might want to take a look at this," August called to them from the doorway facing west.

They crowded out of the arena and congregated outside the entrance. August ducked back into the amphitheater focusing his gaze on the compass. The space the dragon had occupied retained its shape but the tiles appeared colorless. He rejoined his companions wondering if they were about to become the beasts' dinner.

The dragon gauged them through half-lidded eyes; the vertical black slits nearly lost within the scarlet pupils. It studied them with a mixture of curiosity and disdain. It tapped the ground with a foot long talon, the tip clicking sharply on the rock beneath it.

Taman gaped at the winged serpent, its elegant beauty immediately seducing him. Tri-lobed scales as iridescent as dragonflies flowed from the back of its head, down its sides and along its long, whip-like tail. A row of small spikes that decreased in size ran down its face. The dragon's rectangular muzzle was closed but he could still see the knifelike tips of its teeth sticking out beyond the surprisingly smooth appearing cheeks. Its wings, tucked against its sides, were barely visible.

"I am Mercator, Keeper of the Elements," his deep, clear voice broke the silence.

Taman felt the wind, earth, fire and water unite and swirl around him blocking out his friends, the arena and everything else found in the land beyond the mountains…

The smoke filled sky cringed as gleaming bolts of lightning shredded through it, the booming thunderclaps shaking the ground beneath his feet. The range in the far north surrounded a massive volcano spewing lava and fire all over the land. A hot wind touched his soot covered face as he stared at the black lake between himself and the belching peak. Shreds of greenish gray clung to the boulders and sprouted up on the chestnut hued soil. The bitter vapors made him cough and rub at his eyes, robbing his lungs of precious air. He doubled over hoping the image would fade away. It did not.

A brightening took place between the horizon and the clouds. A milky light pushed upward forcing the dirty clouds to cede their hold on the sky. A brisk, cool wind fragmented them then pushed them far into the north. The water changed from black to blue and the tattered strands metamorphosed into bright green filaments. Taman watched as a river of lava flowed into the lake. It hissed and steamed with displeasure but was powerless to stop the glowing finger. The waters began to ripple, the pure energies converging within causing an eddy to spiral upon its roiling surface. The whirlpool began to sink in the center then boiled upward forming a churning waterspout. Taman's clothes and hair were pulled toward it as he grabbed onto a slab of rock to keep from being sucked into the center. The verdant fibers were yanked from their barren places and thrust into the vortex.

The column spun faster and faster, bulging in the center and sending out vaguely shaped appendages. Amethyst, emerald, black, red and a solitary silver sparkle erupted

THE FORTRESS OF DARKNESS

from the lake and disappeared into the daunting pillar. They whirled within for several long seconds then were cast out into five different directions. Their exit slowed then halted the maelstrom. The mist from the roiling waters dissipated revealing the Keeper of the Elements.

Mercator hovered in the dampness his great wings pumping the air in slow motion. He languidly flapped his gossamer fins and flew toward Taman, the whooshing sound loud in his ears. The dragon swooped down then up into the brilliant blue sky, hanging motionless for a moment before taking a breath so deep his neck arched backward while his head dropped near his broad chest. Mercator roared, the deep tone splintering the mountains and pulverizing rocks. Taman twisted around just in time to see the faces of the range slide to the ground and rush toward him in an avalanche of dirt and rubble. The elf brought up his arms in front of his face, the choked cry of panic lodging firmly in his parched throat...

The scene faded leaving Taman standing with his companions once more. His chest rose and fell in quick succession, his hands still crossed to ward off the rockslide. He brought them down and, dropping to his knees bowed low to the dragon. He could see his companions following suit, their movements tentative, and their shared looks of uncertainty marking their obeisance.

"We are..." began the brown elf.

"I know who you are and what brought you here," Mercator interrupted him. "Stand."

The group obeyed him, keeping their stances respectful of the being before them.

"No mortals have ever crossed the range...and lived. The Kaiyeths had a good reason to transport you here." He scrutinized the human beings, some with arms hanging limply at their sides and others with hands clasped in front of or behind them. Their dusty clothing hung limply from their shoulders. The tall elf pushed aside a section of hair with his dirt-encrusted fingers, the scabs on his hands appearing garish in the light. Their heads remained lowered and their eyes shifted nervously around looking at everything but him. He focused his gaze on the demon.

"You reek of the Black Abyss," the dragon stated with no hint of malice in his tone.

Sara flinched and squeezed her eyes shut hoping to stop the tears that welled up instantly. Her stomach flipped and her heart cringed in her chest. She suddenly felt very unclean and was grateful when his attention drifted away from her. She didn't notice August's subtle anger flaring up in his eyes nor that May had abandoned her shoulder and now knelt before Mercator.

The Keeper lowered his head and chuckled, if that was what you could call the sound issuing pleasantly from the back of his throat, inviting May to sit on his muzzle. She scampered up and proudly sat on the horn between his oval-shaped ears, ignoring the astonished looks on the faces of her companions.

"All of you save one staggers beneath the weight of your doubts. That one will either save or destroy you. You must cast aside your shortcomings and concentrate on your task at hand."

"What is that task, Mercator, Keeper of the Elements?" asked Elena in hushed tones.

"Two of the five powers are already in the Vox' hands: you must liberate the remaining ones before he does."

"Where can we find them?" asked Clay. "What shall we do with them if we are successful?"

"You must do so before the next full moon," Mercator ignored the elf's question.

"With all due respect, Keeper of the Elements," Elena's voice filled the silent void, "but you offer us little in the way of direction."

"You will find your answers at Varek-Tor."

"But...Varek-Tor won't exist until..." Sara found her voice, the small sound issuing forth barely audible even to her. August half turned his head toward her but the dragon's commanding presence yanked it forward.

"Eight of you will venture forth," Mercator turned his full attention on a shrinking Sara. "A way out will be provided for you but...*heed my words*...do not speak or go into the water."

May tapped the dragon on the top of his head with her front legs then smoothly alit on the ground, the slight breeze carrying off her silver web. It floated away, gracefully spiraling about until it snagged on a branch. It fluttered several times then hung still.

Mercator narrowed his eyes at the mortals then spread his gauzy wings. He went airborne with one mighty thrust, his sleek body standing out starkly against the sky.

The group watched the Keeper of the Elements take flight and hover over the black structure then disappear in a shimmering cloud that dropped back down into the center of the edifice.

Garadan braced a wobbly Taman while the remnants of Mercator's magic ceased weaving through the brown elf's mind. The silence ensued for a few more moments until Clay spoke up.

"He said eight. There are only seven of us."

"Maybe he's counting May," suggested Taman as the spider resumed her place on Sara's shoulder.

"Somehow I don't think so," replied Whistler.

"What did Mercator mean by a way out...?" asked August.

He suddenly went silent as the sound of running water grew louder by the moment. The groups that had traveled through glass reeds and over treacherous marshlands instinctively scanned the area for a possible new threat. The land between them suddenly split apart pushed away from each other by a dark and shadowy river that ran east to west. The abrupt shifting knocked them all off balance. By the time they regained their footing it was too late to jump to either side. Whistler, Sara and Clay looked over the ribbon of water at August, Taman, Elena and Garadan. Taman looked toward the west and absently poked Garadan in the chest. The elf glanced over in that direction and cocked his head to the side: two empty, long boats floated up the river. They glided soundlessly side by side until they neared both parties, each boat flowing to a stop in front of the companions. They narrowed their eyes at the bizarre objects.

The vessels weren't constructed of wood but of a strange, grayish material that glistened where the water lapped up against it. Both had figureheads, their long arms and fingers sweeping rearward along the sides. The boat awaiting Garadan, August, Elena and Taman had a carved figure of a woman, her eyes closed, and her face serene. Her long hair was twisted into thick braids that covered her breasts. The other was that of a man but his expression was severe and unfriendly. His short hair coiled into numerous spikes all around his head. Both wore boxy lanterns around their necks.

They peered apprehensively into their respective vessels, unsure of what they would find. The only place to sit was on the bottom next to full pouches and several canteens. There were no oars. Each group eyed the distant cliffs separating them from the land of the mortals then back to the skiffs. They stepped in and took a seat, the boats moving toward the center of the river, well within speaking distance of each other. They headed due east, the river's pace quickening with every passing minute. The short grasses along the banks became higher the farther they traveled until they met overhead and formed a canopy of tinkling reeds. The sky was gone and soon a gloomy semi-darkness filled their vision.

"We have less than two weeks before the moon is full," stated Garadan in quiet tones.

"We don't even know where to look for these powers."

"No, Elena, we don't," he replied watching their peculiar world become even darker. He absently gazed into the strange rush along the riverbank expecting to see his men continuing their torment, one hand firmly grasping the side of the boat while the other lay flat on the bottom.

Sara closed her eyes and heard Mercator's words reverberate in her mind: *You reek of the Black Abyss.* She would never be free of that stench nor would she ever be completely clear of Emhella's influence. He had called to her and she had subconsciously obeyed him. Had it not been for August she might have fully given herself to the demon. She chanced a glance at him across the water. August sat at the head of the boat followed by Taman, Elena then Garadan. Sara felt secure as she hunkered down between Clay and Whistler. Well, she, like the others were on this scary and unfamiliar journey for reasons none could, at this point, understand.

"We all had our own agendas and met by coincidence to proceed with this unexpected quest."

"Do you really think it was accidental, Whistler?" asked Taman.

"Everything is interrelated," Sara said softly, her silver eyes focused on nothing in particular. "A shift in one area pulls on the entire fabric that is the land."

"So what happens in Bystyn has repercussions in…say…Windstorm

Harbor?" Clay's voice reached into her demanding her full attention. She nodded.

"We were all meant to be together then," Elena's whispered words made them all look from one to the other.

"Does that then mean that the eighth person is also meant to join our band?" asked Taman.

"I suppose…why?" Whistler narrowed his eyes at the elf.

"Because we are still only seven." He stared at the water below them, the bows of their vessels slicing through the water sending water spraying along its sides. Tiny, icy droplets landing on their exposed skin sent shivers up and down their spines prompting them to move toward the middle of the boats.

The monotonous landscape continued to roll by never offering a hint of whether hours or days had gone by. May scrambled into the bow and secured herself with her web, her actions not lost on her mates. The companions were each lost in their own thoughts, the repetitious scenery and exertions over the past few days lulling them into fitful sleep. August would suddenly awaken to the sounds of hooves; Whistler would rouse as the yellowish mist oozed out of Evan's Peak; Sara stirred from the dreadful demon pit and the ghosts of his men prodded Garadan back to reality. They scrounged through the packs and ate what Mercator had provided for them, careful not to eat too much too soon. They washed down their meager meals with water but did not doze off anymore. The air gradually became cooler and the reeds suddenly parted before them revealing a giant opening in the mountains. Startled by the abrupt wall of rock, all the companions could do was gape openmouthed ever upward until the back of their skulls rested on their backs. They stared back the way they had come, the light disappearing quickly behind them.

Mercator sat atop the compass, the wraiths suspended all around him. The Kaiyeths' features no longer bristled with anger or scorn, instead unease rippled across their ethereal faces. Their silent voices merged, their haunting tones not quite in unison as they reverberated in the dragon's mind.

The mortals are weak and unpredictable, Mercator.

You place too much trust in them, Keeper.

They will break beneath the awesome responsibility…

"Enough!" Mercator's growl dispersed the wraiths but not their grim predictions. "We have no other choice."

The dragon unfurled his gossamer wings, rising until he cleared the top of the enclosure. Hovering over the center, he waved one of his talons and roared deeply. The four elements on the compass began to shimmer then rose up, each of the essences morphing into a vague dragon form. Mercator reached into the water shape and extracted a small amount of liquid. He held it up and looked at it for a moment before letting it float free before him. Mercator inhaled deeply then released his fire, the vermilion flames encasing the fluid until it blazed as brightly as the noon sun. It pulsed with a sizzling energy and spun at a dizzying rate until a dark core began to materialize. The movement slowed then ceased. Mercator concentrated on the round, dark gray rock suspended in the air for a few seconds before taking hold of it. He repeated his actions on the remaining three elements then handed all four over to the wary Kaiyeths. The four indistinct dragon shapes continued to drift nearby.

-8-

Lady Wyntyn crossed her arms as she stared down into the garden. She watched Caladan drape an arm across a senior lord's shoulder while handing him a letter to read. Caladan spoke to the elf and nodded, urging him to finish examining the missive. They spoke for a few minutes then Caladan walked away, the report firmly in the other's grasp. It was the third time in as many days that Caladan had approached a ranking member of the court. His resolve to assume Balyd's position was greater now than before and elicited a frown on her face. It was time to find out what those papers contained. She ordered her aide to summon Caladan.

Lady Wyntyn trusted Balyd even after he had confessed to sending elves out into the land against Aryanda's instruction. She, like Balyd, felt uneasy about being isolated from the rest of the land but was in no position to try to change that. No, that wasn't quite correct. Unlike Balyd, she didn't have the nerve to act against the queen's wishes. She was now thrust into the forefront of elven affairs and had the opportunity to at least gauge what the other members thought about that situation. Caladan and his personal agenda, however, threatened Balyd's respectability and position in the court. Losing the First Advisor was not an option. A knock on the door forced Lady Wyntyn to regroup her thoughts, the slight smirk on Caladan's face as he entered far from reassuring.

"Thank you for coming, Lord Caladan." Her features remained calm even as he offered her a slightly dramatic, almost impertinent tip of the head. She begrudgingly invited him to sit and poured him a glass of wine.

"How may I serve you?"

"I would like to know about the letters you have been giving to the court."

"They simply list my qualifications to assume Lord Balyd's position if the members deem I am suited for it."

"May I have a copy?"

"Certainly, Lady Wyntyn. I will have one sent to you."

He crossed his legs and stretched his arm along the back of the chair, nonchalantly swirling the contents of his goblet. He knew he was allowed to try to sway the court members.

"I appreciate that."

"Is there something else I can do for you, Lady Wyntyn?"

Yes, she thought. You can pack your things because as soon as an heir to the throne is found, I'm going to make sure your days in the castle are over. You won't be going alone, though.

Looking at him through her eyelashes, she muttered, "No, that will be all."

"Good day to you, Lady Wyntyn."

"And to you, Lord Caladan."

Caladan headed for his chambers. They had once belonged to Prince Danyl and it had taken a great deal of persuasiveness—and overt affection—to procure them for himself. He opened the door and felt that particular thrill coursing through his body. He imagined the wielder of the Green Might standing in front of the balcony doors, unafraid of anything standing in his way. His virility attracted the most beautiful women and his command was the envy of every man. Everyone from king to slave would bow low to him fearful of inciting his wrath. Caladan stood in front of the open doors and closed his eyes, willing even the tiniest of fragments of the Green Might into his body. A cold wind blew against his skin, the touch immediately turning his skin into gooseflesh. He opened his eyes, his darting glance probing into every nook and shadow. The air felt thick and heavy. He closed the doors and sat down in a chair across from the scrolled and inlaid desk, rubbing both hands over his eyes and across his brow. Aryanda's sudden death had put a crimp in his plans…or had it?

She had chosen him to replace Balyd and had even announced a date when that was to occur. Her edict stood regardless if she lived or died. That was in his favor. He could not trace his lineage back to the original king but his family had been members of the court for well over a hundred years. He could play the loyalty card to his advantage. Caladan stared at the well-worn leather chair behind the desk imagining the elf that had at one time sat in it. Danyl would have become king of Bystyn had he remained in the city yet he had chosen to live outside its walls with Ramira. His bloodline and the Green Might would have made him impossible to defeat. What a fool to squander such a perfect combination. He could have conquered the entire land and filled his coffers with riches.

Caladan imagined the gifts and acknowledgements, the sounds of cheering rising from thousands of throats as he passed by the adulatory throngs. Rose petals would be cast before his feet and women would place their hands across their breasts while adoring looks shone from their eyes. Men would pump their fists into the air and shout out his name. *Caladan! Caladan! All hail the king!* He flipped a corner of his coronation mantle over his shoulder revealing the sash worn by all the kings since the first Alyxandyr. He looked down and instead of seeing the deep green silk material with the golden threads, he saw only his blue tunic.

Caladan took a deep breath, the roaring of the crowd and the admiring looks fading away. He was standing in the middle of the room holding his fist high above his head while his other hand reached out to his people. He snapped back to the present and placed his fists on his hips.

"I had best get started." He spoke to the empty room and chair behind the hallowed desk.

* * *

Lady Wyntyn read Caladan's letter. It was, as he had said, merely a record of his achievements in the court, most of which had been slightly embellished. There was absolutely nothing contained within it that would make even a fool elevate him over Balyd. The image of Caladan's arm across the Lords' shoulders returned to her mind. He was gifted with a smooth tongue and used it liberally, especially in these uncertain times. He not only had the court to woo but the possible successors to the throne as well. The known potential heirs saw the throne as a reward and not a seat of ruling power. That dilemma chased away the Caladan problem for the moment. She began to think about Bystyn's future when Balyd's revelations echoed in her mind. The city would have no tomorrow if what he said about the demon were true.

Lady Wyntyn left her chambers intent on speaking with Balyd, hesitating as she passed by the entrance to the Great Hall. She faced the massive oaken doors then pushed down on the brass handles and entered. The portals closed softly behind her. She glanced at the arched windows abutting the garden, the light shining through illuminating the tiled floor. The potted trees standing between the windows hugged the wall, their branches expanding and intertwining above the panes. Modest altars to the kings and queens of the past lined the walls the jewelry, swords and personal items gleaming in the light. Their busts stared straight ahead yet she could not shake the feeling they were looking at her. The most impressive piece in the entire room was a huge tapestry hanging at the far end depicting the elves' journey to the as-yet-to-be-built Bystyn. The first kings' queen had woven it while the elves had constructed the city.

She turned at the sound of footsteps then realized it was so quiet in the large, paneled room, it was her own heartbeat she heard. She walked over to the nearest window placing her hands flat against the glass as she gazed out into the garden. She inhaled the piney scent of the rosemary bushes planted alongside the pathways leading away from the doors and heard the faint splashing of a fountain beyond her line of sight. A pair of songbirds was feeding their young in a nest built in the cornice of the arch. A maidservant carried a wide basket filled with flowers into the opposite wing. Life went on as usual. She sighed and backed away from the sunshine and headed for the library, the sun's rays outlining her palm prints.

"Lord Balyd?"

"Coming!" his muffled voice echoed from the far corners of the extensive chamber. He emerged from between two bookcases brushing the dust and cobwebs from his robe.

"Caladan is pressuring the lords and ladies of the court in his own charming way, of course. Here," she handed Balyd the letter.

"He did all of these things, did he?"

"It's not what he has written down that bothers me, Balyd, but what he says to the members of the court." She proceeded to tell him how friendly Caladan became with them and their brief meeting earlier that afternoon.

"Have you found any leads to another heir?"

"One that won't fall for his charisma? Yes and no."

He stepped over to his desk and shuffled through a stack of books until he found what he was looking for: a thin, leather bound journal—the queen's personal log.

"What have you discovered?"

"A vague reference to Tarat's line. Listen. 'The news, if true, is not good. I have groomed Aryanda in every aspect of ruling Bystyn and will not cede the throne to anyone but her. I have dispatched Ansar to insure Aryanda assumes her rightful place.'"

"Wasn't Ansar Queen Tryssa's captain?"

"Indeed he was. It seems as though one of Tarat's descendants came to call but never made it into Bystyn."

"If Tryssa sent Ansar, then the chances of that person being alive are slim. Even if he had spared their life, more than twenty years have elapsed since then and anything could have befallen him," Lady Wyntyn said quietly.

"Or her. Don't you find it odd that Danyl's and Ramira's offspring chose to live away from the city, yet one makes the effort to contact the queen?"

"That was the only mention written in the journal?"

"Yes."

Lady Wyntyn contemplated the fleeting entry. The communication between the individual and Tryssa was short-lived, the result being he or she never entered the city. The queen felt threatened by this person and sent her captain to make sure he or she did not impede Aryanda's ascension to the throne. Aryanda eventually became queen without any other mention of this stranger.

"What would make someone suddenly appear at their family's doorstep, assuming, of course, that this person was somehow related to Tryssa?" asked Lady Wyntyn.

"I would return to my homestead if I were down on my luck, hurt, or sick."

"And if you were a woman?"

Balyd met her gaze and nodded his head. A successor bearing an heir would certainly disrupt Tryssa's plans. Ansar was many things but he wouldn't slay a newborn.

"Balyd, we have to find this person but first we must locate Ansar."

"What if he or she turned out to be evil?"

"Then we finish what Ansar did not do and do our best with what we have."

* * *

Emhella stood with one boot upon a rock the other firmly on the ground absently staring at the glass urn. He flipped the blue stone with his forefinger and thumb, the smooth surface brushing against his fingers. The Kaiyeths would pay for denying him a chance to acquire the magic he had sensed near the mountains. He had secured the other powers long ago, but the tremendous effort he had exerted to collect them left him too exhausted to bring them back. *No matter, they'll be in my possession soon enough.* The dragon had awakened, too but his magic could not stray beyond the mountains. Once he claimed all the magic for himself, he would pay Mercator a visit.

He looked down at the stone and nodded imperceptibly. The foolish mortal had no idea what she wore around her neck. But he knew. He closed his fingers over it and strode out of the abyss and through the yellowish fog encasing the frightful pit. He stopped beyond its sickly glow and gazed out over the desert. The moon and stars shone brightly from the heavens; the miles of undulating silver sands stretched away toward the dark horizon. The Great White Desert was silent.

The journey to this point had been difficult even for him. The remnants of Mahn's evil power had not always been easy to find. Danyl had wielded the Green Might against Mahn before the gates of Bystyn, shredding then scattering the magic over a wide area. It was like a floating cloud of ashes, cascading out of his grasp the moment he managed to snatch a handful. The bigger shreds had wormed their way into any place that was dark and dank; the smaller bits retreated into any crevasse they could find. He detected some in between the barks of trees; others had made their way under rocks and pebbles. He had rummaged through caves, ditches, abandoned buildings and crawled beneath razor sharp brambles to reach those in rotting logs. He had slain imbeciles who had inadvertently picked up the larger gelatinous blobs. He had destroyed an entire house to get into the basement and a handful of paper-thin remnants. His biggest challenge was to retrieve an armful of power from the meadows near the feet of the range north of Bystyn. The Kaiyeths were able to keep him at bay by diving down at him whenever he left the relative protection of the forest. He waylaid a hapless passerby forcing him toward the cache but the spirits tore him to pieces before he could get halfway to the power's hiding place. He was forced to expend some of his own magic to keep them away. He recovered the power but did not escape unscathed. Emhella could still feel the stinging sensation between his shoulder blades where the Kaiyeths had raked him. He had prevailed and was now about to annihilate the humans.

Emhella held his arm in front of him, the gem firmly in his grasp, and closed his eyes. He willed the power up from within his innermost self, grimacing as the blistering energy raced up from his blackened soul out to his hand. Bits of darkness escaping through his fingers dripped onto the sand, the sound it made on contact like hissing vipers disturbed in their nests. He crushed the stone with his fingers. For a brief moment, nothing happened. Then a brilliant silver shaft suddenly erupted from the stone and settled on the dunes. The luminescent track disappeared down into the trough of a dune then ascended the steep sides of another one. Emhella dropped the remnants onto the sand and followed the faint trail into the wasteland.

He walked upon the dunes' ridges, picking his way along the unstable sands. Even he was not immune to being absorbed into the pockets of death. The demon's strides were long and purposeful, carrying him into the desert with ease. He descended one dune then climbed up the next one with little difficulty. He did not sweat nor did he tire as he followed the thread thin beam barely visible in the darkness. He didn't stop until he stood in front of the ruins of a dais. Emhella stared emotionlessly at the broken columns and smashed fountain then brought out his full power and concentrated it on the platform.

The dais quivered and shook, the countless fractures streaking across its dusty surface becoming wider and deeper. It began to splinter then crumble, the chunks rapidly turning to dust. The force of the magic sent the remnants of the columns out into the desert, the whirling fragments exploding into tiny bits, which the sands immediately consumed. Emhella lowered his outstretched arms until they opened invitingly down toward the cavity left by the platform. With one mighty sweep of his hands the sand, debris and anything else that had occupied that spot was shoved aside revealing an oval shaped opening. Steps disappeared down into the darkness. The demon peered into the dim shadows, a cruel smile touching his lips. *I've come to pay my respects, dear Lady.*

The Vox descended into the dark corridor at a rapid pace, the thought of cornering the Lady in her own realm incredibly satisfying. Hers wasn't the most potent of the energies but it was one of the original powers in the land. He coveted those like a thief craving a pouch full of gold. A shimmering half-light intensified the farther down he went. He finally reached the bottom and glanced around at the vastness of the Lady's home.

Columns of crystalline black trees held the desert up, their sinewy branches stretching into the distance. The polished ebony floor and the trees reflected everything around them. Emhella walked forward, his likeness appearing and disappearing on them like a terrible nightmare. He stopped and cocked his head silently waiting for the Lady to give herself away. A faint pulse of power to his right brought a wicked smile to his face. He nodded then headed in that direction, the pounding of his boots echoing within the cavernous chamber. The magic drew him to the far end and the closer he got the more the power seemed to shrink back away from him. He took several turns following the flickering pulse of energy as it desperately sought to avoid him. *You cannot hide forever, dear Lady.*

Emhella rounded a particularly wide tree and stopped in his tracks, the evil glinting from his face. The Lady stood just yards ahead of him, her dainty hand pressed against her mouth, her eyes radiating terror.

The Vox absorbed her fright for a brief moment then discharged his vile blackness at her. She groaned as the force slammed into her then did something the Vox could not comprehend: she nodded and smiled at him. Her form shimmered then disappeared.

"What...?"

Emhella stared at the now empty space in front of him, the bitterness at having been fooled welling up in his throat. The witch would pay dearly for that affront. He turned around and began walking back the way he had come then suddenly halted He glared at the endless rows of trees spreading out all around him, every one of them appearing exactly alike. The gleaming trunks and branches seemed to mock him.

"I will get out eventually, witch."

The Lady of the Sands stood on the crest of a dune gazing down at the entrance to her domain, her back stiff and her skin stretched tautly across her features. The strain to maintain the illusion within her domain was stealing precious amounts of her magic, power that could not be replenished. Emhella's imprisonment would not last but at least her ruse gained the mortals' valuable time. The Vox had defiled her home although that no longer mattered. She glanced up at the sliver of moon then toward the still dark east, a heavy sigh leaving her lips.

* * *

The last of the light disappeared behind them as they rounded the first bend on their underground journey. The two boats floated silently side by side in the darkness, the only sound the swishing of the water displaced by the bows. The vessels curved to the left then to the right, the undulating motion continuing for a long time. The utter blackness left the companions disorientated. The air was cool and slightly damp but it was not what caused the chill in their minds and souls.

Sara groped for Whistler a scant foot or two in front of her. She found and clung to his shirt just as Clay's hand latched on to the hem of her tunic. Unbeknownst to them the group in the other boat sought the same contact.

"Elena?" Whistler finally dared to whisper.

"We're here," she replied in a muffled tone.

Sara felt the dwarf's shoulders relax somewhat, the reaction passing from him to her and on to Clay. *Will the entire trip be without light?* She strained to see anything and slowly focused on a faint glow up ahead. The skiffs drifted toward it, winding around an outcropping before flowing into a vast cavern illuminated by pale orange-yellow globes. There were hundreds of orbs clinging to the craggy walls of the subterranean passage bathing everything in an eerie light. The companions checked on each other before allowing the imposing and beautiful panorama to grab their attention. The more their eyes became accustomed to the light, the more wonders they beheld.

The spheres reflected off the placid waters, giving the illusion that the companions were suspended in mid-air within this limitless hollow. They glanced down and spotted long, thin flashes of silver streaking by that reminded them of shooting stars in the night sky. They drifted along at an even pace, so engrossed in their surroundings they promptly lost their bearings.

They forgot about their dilemma for a brief moment, and even Sara relaxed for the first time since they had entered the bowels of the mountains. She looked up, rubbed her eyes and began to frown. The globs of light were shifting. She tapped Whistler on the shoulder and pointed up at the spheres. He stared up for a long time then became rigid as several of the lights began to bob along in the semi-darkness. A barely perceptible squeaking rippled overhead in the darkness, the sound increasing as more of the pinpoints of light detached themselves.

Garadan narrowed his eyes at the commotion coming to life over their heads. He shifted his attention toward where the skiffs were taking them, hoping they could enter the gloomy openings on the other side of the lake before all the spheres awakened. Their transit was too slow and the lights were rousing more quickly with every passing second. He watched with a growing horror as the lit balls began flying rapidly around the hollow, their frightening shrieks echoing off the stones. One zoomed over his head, the fleeting glimpse of the fanged features and leathery wings enough to make him take cover in the bottom of the boat. The others soon joined him and together they cowered while the large bats flew about in a crazed state. They huddled together, hands pressing against their ears and knees drawn to their chests as the wild cacophony persisted. It was impossible to hear anything and no one dared peek over the side to see how the other boat was faring. Garadan finally did chance a quick glimpse of where they were and was slightly relieved to see they were very close to the breaches on the other side. He glanced at the other vessel and opened his mouth to speak. It headed for the cleft on the right while they continued on to a fissure on the left. Before he could utter a single word, the mountain swallowed them up once more.

The noise began to diminish, the fear of the bats following them dissipating with every passing moment. Whistler, Sara and Clay slowly sat up in the boat. The glowing lanterns illuminated a narrow corridor snaking through the mountain. The waterway turned right then left then seemed to double back on itself, the group believing they were actually returning to the cavern. They could do nothing more than sit silently, hoping and praying they would not die beneath the rocky bulk above them.

Sara sank deeper and deeper into the skiff, the claustrophobic feeling dragging her back to a place she had worked so hard to escape. This place, even without the molten streams of lava and stench was so much like the demon's pit. The overwhelming sense of despondency clawed at her soul; the feeling of being trapped grabbed at her heart. She began to breathe heavily, barely able to conceal a whimper. She jumped as a hand touched her shoulder then squirmed into Clay's embrace.

Clay held her tightly against him, his own fears threatening to bubble to the surface. He had spent his entire lifetime beneath the warmth of the sun and the reassuring gaze of the moon. This space was not meant for humans. He noticed the walls were getting closer together. He could reach out with both arms and brush his fingertips against the rugged rocks. Sara burrowed deeper into his arms, sobbing softly.

Whistler reached out and wiped away her tears. He looked into Clay's eyes and saw the same trepidation he felt. The dwarf took a deep breath and returned to his spot, wondering what was happening to Elena and the others. He stared at the back of the figurehead. It suddenly didn't seem to be as upright as before but, then again, their enclosed space would make anything seem disproportionate. The shape bent to the side trying to avoid an overhanging section of stone. He blinked several times, the thought of going insane a distinct possibility. Did he just see that? The figure turned around and looked directly at Whistler, the hostile features appearing undead as the lantern light glowed eerily on its chest. Whistler began to retreat to the rear neglecting to notice an outcropping of rock before it grazed his arm.

Clay grabbed his tunic to catch his attention then followed his gaze to the front of the boat. The form was just rotating back into place and detaching its arms from the sides. Sara stiffened in his arms and Whistler nearly jumped out of the vessel. They sank deeper behind the gunwales, clutching each other with desperation. This otherworldly being was bringing them into the very belly of the mountain and down a channel that barely allowed the boat to pass. They dared to look past it and gasped at what awaited them. The mountain came together at this point yet the boat did not slow down one bit. The frightened trio drew even closer together, unable to do anything that could save them. They were at this creature's mercy. It turned around.

Breathe deep and hold.

The shape reached into the water and pulled the vessel under, the companions inhaling precious air before the icy waters cocooned them. They clung to each other while being battered against rocks and lugged through tight spaces. The need to breathe tormented their minds. Sara began to struggle, her hands groping for anything to help haul her out of this watery hell. She raked and clawed the area around her, finding rock, flesh and clothing.

Air bubbles began to escape their mouths and soon their lungs were empty.

Garadan watched the other boat retreat into the fissure until the cleft they were floating into obstructed his view. The bat things did not pursue them but that did little to assuage his uneasiness. A sudden light brought his gaze to the front of the vessel then up and all around him. They were drifting through a passageway lined with rock-strewn landings. A glimmer of silver in the water caught his eye then another one. They were similar to what he had seen in the lake in the cavern. One of the things swam alongside the vessel then broke the surface. Garadan narrowed his eyes at the smooth body with the luminescent white stripe down its back. Its head was flat, the dead eyes staring up at him from the ends of dozens of fleshy protrusions. He moved closer to the center of the craft when the beast rolled over onto its back, exposing row upon row of razor sharp teeth.

Elena sat cross-legged and back-to-back with Taman. The contact felt reassuring in the midst of all this strangeness. Her thoughts drifted to Whistler and how long it would be before they were reunited once more. She disregarded her surroundings, the chill air and crushing weight over her head something she could do nothing about. She glanced up at August's profile, illumed by the lamp hanging from the figureheads' neck. His silhouette was slightly blurred by the halo of light but this only enhanced his proud yet humble features. She imagined him thinking about his friends and how they were faring.

A slight bump brought her out of her reverie. She looked to her right and scrambled away from a mouthful of thorny teeth that clamped down where her head had just been. The creature continued to bite at her retreating form then prepared to launch itself onto her. Taman, suddenly jerked out of his slumber and deprived of his support, tumbled backward, arms flailing to stop his momentum. Garadan drew his sword from its scabbard and raised himself onto one knee waiting for the beast to lunge for the dwarf. He did not have long to wait. It arched its back then thrust itself at Elena who brought her arms up to protect herself.

Garadan brought the blade down but it never connected with the creature. He found himself staring into the face of the figurehead, her stern countenance regarding him as if he were a misbehaving child. Her right hand held his sword arm with so much strength he thought she would break his bones. Her left hand grabbed the wriggling monster snapping and biting at anything that moved. She released her hold on him then set the creature loose in the water. It swam alongside the vessel for a while then vanished into the inky liquid.

They journeyed on, one moment moving straight ahead the next bending sharply to the left or right. Sometimes they could not see either side of the river and other times they had to duck to avoid a low hanging rock. No one knew, or could guess, what time it was or how much farther they had to travel.

Mist began to billow up from the water, imbued with the aromas of eucalyptus and lavender. The fragrances soothed away their uneasiness and relaxed their bodies. Their eyelids fluttered several times then closed as the companions sank to the bottom of the boat and fell asleep. The figurehead glanced over her shoulder at them then took her slumbering cargo through a foamy white curtain.

* * *

Captain Hardan escorted Lady Wyntyn in the garden, the early evening breezes gently stirring their clothing as the gravel crunched beneath their feet. Rosemary, basil, parsley and dozens of other herbs released their redolence into the warm air, clinging to anything that passed by.

"It feels good to be away from all that paper shuffling," Lady Wyntyn conceded as she sat down on a stone bench beneath a maple tree. A fountain stood nearby, the water bubbling over three tiers of creatures carved from granite. Birds flew in the uppermost level; foxes and rabbits scurried about in the second layer. Fish, partially submerged within the fountain's basin, swam below them. A cardinal landed in the branches of the tree, its scarlet plumage adding a splash of color to the water.

"You've done more work in one day than Aryanda did in a month."

"She had a bad habit of allotting her work to others, and that's the easiest way to lose sight of what's going on in your realm."

"This isn't just a leisurely stroll in the garden, is it?"

"No, Hardan, it isn't. I'm looking for someone…his name is Ansar. Does he still live?"

"Queen Tryssa's captain? Why?"

"Balyd and I have a weak theory that he may know something about a possible heir to the throne."

Lady Wyntyn relayed what little they knew then waited for the captain to respond. The only sounds for a long time came from the fountain directly in front of them.

"He now captains the western patrols," Hardan began, "and has not been back to Bystyn since Queen Tryssa died. He has no desire to return."

"Why?"

"No one knows."

"I need to speak with him."

"His duty was completed the day Tryssa passed away."

"Then you must convince him."

"Lady Wyntyn..." the captain's voice echoed with exasperation.

"Hardan, if there is a true successor to the Bystynian throne then we must know if he or she is still out in the land somewhere. There is no one in Bystyn capable of ruling this city. We are vulnerable to the outside world unless someone with the proper birthright sits on that dais! If Balyd and I are wrong then we'll try to figure something out but if we are correct? Do you want the likes of Caladan ruling over the elves?"

"That would never happen!"

"Oh really? Imagine one of Aryanda's cousins sitting on the royal seat, Caladan standing beside him as Advisor."

"I'll send a messenger out," Hardan stated after another long silence. He bowed to her and left.

Lady Wyntyn focused on the fountain. The streams of water absorbed the lavenders, melons and smoky blues reflected from the western sky. It would take a courier at least a week to ride out and find Ansar and another week would elapse before the captain returned to Bystyn. *If* he chose to come back.

She rose to her feet and walked back to the castle, groaning inwardly as she spotted Caladan heading for the same entrance. *I am being tested, aren't I?*

"Good evening, Lady Wyntyn!"

"Greetings, Lord Caladan."

"May I escort you to dinner?"

Lady Wyntyn kept a polite smile on her face yet her stomach cringed in his presence. She was not afraid of him but of the irreparable damage he could do to the elves in his quest to further his personal wants. She had nearly fainted with disbelief when Caladan managed to persuade Aryanda to let him live in Prince Danyl's old rooms. Prince Danyl! The bearer of the Green Might, for heavens sake! Lady Wyntyn needed to get away from him.

"Thank you, Lord Caladan, but I have had a long day and will eat a light meal in my chambers."

"Please allow me," he offered her his arm. Lady Wyntyn nodded, the forced smile lost on Caladan. He chatted with her on the way to her rooms, leading her at a more leisurely pace than she wished. They ran into Hardan who glanced sideways at the odd pair walking toward the staircase leading to the royal chambers. The servants bowed low to them and the few courtiers who were still in the castle sauntered over to the pair. Caladan made sure he greeted every one of them. He stood tall and spoke amiably with them never taking his hand off Lady Wyntyn's arm. She finally had enough.

"Lord Caladan, I really must retire."

"Oh, forgive me, Lady Wyntyn. How very thoughtless of me."

He was about to lead her up the stairs and to the guestrooms opposite the royal wing when she deftly slipped her arm from his and bid him a good night. She kept her poise about her until she closed the door to her rooms behind her, a scowl exploding across her face.

* * *

Harald watched the Rock Lords ride by, the grim expressions on their faces getting worse with every passing moment. They rode in from the same direction Tarz and his men had taken about eight or nine days ago. They were on their way to report to Kevlan and Harald wouldn't have wanted to trade places with them for all the freedom in the land. A knowing chuckle escaped Harald's throat.

Kevlan glared at the men who had just entered the Hall and given their reports.

"Were there any signs of a struggle?" he asked in a low and dangerous tone.

"No, my Lord."
"How were they killed?"
One of the Rock Lords drew his finger across his neck.
"Horses?"
"Gone, my Lord."
"Tracks?"
"Only heading north, my Lord."
"Any signs of the dwarves?"
"None, my Lord."
"Send a band north to Evan's Peak."
"Anything else, Lord Kevlan?"
"No. Get out."

Kevlan leaned back into his chair; one hand resting on the fur covered armrest while the fingers of the other drummed against the other support. The door to his chambers closed leaving him alone. So, Tarz slaughtered his men, took the horses and headed north. Why? If he thought he could catch Whistler and Elena without the others why didn't he just send them back? He gulped down some ale. Did he make some sort of deal with an elven patrol? Unlikely. What motivated Tarz to do what he did? Kevlan knew what Tarz had to lose but what did he stand to gain? He drained the rest of the amber liquid then threw the glass across the room. *What the devil are you up to, Tarz?*

-9-

Whistler's strength ebbed from his body, the tenacious hold he had on Clay and Sara slackening until his fingers released them. They slipped from his grasp and floated away, absorbed by the bright light growing larger by the second. He had failed on this mission just as he had failed his people. Something pulled on his body forcing it onward faster and faster. *Death is sure in a hurry to claim me.* He watched as Clay and Sara dissolved into the brilliant white breach, hoping, if nothing else, he would reunite with them on the other side. Moments later found him floating in air, the feel of water and crushing mountain gone. The Dwarf instinctively inhaled precious air, retching out the cold water that had filled his lungs. The feeling of euphoria did not last long for he dropped into another body of water. He flailed his arms and legs, desperately seeking the surface. He bobbed randomly, sucking in air while searching for Clay and Sara. He spotted them near a stand of reeds, their heads nodding in the warm breeze. He was about to swim over to them when two of their backpacks drifted nearby. He managed to retrieve them and towed them to the shore. Clay forced water out of Sara's lungs, her unresponsive body alarming them both. Whistler grabbed her face and breathed deeply into her mouth while Clay continued to press down on her chest.

"C'mon, girl!" Whistler called to the lifeless demon, finally smiling as she began to vomit up the liquid.

"We thought we had lost you," Clay confessed as she inhaled and exhaled, the fear gradually dissipating from her eyes.

"I'm...fine...where are...we?"

Clay gazed up at the mountain, and then froze. He glimpsed the boat just behind the curtain of water, the figurehead wearing a twisted smile. It tossed something into the lake then burst into a million droplets. He wondered what had been discarded, then, he dove into the water, swimming like a madman to get to the object sputtering on the surface. He grabbed May, placing her on his head as he swam back to the shore, cursing the attempt to kill her. He handed the spider over to Sara who examined her for any damage. Clay continued studying the area. They had been discharged from the mountain from about forty feet up, and, as he looked to the right, noticed a barely perceptible opening at the base of the waterfall. This was unfamiliar territory.

"Whistler? Where are we?" he asked.

The dwarf scrutinized the range then turned due south where the last mountain, Evan's Peak, appeared no bigger than an anthill. To the north was a dense forest running parallel to the mountains to the east. There were no signs of their companions.

"We're about a hundred miles from nowhere," he muttered.

"We should look for the others."

"What if they..." Sara couldn't finish her thought, the idea that wild animals or some other danger had taken their lives was too much to bear. She glanced over at Whistler. The dwarf pair had been forced to accompany them on this expedition, even though he and Elena were already burdened with the plight of their enslaved people. The weight on Whistler's shoulders was so much heavier to bear without Elena, especially since her fate was unknown. She watched as Whistler took a deep breath and stared at his hands.

Clay checked their supplies and fished out three canteens, which Sara filled with fresh water. They had enough food for an estimated five days, perhaps even a couple more if they rationed what they had. They decided to survey the area for the others. They split up and explored for more than a mile but found nothing. Clay fashioned a rudimentary trap out of pliable branches and managed to snare several rabbits; Sara found some wild vegetables. Whistler gathered wood and made a fire. They cooked their meal then ate it in silence, their minds trying to make sense of what was happening. Their muscles were stiff and sore from their excursion through the mountain.

The sun began its descent, the darkness beginning to fill with the sounds of crickets and night birds. They could see the shadowy forms of deer coming to drink and knew wolves and other predators wouldn't be far behind. Clay pointed to an outcropping of rock about twenty feet up. It would be a bit of a climb but at least the animals couldn't get to them and they could keep a lookout for their friends. Whistler smothered the fire and led the way up, the trio fast asleep the second they reached the top.

* * *

The boat glided silently from within the cascade of water, the four bodies lying motionless on the bottom. The figurehead turned around and glanced at them, her features beginning to crack the moment she left the spray. She looked over toward the flat rock then resumed her journey. The moon had begun to rise, peeking through the overhead canopy, following her progress along the winding river. She had been born at the same time the Kaiyeths had but her composition was strictly from the pure original waters. She was an *Annoush*, one of two that had ever existed. Her mate would have already transformed out of the vessel shape but she needed to maintain it for a little while longer. The mortals would be in her care until the morning sun rose.

She began to stiffen, the strength it took to remain intact becoming more difficult to sustain. She needed to bring them near Hyssa's realm before sun-up. The farther she traveled the more rigid her skin became. She splashed water on herself but it could not stop the splintering along her face and sides. She looked to her left and noted the faded shades of blues and grays then watched with trepidation as the oranges and lavenders began to glow. She couldn't pick up her pace and she was still a distance from her goal. Her bow bumped into a submerged rock opening up a small, jagged break below the surface. She shuddered as the pain shot through her entire being. She desperately searched for the boundary marker, the ache in her body and the leading edge of the sun spurring her on. The crack in her body began to widen, allowing at first a tiny amount then increasingly more water into the craft. She wanted to look and see how much was accumulating but could no longer swivel her head. Her once moist skin appeared like planks of weathered wood. It began to warp and pull away from her frame just as the marker came into view. She struggled to stay together just long enough to beach herself along the river in a final surge of energy, sliding up under the shade of an ancient willow tree.

Taman was the first to awaken. He leaned on one elbow, and then sat up observing the crumbling skiff, a peculiar rock notched with three flaming intersecting circles near the stern. He stood and gazed down upon his still slumbering companions, grateful none of them appeared to have any injuries. They were in a forest beside a wide stream protected by boughs of ash, maple and oak trees. A huge willow tilted toward the water directly overhead, the graceful fronds swaying gently in the breeze. Birds chirped overhead and insects flew in lazy circles in the soft, golden light of morning. And, best of all, they were alive.

The elf squatted down and gently awakened his friends. Elena, August and Garadan rubbed their eyes and their bumps and bruises as they got to their feet to study their surroundings. Elena stepped out of the boat and looked down at the shattered figurehead sprawled over the pebbly shore. A tear suddenly ran down her cheek as she gazed upon the fractured face. The once serene features now held deep fissures and her down-turned mouth looked more like that of an old woman that had seen too many tragedies in her life. Elena knelt down beside her and touched her weathered cheek in gratitude.

The stream began to rise, forcing the group to collect their pouches and canteens and escape higher into the grass. They watched as the waters rose and covered the craft, a compassionate and fitting end for the help it had given them.

"We need to see if the others are around here," Garadan stated.

"Somehow I don't think they are," murmured Elena pointing through an opening in the treetops. There, in the far distance was the uppermost peak of the range they had just escaped from, its crown covered in ice and snow.

"Well, we'll make a sweep anyway," urged Garadan. They spent hours combing the bordering area but came up empty. Garadan wanted to continue looking and acquiesced only after the others convinced him they were wasting invaluable time.

"What direction shall we take, Taman?" asked August.

Taman sighed then sat down cross-legged on the grass. He closed his eyes and blocked out everything around him, then opened himself up to the magic. At first there was nothing. He left himself exposed for a long time without any contact whatsoever. He started to think there was no magic in this part of the land when, without warning, one pulse erupted in his mind, and then two more emitted their far-off call. He was about to extricate himself from the connection when a lesser vibration caught his attention, this one relatively close by. Taman opened his eyes, the charcoal clouds still roiling into the whites. He could just make out three silhouettes hunkered down in front of him.

"Taman?" Elena called out to him.

Taman shook the shadows from his mind and stared at his companions. They anxiously awaited any news he may have learned.

"Well...I sensed two powers and another, less potent one not too far from where we are."

"Three...are you sure?"

"Yes, August."

"Then...they are all in this part of the land," said Elena, the dappled sunlight shimmering all around them.

"Why don't we follow the river south?" suggested August.

They hiked along the stream until dusk, making camp on the soft grass beneath a willow tree. They ate sparingly but drank their fill from the spring, then lay down to sleep. The days went by quickly yet they never encountered anyone else in the forest. They took turns keeping watch during the long nights.

The group walked on, Garadan leading the way. The moss-covered ground felt good beneath their feet, the spongy vegetation absorbing every impact. The further they advanced into the woods the darker it became, the only light a stark glow radiating from beneath platter-sized leaves. The veins and edges of the foliage shone with a bright luminosity. Curious, Garadan picked up a stick and lifted the edge of the leaf. Clinging to the underside was a large beetle, its body emitting a luminous light. It lifted its head, the brisk screeching sound prompting him to let the leaf drop back into place.

Garadan squinted at an oak up ahead. Its bark, unlike the rich, dark brown trunks of its neighbor, was ashen, almost as if consumed by fire. They walked near it and gazed up into its withered branches. They discovered another tree abutting it had succumbed to the same thing. They noticed the disease or whatever affliction it was had spread in a fluctuating line beyond their sight.

"What in Hades happened to them?" August asked in low tones, looking around nervously for a logical clue.

"Very strange," Elena said her hand reaching out to touch the scorched trunk.

"Not a good idea," Taman's hand pulled hers away from the tree.

"Come look at this," Garadan called to them from a few yards to their right.

They joined the elf as he stood in front of a partially destroyed oak tree, his finger pointing at a strange vine twisting mid-way up its trunk. It was about as thick as a man's arm; one upper offshoot entwined with the lowest branch and the other wrapped around the middle. The two lower growths straddled the tree like some crazed lover refusing to release its mate. Clumps of frilly, pale green wisps sprouted without rhyme or reason all over it. Partially hidden in the semi-darkness was an elongated paddle-shaped bulge. The colorless climber gradually took on a mahogany hue. The oak rustled imperceptibly, its leaves turning brown then curling up then turning to dust before their very eyes. They were so transfixed by the trees' silent death they failed to notice the vine creep around until the protrusion came into view. Apathetic eyes with vertical lids stared coldly at them, its leech-like mouth housing tiny teeth still dripping with sap.

"Sweet mercy!" Elena cried, covering her mouth in shock.

"What in the Four Corners of the land is it?" August muttered while taking several steps backward. He bumped into Garadan who had drawn his sword, the elf swearing under his breath.

"Taman? What is it?"

"I don't know, Garadan."

"Let me introduce myself, then…I am Hyssa and this is my home." Her voice sounded like dried leaves blowing over rocks; her features remained aloof. She slithered up into the nearest branch that connected directly to the next tree, and then reappeared, coiled around the trunk. She studied every one of them, finally focusing all of her attention onto Taman. She inclined her head toward him after many long minutes.

"We did not mean to intrude," Taman apologized then waved his friends on, his gaze never far from the Tree Witch.

"Of course not," she replied following them across the tree limbs, "perhaps you are lost?"

"No, not lost," Taman answered.

"Then why are you in the middle of my forest?" She sniffed the air then added, "You wear the stench of the Annoush."

Taman wore a confused look on his face while Garadan simply shrugged his shoulders. Elena pursed her lips in thought then remembered the river reclaiming the boat. The craft had been smooth and supple when they began their journey through the mountain but had hardened and splintered at its end. The Annoush had given her existence to ensure their safety.

They moved on keeping a close watch on Hyssa. She trailed them along the branches, appearing and disappearing with greater frequency. They had all removed their weapons by now, the metal flashing dully in the dim light. Then abruptly she was gone. They instinctively formed a circle, their backs scant feet away from each other as they canvassed the boughs. She emerged from directly overhead, a lightning fast Garadan pulling his razor-sharp short sword from its scabbard and hacking into her body. The blade bounced off and knocked him off balance. He tumbled to the ground then immediately rolled back up onto his feet, sword at the ready, but she had already vanished.

"The sun's going down…we need to get out of here before it's completely gone," Elena stated as she watched the slanting rays illuminate the treetops.

"Let's go and stay as close together as…" Garadan never finished. Hyssa reached down and grabbed Taman, her stick-like limbs picking him up as if he weighed no more than a feather. She yanked him out of their reach and placed her mouth at the base of his throat. Taman screamed as she bit down, his arms flailing to fend her off while his legs dangled crazily below him. Her teeth sawed through skin and flesh as they eagerly worked their way to his veins. She finally found a blood vessel and sucked the rare treat into her mouth. Her victim's blood coursed through her gaunt frame, its potency making her heady and unstable. She swayed with pleasure, Taman's body flopping lifelessly with the motion.

"Garadan! We have to do something!" shrieked Elena in horror.

Garadan felt helpless, his only weapon unable to penetrate the Tree Witch's surface. Taman would have figured out what to do but she was draining his blood while Garadan stood powerless to stop her. Wait…she kept to the branches…she kept her body from contacting the ground. Could it be? Would that work?

Garadan snapped into action. He seized Taman's feet when the Tree Witch dipped too low and wrenched the elf downward, each tug bringing him inches closer to the ground. August and Elena had no idea what he was doing but they quickly added their weight. Hyssa kept her eyes closed, her indulgence keeping her from reacting to what the companions were doing. They wrenched Taman out of the tree and onto the forest floor, the Tree Witch firmly corkscrewed around him. Her shrieking sounded the moment her body touched the mossy carpet. She twisted and turned but the elf's body pinned her down. Pale smoke began to rise from her writhing form and, as the last of it left her body, they gaped at her charred remains.

Elena dropped to her knees beside Taman while the elves drew their knives and cut Hyssa's body away from him. She pulled back his shirt and grimaced at the perfect circle of teeth embedded on his flesh. He moaned, the perspiration running down the sides of face and into his hair.

The Tree Witch's power drifted up into the sky, the column of haze hovering over the site of her demise for a long time. Those out on the plains to the south of Evan's Peak saw a semblance of a possible fire but those who dwelled far, far away saw something very different.

* * *

The sun bathed Whistler in a soft light, prodding him out of his reverie. His eyelids flickered open yet he didn't raise himself up. He focused on the forest to the east then at the open plains to the south. Scattered here and there were clumps of trees and thickets of brush. He longed for the scent of lemon grass and rosemary as he eased his rigid body onto his feet. Elena would have massaged the stubborn muscles between his shoulder blades while he ate breakfast, chatting amiably about the coming day.

"Morning, Whistler."

The dwarf smiled at Sara who offered him some food, and watched as the spider disappeared in a cleft in the dirt bank behind her. She returned a few minutes later holding a large bug, which she thankfully took behind a mass of rocks. Whistler had never seen May eat and really had no desire to start now. He looked down at the small lake where Clay was busy emptying and refilling the canteens.

"We're separated for a reason, aren't we, Sara?"

"Yes."

"I don't suppose you know why?"

"I'm sure they're fine," she offered him a little smile while touching his shoulder.

"Which direction do we take?"

"You'll have to join Clay and let me find that out, Whistler."

The dwarf looked into her face. He wanted to offer her any help he could but the place she went to in her mind was not for mere mortals. May clambered onto the boulder beside Sara and devoured the last bits of the beetle. The spider looked up at him then turned her attention to Sara. He nodded then scrambled down to meet up with Clay.

Sara took a deep breath then began to relax. The world around her faded away, the icy chill of the river replacing the warm morning sun…

The acrid odors overwhelmed her the moment she crossed into this dreadful region, the frigid air burrowing into her very bones. She concentrated on the immense vortex swirling in the distance. The tiny red lights had multiplied a thousand-fold since she had last intruded upon this place, glittering in every corner of the maelstrom.

She shivered as she hurriedly scanned the dismal whirlpool, every passing second in here feeling like a lifetime to her. She knew what it did to her and how difficult it was to recover from it. She forced her fears out of her mind and continued to look. She finally located two: a red one slightly to the left and a green sparkle to the right. It was time to leave. She started to withdraw when something caught her eye. She was transfixed, staring at it for what seemed a long time.

There was a bulge off to her left...no, more like a ripple blocking out part of the lights. Panic instantly struck her as the very thought of being in here with Emhella consumed her with horror. He had the power to imprison her in this awful place. She wanted to flee but there was something about the shadow that kept her rooted in place. Her time, however, was over and she unwillingly departed...

Sara was careful not to open her eyes right away, yet she still squeezed them more tightly as the sunlight burned through her lids. She covered them with her hands then slowly gazed upon the real world. She was facing south. May climbed up her shoulder and the two of them joined their companions who were already packed and ready to go.

"Which way?" asked Clay.

"There," she pointed to an unseen place parallel with the mountains to their right.

"But...no, that can't be..." Whistler muttered, his eyes wide with disbelief.

"What's wrong?"

"Sara...that's too close to the Rock Lords! Elena and I didn't go through so much difficulty just to walk back into their camp!"

"That's where the magic is," she reminded him.

"We'll just have to be extra cautious," Clay stated reassuringly.

Whistler glared at them, his hands balling up into fists, the tendons and veins sticking out on his arms and neck. Sara's gaze slid from his face to the throbbing artery in his throat. A primeval urge to sink her teeth into that vessel wormed its way out of her subconscious. Her mouth began to water. Her tongue stroked the roof of her mouth. She didn't hear the elf and dwarf argue or even realize that Whistler no longer stood in front of her. She suddenly felt very dizzy. Sara inhaled several times and began to regain her composure. Only then did her mind clear enough to allow her to comprehend what had just happened. She shuddered at the memory.

* * *

The Vox had been searching for the way out for days. His temperament was beyond foul and all he wanted to do was place his hands around the Lady's neck and crush the life out of her. The endless rows of trees grated on his nerves, as did his lack of judgment in descending into her lair. He should have waited until he had reclaimed the powers. He brushed at something on his cheek then stopped short, waiting for the feeble tickle to return. He took a step back, and then grinned darkly as a puff of air touched his face.

"This game is over!" he shouted, the spell she had woven tearing to bits, revealing the steps leading up to the desert.

Emhella bounded up the stairs two steps at a time then stood on a nearby dune. The sun was sinking behind him but all he cared about was finding the Lady of the Sand. His hands clenched in anticipation. "*Where are you?*" he whispered into the shadows.

A faint breeze washed over him carrying with it a faint bitter odor. The pungent smell bore another feature, too, one that aroused his dark powers. His concentration progressively shifted to the east. There, unseen but sensed nevertheless, drifted an insignificant magic. It hung motionless in the sky, a beacon that illuminated that which he had so long labored to capture. Uncertainty wormed through him for one brief moment, then, without another thought for the Lady, he headed east. He made one stop along the way: the demon pit.

* * *

Caladan drummed his fingers on the desktop while he stared out the balcony doors. Balyd still carried on the duties of First Advisor, Aryanda was dead and left no heir, Lady Wyntyn temporarily ruled Bystyn and Hardan controlled the guard. Caladan had managed to convince about half of the court to remove Balyd but even those who supported Caladan believed this current situation was for the best.

He slammed his hand down angrily on the desktop and stomped out onto the balcony. He looked out over the garden below. He had bedded the queen and charmed the court. He had undermined the great Balyd and had been on the verge of taking over his functions. Caladan had fully expected Aryanda to choose him as co-ruler, since she had told him he would sit beside her on the throne. All of this would have already been his had she not died. Now he had to reshuffle his plans. "If only Balyd weren't around," Caladan mumbled aloud. "If he were gone I would become First Advisor." *Hmm…gone. Not a bad idea. How do I get rid of him? Blame him for Aryanda's death? That would be perfect but not feasible. He doesn't go anywhere and has very few visitors. He spends all of his time in the library, a place I think I should visit.*

Caladan left his quarters and walked rapidly through the cavernous halls until he came to the library entrance. He knocked on the door then entered the chamber.

"Lord Balyd? Are you in here?"

"He's meeting with Lady Wyntyn, Lord Caladan. Shall I send for him?"

Caladan looked down on the young scribe and took a step backward as the scrawny elf in the homespun clothes sneezed. He grimaced as the boy wiped his nose on his sleeve.

"No. You're dismissed." Caladan couldn't keep his upper left lip from lifting.

The scribe shrugged his skinny shoulders and left the room, walking away down the short hall.

Caladan turned his attention to the front section of the library and Balyd's desk. The scrolls, books and journals littered the usually neat writing table. Caladan glanced at some of the titles. Most were histories; one held the ruling family's genealogy and two others were standard journals. He picked up a stack of papers and flipped through them. They contained nothing but notes about possible heirs. He found a thin, leather bound logbook at the bottom of the pile and picked it up.

"Queen Tryssa's diary," he said with renewed interest as he flipped through it. He read some of the entries, smirking at her descriptions of some of the courtiers until he came across one directed at his favorite uncle. He frowned and cursed at the dead queen for calling his uncle a 'fop with the manners of a donkey and the face of a constipated pig'. He tossed the booklet onto the desk, the journal landing open to a different page. Nosy, he retrieved it and read what she had written. He placed it flat on the desk and then reread the page.

"Well! It seems Queen Tryssa had a potential successor murdered years ago and by her captain, no less!" Caladan could hardly contain himself, enjoying the knowledge of the dark family secret as a special and unexpected luxury. He held the book against his chest for a long moment then slipped it into his pocket. "If Captain Ansar *killed* this supposed heir, then why is the journal of any interest?"

Caladan walked out of the library, pleased no one but the runny-nosed scribe had seen him, and headed for the main entrance hall.

He hailed one of the guards "Where is Captain Hardan?"

"He's at the barracks, Lord Caladan."

"I need to speak with him."

"He'll be returning in about an hour, my Lord. I'm sure…"

"I want to talk to him now, sentry, and send him to my rooms when he arrives." Caladan lifted his chin and marched up the grand staircase, never once looking back to see if the guard was obeying his order.

The elf raised a brow and considered stalling a while before riding to the barracks located just inside Bystyn's walls. Hardan would be there, meeting with his men and would frown upon being commanded to do anything by a conceited buffoon. A smile erupted across the elf's face. *I could use some fresh air*. He sauntered out through the massive wooden doors, waved away the proffered horse and ambled down the main avenue.

A knock on the door two hours later awoke a dozing Caladan, as an attendant announced Captain Hardan's arrival. The servant poured two glasses of wine and left.

"Thank you for your *prompt* arrival," Caladan said sarcastically as he picked up a goblet.

"What can I do for you?" Hardan asked, ignoring the wine.

Caladan studied the captain briefly, Hardan's unblinking dark brown eyes firmly fixed on him. He could see an uneven scar running along the top of the captain's forehead just beneath his short-cropped hair, and he noticed the muscles rippling beneath the man's tunic.

"I need to find Captain Ansar." He expected some sort of reaction but Hardan remained impassive.

"I believe he's on the western perimeter."

"I have a few questions to ask him, Captain Hardan."

"He's more than two weeks away by horse."

"Then perhaps you should send someone out right away." *Moreover, you should start addressing me by my rightful title, you insolent serf,* he silently admonished the officer. The captain remained immobile and continued to stare fixedly at Caladan, whose fingers began to twitch nervously. He pretended disinterest and focused on a painting behind Hardan before dropping his gaze to the floor.

Hardan finally gave Caladan an affirmative nod before walking out the door.

* * *

Balyd entered his rooms and closed the door. The bags under his eyes added years to his face. His stooped shoulders stole inches from his frame. He poured a glass of wine and stepped out onto the balcony letting the cool night air flow over him. He sat down on a bench and leaned against the stone balustrade. He rubbed the tense muscles on his forehead but the dull throbbing would not go away.

"Evening, Lord Balyd." Hardan's silhouette detached itself from the shadows at the base of the staircase leading up to the balcony. "I hope I'm not disturbing you." He kept his voice low.

"Captain Hardan." Balyd motioned for his guest to join him on the terrace. "Come, sit and share a glass of wine with me." He vanished briefly and returned with another goblet and the bottle of wine, as Hardan vaulted over the balustrade and made himself comfortable on the bench.

"I wonder how my Library Mouse and Garadan are faring." Balyd refilled his own goblet, the two men taking large draughts at the same time.

"I'm hoping better than we are," Hardan watched his wine swirl in lazy circles.

"I can see you are the bearer of more good news."

The captain snorted then told Balyd about his meeting with Caladan. "Where could he have gotten the information about Tryssa and a possible heir?"

"My scribe told me Caladan paid me a little visit earlier and, since I was elsewhere, decided to look through my papers. By the way, when will our caller arrive?"

"Soon and without fanfare. How long do you think Caladan can keep quiet about his discovery?"

"He's pompous, impatient and only half as smart as he thinks he is, Hardan. He's so close to becoming First Advisor, he'll blurt out the right but misinterpreted information at the wrong time."

"It's fortunate for us that Ansar chose to serve so far away."

A branch snapped then footsteps retreated into the darkness below them.

"We have company," Balyd remarked dryly.

"I know, I passed by Caladan's spy when I arrived," Hardan chuckled quietly. "I was going to tap him on the shoulder but thought better of that idea."

"Captain Hardan? Do you know anyone that could pick the gold out of your teeth without your even knowing it?"

"I might, Lord Balyd," the captain smiled knowingly.

"I'll leave you to the details, then. Good night, Hardan. It has been a very long day." He patted the captain on the back and went inside.

Hardan disappeared over the balustrade and down the stairway, and then faded away into the night.

-10-

Taman groaned in Elena's arms, the teeth marks pulsing hotly against the burgundy-hued circle on his skin. Perspiration glistened on his forehead but not along the side of his face. Not yet anyway. Elena rummaged through her pouch and took out a fleshy, green and yellow speckled leaf. She cut it near the end then held the plant over the wound, watching as a clear, thick gel oozed from the plant's end. The dwarf immediately spread the syrupy liquid with her fingertip. It trickled for a few seconds before taking on a shiny cast, the edges adhering to Taman's skin. Elena gently poked at the coating, nodding with satisfaction when none of the clotted mass stuck to her fingers.

"How are you feeling?" she asked Taman.

Taman closed his eyes, the sap's cooling sensation dousing the venom's fire. The Tree Witch had only spent a few moments biting him. He couldn't imagine how much greater his pain would have been had his companions not intervened when they did. Taman's shoulder ached and, as he struggled to sit up on his own brought his hand up to ward off the slight dizziness that came over him. He looked down at the clear bandage covering the bite and reached for it.

"No you don't," Elena softly admonished him. "Your wound will start to itch in a few hours. Let me know when that happens and I'll replace your dressing."

"I'm a little lightheaded...that's all."

"Can you walk?" Garadan offered the elf his hand.

Taman nodded and slowly got to his feet, swaying unsteadily for a minute before regaining his balance. He took August's canteen, drank deeply and glanced down at the ashes. *She had chosen me...was that because of the magic that flowed through me?* He shuddered at the memory of her gnawing through his skin and muscles, her snake-like tongue probing into every breach. *She could have reached my soul with that thing.* He suddenly scanned the area, afraid another such creature existed in the trees. He was achy and tired but the thought of staying in this bizarre and dangerous place compelled him into action.

They continued following the stream hoping it would take them out of this eerie place. The light remained constant, the near-twilight broken only by the occasional shaft of sunlight or the beetles' eerie light from underneath the leaves. Bunches of waist-high ferns grew at the base of the youngest trees, their knobby flowers on long stalks huddling together within the protection of the lacy fronds. No birds flew or chirped in the massive boughs; no squirrels, deer or other creatures stirred along the moss-covered ground. The stream continued to wind away from them. It was hard to determine exactly in what direction it flowed but their choices were limited. The waterway was their only link to their destination. The group would halt for a few hours every now and then to rest and eat, their eyes constantly scanning for signs of any more unusual 'vines'.

Garadan lay upon the soft ground, his head on his pack and one arm placed over his eyes. He shifted his body trying to ease the soreness at the base of his spine and then took several deep breaths. He wasn't sleepy, just drained and feeling a bit anxious. He thought back to the events that had brought him to this moment in time. The unofficial trips off elven lands to gather information; the terrible fate befalling his men and then meeting Taman and the rest of his current comrades was only the beginning. The journey into Mercator's realm, the Tree Witch and their current passage to retrieve magic were complicated things that he, a simple soldier, had trouble grasping. He would never have agreed to come along had it not been for Balyd. Garadan understood and shared the advisor's deep concern for the elves. This conviction was the one thing that gave Garadan the strength to persevere. The odd collection of individuals he was a part of also gave him hope. Perhaps in the future the elves wouldn't have to spy on their neighbors but could simply communicate with them.

Garadan contemplated the fate of his other companions. Had they survived the expulsion from the mountains at the edge of Mercator's realm? Were they following the path he was now on or did they travel another route? Would they ever see each other again? He moved his arm away from his eyes and gazed at Elena. She lay curled up on the springy earth, her hands beneath her cheek. She had dirt caked under her fingernails and road grime made her skin appear dull. Her stringy hair lay flat against her head, one greasy strand hanging over her nose. Garadan knew none of them looked freshly bathed nor would they any time soon. The dwarf stared past Garadan as if watching for Whistler and the others. The elf had no idea where the others were but he doubted they'd be joining his group any time soon.

Garadan turned his attention to August and Taman sitting side by side, as they watched over him and Elena. August's lips were in a tight line, his eyes narrow and focused on something in the murky shadows. His attention swung to the right then over to the left, his body remaining completely still. Garadan studied August's features. The fierce glint in his black eyes was tempered by something the elf could not quite identify. August glanced over at Garadan and, for a split second, the elf thought he caught a brief glimpse of uncertainty lurking just beneath the surface. It was fleeting yet poignant. Garadan watched as August absorbed the smallest details around him without ever seeming to be aware of anything. He offered Garadan a sheepish smile, which the elf returned. Garadan slid his arm over his eyes seeking a few more moments of sleep.

He awoke several hours later, surprised at how dark it had gotten. He looked over where Taman and August had been. They were nowhere to be seen and neither was Elena. The elf stood up and rubbed the sleep from his eyes. His head swiveled from left to right as he searched for his companions. *They wouldn't have left me here! They would have awakened me if...unless there's another Tree Witch around here!*

"Taman? August! Elena? Where are you?"

"We're here."

Garadan turned toward their voices, his relief turning to horror. His companions were indeed nearby but they couldn't have been farther away. Garadan gaped as they twisted their stick-thin forms around the nearby trees. Their mouths were open revealing a circle of short, spiky teeth and forked tongues probing the air around his head. They lowered themselves from the overhead branches, reaching out to him with their twig-like arms. They surrounded him, their distorted paddle-shaped faces inching closer and closer until their tongues flicked against his skin. His hands came up as he desperately sought to push them away but they began to wrap around his body and started to squeeze him. Garadan felt the air being wrung out of his chest, the tears spilling from his eyes running over his crimson cheeks. He tried to ignore the hideous faces peering at him but they moved into his line of sight no matter where he looked. His vision began to blur then darkness mercifully blocked out the dreadful faces...

"Garadan? Wake up!"

Garadan bolted upright, his arms crossed in front of him to ward off the frightening faces. His rapid breathing soon calmed and his hands stopped shaking as he recognized his companions. He ran his fingers through his hair and accepted some water from Taman, drinking while nervously scanning the boughs for any moving vines. He didn't need to be convinced to resume their trek; he bounced up to his feet and, with one last look backward, trudged after his friends.

The days turned into a week, their routine never varying. Their pouches grew thinner every day even though they ate sparsely throughout their journey. They'd be lucky to have another day's worth of food left. They were thankful that at least they had water. The companions hiked on, the stream curving abruptly to the left. The ribbon of water rounded several clumps of roots then suddenly disappeared. Taman noticed first and stared in disbelief at the spot where the stream abruptly ended then over to a scowling Garadan. The life-giving waters had been their guide and now, with virtually no supplies and half-empty canteens swinging from their shoulders, even that had abandoned them.

"It's as if the earth just swallowed it," muttered Elena.

"Maybe it was thirsty," Garadan grumbled sardonically. He put his hands on his hips and looked around. The semi-gloom of the woods seemed to dare him to choose a direction without the aid of the brook. He studied the area ahead where the stream would have flowed on and discerned only more hardwoods and moss-covered ground. A ray of sunlight penetrated through a break in the branches to his right, illuminating several gray rocks. The elf walked over to them, kicking them with the toe of his boot and it was then that he became aware of more stones a few yards away.

"The landscape is starting to change," he said to August. "Is that an opening up ahead?"

August peered beyond the trees, the faint light glowing between the trunks and leaves an invitation he could not ignore. The Herkah and his companions wandered past the hardwoods toward the beckoning light. An imperceptible tangy odor reached them as the oaks and ash gradually gave way to pines. A wet crashing sound reached their ears followed by a faint mist tickling their faces. The light grew brighter, momentarily blinding them as they continued to head for it. They licked their lips, surprised at the large amount of salty spray that began to dampen their skin and clothes.

The white glow extended from left to right now, the brilliance so intense it swallowed up the last line of trees. The booming rumbles were now so loud the group had to shout to be heard. The thought of escaping the creepy forest imbued them with a renewed energy. They began to jog toward the light, eager to leave the Tree Witch's domain far behind them. The hissing spray drenched them, the briny taste intensifying their thirst and leaving salty patches on their skin. The group could no longer speak over the noise of the thunderous breakers, the whooshing and booming obliterating every other sound.

Garadan suddenly skidded to a halt, the exhilaration of surviving another portion of their journey overshadowed by his instincts. The elf grabbed August's sleeve, yanking him to a stop and waving his hand for him to wait. He blocked Taman from moving any farther but Elena had already passed by. The trio cautiously moved forward, stepping beyond the last line of trees.

August tripped on a rock and fell hard on his knees, the impact on the sharp protrusions sending a wave of nausea through him. He sat on the ground and pulled his pant legs up, cursing under his breath when he examined the jagged cuts and puncture marks. He wiped the blood away, his throbbing knees already beginning to swell. He poured some water over the reddening sections then plucked out about six or seven tiny bits of gravel from within the abrasions. He could hear Garadan calling out to Elena.

Taman scratched the back of his neck, his fingernails scraping off some of the dirt and grime covering his skin. His eyes finally adjusted to the light and what he saw astounded him.

The forest behind him ended perhaps thirty or forty yards from the edge of a cliff covered in wild rose bushes. The purple and white blossoms released their scent into the warm, late morning air. The bushes grew in abundance to the north but gave way to another wood to the south. The trees were slender and the ground thickly overgrown with saplings and bushes. The raucous cries of gulls circling in the bright blue sky reached his ears, as did the sound of the surf pounding the cliffs. Taman looked straight ahead and saw that the ground dropped off sharply. He stepped forward tentatively until he reached the edge then gazed out over the ocean's surface.

The vast sea stretched toward the horizon, the slate blue of the deeper regions turning a pale green near the treacherous rocks at the base of the cliff. The white foam and spray sizzled with energy as it thrust itself on top of the uneven boulders. The sunlight reflecting off the white-capped water reminded Taman of a broken mirror, each shard a miniature sun that blazed brightly on its own. The elf felt a peculiar stirring inside. He braced himself for the magic but what filtered through him was different from anything he had ever experienced.

Instead of the usual surge of power, a rhythmic sensation washed over his being. It was slow and steady, cooling and refreshing. It reminded him of standing outside during a summer rain or inhaling the crisp air after the first snowfall of winter. He closed his eyes, inviting the invigorating feeling to continue. The energy emitted by the ancient ocean reached up and surrounded him, the sea greens and deep blues alleviating his burden. The soothing swells promised to remove all of his problems and responsibilities; all he had to do was walk to the edge and immerse himself in their restful embrace. Taman crept closer and closer to the edge, the foamy spray drenching him yet he never turned from his projected goal—the fall from the edge into the peaceful ocean.

"Whoa," Garadan grabbed Taman's arm as the elf stood a few feet from the rim of the cliff. "Where do you think you're...?"

Garadan noticed Taman's eyes, the expected gray clouds marking his entrance into that peculiar in-between world replaced with crimson. Taman strained in Garadan's grasp, the lure of some unknown magic seducing him forward. August hobbled over and seized Taman's other arm, the two of them dragging Taman back from the brink. Garadan shook the elf until the cobwebs of whatever vision he had had dissipated.

"Taman?"

"Yes, I'm fine...now, Garadan. Have you found Elena yet?"

"No," August wiped away the sweat from his face. "She can't be too far away."

Elena saw her friends' shadowy forms to her left but the deep rumbling and loud splashing made it impossible to hear them. She brought her hands up to shield her face, the penetrating light blinding her. She slowed her pace, carefully feeling ahead with her toes before taking any further steps. The spray drenched her. She rubbed her burning eyes wishing just one surge of water was fresh and not salty. She took a few steps to the right then left and moved a few feet ahead. The ground was soft, sandy and began to shift beneath her boots. Elena froze, the certainty of what was predestined etched into her mind. She held her breath, trying to transfer her weight backward and from the edge of the cliff. She was a second too late. The ground gave way beneath her and she slid down a steep hillside grasping at anything her fingers touched. Rocks and sand cascaded down on top of her head and shoulders. Her eyes, already irritated by the salt spray, now began to fill with grit, as did her mouth as she screamed for help, hoping her companions would hear her voice. Elena finally skidded to a stop, her heartbeat pounding in her throat. She gulped in the moist air and removed enough of the sand from her eyes to study her predicament. *It can't be that bad, you just survived the worst of it.* She glanced down and panicked.

* * *

Whistler led the way south, his unintelligible mutterings trailing behind him like the stench of pungent food, which Sara and Clay passed through. They couldn't blame the dwarf for the bitterness erupting from his soul but they had no choice but to follow the road fate had placed them on. His grumbling eventually subsided although his sour expression remained unchanged. The sun rose steadily in the sky and reflected off the rose-colored granite sending shimmering bands of heat upward like flames from an open fire. Sweat rolled down their bodies and soon bonded tunics to skin. May had taken refuge on Clay's shoulder, frequently flicking away the beads of perspiration that dripped off his head. They could see the very end of the range to the south but it was still many days away.

"Tell us about this Varek-Tor tower, Sara," Clay asked, breaking the silence.

Sara swallowed hard, the knowledge she possessed about the tower frightening even in the daylight. She contemplated what to say and how to say it without evoking any fear, and then realized it was a terrifying revelation no matter how she revealed it.

"It's not really a 'tower', Clay, "she began tentatively.

"Then what is it?" Whistler asked, his anger forgotten.

"It's a gateway…an access for the demons."

"What exactly does that mean, Sara? That 'gateway' was in ruins, remember?" Whistler grabbed her arm and stopped her in her tracks.

Sara stared into his gray eyes, sensing his apprehension. "I don't know why it was shattered," she replied, her voice quavering.

"Are you telling us that Emhella will succeed in opening that terrible portal?" Clay could barely breathe, let alone utter those words.

"Then what's the point in seeking out the magic? To hand it over to him when he deems the time is right?" Whistler's grip tightened on her arm, his fingers digging into her flesh. He felt her flinch and saw her silver eyes well up. He released her then turned his back on them both.

"I can't answer that…"

"'Can't' or won't? If I had known that was going to happen I would have stayed with Elena and attempted to worry about my people, not go on this meaningless mission!"

"I will not abandon this task until I have either succeeded or died trying!"

Clay stared at Sara, the determination in her face stronger than the fear flickering in her eyes. She knew the consequences of failing and now they did, too. He remembered how much the Kaiyeths had detested him, their cruel handling as they transported him into Mercator's realm still sharp in his mind. The dragon had looked down on them as well. August and the others, he was sure, were in the process of fulfilling their part in this plan. *Well, we're in the middle of this mess so why not finish it.*

"We have a long way to go," the elf said resignedly then set off not bothering to look back to see if they were following. May nuzzled his neck, the contact offering Clay some measure of comfort.

Whistler was the first to meet up with Clay. The dwarf walked sullenly by his side. Sara eventually caught up with them treading unobtrusively a few steps behind.

The sun rose overhead until they seemed to trip over the squat shadows crowding around their feet. The dry ground made walking easy although they had to step around accumulated piles of different-sized pebbles. They were the color of old bones exposed too long to the weather, some with faint cracks and many beginning to splinter into pieces. Clay glanced down and felt that the same thing was happening to them. Whistler hadn't said a word in hours and Sara still trailed behind, lost to everyone, including herself.

The sun disappeared behind the range, the lengthening gloominess enveloping the travelers in darkness. The stone kept emitting the heat it had absorbed during the course of the day as the sky gradually faded into night. They could see the evening clouds over the peaks, the warm hues chased by the twilight from the east. It was time to make camp for the night.

They found a cluster of scrawny trees hugging a small pool of water and headed in that direction. The water in the pond was cold and refreshing. They filled their canteens and shared a meager meal but never said a word while they ate.

Whistler took off his boots and flexed his toes. The night air cooled his tired feet and eased some of his bad temper away. He turned his boots upside down and shook out bits of gravel then reluctantly put them back on. He finally looked at Sara. She sat a short distance away from Clay, her knees pulled up to her chest, her forehead resting on her kneecaps. Sara's breathing was long and even and it occurred to him this was the first time he could remember her actually sleeping. She had always been the one to keep watch over them while they slept. Her exhaustion was due to not just the exertions of the past couple of weeks but also to the tremendous strain she endured to journey into that nether world. The monumental task she had accepted, and would probably fail at, did not deter her one bit. It was a duty she truly believed in. How was her objective any different from his intention to free his people? She suddenly seemed so vulnerable. Like he, himself, was.

Elena understood him better than he did. She realized his goal, his very reason for remaining alive against all of the odds, would probably never come to fruition. If he believed that then he might as well let the Rock Lords beat him and the Dribbies rip him apart and consume him. He took a deep breath but he could not exhale away the guilt.

"Whistler, are you all right?" Clay took a seat beside the dwarf.

"No, not really. I've been a fool, Clay. A stubborn, short-sighted idiot." Whistler lifted his gaze toward the sleeping demon.

"We all play the 'fool' sometimes, my friend. It's what makes us mortal. Besides, I don't think that Sara took what you said to heart."

"She's a brave girl."

"She's that and more." Clay nodded affirmatively. "Get some rest. I'll take the first watch and wake you in a couple of hours."

"Good-night, Clay."

"Sleep well, Whistler."

Clay unsheathed his sword and placed it across his lap. He had no idea what sort of four-footed hunters lived in these parts and he didn't want to fumble with his weapon if one appeared unexpectedly. He couldn't help but smile a little at Whistler. The dwarf chewed over his thoughts as if they were made of gristly meat, finding out the effort needed to extract the edible parts was more difficult than he had anticipated. Elena would

THE FORTRESS OF DARKNESS

simply cut away the tough ends. Whistler dared the world to beat him; Elena convinced the world it was wrong. They would lead the dwarves well. Clay looked over at Sara, frowning as she twitched in her sleep.

Sara pulled the sheet over Eppe's face concealing his ashen skin and drawn features... She glanced over her shoulder at the mound of dirt covering his body as she walked away from the only home she had ever known... Sara was suddenly staring down into an amphitheater, the huge slabs of flat rock in the center buckled and broken. She spotted the remains of stairways and footbridges that intersected all along the sheer cliffs a short walk from where she stood. She hiked down into the stony hollow, following overgrown pathways and scaling precarious ledges until she stopped in front of a collapsed entranceway. Her mind begged her to turn away; her feet propelled her forward. She picked her way over boulders and lintels and entered a vast chamber. A low thrumming sound hypnotized her and drew her deeper into the complex...

Clay shivered as the cold mountain air seeped down from the rocks and enveloped him. He glanced up at the pale peaks illuminated by a quarter moon and countless stars wondering when this was all going to end. A branch snapped to his left. He grasped the pommel of his sword and rose up into a crouch waiting for whatever made the sound to show itself. He didn't have long to wait.

A low growling sound broke the silence; the slow, serpentine movements of a dark shape emerged from out of the gloominess. It reminded him of spilled ink trickling across a desk. The indistinct form took on a more solid appearance until Clay was only a few yards away from a heavily muscled beast. The hair on its back stood straight up forming a low row of spines; its long fangs glinted even in the near darkness. Clay took a step back, the brute never taking its yellow eyes off him.

"Whistler...Sara...we have company!"

The dwarf and the demon materialized by his side within seconds, weapons at the ready.

Whistler stared at the creature's rectangular jaws and grubby coat, the raised shoulders and lower haunches prepared to spring on them. Dribbies had escaped from the camp on a few occasions. Most came back but the meanest ones never did. The dwarf knew they had formed small packs in the camp and would undoubtedly do the same in the wild.

"What is it?"

"It's a Dribbie, Sara. And there might be more around here."

No sooner did those words leave his mouth when another one yowled in the distance. A third one answered its call and the companions dared to hope there weren't other Dribbies in the area. Sara unsheathed her black daggers, twirling them at her sides as she waited for the other hybrids to join the one facing them. It licked its chops, striking the ground with a huge paw that could easily cover their faces.

"Are the ones in your camp this big?" asked Clay as he spun around to confront the sounds coming from behind them.

The Dribbies circled the trio, their glowing eyes disappearing and reappearing as they moved in between the rocks and brush. The beasts suddenly went still. The companions gripped their weapons while they strained to see into the dimness encircling them. A small rock bounced down to their left then came to a stop. A bush shook nearby as one of the Dribbies brushed past it.

"Not this big and not this smart," replied the dwarf as he turned toward the noise.

Whistler's voice was the catalyst inciting the brutes to attack. The snarling grew louder and seemed to come from all around them. Without further warning, the Dribbies vaulted out of the shadows and bore down on the three friends. Their stench and fetid breath seemed to envelope them in an invisible fog. Each of the companions had to exercise a great deal of self-control not to retch.

Clay swung his sword but did not connect with his first attempt. He hacked away at one of the creature's heads, his lips pressed tightly together as he brought his weapon down forcibly. It yelped in pain, its ear stuck to the blade. It backed off, then lunged at the elf once more but this time it wasn't as fortunate. Clay sliced along its exposed belly, the Dribbies' steaming innards cascading from the wound all over the front of his own body. He detached its intestines from his arm and flung them away with disgust, then plucked its stomach off his shoulder. The reeking contents oozed onto his tunic and dropped him to his knees. He vomited until his gut was empty then focused on Whistler and Sara.

Sara slashed and stabbed her foe with such a vengeance that the Dribbie whimpered with fear. It struggled to escape but the demon had just about severed its right leg. It dragged its useless limb whining in pain and fright, its massive head constantly looking backward in terror. The hybrid heaved itself in between two boulders, the demon a step behind it. After a brief pause, the Dribbie wailed once then fell silent.

Whistler jammed the hoe blade into the Dribbies mouth, grinning at the sound of shattering teeth. The beast roared with fury and knocked his entire body into the dwarf. Whistler staggered beneath its weight and fell backward, the impact with the ground jarring him. The brute was on top of him a split second later. Whistler's great strength barely prevented the maddened creature from ripping out his throat. In his peripheral vision, the dwarf could see Sara and Clay coming to his rescue. Whistler kicked the Dribbie in the mid-section. The beasts' ribs cracked and it suddenly began to gasp. It relinquished its hold over the dwarf, which gave Whistler the opening to bury the blade in its skull. The creature collapsed in a heap, twitched several times, then lay still.

Clay helped him to his feet then stripped off his tunic, grimacing at what clung to it.

"Do you know how many flies will be chasing you tomorrow morning?" asked Whistler, not knowing whether to laugh or keep his distance from the stench emanating from the elf and his clothing.

"Very funny."

"Sara," he took a step closer to the demon girl, "I sincerely apologize for my outburst."

"I understand, Whistler," she replied placing her cool hand on his arm.

"We should leave this area in case there are more Dribbies out there," suggested Whistler.

They grabbed their pouches and walked south along the open ground, May now riding on Sara's pack. Insects chirped in the scraggly grasses at the base of the mountains; melancholy birdsong filtered toward them from the boughs of the spectral bushes. Clouds began to roll in and obliterated the sparkling heavens and still they hiked on. They finally stopped and rested a couple of hours before dawn, too exhausted to continue any farther. They crawled beneath the low-hanging limbs of a gnarled old pine and fell into an exhausted, dreamless sleep.

***

Far below Elena was a collection of rocks sticking up out of the sea. Their black, serrated tops were wet with the pounding surf; their sides covered with pale blue flecks. The waves smashed into them, the impact sending towering columns of water so high into the air she was soon completely soaked. The sun reflected off the vast ocean spread out before her, the intensity stabbing at her eyes like spikes. She looked up and cringed. She had fallen maybe twenty feet down, the uneven notch at the top of the crumbling cliff's edge still releasing bits of debris and dirt. Roots poked out of the side of the cliff here and there. She reached up and tried to grab the nearest root, her fingertips inches away from it. She stretched carefully until she was on her tiptoes, immediately crouching down and hugging the side as her unstable platform of stone and rubble shook precariously beneath her. If she could reach one handhold that would hold her, she could attempt to climb up but the nearest one was just beyond her reach. The ocean doused her once more but this time she covered her face with her hands the moment she heard the whooshing of the wave breaking across the rocks.

"Elena? Where are you? Answer me?"

"I'm down here, Garadan!" she called back, the elf's voice flooding her with relief. She moved as far away from side of the cliff as she dared then waved her arm as vigorously as she could.

"Are you hurt?" Garadan asked as Taman and August joined him. They peered over the side and spotted the dwarf huddled against the cliff. Rocks and other fragments lay strewn all around her. The little avalanches of sand and soil spilling by her disappeared into the three hundred-foot drop below.

"No, just a few bruises and cuts."

"We'll find a way to get you back up here…stay where you are."

"I don't think she's going anywhere soon, Garadan," Taman stated, hobbling after the elf and Herkah as they moved away from the brink. "It's too bad we don't have any rope."

"We'll have to find something, maybe we can find a sturdy branch to get her up to at least those roots sticking out of the side," Garadan was scanning their surroundings looking for anything that would bear her weight. They scrounged around for a while, picking up then tossing aside several boughs before finding a sturdy limb. They dragged it over to the rim then dangled it as close to her as they could guide it.

"Take hold of this and use it to balance yourself until you can reach the roots, Elena."

Garadan and Taman held the branch tightly in their hands, keeping it as steady as possible while Elena left her position. She grasped the bough and began to pull herself up, the first handhold still too far over her head. Her perspiration mingled with the mist spurting upward, both stinging her eyes. She struggled on, her body cramping with the effort of trying to reach for a safe grip. She finally connected with the closest root and latched onto it.

Elena looked up at her companions, her wide-open eyes begging for help. They could do nothing for her until she neared the final third of her ascent. She shook the droplets from her blotchy face then lifted her shaky hand up to the next support. She winced as the rough surface abraded her sore and blistering hands. Her progress was slow; it took many minutes to climb up to the first root. Elena's breathing became raspy, her tired muscles complaining with every movement.

"She needs help," Garadan whispered to August, "but there's nothing we can do until she climbs a little bit higher."

"You're doing well, Elena," August shouted down some much-needed encouragement as she seized the next protuberance. He jerked involuntarily as her grip slipped and she slid backward to the first root.

"I'm going down to help her," Garadan stated, swinging his lean frame over the edge. He cautiously scrambled down the side, his body wrenching awkwardly as the loose surface gave way beneath his feet. He held on firmly, the broken ends of the roots poking into his palms until they became slick with blood. He managed to move down to within a few yards of the dwarf.

"I'm sorry to put you in this dangerous predicament, Garadan."

"Here, take my hand." He wiped his fingers on his trousers before offering it to her. She needed to climb up to him before she could take his hand but his presence renewed her resolve. She advanced a little at a time, reaching Garadan after only a few moments. He clasped her hand and heaved her up while holding onto the nearest root. They pressed on, gaining inches as the edge loomed closer and closer over their heads. Taman knelt at the top; August bent over at the waist careful not to rest his hands on his aching knees.

Taman stretched to take hold of Elena, August clutching the back of her tunic as the two of them hauled her to safety. Garadan quickly followed her up to safety, the dwarf and soldier panting as they rested on their backs.

Elena attended to Garadan's hands then took care of her own, the salve easing the stinging pain. They decided to share the rest of their food before setting off once more beneath the noontime sun.

They kept the line of cliffs to their left as they traveled south, the scent of wild roses and salt air invigorating them. The group headed for the woods about a half mile away, the black-speckled white birch trunks and young pines much more inviting than the oppressive oaks they had just escaped. A few puffy clouds drifted lazily across the turquoise sky, occasionally blocking out the sun. The day was warm but the sea breeze kept them cool and comfortable. They neared the outskirts of the forest and found a rutted trail winding up the gradual incline. August was the last one in line and stopped to look back the way they had come. There were no signs of anyone following them, only the gulls dropping shells onto the flat exposed rocks. He shuffled after his friends, limping slightly from his knee injuries. They hiked along the meandering path, wondering where it would lead them. The breeze filtering through the young trees dried their perspiration and rustled the leaves around them. Birds chirped overhead and small furry creatures scampered out of their way as they progressed. The welcome sound of running water grew steadily louder and, as they rounded a bend, they spotted a stream to their right. They emptied the stale water from their water skins and refilled them with the cold water, then washed away as much of the dirt and grunge as possible.

The group walked for another hour until long shadows began to darken the woods. The wind that had cooled them during their trek now sent shivers up their spines. The effort needed to lift their legs increased and their growling stomachs demanded food. It was time to stop for the night. They made camp on an outcropping of rock several feet up from the trail. A partial overhang and the side of the hillock offered them protection from the elements and any four-legged creature out hunting during the night.

Garadan and Taman managed to kill a small deer that had been drinking at the stream, the fresh venison the first they had had in a very long time. Elena gathered firewood and found some wild vegetables along the way. They took a chance building a fire hoping their remote location and the encircling hills would hide the smoke.

The aroma of cooking meat made their mouths water. They ate their fill, curing the rest of the venison as best as they could before packing it away in their pouches. August let out a sigh of relief, which turned to a groan as he gently massaged his knees. They ached not only from the jarring impact earlier in the day but from the constant climbing. He watched Elena rub her calves and Garadan stretching out the kinks in his muscles.

"We'll take turns keeping watch," August said, "I'll go first." The others tried to make themselves as comfortable as possible, the stone platform's rough surface gouged by wind and rain. Their exhaustion prevailed and the bumpy ground was soon forgotten.

August leaned against the coarse hillside and stared out into the darkness. Crickets chirped and night birds sang their lonely songs. He heard branches breaking somewhere close by then the brief shriek of a hapless animal followed by a low snarling. There was a reassuring sensation rippling through the trees, one that promised security. It urged him to sleep without fear of being bothered. August gratefully surrendered to it.

The fog floated silently toward the shore, shrouding the cliff in a thick blanket of white. It crept up the cliff side and stole into the forest, minute droplets clinging to everything it touched. It curled lazily around trunks and seeped through the branches, rising upward toward the ledge. Elena shivered and August shifted his aching knees. Garadan woke up first and began to rub his arms. He caught a glimpse of a dozing August and tossed a pebble on his chest. The Herkah bolted upright, rubbed his eyes and stared into the white, soupy mist. His face reddened and he shrugged his shoulders apologetically.

"Rise and shine, Library Mouse," Garadan nudged Taman's leg with the tip of his boot.

The elf gazed over at Elena, his fingers reaching for the bite mark. She nodded her head, grabbed her small pouch and attended to the wound. The flush was fading but the incisions retained a waxy appearance. The dwarf smeared the salve over the injury and waited for it to dry to her satisfaction. She tested it a few minutes later and motioned for him to pull his tunic back into place.

"Can't see a thing out there," muttered August, "I wonder when this fog will burn off?"

"It'll be a while, I guess," Garadan passed out slices of meat and cut the last of the cheese. They needed to find some fresh supplies soon.

They waited for the thick vapor to fade away. Garadan dozed; Taman gazed out into the whiteness; Elena hummed softly to herself and August examined his knees.

The swelling had gone down and the abrasions were showing signs of healing. He flexed first one knee then the other without any real discomfort then propped himself up against a smooth boulder.

The sun's rays finally penetrated the haze late in the morning. The group was eager to move on and quickly descended from their rocky perch. They followed the faint trail as it wound around hills, dipped down embankments and rose up again. An afternoon breeze blew in from the ocean stirring the leaves and smaller branches. It cooled their heated skin and brought with it the tangy aroma of the sea.

The ground began to rise steadily, the gray rocks and knobby roots hindering their ability to climb with any speed. They rested in the trough of two knolls in the late afternoon and shared a quick meal. A brook bubbled near the base of the mound inviting the travelers to wash themselves as much as they could and refill their canteens.

Garadan walked beyond the twin foothills and headed for the vast waterway on the other side. He squinted as he looked out over the white-flecked waves then glanced down at the breakers smashing against the rocks. A movement to his right caught his attention. There, maybe a mile away was a boat, its blue and white striped sails dropping to the deck. The vessel rounded a craggy shelf topped with trees and disappeared from view. *Maybe we can find some provisions there.*

He rejoined the others and told them what he had seen. They would need to be cautious yet they were grateful there were other people in the area. It had been so long since they had encountered anyone else. They set off again, the path continuing to climb until it reached a hollowed out hillside. The light was beginning to fade, the lengthening shadows distorting and blurring the way. They opted to spend the night rather than risk a fall.

Their night was uneventful and they slept well. They set off at dawn after eating the last of their food, hopeful they'd be able to procure more before the day was over. They made good progress and, near late morning, came upon a break in the trees overlooking the ocean. They crouched down and studied the village at the base of the cliff. Ramshackle one-story buildings were crowded together between the beach and base of the hill. Their drab plank walls, with thick glass blocks stacked together to form windows and shale rooftops were in sharp contrast to the gardens growing all around them. Sunflowers, their huge heads hanging as if in deep thought, grew beside each house. Vegetable plots and bright red, blue and yellow flowers took up most of the limited space between the homes. Climbing roses, morning glories and other vines claimed porch posts and trellises. Women hung out their wash; children ran and played with each other and the large, longhaired dogs. A few men were busy gutting and splitting fish then placed them on ventilated partitions to dry.

The group watched as a dozen men rowed their skiffs out just beyond the headland, nets piled up in the bows and buckets behind in the stern. The weather-beaten boats rolled up and down the swells with ease. The men stood in the center of their crafts and effortlessly cast out their nets, their legs moving as one with the wave action. The netting was in the water for only a few minutes before the men began to haul them up. Their boats quickly filled with flopping fish.

"Do we barter or borrow from them?" asked Garadan.

"They look peaceful enough," August said.

"We really should be seen by as few people as possible," uttered Taman. "What's wrong with the men?"

The group watched the men in the skiffs point back to the shore, the breeze carrying their shouts of alarm across the water up to their vantage point. The fishermen hurriedly rowed back to the beach, their muscles straining against the oars.

The women dropped their laundry onto the dirt and hastily rounded up their children. The men gutting the fish sprang into action. They grabbed their families and rushed to get them down a rocky embankment toward a series of caves beneath the bluff. The craggy rocks were hard to climb over and down, leaving the escapees exposed for a few brief moments. That was all the time the arrows needed to find their marks. Two plummeted into the heavy surf while a woman reached out to clutch her lifeless child before she, too, went still. The headland blocked the companions' view but that did not stop them from nervously gripping their own swords. Whatever approached these people could just as easily confront them as well.

"There," whispered Garadan.

Soldiers wearing white tunics over their breastplates surged into sight, short, white feathers dancing wildly on top of their conical helmets. They carried long spears in one hand and short, slightly curved blades in the other as they pursued the fleeing villagers. The old and infirm fell beneath their swords first as they sacrificed themselves to allow the young and women to escape. The detachment's shirts were soon soaked in the blood spurting from the withered arms, necks and chests of the elderly. The unit kicked the hacked off limbs out of their way and lashed out at the dead and dying as they chased after the residents fleeing for their lives.

Dozens of soldiers met the men disembarking in waist high water, their fishing knives no match for the well-armed intruders. The unit used their spears against them, the notched heads slicing straight through to the other side of the bodies. The encounter was brief but devastating. Three soldiers wearing blue tunics and feathers in their helmets moved onto the beach. They spoke with several of the fighters then looked back toward where they had come from. The men bowed as a single man walked past the edge of the headland, his blue and white striped tunic covering a chain mail shirt that hung halfway down to his knees. He wore three long plumes in his helmet: a blue feather between two white ones.

He placed his gloved hands on his hips while surveying the bloody slaughter all around him and nodded his head in satisfaction. He directed their attention to several of his wounded men then pulled out his sword to parry an invisible enemy. He sheathed his blade and strutted back out of sight, the soldiers setting the village ablaze before following after him. Some of the men playfully slapped each other on the back, their spears resting jauntily on their shoulders.

Everything grew quiet then a baby wailed from some place unseen. Elena squeezed her eyes shut as the crying abruptly ended, a tear sliding down her dirty cheek. Carrion birds circled overhead and spiraled closer to the corpses, finally landing to begin their grisly feast.

"Let's go," Garadan ordered tonelessly, his features tight, his eyes flashing with a myriad of emotions.

-11-

"Come in," Balyd called out in response to a light tap on his door. It was nearly midnight and he wondered who would be visiting him at this late hour. A tall elf with a leathery face entered and offered him a slight bow. Balyd stared at him, a faint memory worming its way to the forefront of his mind. "Captain Ansar?"

"Yes, Lord Balyd. You sent for me?"

"Ah...yes. Please sit," he waved Ansar to a chair in front of the fireplace. "Would you like a glass of wine?"

"Thank you."

Balyd poured the deep purple liquid into the goblets then handed the captain one before taking a seat across from him. The First Advisor was at a loss as to how to convey the information to Ansar and how to convince the captain to reveal what, if anything, he knew about the stranger from years ago. Was his allegiance to Queen Tryssa as strong now as it had been back then?

"What can I do for you, Lord Balyd?"

"We...I have a slight dilemma on my hands, Captain Ansar, one which I think you might be able to help me with." The captain waited patiently for Balyd to continue. The First Advisor took a chance and revealed the truth about the demon, Aryanda's death and Garadan and Taman's mission. Ansar never moved nor spoke the entire time. The captain remained silent long after Balyd had finished.

THE FORTRESS OF DARKNESS

"Those are ill tidings, my Lord."

"Yes, they are, Ansar, but if an heir to the throne isn't found soon, the elves' situation will become noticeably worse."

Balyd watched as Ansar's features fluctuated from surprise to suspicion then to indecision. His shoulders stiffened. It took a moment for him to regain control with a neutral expression on his face.

"Why did you ask me to come here?" He placed his glass on the oaken table between them.

"I found one of Queen Tryssa's journals," Balyd leaned back in his chair. "And it made mention of a woman who had come to Bystyn approximately twenty years ago. I read in this journal you went to see this stranger."

Ansar swallowed but said nothing.

"Who was she, Captain Ansar? Why did she come to this city?"

"She was ailing and wanted to give birth amongst her own people."

"She was of elven blood?"

"Yes."

"What happened to her, Ansar?" Balyd spoke in low tones.

"She died before the delivery could take place."

"And the baby?" Balyd's hope for a legitimate heir began to fade; the thought of Caladan manipulating the next ruler to serve his needs sickened him.

Ansar stared down at his hands clasped in his lap. He remembered that night well. Indeed, he thought of it every single day. He had disobeyed Queen Tryssa, the very person whose life he was sworn to protect and be faithful to in every possible way. He knew eventually there would be consequences, no matter how much time had elapsed since that fateful night. The keys to Bystyn's future were his to keep secret or to pass along to Balyd. Ansar took a deep breath, drained his goblet and revealed to Balyd what had happened that night more than twenty years earlier.

"I was summoned to Queen Tryssa's chamber around dusk. She was tutoring Aryanda who was not quite seven years old at the time. Tryssa dismissed the princess. She held a letter in her hand, the folds sharp but the edges tattered. She held out the note and stated an impostor had arrived outside the city and wanted to speak with her. She claimed this individual threatened to usurp the elven throne and the only way to protect Bystyn and the elves was to get rid of this person. The queen informed me this pretender was being held prisoner in a hunter's cabin about half an hour from the city. I rode out to comply with the queen's orders.

"I had no idea what I would find but I never expected to come face to face with a young woman heavy with child. Her delicate condition only served to underscore Tryssa's command to terminate this stranger. She was in the first stages of giving birth when she began to slip away. She looked me in the eye, beseeching me to care for her unborn baby, then her lids closed and she stopped breathing."

"What of the baby, Ansar? Did it survive?"

"They *both* lived, Balyd, although I had to cut them free from her belly."

"She had twins?"

"Yes."

"You didn't kill them, did you, Ansar?"

"I am not in the habit of slaying children, Lord Balyd. I gave them to my second in command, Altac, and told him to take them away."

"I didn't mean to insinuate you to be a slaughterer of innocents. I apologize, Ansar. Do you know where he took them?"

"No and before you ask, Altac died several years ago taking his secret with him to the grave."

"Were they boys or girls? What did they look like?"

"I know the fair haired boy with the green eyes that I held was healthy. Altac took the other one before I could see it." Ansar suddenly went still, his mind drifting back several weeks. A face began to materialize in front of him, a vaguely familiar face that time could not erase. The color began to drain from his countenance.

"Ansar? What's wrong?"

"I...I think I might have seen one of them not too long ago."

"Where?" Balyd slid to the edge of his chair, the mere thought that a possible successor still lived and was near elven lands making his pulse race.

"He was traveling with a man and young woman along the western border region more than a month ago. I asked what his business was and he told me he wanted to go to Bystyn to seek out his kin."

"And?" Balyd leaned so far forward he was on the verge of falling off the chair.

"I ordered him to leave."

Balyd's eyelids drooped, his hands plopping heavily onto his lap.

"I believed it was for the best at that time, Lord Balyd. If I had known about Queen Aryanda's fate I might have escorted him into the city to prove or disprove my presumption."

"What made you think it was one of the stranger's children?"

"He bore a striking resemblance to the picture of Prince Danyl."

Balyd picked up his glass and drank it dry then refilled it once more. He let out a long, slow breath, the painting of the bearer of the Green Might filling his vision. It hung with the other family portraits in the hallway on the second floor leading to the royal rooms. It had been completed many years after the great battle against Mahn and his army. Ramira's image had hung beside his but King Ardall, Queen Alyssa's successor, removed it after Ramira passed away. No one knew why nor did anyone know where her painting was stored. *My little Library Mouse probably knows where it is.*

"Shall I look for him, Lord Balyd?" Ansar quietly asked.

"No," Balyd massaged his throbbing temples, the wine beginning to course through his system. "Will you stay in the city for a while?"

"I'll remain in the city until you no longer require my services, Lord Balyd."

"Ansar, one of the lords at court, Caladan, is also seeking you out to question you about this situation. He does not have Bystyn's best interests at heart."

"I know who he is and of his intentions, Lord Balyd. Captain Hardan has made room for me in the storehouse beneath the southwest tower. It's rarely used. I wish you a good night, sir."

Balyd nodded and watched him leave. *At least one is still alive.*

* * *

Sara awoke first, immediately covering her nose and mouth with her hands as she scrambled away from the sleeping elf. Clay's arm covered his eyes; one of his legs was straight, the other bent at an angle. He was smeared with blood and encrusted with bits of entrails; the only area not affected was where his shirt had been. She stifled a giggle as he awakened, the bewildered look on his face gradually changing to revulsion.

"You're walking downwind of us until you find a place to wash," Whistler stated as he extricated himself from out beneath the bough. He searched the area to the south where Evan's Peak stood perhaps two days away. The only thing that moved across the ground was dirt kicked up by the wind.

Sara joined him shaking her canteen, the sloshing echoing hollowly in their ears. She pulled out a chunk of cheese and a handful of nuts and gave them to the dwarf.

"That's all I have," she said.

Whistler shrugged his shoulders, grinning at the approaching elf. Clay scraped Dribbie pieces off his trousers with one hand while shooing away the flies with the other. He wasn't very successful with either task. They shared what food they had, the demon girl and the dwarf keeping their distance from the malodorous elf. They set out at a brisk pace and covered many miles by the time they stopped to rest about noon. Evan's Peak loomed larger and larger with every passing hour.

The sun began its descent bathing their surroundings in soft peach and gold tones. A few hardwoods were interspersed between the pines and blueberry bushes hugging the ground. There were wild apple, plum and hazelnut trees, but their fruits were not quite ready to eat. Where there was vegetation there was water. The tributary wasn't hard to find. They ran over to it, falling to their knees and dunking their heads into the refreshing water. Clay's skin erupted in gooseflesh but he didn't care—he was finally going to get rid of the nasty coating. He washed himself then his tunic and hung it across a bush to dry.

Flashes of silver darted in the water. Clay fashioned a makeshift net out of slender twigs held together by blades of thick grass. He tried scooping them up but the fish dashed out of the way the moment he came near the water.

"Here," Sara grabbed the net and deposited a few crumbs from her pouch into it then placed it in the stream. She dipped one end slightly under the surface and waited. It didn't take long. The fish were attracted to the stale bread and cautiously swam into the net. Sara flipped the rim up several times then handed the net with five fish in it to Clay.

"I'll get some firewood," said Sara.

Clay repeated her movements and was delighted to catch several more before the fish shied away from the net altogether. He gutted them and grimaced at the memory of the Dribbies' insides adhering to his skin and clothing.

They ate their fill and wrapped what remained in some broad leaves Sara had picked. The companions foraged for whatever was edible and added the nuts and roots to their pouches. May disappeared into the branches in search of her own meal, returning a little while later to resume her place on Sara's shoulder. Whistler took first watch, sitting with Clay's sword firmly in his grasp. Clay took his place shortly before midnight then Sara took her turn, watching over her friends until sunrise.

The pattern continued until they rounded Evan's Peak. They stared down at the broad vista before them, Whistler with narrowed eyes, Clay and Sara gaping at the endless terrain below. Thick forests grew to the west and a dark green smear was visible on the horizon to the east. The south was a wide plain interlaced with hundreds of streams, rivers and tributaries. Tall yellow grasses sprouted up amongst knots of slender trees and squat bushes here and there. The plant life changed into prairie lands beyond the widest of the waterways.

Whistler knew that area intimately. He and Elena had hopped over, waded through and nearly frozen to death in those waters. Elena had nearly drowned there a few weeks earlier and here he stood right back where they had started. What next? A group of Rock Lords ready to take him prisoner and send him back to camp?

* * *

Tarz sat in the shade of Evan's Peak, the morning shadows growing shorter as the hours passed. He had lost the dwarves' trail near the mountains but where there should have been two sets of footprints there were seven. Did Whistler and Elena run into friend or foe? Where did they go? They had churned up grass and dirt but there was no sign of any fighting. The tracks simply ended.

He scratched his cheek while scanning the open plains to the south and east. The land sloped away from his position, giving him a slightly elevated view. There, far in the distance, a group of riders headed steadily toward him. Kevlan, it seemed, had heard about his dead men and had sent another patrol out to investigate. Tarz was glad he had tethered the horses out of sight inside the main room at Evan's Peak. He kept himself hidden within the gloomy recess of the entranceway, watching the horsemen gradually looming larger as they came closer. He was so intent on watching them he failed to notice the crashing in the woods to his right. It wasn't until deer and rabbits broke through in a panic, and birds shot skyward that he paid any attention to what poured out onto the plains.

Tarz' mouth dropped open, his eyes wide with astonishment then fear as the barrel-shaped creatures with spindly arms and legs broke through the tree line. Fangs gnashed wildly at the air, some of their maws filled with bits of bloody fur and bone. The animals scattered, the fiends pursuing them with a frenzy bordering on madness. The brutes caught and immediately ripped apart the slowest of the creatures, their brief shrieks of terror sending a pulse of pity even through Tarz. *Nothing deserves to die like that*, he thought, unable to move.

Tarz turned back to the rapidly approaching Rock Lords. Tarz wanted to warn them but the sheer brutality of the monsters kept him rooted in place. They would swarm over him within minutes if he revealed his location. All the Rock Lord would be able to do was to witness the butchery that even now began to unfold.

The creatures' interest shifted from the woodland animals to the approaching men. They spun around and raced toward them, gangly arms and legs churning up dust. The Rock Lords straightened up in their saddles as they tried to figure out what was going on then jerked the reins of their horses until they skidded to a halt. Rising clouds of grit concealed them. Tarz could see their vague outlines becoming more visible as the dust began to settle. The horses began to stomp their hooves, their ears flat. They snorted and whinnied nervously then began to rear up and strain against the reins. The Rock Lords could barely control them, whipping them fiercely. The steeds didn't seem to feel the blows. Tarz could see the whites of their eyes even from where he hid. They raised their forelegs high into the air and bolted north in Tarz' direction.

Tarz swore under his breath as he inched farther into the niche behind him. His own horses were becoming restless, the sounds and smells of danger reaching Evan's Peak. If his animals did not remain silent, he was doomed. Two hundred yards separated him from the advancing groups. Then one hundred yards. The creatures launched themselves on the Rock Lords and their mounts when they were no more than a few yards away. Tarz flinched involuntarily as the things uncurled their claws and raked their razor-sharp talons across the Rock Lords' chests. Blood spurted out from the dreadful wounds, the men screaming in agony as they sought to escape the fiends. One Rock Lord managed to slice into his attacker but the dark blood gushing from the creature scalded his exposed skin. His cry excited the thing and, even though its arm dangled only by a few tendons, it ripped open the Rock Lords' throat. It looked up at its horrifying brethren, bits of gore swinging from the sides of their jaws.

Tarz gaped at the massacre, man and horse succumbing to the mindless obliteration. He watched as the creatures feasted on the dying, returning to the dead only when the Rock Lords lay absolutely still. Tarz' mouth was dry and his body cramped from crouching in the entranceway. The rising sun chased away the darkness in which he hid but he dared not move. His calf muscles ached; beads of sweat ran into his eyes. His sodden leather vest clung to his brawny form. *Must…move…can't squat much…longer!*

The fiends continued their gruesome feast until they suddenly stopped and turned to the south in unison.

Tarz fell forward on his knees and leaned over as he grabbed the back of his thighs, massaging his muscles back to life. He cautiously dared to look over at the horrible scene. Man and animal lay strewn in grotesque heaps, their twisted corpses barely recognizable. Tarz turned his head and threw up onto the ground.

* * *

They trod through the village, the soldiers' efficiency apparent no matter where they looked. Their presence scared away the carrion-eating vultures in their immediate path but not the ones several yards to either side. August glared at them as they squawked and fought over the corpses. Elena put her hand against her mouth as she espied a dead mother holding her baby protectively in her arms. Its tiny hand rested on the woman's breast but it did not move. Dead bodies lay in heaps where they had fallen; some driven through with swords, others riddled with arrows. There were no survivors.

"We need to replenish our supplies," Garadan stated quietly.

"Shouldn't we do something?" Elena's voice sounded loud.

"If we bury them and the men come back, they'll hunt down whoever did that deed. The last thing we need is company," August wrapped his arms around Elena and held her for a few moments.

Taman stared transfixed at a high promontory farther to the south, a jagged structure clutching the very edge of the cliff. It appeared to balance precariously along the edge even at this distance. Taman felt the magic begin to stir but it did not pull him into that daunting in-between place.

Garadan proceeded to scrounge for anything edible. His companions did the same, silently mourning for the villagers and thanking them at the same time. August found an underground storage room and entered it. He placed his hands on his hips then called out to Elena. She joined him, a sad smile forming on her face. "I'll carry out whatever you hand to me," he said.

Elena nodded and reached for a bag of rose hips, slabs of cured bacon, several loaves of dark bread, a large block of cheese and a sack of dried fruit and nuts. Her fingers lingered on a jar of strawberry marmalade, her mouth watering as she stared at the berries pressed against the glass. A pot of blueberry preserves rested beside it. She turned around and took inventory of the rest of the root cellar, as August awaited her decisions.

"That will be about all we can carry," she said stepping up out of the chamber.

They divided the food and realized they had room for a little more.

THE FORTRESS OF DARKNESS

August made one more trip down to the storage area. He emerged, one of his tunic pockets bulging, carrying another sack of fruits and nuts. They completed their task and headed away from the beach, seeking what protection they might find in the forest.

A cold, acrid breeze washed through Taman's soul, its leading edge composed of tongues of fire. He cocked his head, unsure if the faint sound reaching his ears was the wind or long forgotten whispers. The subtle undertones reverberated inside his head, their seductive vibrations worming their way through his body. Taman closed his eyes and leaned his head back, a slow smile spreading across his face. The fire suddenly flared startling Taman out of the trance. He concentrated on the gloominess around him, recoiling as his distorted features abruptly emerged from the murkiness. Lightning erupted around his head; forked tongues flicked hungrily from his mouth and tears of blood trickled out from his vacant sockets. Taman ripped himself out of the dreadful vision.

"We have to travel south," Taman stated, crossing his arms and sticking his trembling hands into his armpits.

"That's the way the enemy traveled."

"I know, Garadan. I wish it were another direction but what we seek is on a precipice a few miles away from here."

"Your eyes are like dark storm clouds." Elena shivered though no cool wind touched her skin.

"We're close to a magic, aren't we?" August's voice resonated with a tinge of fear.

"We're close to something," she replied.

They followed a deer trail as it meandered past birches, maple and oak trees. Tufted waist-high grasses grew abundantly, warmed by the dappled sunlight. A blue jay's grating call echoed beneath the summer leaves. Another jay answered from off in the distance. Other sounds of far-off rustling were faintly audible. They trudged on, the horror of the massacre miles behind, their unknown fate before them.

The companions panted as they labored up the sloping grounds into the hills. They clambered upward, grabbing onto roots and trees for support, the valley beneath them growing steeper and more distant by the hour. A dull gray light penetrated the forest, a permeating dampness foretelling an uncomfortable night. Dim shadows distorted the hillside. Garadan placed his foot on a short ledge of rock only to break a flattened branch, which sent him tumbling past his companions. August reached out and snatched the back of his tunic, holding on long enough for the captain to regain his footing. The sound of rain pattering on the leaves hastened their search for some sheltered place to spend the night.

They hiked a little farther and spotted two huge, moss-covered boulders ringed by pine trees, their interconnecting boughs keeping the area underneath dry. The companions crouched down then scrambled into the protected space dragging their pouches in behind them.

August glanced up at the ancient trees, their redolence washing over him. The branches hung low but he could stand up without hitting his head on the lowest one. He stood and turned around to face the break between the two granite slabs. The branches and trunks of several more pines created a partial obstruction between the front and back sides of the hill. He was about to explore the other half of the knoll when a flash of blue appeared. He peeked through one of the boughs. There, not thirty feet on the other side, were the men who had butchered the villagers. They were arriving in single file, having taken a parallel route toward the tower on the cliff. He signaled to the others then put his finger to his lips.

Garadan leaned forward and peered through to the other side, the dusk settling on the woods beginning to blur the landscape. He watched as several men built a fire in an open area. Others tossed their bedrolls on the ground and wearily lay down. The officers waited for their aides to pitch their tents while the leader watched from off to one side. Garadan ducked out of the way as one of the men approached and urinated on one of the nearby trees. Another man soon joined him.

"Hey, do you remember Lilly from the tavern?"

"The redhead with the ample bottom?"

"That's the one," replied the first man. "She took me up to her room the night before we came out here."

"What happened?" the second man asked.

"Well, her backside isn't the only thing that's ample..."

Their laughter drifted away as they rejoined the others, and Garadan was grateful he wouldn't be privy to the details. It was too dark to try to sneak away, especially in unfamiliar surroundings, but the close proximity of the men dictated they had to do something. How long would it be before matters demanding greater privacy brought one of them to the other side of the boulders? The elf looked questioningly at his companions. They huddled together, their heads nearly touching as they whispered in the near darkness.

"Any ideas?" murmured Garadan.

"The chances of us being found out here are, unfortunately, high," stated August.

They sat silently as another soldier came to relieve himself, the slight breeze carrying with it his pungent odor.

"Hey! You there!" a voice boomed from beyond the barrier, "Where do you think you're going?"

"Uh...to..." uttered someone from very close by.

"Go downwind you imbecile! We're trying to eat and sleep here!"

The second man grumbled several unintelligible words but his footsteps faded away into the night.

"We should stay," suggested August. "At least we know where our enemy is."

"At least we won't be exposed to their personal habits any more," Elena added, wrinkling her nose.

They divided the watch into three-hour increments, Elena taking her turn first. Most of the men had settled down by the time Taman took over. August had the last shift. He could hear them snoring and an occasional cough, their trips to the bushes sounding loud in the night. More than one broke wind, the different lengths of duration forcing August to suppress his laughter. *What do these people eat?* He wordlessly roused his companions near daybreak; the men on the other side were already packed up and ready to leave.

The group waited for nearly an hour before setting out, departing just as the first raindrops fell from an overcast sky. They put on their cloaks and pulled their hoods up over their heads. They stayed on the winding path that ran parallel with the men wearing blue, wary of encountering any stragglers. They continued for most of the morning, the drenching rain abating near noon. After briefly stopping to rest, they moved on until the sky began to fade to gray. The trees began to thin out and there, rising up on a narrow promontory to their left, was the tower. The group edged over to an area hemmed in by pines and boulders and stared up at the structure.

The tower stood out starkly against the evening sky, the irregular shape widening slightly near the foundation where it merged with the cliff. Grasses grew between the rocks at its base; gulls circled then landed on the open sections of ground, their raucous cries reaching the watchers' ears. Spray shot up the jagged side of the precipice as if trying to wash the fortification off the cliff and pull it into the sea. A narrow pathway from the mainland crossed over a rough-hewn archway through which white-capped waves rolled. Stars became visible in the darkening sky.

Taman didn't move nor could he tear his gaze away from it. An unearthly glittering red mist seeped upward from the ground. The scarlet tendrils formed into many twisted strands rippling up the structure like gigantic snakes. They coiled and spiraled until they reached an opening at the top where they suddenly joined together and disappeared into the breach. Everything grew still, even the breeze.

Taman held his breath, his heart pounding in his chest. Then a brilliant blood-red light exploded from the pinnacle of the tower. The corona radiated outward and slammed into Taman. The magic coursed through him, its fiery touch searing everything it touched. It squeezed his lungs, found his soul and attempted to raze his mind.

Elena, Garadan and August were surprised when a small, reddish light flickered to life in the gap at its peak.

"That's the oddest lighthouse I've ever seen," August murmured, "I've never known one to have a crimson beam before."

"Look, over there," Garadan pointed to numerous fires near the base of the tower.

"Our friends from the woods?" asked Elena.

"Possibly," replied Garadan. "Taman, what…"

Suddenly, Taman collapsed to the ground gasping for air. Elena desperately searched for an obstruction but his airways were clear. Taman's back arched, his fingers frantically digging into the dirt terrified them all, especially his black eyes infused with gleaming sparkles of crimson. His face slowly drained of color as he thrashed back and forth, the likeness he had seen earlier demanding to be released.

"What's wrong with him?"

"I don't know, Elena," Garadan grabbed Taman's shoulders while August tried to keep his lower half as still as possible. They fought to control Taman's writhing body. August grimaced at the cramp forming in his leg but moving it would free the elf's arm. He gritted his teeth and held on.

Elena glanced up at the stone edifice, the red shaft of light pulsing more strongly. There were no obstructions between where they were gathered and the tower. She looked down into Taman's unblinking eyes, the flashes of red getting brighter and spreading rapidly. *The magic drew him here; could it also be doing this?*

"Bring him behind those rocks," she ordered. Garadan and August stared at her in confusion then hurried to move Taman. The red in his eyes began to fade but did not go away. They transferred him farther down the hillside then several more yards down the embankment before he slowly began to relax. Taman took several deep breaths for quite a few minutes before he was able to sit up on his own.

"How are you feeling?" the dwarf asked.

"Like I was being burned alive." He coughed deeply. He shoved the hallucination of his grotesque head into the far corner of his mind.

"And you want to go to the tower?"

"I have to, Garadan. That's where the magic is being kept."

"It almost killed you!" Elena couldn't believe he still wanted to go into the fortification.

"Taman," Garadan forced the elf to look him straight in his eyes, "It drastically affected you from a few miles away! What do you think will happen if you go inside it?"

"We know what will come to pass if I don't."

August exhaled sharply. Garadan looked over his shoulder at the promontory, the edifice now becoming lost in the shadows of the darkening sky.

Elena untied the strip of leather binding her hair and used her fingers to work out the worst of the tangles. She scratched her head then retied her locks. "Is there anything you can do to protect yourself from this power?"

"I don't know, Elena."

"Well, that isn't the only problem we have," Garadan stood up and placed his fists akimbo. "Our friends from the other night are camped at the edge of the point."

"Maybe they're just stopping for the night," suggested August.

"Let's hope that's true," Elena said. "That would be a good idea for us, too."

They made themselves as comfortable as possible, mindful of staying out of the magic's path. They took turns keeping watch but those who lay down had a difficult time trying to sleep.

-12-

Whistler, Clay and Sara caught sight of the Rock Lords through the waist high grasses as the riders neared Evan's Peak. The trio quickly hid amongst a cluster of trees and boulders, their weapons at the ready. May crawled onto Sara's shoulder and began to yank on the girl's hair. Sara tried to soothe the spider but May's anxiety increased steadily as the minutes ticked by. Sara was about to scold her when an abrupt coldness wrapped itself around her. At first, she thought the frigid air had oozed down from the mountain but the icy chill did not affect her companions. May became more persistent then disappeared up into the branches of a tree. *This does not bode well,* Sara thought.

The Rock Lords unexpectedly came to a halt, their faces at first confused then completely terrified. They turned their mounts around, frantically digging their heels into the sides of their frightened animals. Whatever had prompted them to escape was closer, or faster, than the men had anticipated. All of a sudden snarling whirlwinds of teeth and claws attacked man and beast, their screams of terror and pain reverberating off the granite cliffs and into the trios' ears.

Sara smothered her own involuntary whimpers with her hands. Clay grasped his sword while Whistler's hatred for the Rock Lords vanished behind a veil of sympathy for those suffering such a horrible death. The carnage lasted a short time. Whistler started to rise but Sara grabbed hold of his tunic and pulled him back down. He opened his mouth to speak and only her definitive hand movements stilled his tongue.

They waited for a long time until the last of the demons had eaten its share and re-joined its dreadful kin. Sara got to her feet and crept toward the area of the slaughter. Large birds circled overhead seeming to grow bigger with every passing swoop. Whistler and Clay walked by her side, May perched on the elf's pack. They finally reached the point where they could see over the last of the sedges, the scene even more horrifying than they had imagined. It was easy not to look down.

Something moved behind the carcass of a horse. They clutched their weapons and advanced toward the movement. A Rock Lord vomited onto the ground, his back toward the trio.

"Are you hurt?" Clay called out to the man.

The Rock Lord staggered to his feet, turned around, and wiped away the last of the spittle from his lips. His expression went from distress to confusion to astonishment in a fraction of a second.

"Tarz!" Whistler rushed forward, his cheeks flushed red as he faced his adversary. Tarz' features appeared dazed and devoid of hatred, his body limp and unsteady.

"Whistler?" Tarz stared at his quarry standing just a few feet away from him then over to his companions. The Rock Lord shuffled to a nearby boulder and sat down heavily, his gaze fixated on the corpses.

Clay walked over to Tarz and squatted down beside him, the Rock Lord waving away the proffered canteen. "What were those things, Sara?"

"Demons."

"They're heading in the direction of the camp," Whistler stated anxiously. "We have to do something, Clay."

"We'll never reach them before the fiends do, Whistler."

"We have to try. There are too many lives at stake."

Whistler looked down on Tarz, the loathing for his captors beginning to take charge once more. He could slay Tarz before either Sara or Clay could intervene and there would be one less Rock Lord in the land. He glanced over at the mangled bodies, their cries of pain and fear still ringing sharply in his head. He felt no satisfaction in their deaths nor would killing

Tarz offer him any closure. He decided he could always deal with him later, if need be.

"What were you and your men doing out here, Tarz?" asked Whistler.

"These weren't my soldiers," he replied waving his hand at the dead.

"Why are you here, then?" pressed Clay.

"My men and I were sent by Kevlan to find you," he locked eyes with the dwarf, "but you found me instead."

"What were you going to do? Take me back?"

"Yes."

"Huh. Kevlan's dog fetches for him…what kind of treat did he promise you?" Whistler's compassion was rapidly dissipating.

Tarz cocked his head as he studied Whistler. The dwarf's steady gaze bored right through him but the Rock Lord refused to look away.

"Kevlan is a fool who should have had you eradicated years ago. You were a diversion, a mouse he could play with then eventually kill. All he managed to do over the years is to make you more dangerous and himself less effective."

Whistler crossed his arms and smirked. "So you obeyed your master and went looking for me, your men torn to pieces in the meantime?"

"I already told you these aren't my men."

"Where are *your* men, then?" asked Clay, tired of the charade.

"I slit their throats the moment we entered elven lands."

"What were you doing on elven lands, Tarz?" asked Sara.

"We were sent to warn the elves about two plague infested dwarves."

Whistler's face darkened, the smoldering look in his eyes seconds from erupting into geysers of fire.

"Your proof?" inquired Clay.

"These men were sent to find out what happened to me and my men, elf."

"If there's even a hint of there being someone else with him, slay him before he has a chance to act first," Whistler whispered to Sara and Clay.

Tarz held his index finger up indicating they should wait a moment and headed for the entry into Evan's Peak. Whistler was galled the slaver would defile his ancestral home with his presence. The friends checked their weapons in case Tarz reemerged with a surprise but the Rock Lord came back out with three horses trailing behind him. The animals smelled the blood, the whites of their eyes showed as they tried to rear up and flee but Tarz managed to control them.

"Would he do such a thing, Whistler?"

"He'd offer up his own mother, Sara. Three horses—one for each of us," Whistler reached for the reins.

"I think not, dwarf. I came out here to get you back to the camp and that's what I'm going to do. I haven't spent the past few weeks searching for you along the northern mountains for nothing."

"Why, Tarz? Why do as you are told for someone you have no respect for? What treasure did Kevlan promise you?" Whistler's curiosity demanded to be satisfied.

Tarz remained silent.

"I'm the 'treasure'," Whistler chuckled, "and you had no intention of handing me over, did you? I was going to be your means to seize the Hall. How very clever and ambitious of you, Tarz. Replace one slaver for another one."

"I hate the dust, heat and missed opportunities to the east," growled the Rock Lord, "along with the meager and tasteless food. I don't care about you or a pack of demons, Whistler."

"The demons should concern you," Sara spoke after a brief lull in their conversation. "They are controlled by a demon called 'Emhella' and it is his plan to collect all of the magic in the land."

"For what purpose?" Tarz was beginning to regain his composure.

"To let all the demons loose upon the land. These monsters will be able to prey on all people at will. Your desire to overthrow Kevlan and place yourself as head of the Hall will never be realized if that comes to pass."

Tarz shook his head. If he hadn't seen the fiends and their butchery for himself, he would have simply killed the elf and the girl with the strange eyes and taken Whistler. He looked to the southeast. The demons were already out of sight. It would take less than a day to ride to Whistler's old encampment and less then half a day to reach the Hall. If they hurried, they would be able to warn everyone about the demons. He glanced over at Whistler. The dwarf glowered at him, his hand tightly gripping the hoe blade.

"Why are you heading back to the camp, Whistler?" he finally asked.

"Because there is something there the demon wants," Sara answered for the dwarf.

"What would that be?"

"Careful, Sara," warned Whistler.

"Magic. He already possesses two of the five powers in the land and seeks the remaining three. One of them, we think, is near the Hall."

"How very interesting," stated Tarz.

"Before you get any foolish ideas, Tarz, I must tell you that the magic cannot be wielded by just anyone."

"Is that a fact, Sara?" Tarz rubbed the sweat off his shiny head with both hands, drying them on his trousers. "So...what will you do with it if you find it in the compound? Tuck it into your pocket?"

"We won't know until we locate it," Clay chimed in.

"You present a lot of maybes and what ifs."

"What are you going to do, Tarz?" Whistler's impatience was nearing its limit.

Tarz stretched his head to the right then to the left, the perspiration running down his thick, powerful neck. He handed two horses' reins to Clay then jumped up on his own mount. Whistler hopped up onto one horse while Clay and Sara shared the third one. They stared at one another for a few moments then raced the horses toward their destination.

* * *

Harald stood inside the tool shed, a sturdy building in the center of the compound. It was nearly empty, the repair work to the huge beams supporting the roof requiring almost everything to be removed. Hooks for the tools ran all the way down along the left side of the wall, and the back wall was filled with workbenches and sharpening stations. Dozens of wheelbarrows leaned against each other and the right wall. Most of the equipment was still out in front of the shed.

Harald stepped back outside into the oppressive heat to take inventory of the returning workers' gear. It was his job to check off each implement on a list as each laborer turned his in. What little rain that usually fell this time of year had not yet arrived forcing the dwarves to carry water from the slowly evaporating river a few miles to the south. It was tedious work the Rock Lords made even more difficult. The dwarves pulled two-wheeled carts over the uneven terrain; the only rest allowed was when they stopped to fill the jugs with water. A pair of Rock Lords and their Dribbies flanked Harald, their whips and clubs at the ready. The dwarves dragged the tools behind them, the furrows in the dirt crisscrossing one another, their glassy eyes focused on the dusty ground. They formed a straggling line as they waited to hand over their tools, many using the handles to lean on. Harald used a dirty rag to wipe the sweat off his face then blotted a few drops from his list.

"You!" the crack of a whip broke the silence. "Scrape that dirt off the shovel!"

Harald looked over at the aged dwarf, his white hair matted to his head and his ragged shirt hanging loosely from his thin chest. Blood appeared on his sunken cheek, the whip barely missed his eye. The old dwarf turned the shovel around and, with gnarled fingers picked off the tiny clumps of soil before handing the tool to Harald. Harald watched him shuffle away, his bent form and depressed spirit something all the dwarves would someday face. *Whistler! Where did you go? When will you come back and relieve us of this nightmare?*

Harald glanced up at the long line waiting to hand over their gear then beyond it. Several Rock Lords came galloping in at full speed shouting at the top of their lungs. The dwarves and their guards turned to face the riders. They sped up the main street, their terrified mounts sending chunks of soil into the air. Harald gaped at the cruel claw marks along one of the horse's sides, its blood spattering him as it hurtled past. The panic-stricken features of the rider and his frightened shouts sent chills up his spine.

"Run! Devils on the way...run and hide!"

"Lock this up and go to your cabins," one of the guards ordered before they headed back the way the horsemen had come.

Harald held the bolt in his hand but his attention was riveted on the dusty plains beyond the edge of the camp. The guards were nearing the last few buildings when they stopped, turned and ran back. The Dribbies yanked the leashes out of their handlers' hands, whining and yelping as they ran up the street. The Rock Lords split up, each one running down a different alleyway. Faint snarling and howling noises drifted toward him, sounds not even a Dribbie could make. Harald felt the hair on his nape rise and his innards twist into knots.

"Everyone! Come to the shed!" Harald screamed at the top of his lungs, "Hurry! *Hurry!*"

The dwarves raced to gather as many people together as possible. They helped the infirm and those weakened by too little food and too much work into the building where Harald and a few others ushered them inside. Dozens of dwarves avoided colliding with Rock Lords both on foot and atop frightened horses as they streamed toward the structure. No longer leashed, the scared Dribbies attacked anything that moved, biting one moment then scurrying away the next with their tails between their legs. Horses threw riders then bolted away; dwarves and Rock Lords pushed and shoved each other to rush away or enter the shed. There was yelling, shouting and thick dust rising everywhere, obscuring everything.

Harald coughed and tried to wipe the fine particles out of his eyes as he pushed frightened stragglers inside the building. The minutes seemed like hours and his fear increased with every second. Then, from somewhere close by, he heard a sound that prompted him to retreat into the building and slam the door shut. He slid the heavy bar across through the iron brackets and listened to the menacing growls and frenzied whimpers intensifying outside. Someone banged on the door begging to be let inside, his pleas swiftly silenced. Harald backed away from the tearing and ripping sounds and shuddered as fingernails ceased scratching on the doorway.

Those inside the building knotted together, their bodies trembling and chests heaving as they faced the well-built walls around them. Harald looked around and guessed there were sixty or seventy dwarves and about a dozen Rock Lords present. Whatever lurked beyond the walls continued to slaughter those still outside but now began to strike at the shed. There was only one small window up near the roof and it was open.

The grime on Harald's face smeared as he wiped away the perspiration. The muted light glowing faintly around the window disappeared behind a shadow, and then a malformed head peered down at them with its hideous eyes.

"Grab anything that's sharp," he barked, "and keep those unable to defend themselves in the middle."

They strong grabbed hoes, rakes and pick axes then formed a circle around the vulnerable. Some peered up at the opening while others watched as the creatures tried to work one of the planks loose from the outside. It held but the thing scrabbling down the rough-hewn wall inside screeched to its evil brethren. The dwarves blocked their ears to keep out the high-pitched shrieks. They ignored the barrier, intent on protecting themselves from the fiends squeezing their misshapen bodies through the opening. They crawled down the walls as effortlessly as insects.

The dwarves attacked the demons, hacking and stabbing at their hideous bodies. They screamed in agony as the fiends' black blood splattered on them, immediately blistering their skin. One of the Rock Lords shattered a demon's skull with his club while a dwarf fighting beside him swung a rake into another monster. The dwarf twisted the handle and forced the iron teeth into its midsection, then yanked out its entrails with one quick jerk of the handle. It howled in pain and fury until the Rock Lord smashed its head. The demons clawed and bit anything that moved, even each other, the need to slaughter their sole reason for existing.

Harald glanced up at the dark gap then screamed as blood landed on his cheek and neck.

***

Elena reached out to her left, her fingers seeking the rock-hard body she had slept beside for so many years. Her hand moved through empty air, the forlorn feeling bringing her to wakefulness. She opened her eyes and stared at the bare ground. It wavered for a moment then disappeared, replaced by an image forever etched into her mind...

She had awakened the day after they had first been intimate. Whistler's passion for her had been gentle yet all consuming; a controlled fire that burned without scorching. It reached down into her very soul and bound them together, the connection beyond the reach of the Rock Lords or even of death.

Whistler wasn't in bed with her. She sat up, rubbing the sleep from her eyes when suddenly she spied him as he walked toward her with one arm behind his back and wearing a huge grin across his face. His eyes twinkled with a rare joy as he held out his hand and presented her with a small cup filled with honey. She had placed her hand across her mouth to stifle a giggle when he peered into the mug and plucked out a bee, which promptly stung him on the finger. They had laughed while she removed the stinger then dabbed at the swelling with a cool cloth. She didn't have the heart to tell him she disliked honey, but she spread it across her bread and ate it every day until it was gone...

"Elena?"

The dwarf blinked her eyes several times and smiled at August crouching down beside her, a mug of tea in his hands. He handed it to her then reached into his pocket and pulled out the jar of strawberry marmalade. She offered August a warm smile of appreciation. She opened the lid and scooped out a mouthful of sweetness.

They ate breakfast then returned to observe the tower. Taman peeked through the trees and brush but there was no sign of the red mist.

"What happened to you yesterday?" Garadan asked Taman.

"I think the power was seeking a host."

"Do you think it'll try that again?" inquired Elena, frightened at the thought of that vapor infusing itself into one of them.

"It has already determined that none of us are suitable," replied the elf. "We have to go and get it."

"But...the soldiers, they're still camped on the mainland side of the causeway!" said Elena. "There's no other way to get to the structure."

The sun illuminated the craggy cliff, the deep fissures rising vertically up from the hissing waves crashing against the boulders. The areas near the ocean were concave and would eventually erode all the way through.

"A diversion," suggested Garadan. "Get them to chase us while somebody grabs the magic."

"We don't know the land, Garadan," August reminded him. "Besides, whoever retrieves it will still be seen."

"Not if we cross at night," proposed Taman.

"How are we supposed to maneuver across the land bridge in the dark?" Elena stared upward, calculating distances.

Garadan scrutinized the causeway. The camp spread out at the forefront of the peninsula of bare land near some trees and bushes and, just beyond was an open area. Boulders and rangy grasses cluttered the section leading up to the tower. The only place offering no cover was between the soldiers and halfway out onto the precipice.

"All of the guards won't follow us but those that stay behind will undoubtedly watch," August stated. "You might be able to sneak past them if you're fast enough."

"Taman, how are you going to handle the power?" asked Elena.

"What do you mean?"

"How will you control it?"

"I'm...I don't know. Mercator instructed us to collect the magic but he never said how."

"Well, we can at least piece together some sort of plan," Garadan began. "Taman and I will slip down near the edge of the camp near sunset and hide until dark. August and Elena will head south and skirt the encampment. You two will have to draw their attention away long enough for us to get to the reeds and boulders. We'll take the power and meet up with you."

"Garadan?"

"Yes, August?"

"Won't you need another distraction to get back across the causeway?"

"We'll have to make it on our own, my friend. It would be too risky to have you and Elena circle back to help us. Besides, the guards won't be expecting anyone to walk from the cliff."

"It might be a good idea to survey the area a little bit."

"We don't have time, August."

"We have most of the afternoon, Garadan. I could head south for an hour or so then loop around and be back before nightfall."

"*We* could be back before nightfall," corrected the captain.

"I think August is right," Elena interjected, "it would be far better to know what's out there if we have to make a hasty retreat."

"It's settled, then," August grabbed his pack and stood up, "I'll be back in a few hours."

Elena rummaged through her pack and handed each companion one of the fleshy yellow and green speckled plants and two smaller leaves each.

"This one," she pointed to the plump leaf, "will soothe and clean a wound. These," she held up the thumb-sized bits of green, "are to be chewed and will give you extra energy when you need it the most."

Garadan, Taman and Elena watched August slip away then turned their attention to the strangers at the bottom of the hill. Half of the men marched away by early afternoon, the rest left shortly thereafter. August had not yet returned.

* * *

Approaching cautiously, August kept the hillocks between himself and the men for over two miles before the ground flattened out. The graceful birches, poplars and young maple trees growing on the level land offered him some cover, as did some low-growing shrubs. August scanned the area, the rays filtering through the trees offering him ample light to make out many details. He noticed poison ivy clinging to a partially collapsed rock wall farther up ahead and, upon closer inspection, found overgrown pockets of vegetable plants scattered here and there. A hut slowly strangling beneath the weight of thick vines caught his attention, the stems weaving in through the broken windows and splintering floorboards. The creepers pushed out through the rotted roof and wound around the lopsided chimney.

He walked toward the wall and peered over to the other side. A wide pathway meandered past the property. Grass grew in a thin strip down the center, the dirt on either side compacted by heavy use. He decided to follow the road for a while before returning to his companions.

He sipped from his canteen, wiping his mouth with the back of his hand as he walked on. Insects chirped on either side of him and birds twittered in the branches overhead. He had traveled for about half a mile when the woods to his left suddenly opened up. He crouched down and peered through the last of the undergrowth at a pale gray wall. He cautiously worked his way toward it then flattened himself against it and looked up, immediately wishing he had opted not to survey the route.

A guard leaned against his spear at the corner of the turret, casually looking out past August to the path. August's decision to leave the road where he did was sheer luck. Leaving the road a few yards farther on would have placed him directly in the sentry's line of vision. August had seen enough. He was about to head back when the sound of voices and boots treading heavily on hard ground reached his ears. He slithered down into a crouch and backed away from the guards' line of sight just in time. A contingent of men marched past him wearing blood-spattered white tunics and feathers in their helmets.

August waited for nearly a half-hour to make sure there were no stragglers before slipping back onto the road. He dove for safety twice more as smaller groups of men ambled past. He passed a shadowy farmhouse, the empty windows and fallen door reminding him of a skull. He shivered and increased his pace, the sun sinking more rapidly than he wanted it to. His stomach growled and his parched mouth demanded water. Sweat began to drip down his face even though the night was cool. He should have been back hours ago, before his absence altered their plan.

Stars became visible in the purple sky. Howls and grunts emerged from the darkening woodland. He couldn't have traveled that far from the others. He should already have met up with them. The men leaving would cancel out the need to create a diversion unless some of the guards remained behind. The last of the light disappeared replaced with a dismal fogginess and then it started to rain. He cursed under his breath and looked about for some suitable shelter. He could just make out the dilapidated hut he had seen earlier and headed for it.

August placed his foot on the step and eased his weight onto the board. It snapped in half, the sharp cracking sound echoing throughout the woods. He pulled his foot out and ducked down but there was no one around to hear. The rain became more intense, slanting down from the west. He walked around to the east side of the building and spotted the outline of an eave. He decided it was better to be outside than to take a chance the cabin might fall down on his head during the night. He lay on the moss-covered ground and pulled his hood up, the bushes and briars around the lean-to keeping him well hidden. A terrible odor awakened him near midnight. August could have sworn he smelled burning hair and meat. The stink became stronger as the night progressed, eliciting a number of chilling thoughts. He finally gave up trying to sleep and stared into the forest for the rest of the night.

He wondered how Clay and Sara were faring. Nearly two weeks had passed since they had traveled through the mountains to the north. August missed them both very much but his mind strayed to a pale and delicate face with shining silver eyes. The corners of his mouth turned up a little at the memory. He had no right to think of just Sara. His friends and companions were out there, possibly in danger, and he was sitting here wondering how she was coping with everything. He sighed, the feeling of helplessness worming its way into his mind.

* * *

"We should go look for him," Elena pleaded with Garadan and Taman, "he could be hurt or worse, captured."

"We want to know how he's faring, too, Elena, but we have the perfect opportunity to get the magic!"

"Taman is right. We go to the tower, take it, and then go meet up with August."

"Let's hurry," she said after several long moments.

The trio scampered down the hill, careful not to walk too close to the edge. The drop down to the jagged rocks and pounding surf would have seemed like an eternity. They grasped onto branches and roots during the steep sections as their feet dislodged stones and chunks of soil. Garadan stepped onto a decaying trunk perched near the bottom third of the hill. All three skidded down the side, the dirt and debris-laden avalanche nearly burying them at the bottom. They spit the soil out of their mouths and shook it free from their hair and clothes. Garadan checked the area for any laggards before they moved on.

The sun was setting when they reached the lengthening shadows shrouding the entrance to the causeway. Charred pits held still glowing ashes and animal bones. A once-white feather swirled back and forth in another singed hollow. The grass lay flat in some places and torn up in divots in others.

"Elena and I will go in," Taman said in low tones, "you wait here."

The companions eyed the tower rising about a hundred yards ahead of them. The setting sun's rays fell upon the black rock but even the soft, golden light could not penetrate the bleak surface. Elena and Taman inhaled and exhaled deeply then moved forward.

They walked carefully, treading over loose stones and cracks on the cliff's surface. They pressed on, the edifice looming larger with every step they took. They stopped and turned around but their companion was lost in the shadows behind them. The dwarf reached out and slipped her hand into Taman's, squeezing it reassuringly.

They continued on, eyeing the narrowing pathway. More and more of the ocean came into view on either side of them. They could taste the salty mist and feel the precipice shaking with every wave crashing against it. They were about fifty yards away when the trail tapered to a couple of yards across, the worn away arch directly beneath. The moon gradually materialized within the rich fading hues, its weak light barely discernible in the sky.

Taman placed first one foot then the other on the stone bridge, testing it with his weight before moving on. It held firm but bits of debris trickled down with every wave's impact. The wind swirled all around him showering him with droplets cast up by the force of the sea. A powerful gust of wind nearly knocked him into the churning sea below. He dropped into a crouch and waited for it to die down before covering the last few yards to the other side. Adrenaline raced in his veins as he wiped away the water from his face.

Elena swallowed hard and took her first step, the buffeting wind pushing at her from first one side then to the other. Her eyes were wide and her breathing came in quick gasps. The tower blocked out the stars,

THE FORTRESS OF DARKNESS

a black rift in the heavens sending a shiver of fear through her. She glanced down at the ocean, the glowing foam hissing as it beat against the rocks. It was an unearthly light, not white but a pale, icy blue. She concentrated on the unstable span beneath her feet. The erratic drafts pushed at her from all sides. She fought to maintain her balance then decided to crawl the rest of the way. Taman helped her up, the two of them holding on to each other to catch their breath and calm their nerves. There were only a few yards between them and the tall spire perched at the edge of the cliff. The walls looked smooth yet cracks spider-webbed all along its sides.

It was fortunate they decided to linger when they did.

Taman watched the red mist emerge from the ground around the base. It formed itself into thick tendrils and slithered up the tower, erratically following the cracks to the top. It crept into the opening at the very top without acknowledging the mortals clinging to one another. The elf exhaled with relief. He looked at Elena, a strand of loose hair whipping around her face and nodded.

They walked around the base searching for an entrance. Nothing but impenetrable rock greeted them. They inched their way toward the side overlooking the ocean, mindful of the few yards separating them from the hundred-foot drop. The faint moonlight didn't so much illuminate the opening as much as it thrust it into deeper shadow. Taman took a deep breath and headed for it, his hands reaching out in every direction to detect any overhanging rock. Elena grabbed onto his tunic and followed him in.

A diffused red light lit the interior of the tower growing more intense as it neared the top. In the center stood a spiral staircase carved out of the core of the rock, the uneven steps disappearing into the crimson glow at the apex. The walls were coarse and unadorned, the deep recesses emitting sharp snapping and irregular grating sounds.

Elena shuddered with trepidation, her grip on Taman tightening. She glanced at the elf's profile, the red radiance giving him a surreal appearance. His features were more pronounced one moment then blurred the next but the only thing that didn't change were his eyes. The roiling gray clouds had returned and smothered the whites. He focused them on the uppermost portion of the structure.

"Stay here," he said then moved toward the staircase, Elena's hands still clutching the air where his tunic had been moments before. Taman did not see her back up. She pressed her body against the bumpy wall, waiting fearfully in the shadows of the tower.

Taman picked his way over the debris as he headed for the flight of steps. He reached the center after a few minutes, the winding steps partially enclosed by a waist high wall that was broken in many places. He placed his foot on the first step and began to climb, always scanning the path ahead. The staircase kept coiling ever upward, the elf occasionally hanging on to overhangs in the core to steady himself while scrambling up over several missing steps. He glanced over to the entranceway searching for Elena but her figure was lost in the shadows.

He continued on, the stairway becoming narrower the farther he ascended. A chill seeped downward, the cold air infused with musty and slightly acrid odors. The luminosity shining from above deepened until it took on the hue of freshly spilled blood. It bathed him in the same colored light until everything he looked at was an intense crimson shade. He stopped climbing near the top then poked his head through the opening.

The only thing he saw in the open space was a flat-topped stone altar in the very center. The dim light of the moon reflected off something positioned on top of the slab. Taman walked over to investigate. He shivered as he stared at the flattened glass urn with the broken seal, flames fashioned from silver extended from the base to the band around its neck. The crimson haze flowed out of the partially unfastened mouth and snaked down the stone table. Its freedom was short-lived because the bottle seemed to suck the magic back inside of itself moments later. Taman squinted at the glass container. There was something along its rim. He moved closer then trod around to the other side for a better view. The black, brittle wax seal had split in half, barely clinging to the lip. It reeked of sulfur and rot and drew him toward the black void.

Taman fought the pull into the in-between world but the demon's power was too strong. The rock upon which he was standing began to lose its hardness and the haze faded to a garish pink hue. The frostiness in the tower was preferable to the iciness of the void.

"*Can't...let it...take hold of me!*"

The frozen air oozed down into his lungs threatening to encase his words in ice and forever lock them in his throat. He struggled against the river's powerful current, the sweat freezing to his skin. He dropped to his hands and knees, his face twisted in pain and a fearful grimace. All of his tendons stood out in the gaudy light as he exerted every ounce of energy to withdraw from the abyss.

The infinite darkness finally released him. He fell to the floor with a thud breathing in deep draughts of air. He raised his spinning head and approached the urn, gazing at it for a while before reaching out, his fingers poised over the neck and lid. He waited for the red mist to retreat into the urn then grabbed the container and slammed the lid tightly into place. He touched the seal and immediately let go. Tiny blisters erupted on his fingertips, the searing pain shooting up his arm. He stuck his thumb and forefinger into his mouth to relieve the pain. Taman stared long and hard at the sinister ring that had been on the urn and thought of the evil that had handled it. Lightning flashed and muted thunder faltered in the distance. Rain suddenly poured from the heavens and spilled through the window instantly forming a large puddle. It surged toward the altar then down the staircase.

Taman looked down at his reflection in the water and cringed at we he saw. Dark circles reflected his shadowy sockets and the furrows on his forehead appeared sinister. A brilliant flash of lightning and an immediate crash of thunder seemed to accentuate his ghostly façade.

"Taman?" A faint cry brought him out of his reverie. He tucked the urn into his belt and left the chamber. He never looked back as he carefully descended the treacherous staircase. He spotted Elena at the bottom, her hands clutching her elbows, the lines on her face appearing deep in the eerie light. She rushed forward and grasped his arms.

"What happened up there?"

Taman was about to answer her when an ominous rumbling reverberated through the cliff. The rock foundation shifted ever so slightly. Fine, powder-like debris sprinkled down on their heads. Elena sneezed; Taman coughed. He seized her hand and yanked her back toward the entranceway. The stone around the exit cracked and dropped forcing the pair to twist sideways to get around it. They ran around the base of the tower, the heaving ocean drenching them with spray. The salt water stung their eyes and the downpour plastered their clothing to their skin. They kept close to the structure until small rocks and loosened sections began to bounce down its sides. One hit Elena's thigh sending her sprawling onto the rough ground. Lightning erupted all around them illuminating the bizarre scene. Taman immediately helped her up. They ventured closer to the rim of the cliff until large chunks broke off and plummeted into the roiling sea below. The elf shoved Elena away from crumbling edge seconds before it gave way, his foot slipping off the brink and into the air. He rotated to his right, the force of his weight launching him away from the lip. He fell onto the ground wincing in pain as sharp pebbles cut into his left side. He staggered upright, limped forward and they continued on, the platform dwindling in size.

They skidded to a halt in front of the stone bridge.

"You go first!" he shouted but she could barely hear him over the falling rock and thunder. She looked at him, her head cocked to the side so that she could hear him better. Taman pushed her onto the bridge and gestured for her to hurry.

Elena scurried across as fast as she could. She thought she sensed Taman moving behind her but feared turning around for even one second to double-check. She concentrated on the murky link to the mainland below her feet and allowed herself brief peeks of her goal up ahead. *Just a few more feet...* The mountainside suddenly lurched.

She cried out, dropping into a crouch, her fingers digging for a handhold. She scratched until her nails cracked, the oozing blood causing her fingers to slide over the surface. Her heart beat wildly; tears rolled down her face. She pitched back and forth, the scream in her throat ready to split the night in two. Then, a pair of hands came out of the darkness and steadied her. Elena found strength in his touch and stood up. She scampered across the last few feet, hurtling onto the mainland just as the bridge collapsed beneath her.

"Taman!" she shrieked as she landed in a clump of grasses. She bolted to her feet and ran back to the edge.

Taman could wait no longer. They both had to use the bridge at the same time if they had any hope of escaping the collapsing point. He saw Elena's form in front of him then the elevated rock path began to buckle and shake. He caught up with her, encouraging her to resume her flight. She did and had made it across the second the stone ramp shuddered once, then twice and shattered beneath him. He dashed forward, his hands clutching for anything that would catch him but all he grabbed was air. His horizontal motion transformed into a vertical one. He was falling, falling to his death. His body would splinter upon impact and the sea would pull him into her depths. It was over, for him, at least, at last.

An iron grip slowed his descent into the inevitable, his shoulder snapping out of its socket bringing him completely back. He grimaced in agony as he dangled by his arm over the precipice, the ocean vomiting up volumes of water and spray to hasten his plunge to death. Taman's face grew hotter by the moment, the fierce, stabbing pain shooting through his whole body. *Must have…gotten hand caught in a fissure…need to release it!* The sharp edges of the cliff tore at his clothes and sliced into his skin as something suddenly hauled him upward. *Elena! Did she have the strength to get him over the edge?*

Taman steadied himself with his other hand, the abrasions washed clean by the rainfall. The water cooled his overheated face and body but could do nothing for the throbbing in his shoulder. He squinted as his head peeked over the edge then offered Garadan and Elena a pain-filled smile. They each grabbed one arm and towed him over the rim then away from the crumbling cliff. Garadan seized his hurt arm and gave it a decisive tug. The trio could hear the shoulder pop back into the socket even with all the noises exploding around them. Taman took in deep draughts of air, his perspiration mingling with the rain and vapor.

"Let's go!" shouted Garadan as he and Elena helped Taman off the parapet. They passed the camp, the fire pits filled in with water and the now-filthy feather partially stuck in the mud. They didn't care where they spent the night as long as it wasn't near the causeway.

-13-

Whistler and his companions reined in their horses a few miles west of the compound, the circling buzzards flying ever closer and more tightly over something in the distance. Then, one by one, they landed. Tarz sat ramrod straight on the back of his horse. Clay swallowed hard. May nuzzled an apprehensive Sara. Whistler's eyes narrowed. They moved forward as one, the closer they came to the sprawled heaps the stronger the smell of death became. The huge birds with the featherless heads and necks took to the sky, their harsh cries loud even from a distance.

They halted about a dozen paces away. The scene mirrored the one in front of Evan's Peak. The churned up ground and discarded, partially gnawed limbs led toward the compound. The scavengers descended upon the macabre feast off in the distance.

"Why are they moving in this direction?" Tarz demanded after a long silence.

"They are the least of your worries, Tarz," replied Sara.

"What do you mean?" he ordered.

"They are at the forefront of an even greater evil," stated Clay as he mounted his horse. "What follows will make this seem trivial."

"The demon Emhella will not be far behind, Tarz. We must secure the magic before he does or every living thing will meet this same fate."

"Why not find the power and use it against him?"

"Each power was created to conform to a specific Race, Tarz. It won't respond to another's touch."

"Then why is he seeking them, Sara?"

"We don't really know the answer to that question, Tarz," Clay said, his hesitant voice filled with a weariness not solely due to the long journey.

"What about them?" asked Tarz pointing at the corpses.

"They are the lucky ones," replied Sara.

The trio rode alongside the gruesome trail. The camp lay approximately two miles farther east and none of the riders dared speculate what they would find there. They caught glimpses of low, hulking shapes in the distance but could not see any movement.

"No patrols," muttered Tarz.

Whistler felt his stomach tighten. The Rock Lords continuously made the rounds of the perimeter of the camp yet no sounds drifted out to them, not even the Dribbies' choked growls. Carrion birds suddenly took flight from the compound.

"Sweet mercy," Clay breathed with dread. "We're too late. Whistler?"

The dwarf stared in horror at the silent buildings looming larger with every passing moment. The wind blew from the west kicking up dust devils and pushing small, round clumps of grasses down the streets. Whistler pulled out his hoe blade as they rode past the first of the buildings. He could hear metal blades sliding out of scabbards and see the sun's rays glinting off Clay's and Tarz' weapons. Their distorted silhouettes continued to lengthen until their disfigured heads and shoulders fell upon the first of the bodies.

The Rock Lords and dwarves had suffered equally. Hooves and feet had dug up large portions of the road revealing the darker sod below the firmly packed tan soil. Red stained drag marks discolored the dirt; bloody handprints covered doors and broken windows. They moved further into the compound, the grisly scene repeating itself. They halted near the tool shed, the faint hope of finding any survivors fading with the daylight.

"The fiends are moving very quickly," noted Sara.

"They would have reached the Hall by now," Tarz stated.

"Is anybody here?" shouted Whistler. "Anyone?"

The wind blew in between the buildings carrying with it the sound of faint weeping and muffled whispers.

"I am Tarz. Are there any Rock Lords about?"

Something slid along the storage shed inner wall to their left and crashed to the floor. Metal crashed into metal, the reverberation harsh in their ears. The trio flinched; their horses shied away from the structure. Footsteps neared the door then the sound of wood sliding across wood emanated from behind the entry. The heavy door creaked open. A ghostly face peered from the dark gap.

"You are all in danger! Run...hide!" a voice shrieked from within, the panic barely contained.

"It's over, the fiends have gone," Whistler calmly called out to them. His heart pounded in his throat as Harald slowly emerged from the building. Harald's forehead, left cheek and neck were raw and blistered, his clothing shredded and befouled with blood and clumps of greasy black fur. Many dwarves and a handful of Rock Lords slowly emerged from the shed, most unharmed. Harald looked over at Tarz, confusion and mistrust radiating from his eyes.

"It's all right, Harald," Whistler walked over and embraced him, "we all share the same dilemma. How many are hurt?"

"About a dozen. There are seven dead inside, Whistler."

Whistler and his companions watched as the building emptied out, the horrified faces of both dwarf and Rock Lord growing as they absorbed the atrocity in the streets. A dwarf knelt on the churned up ground holding the body of her loved one. Other dwarves identified their family and friends and soon the sound of weeping rose up into the otherwise quiet air.

"We'll tend to the wounded and care for our dead," Whistler said, his haunted gaze sweeping over the terrible scene.

They spent several hours collecting the bodies, first by the fading light then by torches. They placed all the bodies in a pile and burned them, the stench being driven eastward by the wind. Wolves lugged away those who had fallen at the perimeter, their howls echoing beneath the star-encrusted heavens. A charcoal gray wall began to blot out the stars as it moved in from the west. Thunder rumbled way off in the distance then grew silent. Rain began to fall onto the camp for the first time in many weeks. Some of the dwarves and Rock Lords finished their gruesome task while others cleaned out the storage building. Some of the dwarves worked on the shed, bringing in bedding and food, reinforcing the window and door in case the demons returned. They all finally crowded together inside near midnight, the steady rain washing away the nightmare out in the streets.

Tarz, Whistler, Harald, Clay and Sara sat around one of the fires outside, the flames reflecting off the makeshift awning. The dark circles under their eyes stood out starkly against their ashen faces. Whistler recounted his and Elena's flight from the compound, their meeting with the elves and the others, and the trip over to Mercator's realm. Clay described the trek to Evan's Peak, how they met up with Tarz and the terrible spectacles that led to the camp. No one spoke for the longest time.

"I knew you'd come back, Whistler."

"That was my only priority, Harald, but this isn't what I had in mind when I left."

"More demons will come," Sara stated, trying to rub the tiredness from her face, "but this time their master will be at the forefront. What happened here today is nothing compared to what will occur when he arrives."

"What will we do?" asked Harald dabbing a wet cloth against his raw skin.

"We can't stay here," Whistler and Tarz said at the same time. They exchanged a quick glance.

"We have to try and find a safe place for everyone," the dwarf muttered, as if to himself.

"Evan's Peak," muttered Clay.

"What?" asked Whistler.

"Evan's Peak. The demons traveled east...here, look." Clay drew a crude map in the dirt marking Bystyn, Evan's Peak, the compound and, with a little help from Tarz, the Hall and Daimoryia. "The demons killed the Rock Lord party here, at the base of Evan's Peak. They moved to the south and east to the compound, here, and seem to be heading to the Hall, here."

"What's your point?" asked Tarz.

"Did they ravage the elves in and around Bystyn? If they didn't then will the second wave led by Emhella wreak havoc on them?"

"Emhella's prime concern is retrieving all of the magic," Sara chimed in. "Once he has them his monsters will be free to roam the land and kill at will."

"Maybe we can arm ourselves against them," suggested Tarz.

"You've seen what they are capable of," Whistler's contempt for the Rock Lord surfaced shortly.

"What if the demons come back?" Harald's voice shook with fear. "What are we supposed to do? Lock ourselves in the storage building again?"

"If that's what we have to do to survive then yes," replied Whistler.

"We need an alternate plan, dwarf."

Whistler turned toward Tarz, the familiar vitriol rising in his throat once again. The Rock Lord was right, however. They needed a strategy in case more demons made their way into the camp. Whistler sighed heavily. He would have to accompany Tarz, Sara and Clay to the Hall and get hold of the magic. It would be up to the survivors to fend for themselves while they were gone.

Harald, I need you to be in charge while I'm gone. It'll be up to you to make sure our people stay safe. Tarz will assign one of the Rock Lords to work with you, won't you, Tarz?"

"Kemat!" Tarz called one of the remaining Rock Lords over to them after a few moments of silent thought.

"Yes, Tarz," Kemat offered him a curt bow.

"How many men are left in the camp?"

"Seventeen. Most fled when those things came in."

"You and Harald will insure the safety of everyone who is left, understand?"

"Work with the slaves?" Kemat's eyes widened, his expression incredulous.

Tarz placed his hand on Whistler's shoulder as the dwarf rose to confront Kemat, his face beginning to turn crimson. "You will do as I command or I'll slice your throat open right here and now."

Kemat nodded, the low, raspy threat not lost on him. The Rock Lord gave Tarz an even tighter bow and left to pass the command on to his men.

"When do we leave for the Hall?"

"Sunrise tomorrow," replied Clay, "and we had best be cautious or our bodies will become food for scavengers."

They were ready to leave before the first faint rays stained the murky sky. Thick gray clouds bulging with rain seemed to brush the treetops in the distance, the heavy air threatening to smother them. The wind had shifted from the northeast during the night bringing with it an unexpected chill. Whistler leaned over and gave Harald a pat on his shoulder. Harald was awake instantly, a half-smile on his face.

The four companions headed east toward the Hall. No one looked back. It didn't take long for them to see the leftovers of the fiends' slaughter. Thankfully, however, predators and scavengers had dragged away most of the evidence leaving dried puddles and pieces of cloth. They stayed on the dirt roadway leading to the Hall. Years of carts passing along the thoroughfare left deep grooves in the hard soil, and the animals had eaten all the leaves and grasses along the road. What stood out the most, however, was the silence. No birds, insects, or creatures broke it.

They halted at noon and let their horses rest for a while. The carnage had ceased by this time though none of them believed it had ended all together. They had no idea what lay in store for them once they neared the Hall. Did the demons circumvent the Hall or did they butcher everyone within it? If the fiends had slain everyone in the Hall, had they moved on or were they still there?

Thunder grumbled ominously in the distance goading the rain to fall from the gloomy underbellies of the clouds. The foursome donned their light cloaks and flipped their hoods up seconds before the first droplets fell. The rain started lightly then came down in torrents. There was no place to seek shelter from the deluge so they mounted up and continued. The soil could not absorb the water and quickly turned to mud. The horses slogged through it, the mire covering both animal and rider. Tarz shook his head in disgust and pointed toward a cluster of trees off to their right. It took ten minutes to reach them.

They crowded together beneath the wide boughs but even the dense branches couldn't keep the downpour at bay. They stood underneath, forced to tolerate their soggy clothing. The horses snorted irritably, the riders' temperament not much better.

Clay stared off into the distance lost in thought. It occurred to Clay that he had never asked what August did with his time while he was on the island. August was just at the pier whenever Clay had sailed into port, ready to follow him wherever Clay chose to go. August never complained about the direction Clay chose for them to travel, he would simply shrug his shoulders and wave Clay on ahead.

Clay glanced over at Sara. She and Taman carried heavy burdens, which Clay could not or wanted to imagine. That didn't stop August from liking the demon girl, though. He accepted her for who she was and that was something Sara had to learn about herself. Perhaps the feelings she had for August would eventually allow her to open up to him. August, he knew, would wait forever for her to do just that.

Sara closed her eyes and concentrated on that frightful place beyond the realm of the present. She dreaded standing on the shore of that fearsome river but she needed to pinpoint the magic. She waited for a long time at the brink of that ominous place but it refused to grant her access. She exhaled slowly; relief at not having to enter it began to flood through her being when a vague emerald mist flashed to life. It flickered as briefly as a firefly then was gone. May crawled out from the pack and up into Sara's hood. Sara reached up and tried to coax her onto her hand but the spider remained on her shoulder. May's listlessness had grown with every passing mile and her sporadic forays for food left Sara uneasy. The spider hadn't hunted for many days now yet she managed to grow gradually larger and larger.

Sara grabbed a bug flying by and offered it to May but the spider pushed it away with one of her legs. Sara tried again then frowned as May climbed down her arm and burrowed into Clay's pouch.

"Is she ill?"

"I don't know, Clay," Sara lifted the flap and peered down into the pack at the lethargic spider, "she hasn't eaten anything for a while."

Clay peeked inside; May languidly looked back up at him. He lowered his finger and received a half-hearted pat in return. He gave Sara a reassuring smile.

"She's just as tired and anxious as we are, Sara."

"You're probably right," she replied in a small voice.

The rain abated in the late afternoon. The foursome decided when it cleared to mount up and continue on their trek to the Hall. The sun poked through the clouds and heated the waterlogged land, a fine haze forming all around them. The humidity became oppressive. A tree-lined pathway awaited them up ahead; the cool shadows a welcome relief to the travelers.

"How much farther, Tarz?"

"We should reach the Hall soon, Clay." Tarz replied as he studied the road ahead.

"What's wrong?" demanded Whistler.

"There should be patrols along this thoroughfare."

No one asked the question screaming in their heads but they did scan the dirt trail for evidence they wished they wouldn't find. They saw nothing but that did not stop the fear they all felt. They moved on, the horses snorting nervously and jerking their heads from side to side.

The trees began to thin out and the path widened until it split off into several directions. Tarz kept to the middle-most route, his eyes constantly searching the area around them. They rode out onto a wide expanse of ground where a tall, octagonal building sat in the center of the open section. Dark wooden planks encased the first floor; dirty gray plaster swirled to create spiny points covered the upper half of the structure. Three dark and empty slit windows ran along each side on the upper floors and double that amount were on the bottom story. Poles holding limp banners marked every corner along the top of the building. Numerous rough-hewn houses sat clustered off in the distance; dwellings covered in stucco and edged with dark wood surrounded the Hall. There wasn't a single, well-planned roadway into or out of the city. They saw nothing but a series of worn paths that meandered throughout without rhyme or reason.

"It's like they abandoned everything," Clay finally broke the disconcerting stillness.

"Is anyone here?" Tarz shouted.

Irregularly shaped humps lay scattered beyond the first few rows of buildings. The only things that stirred around the lumps were large birds and a few animals. Mourning doves took to flight, their wings whistling noisily against the subdued background. Tarz called several more times with the same result.

"Could the demons have killed everyone here?" asked Clay twisting in his saddle to look around.

"I doubt it," Whistler stated, "there were those back at the camp who managed to survive by running into the woods."

"Let's go," Tarz said, his voice low and threatening.

They crossed the grassy stretch and neared the Hall, the peculiar outlines taking on a terrifying yet expected appearance. The foursome tried not to look at the tainted plaster on the houses near the hall, but couldn't ignore the handprints smeared along the walls. They halted several yards away from the entry into the Hall, the huge wooden double-doors standing slightly ajar.

"One of you must stay outside," Tarz ordered as he dismounted and walked up to the doors.

Whistler and Sara got off their horses and followed Tarz to the entrance leaving Clay to stand guard. Tarz pushed on the door but something was wedged against it from the other side. Whistler added his brawn and the two of them managed to open it far enough to squeeze through.

It took a few moments for their eyes to adjust to the gloominess; the few torches still lit casting about a murky light. The room reeked of death. The metallic taste of blood and the potent smell of urine hung heavily in the air. They each headed towards a brand, tripping over bodies and slipping on the sticky liquids along the way.

Sara carefully tiptoed over the vague outlines sprawled on the floor, her torch just a few feet away. She reached up, her hand inches from the holder when something grabbed her foot. A choked scream erupted from her throat as she immediately withdrew her black blades.

"Wait!" Whistler called out to her as he held his torch over the bulge on the ground.

THE FORTRESS OF DARKNESS

A Rock Lord holding in his innards with one hand grasped Sara's foot with the other.

"Help...me..."

Tarz stared dispassionately down at the poor wretch then brought his sword down across the dying man's neck. Air escaped from the gash as the man lay still.

Sara peeled the Rock Lord's fingers off her ankle and snatched the torch from the wall bracket. She turned around until the faint green haze glinted fleetingly before her eyes. She walked in the direction of the obscure light, her focus straight ahead, and her feet treading over the bodies without ever looking down.

Whistler and Tarz glanced at each other then followed her down the hall to the throne room. They withdrew their weapons, cautiously passing dark recesses and partially open doors. Sara never turned her head in either direction. She stopped at the closed entry to the heart of the Hall then pushed down on the hefty bronze handle. It wouldn't budge.

"It must be barred from the inside," Tarz whispered to the dwarf.

Whistler didn't respond. The demons certainly wouldn't bother to lock it, which meant that some of the Rock Lords might still be alive. This reunion should be an interesting one. *Well, Kevlan, the object of your obsession is right outside your door.*

"Is there another way in?"

"Follow me," Tarz spoke quietly as he led them to a column to the left of the main doors. He turned to the side and squeezed himself between the pillar and the wall. Whistler and Sara followed suit, the demon girl slipping behind them, peering out over the main entrance hall one more time before rejoining them. The only light penetrating the passageway came in through the cracks around the support beams by the ceiling. Odd patches of light illuminated bits of dust and gauzy spider-webs. Rats scampered out of their way, occasionally running over their feet in the process.

Something crunched under Whistler's feet, and his mouth turned down with disgust. He kept close to Tarz' vague outline as the Rock Lord continued. The dwarf focused on the back of Tarz' indistinct head, the urge to bring down his hoe blade on Tarz' head nearly overwhelming him.

How wonderful would that be? To kill one of his enemies within the mighty Hall! Whistler was so engrossed in his daydream that he failed to see Tarz' unmoving silhouette. He bumped into the Rock Lord, Sara knocking into Whistler a second later.

Tarz hissed a warning. They stood silently in the murky passage, listening intently for any danger. Grunts and low growls traveled down the stuffy passageway. Two distinct cracks followed by sucking sounds reverberated down the corridor.

Whistler forgot about Tarz' split head, concentrating instead on the demons up ahead. He felt Sara's hand resting on the small of his back then heard the sound of her dagger blades sliding out from their sheaths. There was barely room to maneuver down the passageway; a battle with the fiends would prove to be interesting at the very least. He heard the snarls becoming muffled then ceasing altogether. They moved forward cautiously, Tarz ready to defend them from the front and Sara's knives protecting them from the rear. Daylight bounced off the wall up ahead growing brighter the farther they traveled. It lit up the small alcove in front of the partially open door to the right, the scene as grisly as the others they had seen. They hugged the wall the last few yards before the doorway, careful not to disturb any remains.

Tarz eased forward, peeking into the throne room. Two demons picked through the dead. They defiled the throne by throwing up what they had eaten. Tarz took a deep breath and immediately regretted doing so. It took a great deal of control to keep what little he had in his stomach. He turned to his companions and held up two fingers. Sara and Whistler nodded in response.

They eased their way into the chamber, the fiends ignoring everything around them but the corpses. The trio crept up behind them, their blades ready to destroy the monstrous creatures. A few more feet and the deed would be done before the demons even looked up. Then Tarz slipped on a pool of deep crimson and came crashing down on his backside. The fiends were on top of him in a split second.

Whistler's hoe blade smashed into one of their skulls. Tarz' features twisted in agony as the black blood burned into his flesh. Whistler kicked the demon away with one foot, its evil brethren abandoning the

Rock Lord for the dwarf. It raked Whistler's chest shredding his tunic and flesh with one swift motion. The dwarf grabbed a nearby sword and swung the weapon at the fiends' head but he tripped on a body and fell to the floor. The demon launched itself on top of him but never made contact. Sara's black knives had separated its head and leg. The sections seemed to hang in the air for a moment before dropping with a wet thud to the ground.

Whistler watched Sara as she stared at the fiend, her gaze intensifying as the creature twitched once then became still. She lifted her eyes until they met his, the brief flicker of cruelty distorting her delicate beauty. She glanced down at the bodies and for a fleeting moment, the dwarf believed she would squat down and partake of the gruesome banquet. Sara lifted her arm and wiped away perspiration, her features returning to normal when she dropped her arm back to her side. Whistler swallowed hard then checked on Tarz.

A short-lived glimmer pulsed in front of her eyes, the crisp green tinge existing outside the in-between place. *Just like the other magic*, she thought. She walked around the room willing the magic to show itself to her. She slowly spun around until she faced the throne area.

"Hold still," the dwarf ordered while he poured some clean water over the blistering skin.

"Hurry, Sara," Tarz said then clenched his teeth as Whistler gently rubbed some of Elena's plant gel over it, "there may be more of those things around. Easy, dwarf!"

Sara nodded and stepped over toward the king's chair. A large chest stood just behind it. She walked up to it and peered inside. Necklaces of gold and silver links lay tangled together with bracelets, golden statues, a crown studded with blue stones and finely designed candlesticks. Three other containers held coins and bronze medals while a plain pot holding handfuls of precious gems sat in front of them. She dug through the riches, pulling out strands of pearls and fistfuls of earrings, rings and other jewelry until she spotted a faint emerald shimmer at the very bottom of the box.

Her hands shook as she retrieved the flattened urn, the beautifully hand-chased silver trees running up from the base firmly clamping the lid in place. She forgot to breathe, the smoothly swirling contents hypnotizing her. Her hands began to tremble at the very thought of holding one of the most potent powers in the land. The Green Might was not hers to wield but that did not diminish the surge of energy that coursed through her body. Something deep within her responded to it for a split second only but that was enough to send a tremor of exhilaration down into her very soul. She could not tear her gaze away from the magic until Whistler touched her shoulder and gave it a gentle squeeze. She looked over at the blurry dwarf, his image becoming more distinct with every beat of her heart.

"We have to go, Sara." He stared into her face, the rapture dissipating from it like the sun burning away the morning fog. He glanced at the urn then felt a pang of apprehension as she carefully tucked it into her pack.

They helped Tarz to his feet then walked over to the main entry. Sara and Whistler lifted the heavy wooden bar off one end while Tarz yanked the door open. They exited as one, much to the relief of Clay as he stopped pacing back and forth in front of the Hall. The elf glanced at the Rock Lords raw chest then over to Sara's flushed features. He threw a questioning look at Whistler who could offer him nothing more than a subtle shrug of his shoulders.

"Now what do we do?" asked Whistler. "Sara?"

"I...don't know. Mercator just said to get the magic before Emhella did; he never mentioned what to do with it once we had it."

They were silent as the day began to wane, standing in a city whose residents lay butchered or hid in the surrounding countryside. Tarz stared at his home. Clay waited for Sara to speak. Whistler scanned the area for any threats.

"We need to find some shelter for the night," Whistler stated, "perhaps one of the more defensible houses."

"Stay here?" Clay exclaimed in disbelief. "What if those things come back?"

"The better question, elf, is where are they now? They have already wreaked havoc upon Kevlan's Hall and moved on. Do you wish to meet up with them in the woods during the night?"

"He's right, Clay. We have a better chance of surviving in one of these buildings," Whistler agreed with Tarz.

They chose a solidly built dwelling without windows on the first floor and led their horses inside. They scrounged for food as best as they could then barred themselves inside.

"I owe you a debt, dwarf."

"You're obligation is to my people, Tarz."

"I will honor my earlier word, dwarf."

The light faded away, the group taking a chance by lighting one candle. The idea of sitting in complete darkness was not something any of them relished. They took turns standing watch but the scavengers fighting and howling outside stole their desire to sleep.

Sara lay awake, the unfinished vision surging to the forefront of her mind.

She walked through the first chamber past wooden furniture crumbled nearly to powder, piles of dried leaves and animal droppings. She stared at the ragged scraps of tapestries, a few clinging to rusted rods hanging at a slant from the dusty walls while most of them lay in moth eaten heaps on the floor. Shafts of blue-gray light filtering in through the cracks in the walls illuminated the long, fine strands laden with dust dangling in the corners. Disembodied voices drifted amongst the fine particles suspended in the musty air, the words muffled by more than the dense stone encasing them. The cacophony echoed hollowly within her mind as each voice sought to be heard above the others. Indistinct shapes materialized down the corridor from where she stood, their ethereal forms moving in slow motion toward the back of the passageway. Sara trailed after them, the traces of fear they left in their wake beginning to rouse something buried within her soul.

The shadows led her to a constricted foyer, the vaulted ceiling angling sharply downward. Their heads bobbed wildly as they scampered down the steps, the way snaking ever closer to the sound of the surf. She was closing the distance between herself and the stragglers who sensed her nearness. Panic replaced fright, which triggered a sudden increase in the quarry's speed. Shouts and screams burst like bubbles before her, each 'pop' releasing the residue of their terror. She closed her eyes and inhaled the emotions, the trepidation as sweet as honey on her tongue...

"Sara...Sara wake up!"

Sara bolted upright, her confused gaze resting on the backs of her companions.

"Is anybody in there?"
The voice startled them and, as one, they ran to the shuttered window and opened it, straining to see the face of their visitor.

-14-

Emhella strode confidently along the elves' southern border encircled by hundreds of grunting and bounding demons. The fiends' macabre romping elicited a merciless smile for in two short days he would unleash them upon all the mortals. He glanced over his left shoulder near where the unseen city of the elves stood. Bystyn would be the last place to feel the fury he had kept bottled up inside of him for the past two and a half centuries. Moreover, he would use their own magic to devastate them. Emhella removed the compressed bottle from within his robes and held it up to the light. The ancient coating of grime obscured what lay inside. He used a corner of his cloak to wipe away the residue then nodded with satisfaction at the amethyst sparkling behind the undulating dunes etched out of silver. He would collect its two mates and these three combined with the black power already residing within him would be enough to harness the *Riannian*. Long had the single drop of the pure magic been lost in the land. Long had he sought it.

The Riannian was the source of all magic, the mighty urn from which all other magic was poured. The elves, Daimoryians, demons and even the Lady of the Sands shared in this power. The difference between them was how they manipulated the magic. The Daimoryians, once a war-like Race, infused their power with the blood of their victims. The elves instilled the Green Might with their respect for the land. Soon he,

Emhella, would defile all the powers and spread his malevolence across the land.

He jammed the bottle back into his pocket and walked on. The Herkah's body that he possessed pleased him immensely. It was strong with incredible reflexes; the multitude of scars a testament to his courage. His spirit also impressed him; the hostility it managed to lash out at the Vox was growing more infrequent over the centuries but never quite disappeared. Emhella understood the demon's fear of Allad and the Vox that had coveted him. It's too bad the other Vox had not been strong enough to defeat him and take the body for their own. He, Emhella, had vanquished the other high demons and now stood upon the land as the only Vox left.

Emhella slowed down then stopped. He nodded with satisfaction as his plan's final pieces fell into place. He faced toward the east and concentrated on the red magic held prisoner inside the tower.

* * *

Balyd mingled with the court outside the hall, chatting intermittently but mainly remaining quiet. It was nearing sunset, an odd time for a meeting but the only time everyone could gather. He spotted Hardan across the way walking with a young elf that wove through the crowd unnoticed, until he bumped into a haughty Caladan. The elf apologized profusely, but Caladan barely glanced at him and continued to orate to the few lords and ladies standing nearby.

Balyd entered the counsel meeting with a deep sense of foreboding. Weeks had passed since the queen's death and the counsel had not yet agreed upon her successor. Caladan had spent a great deal of time with the members of the court trying to convince them he, and not Balyd, should wear the mantle of First Advisor. He had made veiled promises of prestige and leverage for anyone who would support him. Many of the courtiers were tired of arguing over who would take the throne and wanted nothing more than the stability a sitting ruler offered. Half of the counsel supported Dalk, the queen's closest cousin, while the other half were willing to wait a little longer in case another, unknown family member surfaced. The latter however, were not in the mood to delay for much longer.

Balyd entered the hall and took his seat on the right side of the chamber with the other high-ranking officials. The chairs on the left side filled with minor officials and, much to his dismay, Caladan. Balyd studied the elf. Caladan stuck his pointy chin out, his lips pressed into a tight line while his eyes scrutinized everyone present. Balyd frowned at Caladan's fruitless attempt to appear dignified. *Pompous ass,* Balyd thought to himself.

Everyone rose and offered Lady Wyntyn a respectful bow as she walked to the center of the assembly room. "Good morning. We need to decide who shall rule Bystyn and its denizens," she began. "Lord Dalk is, as it now stands, the only royal who has some backing. We are still sweeping the land in our search for the possibility of another member of the family who has chosen to live outside Bystyn's walls. If…"

"Lady Wyntyn," Caladan's interruption was the height of rudeness as he stepped in front of those seated beside him.

"Lord Caladan?" Her stern face fazed him for a moment only. "You have something important to add to this conversation?"

Caladan's face flushed but he did not back down. "Yes, Lady Wyntyn, I do. With all due respect, we've been discussing the same issue for many weeks now, weeks during which our patrols have found no other living family member." He glanced over at Balyd then to Hardan standing to one side of Lady Wyntyn.

"What do you suggest, Lord Caladan?"

"Perhaps we should get on with our lives," he tugged on his robes, "and inaugurate Lord Dalk as king of Bystyn."

"And you as First Advisor?" she smoothly asked.

"That and many other decisions fall to the new ruler, not to me, Lady Wyntyn."

"I see. What if Lord Dalk does take the throne and a member is subsequently found, Lord Caladan, what then?"

"It will be up to the elves and this court to determine whether or not he or she is capable of ruling," he stated, his Adam's apple bobbing up and down. He remained standing, waiting like an old busybody with a secret.

"You wish to add something else, Lord Caladan?" There was little warmth and even less patience in Lady Wyntyn's voice.

"Yes, Lady Wyntyn."

"Then speak, Lord Caladan."

"I am merely suggesting we install Lord Dalk as king because there are no heirs left."

Balyd's hands formed into fists on his lap but he kept his features calm. He dared not glance over at Hardan but he could well imagine the distaste for Caladan slowly flooding into his face. Lady Wyntyn retained her composure.

"And you base that statement on what, Lord Caladan?" *You read the same information that we did and took it at face value*, she thought. *You really are a fool.* The sour taste in her mouth intensified with every passing second.

"There is a little known entry into Queen Tryssa's diary indicating a possible successor did attempt to contact her, but it was revealed no link to the royal family could be found."

Balyd stared at Caladan. The oaf spoke clearly and concisely, his head erect and his shoulders back yet all this could not give him the aura he so coveted. He was incapable of keeping his mouth shut and his focus on caring for Bystyn and the elves. His words were only partially correct but they were enough to sway anyone in the court who had not completely made up their mind. If Dalk were crowned king and chose Caladan as his First Advisor, it would be difficult to remove them when the rightful heir finally came forth. He studied the reactions of some of the members of the court in the hall. Those who had served for a long time reflected a restrained disappointment and dislike for Caladan; the younger group nodded as they whispered amongst one another.

Lady Wyntyn cocked her head to one side as if she were mulling Caladan's information over in her mind. She sensed Caladan was waiting for her to make eye contact with Balyd to confirm some sort of theory running amok in his head.

"Do you have proof of this?"

"Yes, Lady Wyntyn, I do," he proclaimed as he stuck his hand in his pocket. He hesitated for a moment, the look on his face morphing from triumph to distress. "It was right here...in my robes...someone must have taken...that thief! He stole it from me!"

"Are you through with this drama, Lord Caladan?"

"Lady Wyntyn, I would never disrespect this court! I had the booklet up until we were ready to enter the hall then someone, that young elf, knocked into me and took it."

"Do you see him in this chamber?" she asked with growing impatience.

Caladan looked around the room but the young elf was nowhere to be seen. His eyes grew wide and his face reddened with every passing moment.

"Ansar was the one who killed the supposed heir," he blurted out, cringing at the rumbling from the guards.

"You accuse Captain Ansar of murder?" Hardan demanded.

"Yes...no! The queen ordered it!"

"Now you drag the queen's name through the dirt?" someone shouted out from behind him.

"No! She was just protecting the city!" Caladan spun around, his eyes pleading with the nobles to believe him but they slowly backed away from him.

"Who else will you accuse, Lord Caladan?" Lady Wyntyn asked in an even tone, the challenge not lost on Caladan.

He needed that damn book to prove he was telling the truth but it was gone. Or was it? Balyd knew about the entries. Who else would he trust with this information? He willed himself to calm down and think but the dozens of pairs of eyes boring into him would not allow that luxury. He needed a plan.

"I ask for forgiveness for my thoughtless accusations, Lady Wyntyn, and will gladly remove myself from this meeting." He bowed and left, headed for his rooms.

"I'll never find that little pickpocket or the book," he muttered to himself as he ascended the staircase to his rooms. He slammed the door shut behind him and nearly threw himself into the chair behind the desk. Balyd had made an idiot out of him in front of every important person in the city. Lady Wyntyn hadn't helped matters much, either.

Caladan glanced out the balcony doors, the fading light infused with diluted blues, yellows and grays. Thunder rumbled in the distance. He continued to stare out into the gloom, his thumbs drawing lazy circles around each other.

He watched with amusement as a piece of the night seemed to detach itself and hover just beyond the jamb. *I'm more exhausted than I thought.* He cocked his head to one side as the haze began to take on a vaguely human form. It floated in the dimness, its edges drifting like tattered spider-webs in the cool evening air. Caladan's thumbs stopped moving as the candles and lamps went out one by one. He pushed back against the chair as the mist floated into the room and drifted over him, his eyes ready to pop out of his head. Perspiration exploded over his entire body, a pathetic whimper lodged in the back of his throat.

The vapor spread out but the head retained its shape, a pair of indistinct greenish globs boring into his very soul. Caladan could do nothing to stop the tears from flowing down his cheekbones. His hands shook uncontrollably as they grasped the armrests. A chill swept into the room carrying with it the musty stench of a sepulcher. He shivered as it brushed against his skin. Gooseflesh erupted all over his body. The haze suddenly spread to every corner of the chamber. Caladan could take no more. He vaulted out of the chair and into the hallway as fast as his legs could take him.

* * *

August stepped onto the worn path with his fists resting on his hips as he tried to make a decision. Should he head back to the others or wait here for them? The soldiers were no longer an issue. Did his companions manage to get the magic already? If they did, which way did they go? They could just as easily have headed west or, knowing he had come in this direction, they might follow suit.

"You can't stay here, August," he muttered to himself as he pushed his hair off his forehead. "So pick a route."

He chose to return the way he had come. If nothing else, he would be able to find his friends' trail if they had traveled elsewhere. He made good time, reaching the bluff overlooking the causeway by noon. He looked carefully for his friends; the only sounds greeting him were birds, insects and the wind. There were no signs of any scuffles. The only recent trail was the one he had just made. There were no more than three sets of footprints so August followed the tracks south. The tracks veered southwest about a mile from where he had spent the night and merged with a deer path. He had walked for about an hour when he spotted several strands of golden filaments caught in a branch about chest high. He plucked them off and held them up, a smile spreading across his face. He took a drink from his canteen and increased his pace hoping he'd run into them before sunset.

The afternoon wore on without any more signs of his companions. He was beginning to think he had missed a clue when the trail gave way to grasslands. He looked backward before resting his gaze on the woods across the plain. He glanced down, noting the trampled grass beneath his feet. He continued on, his stomach growling but his mind determined to meet up with the others before eating anything.

The long shadows reaching out from the trees swallowed him. He entered the woods, keenly aware of the silence as he walked beside their slender trunks. He peered from side to side, his hand resting on the hilt of his sword. He could see the streaked sky straight ahead but that did not assuage his apprehension. A sudden snapping and breaking of branches erupted to his left and he immediately squatted down behind a tree. He tried to calm his breathing as creatures casting thickset shadows grunted and shrieked within a stone's throw of his position. They were heading in the opposite direction and August prayed they wouldn't detect his scent.

He ran toward the fading light the moment the last of the demons sped by. He did not intend to be alone in the dark with those things running around in the woods. A pang of dread wormed its way into his chest. Had these fiends encountered his friends? Sweet mercy! What if they were dead? What if they were still back along the causeway? What if…?

August tripped on a root and went tumbling forward several yards before landing awkwardly at the edge of the woods. He groaned as he touched his cheek, the blood on his fingers appearing black in the last light of day. He got to his feet and stared at the scene before him, not sure what he was seeing.

Buildings sat at the boundary between the trees and the plain to his left and, a few miles to the southwest lay another series of structures.

"I hope you're friendly," he mumbled heading south along the forest.

He hiked for less than ten minutes, the odor of blood growing stronger the closer he approached. He slowed his pace then stopped, the grisly scene before him stealing away his strength. He remembered the demons speeding through the woods and shuddered. They must have passed through this place then moved on to their next destination. His chest suddenly tightened up as he gaped at the remains.

"Please...please let none of them be Elena, Garadan, or Taman," he whispered uneasily.

He looked at each body, the thought of one of his friends lying amongst these poor souls almost too much to bear. He zigzagged across the area but the light was too faint to recognize any features. A light flickered inside the second floor of a building to his left. He decided to take a chance and walked over to it. Meeting up with whoever might be inside was preferable to what lurked in the darkness.

"Is anybody in there?"

He heard scraping noises then footsteps before one of the shutters was thrown wide open. Three shapes crowded into view, their obscure forms unrecognizable in the darkness.

"Elena? Garadan? Taman?" he tentatively called up to the shadows.

"Augie? Augie!"

A familiar voice called down to him before disappearing from view. The door crashed against the side of the building as a dim shape flew out toward him. August took a step backward, unsure of what was happening until the figure joyfully cried out his name once more.

"August! I'm so thankful you're in one piece!"

August's face lit up as Clay embraced him. The Herkah picked Sara up in his arms and spun around, the demon girl clinging to his neck. He finally put her down but their hands remained firmly clasped. Clay slapped him on the back several times, relief showing plainly in his face.

"Where are Elena and the others?" she asked peeking around him.

"I suggest you three come up here," Whistler called out to them.

Sara, Clay and August hurried over to the house barring the door behind them. Sara led them to where the dwarf and Tarz waited for him, Whistler giving August a hearty embrace before asking about Elena and the others. August eyed the stranger who watched the reunion.

"Tarz, this is August, one of the original members of our quest," Sara introduced them.

Tarz studied the newcomer, smiling inwardly as August met his gaze without flinching or looking away from the eye contact. There was an undercurrent of danger running through him even though his features were calm. Tarz nodded toward August who returned the gesture.

"What of Elena?" Whistler persisted.

"The four of us were together a little more than a day ago," August began, sitting down on the floor, the others gathered around the candle. Tarz stood vigil by the window. August recounted what had happened since their separation nearly two weeks ago, the incident with Hyssa bringing a frown to Sara's face.

"I was forced to spend the night outside a city just to the north and east from here…"

"Daimoryia," Tarz interjected.

"Daimoryia," August repeated then continued on, "and when I finally returned to where I had left the others they were gone. I found their trail and followed it here. I was within the outer perimeter of this place when a handful of demons scurried by." August paused for a moment then asked, "I take it this…this carnage is their handiwork?"

"Yes, and tell us, which way did they travel?" demanded Whistler.

"Back the way I came," August replied. "I hope the others…" He could not finish his sentence, the alarmed look on Whistler's face stilling his tongue. Clay recounted their part of the journey. August listened intently.

"We'll look for them in the morning," Clay stated, looking sheepish as if he were secretly feeling a twinge of guilt and fear.

"Where's May?"

"She won't come out of the pack, August," Clay replied peering into the pouch.

"Is she ill?"

"No, just...sluggish," Sara said quietly, sticking her hand inside. May tapped her finger then retreated into the far corner of the backpack. She pulled the bottle out of her tunic and held it out to him. Clay narrowed his eyes at the container then glanced questioningly at Sara.

"Is that what I think it is?"

"The Green Might is a long way from home," she said handing him the urn.

Clay finally took it, the whirling emerald vapor capturing all of his attention. He couldn't take his eyes off it, the intermittent blips of silver hypnotizing him. He gazed into its depths and was astonished at what he saw. A face with features not unlike his own looked back at him and seemed to nod. He felt a peculiar vibration run up is arm a few seconds later, the sensation not lasting long. He gave the urn back to Sara, the tingling in his arm dissipating but not going away completely.

"We should try and get some sleep," Clay suggested.

Sara settled down between Clay and August, one hand resting against the elf's back while the other clutched the urn. She began to doze, hovering on the brink of forgetfulness. The Green Might began to swirl within the bottle.

The wind buffeted against her as she sped on, cutting through the darkness like the prow of a boat slicing through water. The air was cold but not uncomfortable; the feeling of weightlessness both disconcerting and agreeable at the same time. She heard strange voices, the unintelligible languages harsh in her ears. Sara opened her eyes and blinked several times as she strove to get her bearings. She was moving through an odd tunnel, the darkness that enveloped her slowly giving way to sepia tinted images...

Mercator's maw was inches from her face... Emhella's fatherly voice called out to her, his black eyes glittering with disdain... The artery in Whistler's neck beckoned her to bite into it... Her black blades sliced down into the thief's chest... The pony screamed in pain as she bit into its neck...

Sara moaned softly in her sleep.

August raised his head, the barely audible groan disrupting his slumber. He reached over and adjusted Sara's blanket, his hand lingering on her shoulder. He eased his body against hers and draped an arm over her before dozing off once more.

A voice slipped uninvited into her mind. She shuddered, cringing from its source but unable to banish it.

Sara.

No.

Come to me, my child.

I can't...I won't.

You can and you will. You are not human, Sara, and you never will be. They will always fear and loathe you for what you truly are.

My place is here, with them.

Stay with them and die. Come to me and live.

No...

Sara's body barely twitched as the images began to form in her mind. Demons surrounded her naked body, their twisted and gnarled forms dancing with a maniacal glee, their matted bodies sending a shiver of pleasure through her. She glanced to her right and smiled as Emhella walked over to her, a limp but still living Clay in his arms. He laid him on the ground and stood back, watching her as she knelt beside the elf and reached out to cup his chin. She moved his head to one side and focused on the throbbing vein in his neck. She licked her lips then bent down and bit into his flesh. His warm blood filled her mouth, its sweet taste stimulating more than her hunger. Clay's form became blurry, his features lost behind a gauzy curtain of desire, his identity forgotten. Emhella began to caress her shoulders, his fingers slowly stroking her skin. She turned around to face him, exhaling slowly as he licked the blood on her chin. She opened her mouth when a searing bolt of energy shot through her body.

Sara's eyelids snapped open, her lips brushing against Clay's exposed throat. The elf snored softly, oblivious of the teeth resting against his skin. Sara stifled a whimper, the horror she felt reverberating through her in nauseous waves. She did not move away from him as the voice inside her mind continued to coax her into sinking her teeth into his flesh.

Scratch his skin and try a drop, Sara. You could drink him dry before he awakes. It's who you are, Sara.

She stared at Clay, his facial appearance and skin blending until nothing but irrelevant flesh remained. Her heart beat a little faster and her breathing increased.

Bite, Sara, bite down!

Sara yowled softly as the corner of her tooth gently broke Clay's skin. A tiny droplet of blood beaded up. Her tongue snaked out of her mouth and lapped it up. A feral thrill rushed through her, the sensation coursing through her with lightning speed. It reached every corner of her body then hastened into her very soul. It pierced into her spirit and released the malevolent essence she had striven so hard to suppress. The smell of the elf's blood wafted into her nose, the thick metallic odor gradually banishing the shrinking human part of her. She bit down on her lip, her eyes never wavering from the trickle of blood staining Clay's tanned neck. She wanted more.

August shifted beside her and tugged the blanket up over his shoulder. She could see Whistler's silhouette in the chair beside the door, the sliver of moonlight illuminating his throat. Tarz was somewhere on the second floor, the last watcher of the night. She could take them all with ease and drink until not one drop remained in any of them.

Something brushed against her arm. Sara glanced down at May, the spider rubbing its leg on her skin. It crawled up until it sat upon her chest. Sara couldn't move. She stared at the spider as it leaned forward and gently tapped her over her heart. Sara looked at May, images of Master Felix, her quest, and August materializing before her eyes, her wicked thoughts and deed fading away behind them. Shame crept into her cheeks; guilt forced her to drop her gaze. A tear rolled down from the corner of her eye. Emhella's thoughts punctured through the moment, shredding her memories.

You have tasted the blood of your enemies, Sara. You are now unclean in their eyes. You are now truly who you are meant to be.

No...

They will renounce you now.

They are my friends.

They will never trust you again.

Sara couldn't tear her gaze away from the thin crimson rivulet on his throat. It beckoned her to indulge in another sip and fill her mouth with its sweetness.

You might be able to explain the bite away, Sara. But what of the hunger radiating from your eyes? Will you be able to conceal that?

She glanced over at a patiently waiting May. The spider had witnessed her terrible actions. There was always an onlooker watching sins being committed.

I can't stay here.

Come, Sara.

Sara scooped May off her chest and gently placed her on Clay's side. She rose from the floor and moved silently out of the house, cradling the urn in the crook of her arm.

May clambered onto Clay's shoulder and watched her leave, her head cocked to one side.

-15-

    Elena, Garadan and Taman followed the same path they believed August had taken. The trio scoured the area looking for any traces of his passing but found nothing. They, too, inadvertently stumbled upon Daimoryia, immediately heading west and walking past the dilapidated cabin where August had spent the night. They trod along the trampled grasses, meandering back the way they had come before the trail straightened out.
    "Ouch!" Elena hissed as her hair caught on a branch. She grabbed her ponytail and undid the snag.
    They stopped to rest wondering where August and their other loved ones were, and if they would succeed in the task Mercator had assigned them.
    Taman took out the urn and held it up to the light, the sun's rays unable to penetrate the soupy, blood-like contents. The intricately designed silver flames licked up the sides of the bottle. He could have sworn he saw them flicker back and forth. He stowed it back in his tunic pocket and placed his elbows on his knees, staring without seeing at the treetops growing up over the thorny brush to his right.
    He focused on an odd-looking tree in between two pines. The top and first few branches were missing then, as he focused on it realized there were slits carved into it.
    "Garadan, what do you make of that?" he asked pointing towards it.

"Man-made," replied the elf after a few moments.

"I think that's Kevlan's Hall," Elena stated.

"Is that good or bad?"

"Nothing about Kevlan's Hall is good, Taman."

"Then we'll have to sneak in and see, won't we?" Garadan replied as he picked up his pouch. "Let's go find out."

They hiked for a short period of time, the fading light adding to their uneasiness. This feeling only intensified as they nearly stumbled upon the first of the bodies. Elena covered her face with her hands as the horrific scene spread out before them. Garadan shuddered.

"What in the four corners of the land happened here?" mumbled the elf.

"Demons," Taman barely spoke the word, his charcoal eyes widening with understanding. "Emhella is on the move…he is searching for the magic and has sent his evil spawn on ahead."

"August…" Elena's voice trailed off but her features remained filled with fear and concern.

The sun dipped even lower in the sky, jealously taking the light with it.

"We need to find shelter for the night," Garadan stated as he scanned the area, "and it might as well be in one of those buildings."

"But the fiends!"

"Would you rather be out here in the open?"

Elena shook her head.

"Then we find a house that we can blockade and defend if they choose to return." Garadan walked forward, picking one of the structures with the fewest windows. They entered the building and secured the door and window as best as they could. They overturned a trestle table and pushed it against the door, feeling somewhat protected once it was in place. The window was deep. They filled the recess with items found in the room and stuffed everything from a child's chair to small throw rugs into the niche.

They mounted the staircase to the second floor, the silence accentuating their footsteps, which echoed hollowly in the hallway as the companions checked the four rooms on the second floor. The rooms were all empty. They chose a room to the left of the top of the staircase.

"I've never been so tired." Elena wiped at the grit on her face. She slid into an upholstered chair, kicked off her boots, and wiggled her toes.

"What do we have left to eat?"

"Not too much, Taman," replied Garadan. "I'll go downstairs and see if there is anything in the larder."

Elena watched Taman take out the urn and hold it up at eye level, the crimson contents swirling sluggishly within. The dark color in the corneas of his eyes began to swell and soon seeped into the whites. Elena, mesmerized, sat up in slow motion, staring at the transformation in Taman's face taking place in front of her eyes.

The magic filled his vision, the eerie river swallowing everything around him. He stood alongside the current, the waters seeming to rage past him no more than a foot or two away. Steam hissed off the surface and collided with the same frigid air making him shiver. His breath concealed the scene every time he exhaled, the panorama getting closer every time it dissipated. The red magic stirred to life as it sensed the river of darkness. It flared and shimmered as if signaling the current to set it free. Taman's hand slowly slid to the mouth of the urn, his fingers stroking the wax ring around the neck. The red mist vacillated with an eager intensity as his fingers rested on the seal then grew dim as they moved away from it.

Taman tore his gaze away from the magic's seduction and gazed at the river. He shielded his eyes from the lights suddenly erupting just yards away. A brilliant green pulsed nearby, the dazzling crimson quickly pulsating in response. There, off to one side was a tiny bead of liquid silver. The droplet retreated. His hands began to lose interest in the urn.

Taman's foot inched forward.

The oily surface suddenly became choppy, the tiny red lights exploding all around him. They crowded toward him in bunches, their shapes resembling spiny barbs. He shuddered as the icy air wormed its way into his flesh to burrow down into his bones. He lost the feeling in his hands, his fingertips frozen to the top of the urn the only thing keeping it from the current's embrace.

Taman's foot moved a little bit more.

The water lapping against the toe of his boot froze on impact forming a layer of rime on the leather. He couldn't tear his gaze away from the silver bead. He wanted it.

The tip of Taman's boot disappeared into the water.

A flash of blackness darker than the deepest abyss flared close by. It reeked of sulfur and sent waves of frigid air right through him. It raked across his psyche like a rusty plow churning up hard earth. Taman took a step back as he recognized what the origin of this newest magic was, his nerveless fingers relinquishing their hold on the urn. He didn't care that it was falling into the slimy current; all he cared about was fleeing from the terrible monster that shared the in-between place with him.

Elena lunged across the room, catching the glass holding the ancient power a split second before it crashed to the floor. She rolled to the side and caught the back of Taman's legs sending him crashing to the floorboards. The elf's forehead bounced against a sturdy table but Elena managed to grab onto his tunic to keep his head from smashing against the hearthstone.

"What happened?" Garadan demanded as he bounded into the room.

Taman sat up and dabbed at the scrape across his forehead, the whites in his eyes visible once more. He swayed unsteadily for a brief moment then went rigid, his face draining of color.

"Taman, you didn't drop it…"

"He's here!"

"Who's here?" Elena asked in a shaky voice, the answer already manifesting in her mind.

"Emhella."

"In this house?" Garadan's low tones reflected Elena's apprehension.

"No…but he's not very far away."

"Why would he travel in this direction?"

Elena held up the urn to Garadan in response.

"The Green Might is nearby, too."

"Wonderful," Garadan breathed the word as if it were an annoying insect buzzing around his head.

"Taman, what are we going to do with this?" She handed him the urn back.

"We can hide it," Garadan offered.

"He'll find it."

"What does Mercator expect us to do with it then? Wield it?"

"None but one of Envia's descendants can do that," Taman replied, his brow stinging, the dull throbbing in his head feeling like a blacksmith banging away on an anvil. Hyssa's scratches began to itch. The residue of the in-between world settling on his mind and soul burned like live embers. Elena placed a cool compress on his forehead and held it there.

"Do you think we were split up so each group could retrieve these two powers?" Elena asked, after a long silence. She lifted the cloth to check on the bruise forming over his eyebrow. The gash wasn't deep but the swelling was distorting it. For a brief moment Taman's features melted away then reformed into Whistler's face the day he had revealed his intention to escape and seek help. His bright eyes had glittered with a fierce resolve and this determination had given her hope. She reached out and tenderly touched the face that resembled the one she desperately wanted see once more.

Garadan and Taman blinked at her several times as her words sank into their tired minds.

Garadan's attention drifted over to the window. The first faint hints of light peeking through the shutters fell in pale puddles of soft apricot and gold onto the worn floorboards. Birds abandoned their roosts, their noisy chatter and beating of wings increasing as the sun sought to command the heavens once more. He took a deep breath.

"Are we running *from* or *to* Emhella?" Garadan asked his voice low and unsure of what was happening. Visions of wandering through haunted grasses on the way to meet Mercator appeared and disappeared in his mind.

Elena rinsed the cloth in a basin of water and reapplied it to the elf's forehead before distributing some food. She handed everyone bread, cheese and strips of smoked meats before sitting down to join them. They finished their breakfast then collected their things and left the safety of the house.

Bits of blue sky peeked through the overhead boughs but the sun had not yet burned away the fog meandering along the ground. The haze clung to the trunks and houses, its milky white appearance concealing the horrors littering the ground. Progress was slow as they picked their way over the sprawled shapes that materialized scant feet before them. Elena tripped over something and landed on all fours in a sticky puddle. She stifled a cry, gratefully taking Garadan's hand as he helped her up. The last line of trees separating them from the plains loomed ahead. They walked through the knee-high brush and grasses and out onto the plains dotted with thorny bushes and stumpy trees. The sun illuminated Evan's Peak to the northwest and the faint smudge of a forest line hugged the horizon to the west. The woods they had just vacated ran in a curved line to the north then curled to the north then west. Weeping willows, swaths of reeds and other water loving plants stretched away to the south.

The sun beat down on their backs as they stood motionless at the edge of the plains. Uncertainty rooted their feet; resolve finally prodded them forward.

"How far to the compound, Elena?"

"Less than a day's walk from here, Garadan," she replied looking at him from the side, "are you sure you want to go there?"

"We have no choice," he stated. "If the others have managed to secure whatever magic they were sent after emerge from these same woods they'll probably go there as well."

"Or perhaps they'll go elsewhere," she retorted.

"The Elven Might is near," Taman reminded her.

"So is Emhella, according to you," she countered, inwardly praying she'd see Whistler again soon.

"What do you suggest, Elena?" Taman stopped and faced the dwarf.

"I'm sorry, Taman, I just can't believe that we have gone through all of this just to meet up with Emhella and lose what we have gained."

Taman said nothing. He turned and continued walking toward the camp, his shoulders slightly hunched and his eyes focused on the ground. Garadan and Elena exchanged a long look before following him.

They moved on taking few breaks along the way. The sun shortened their shadows yet they did not stop. The miles disappeared behind them in the dust they kicked up, the southwesterly breeze doing nothing to cool their heated bodies. They squinted into the sunlight, searching for shade.

Elena glanced toward Evan's Peak just once during their trek. Her defenses slipped leaving her vulnerable to the distinct possibility that none of the dwarves would ever live to set foot in that hallowed hall. Whistler had glared at the mountain, daring it to judge him and waiting for him to fail. He would have crawled on his hands and knees over broken glass to prove himself to the ghosts of his ancestors. Elena understood his passion, his drive to resurrect the hall and his stubborn denial of the futility of trying to do so. A brief pang of despondency rippled through her being and it only became bearable when she tore her gaze away from Evan's Peak.

Their shadows disappeared behind them. Garadan narrowed his eyes at the squat buildings no more than a mile or so away. Without a word, they increased their pace and arrived at yet another grisly scene. Elena placed her hand against her mouth as she recognized both dwarf and Rock Lord, her silent tears stark against her dusty face. They called out several times without receiving any sound but the wind moaning through the compound. The trio checked a number of shacks then noticed the tool shed. They went inside noticing the dead demons.

"Somebody survived," Garadan stated picking up a half-eaten loaf of bread.

"Garadan...listen," Elena hushed him. "Someone's out there."

* * *

Harald led the dwarves and Rock Lords into the swampy region south of the compound rather than north to the mountains. He had an uneasy feeling about traveling toward Evan's Peak, preferring the dense expanse of the marshlands to the open plains. No one, not even the handful of Rock Lords, complained. They were all just relieved to be away from the camp. There were plenty of dangers here, too, but at least they could avoid the venomous snakes and poisonous plants.

They made camp beneath the huge weeping willows lining the narrow river running east to west several miles south of the compound. The stream emptied into the fens about fifty yards away leaving the area high and dry. Harald looked from one face to the next. Everyone appeared haggard. The Rock Lords sat huddled together, their arms resting on their raised knees. Some of the women cried softly for their fallen friends and family members. Most of the men stared off into space, occasionally glancing Harald's way for some measure of reassurance. Harald gave them a tight nod in response.

He waited until everyone had settled down then moved over to one of the trees, the long fronds brushing against his head and shoulders. He braced himself against the trunk then eased his weary body down, sighing with relief as the soft earth embraced him. He thought about setting up sentries, but there was little they could do if the demons attacked. All they could do was wait.

* * *

Emhella paused at the outskirts of the compound, the wind his only companion. The early morning sun peeked over the tree line to the east, challenging the dark stains of night to the west. He scanned his surroundings, the view unobstructed for many miles in every direction. He nodded with satisfaction. This would be the perfect place to establish his reign. The demons would return soon and Sara was close by. He could feel the power of the Green Might even though it was firmly contained within the glass.

It had been the wildest of the powers to corral, freed from the confines of Danyl's body but protected by Ramira and the Source of Darkness. The Green Might had hidden itself well but in the end, he, Emhella, had discovered its hiding place. The Elven power had sought refuge at Evan's Peak, the dwarves completely unaware of its presence. He had thought about destroying Evan's Peak and its inhabitants until he witnessed a skirmish between the dwarves and the Rock Lords. Seven and his people had been instrumental in defeating Mahn. Emhella decided perhaps their repayment should be much more humiliating and lasting than simply obliterating them.

Emhella had slipped into the mountain in the middle of the night, a speck of darkness mingling with the shadows. He had crept into the king's chamber and slain him, then proceeded to eradicate the entire family. He vanished before the morning light revealed the atrocities. The ensuing chaos spilled out onto the plains attracting the attention of the marauding Rock Lords. It didn't take long for the news to travel to the Rock Lord Hall and took even less time for them to mount a devastating strike against the dwarves.

A harsh smile spread across his face at the prospect of finally having Sara firmly under his control.

Your ancestors destroyed Mahn but that gave me the opportunity to succeed where he failed. I will not make the same mistakes and you, the heir to the legacy of Danyl and Ramira, will be my guarantee.

A hooded and cloaked form headed in his direction, passing through the center of the camp looking straight ahead. Emhella crossed his arms, his feet planted firmly on the ground as he awaited his visitor. The slight shape stopped several yards in front of him, a pale hand snaking out from within the cloak to push back the hood.

Sara kept her eyes averted from the monstrosity standing before her. She could still taste Clay's blood, the flavor mouth-watering yet repulsive at the same time. She had surrendered to her demon roots and would now pay the price for her treason.

"You have something for me?"

Sara pulled the flask out from within her tunic and held it out to him, recoiling as his hand brushed against hers. She gathered her courage and looked into his eyes. For a brief instant, she saw despair emanating from behind his piercing gaze. The moment passed and the ghost within faded away.

Sara sought some measure of solace beneath the boughs of a pine hoping Emhella would ignore her. She drank from her canteen, discreetly rinsing out her mouth and spitting the traces of her sin onto the ground. She leaned back against the rough trunk and closed her eyes.

Surprised voices then shrieks of horror drifted back up the corridor. The crowd came to a sudden standstill, those in the rear bumping into the unmoving throng. Within seconds the mass turned around and surged back up the steps. She stared at the abrupt reversal, turning around and running as fast as she could to avoid being trampled. Hands pushed against her back, the erratic contact making her lose her footing. She twisted toward the right and pressed her back against the wall panting as the swarm of bodies streamed by. A woman clutching a baby tripped on the top step, her upper body landing painfully on the floor. She remained frozen for a moment then screamed as something yanked her back down the stairs leaving her baby crying and flailing its arms and legs.

Silence ensued. Sara looked down at the child and, after a long hesitation, picked it up. She held it out in front of her studying the red-faced infant wailing for its mother. Sara stared dispassionately at it, its innocence alien to her demon side. The baby finally stopped crying, its red-rimmed blue eyes fixated on Sara's features. She brought it close to her face, her mouth watering in anticipation. Sara placed her lips on its velvety skin and was about to bite down when the baby's delicate fragrance wafted into her nose. She looked at the infant, its tiny fist jammed into its mouth and smiled. Sara took a deep breath then laid the child on her shoulder.

That was the wrong choice, Sara.

Sara's lids snapped open the instant a hand grabbed her by the throat and wrenched her up off the ground. She dangled within Emhella's grasp, unable to breathe as she pounded his powerful forearms with her fists. His gaze bored into her, his ruthlessness radiating from within his merciless eyes. Her struggle did not last long. Her vision began to fade; her lungs demanded she fill them with air. Sara's resistance slowed then ceased. She twitched once then went limp.

Emhella glared at her with disdain, tossing her lifeless body aside with disgust.

* * *

"Sara? Sara! Where are you?" Augusts' words echoed dully in the house.

"Tarz, did she pass by you during the night?"

"No, dwarf, no one went by me."

They exited the house, the fog swallowing up August's figure but not the hollow echoing of his shouts. Concern and uncertainty reflected off Augusts' face when he finally reemerged from the soupy mixture. Whistler brought out the horses.

"Why would she just disappear?"

Tarz stood beside Clay and stared at his neck, the dried trickle of blood noticeable in the ghostly half-light. He grabbed the elf's tunic and yanked him closer.

"Leave him alone, Tarz," Whistler warned reaching for his weapon.

"Somebody was thirsty last night, dwarf. Here, look for yourself." He grabbed Clay's jaw and pushed it to one side as Whistler and August focused their eyes on the single puncture wound.

"She couldn't…"

"She did," Tarz confirmed releasing the elf with a quick shove. He ignored the dark glance Clay threw his way. "I guess she grew tired of eating moldy cheese."

"That's enough, Tarz," August glared at the Rock Lord.

"It seems as though she was planning to drink us dry, a little at a time."

"I'm warning you," August hissed through his teeth.

Tarz studied August, the dangerous undertones in his words paling beside the anger emanating from his glittering eyes.

"You're in love with her!" he uttered, a look of surprised bemusement on his face.

"Tarz!" Clay's tone severed the precarious connection between the Rock Lord and the Herkah. "She took the flask," the elf informed them.

"A present for her true Master…"

August's fist instantly stilled Tarz' tongue and dropped the Rock Lord to the ground. Whistler and Clay immediately grabbed his arms to keep him from continuing to punch the Rock Lord.

"*Enough!*" Whistler roared, startling a flock of birds into flight.

"Sara was the one who sought help to defeat Emhella," Clay stated, "I doubt very much she'd get to this point only to betray us." He watched as Tarz got to his feet, his fingers probing his bruised jaw. Tarz remained silent.

"What do we do now?" the dwarf asked.

"We head back to the camp," Clay replied, their options gone along with the magic.

They mounted the horses, Clay and August sharing the same animal, and moved out without speaking, the losses they had endured weighing heavily on their minds. Tarz' comment might have been unkind but it did bring up a disturbing scenario. Clay, Whistler and August remembered how she nearly obeyed Emhella right before the Wraiths whisked them over the mountain. Had he been successful in luring her to him now?

Clay glanced at August, the Herkahs swarthy countenance still flush with anger. The elf absently picked at the puncture wound causing it to bleed. He held his finger up to his face and stared at the crimson smear. *Why would you do this? Why now, Sara?*

Grasses and hardwoods gave way to underdeveloped trees and coarse clumps of weeds, the hard ground unable to support any other growth. The wind lifted the dust kicked up by their animals' hooves, obscuring the Rock Lords' stronghold behind them. The day passed quickly, the compound rising up along the horizon late in the afternoon. Nothing moved. The riders drew their weapons as they scrutinized every shadowy recess they passed.

Silence reigned in the compound, even the vultures and crows had ceased feeding. Whistler's attention was riveted on the shack he had lived in with Elena. They passed the tool shed, squinting at the sun's penetrating rays. Dust devils danced in the middle of the street, the crosswinds pushing them randomly from side to side. The sound of a shutter creaking on rusty hinges reached their ears. A door suddenly slammed shut to their right startling both horse and rider. A rustling sound from behind brought them to a halt. They cautiously turned around and stared at the shed.

"Is anyone there?"

"Whistler?" a tentative voice replied from within the building.

"Elena? Is that you?" The dwarf scrambled off the horse just as she flung open the wooden door revealing their missing companions. Whistler and Elena held tightly to each other. He stroked her face and hair; she held his face in her hands. Within moments, everyone but Tarz was shaking hands and slapping each other on the back.

"Where's Sara?" Elena asked, looking concerned.

"She was with us until last night," Clay said, "and disappeared sometime in the early morning hours."

"Let's go inside," Tarz interrupted. "This silence is making me edgy." They went inside the tool shed, a small fire illuminating their tired figures. They shared a cold meal while recounting what had happened to them since they left Mercator's realm. Each one listened intently to what the others had experienced. Taman produced the flask containing the red magic for them to see, holding it out to reflect the firelight.

"We had the Green Might..." Clay's voice had dropped to a whisper. "But Sara took it with her when she left."

August glared at Tarz as if daring him to make a comment but the Rock Lord sat cross-legged lost in his own thoughts.

"And May?" asked Elena.

She watched Clay as he carefully lifted the flap of his pouch and reached inside, withdrawing his hand, holding up the spider. May clambered onto his shoulder and lay down, her attention focused on the bite mark on his neck. She reached out and touched it with one of her legs then moved her body over until it concealed the wound.

Taman glanced out the window at the moon surrounded by one rust-hued halo. Emhella's power would peak in two days when two more coronas encircled the full moon. He rubbed his face, the accumulated grime scratching his skin, and watched the flames expanding and contracting hypnotically.

Elena's gasp caused the group to focus on Taman.

The in-between place pulled him into its icy embrace without any warning whatsoever. The green and black magic hovered just beyond his reach, as did the silver sparkle. Taman recoiled from all three energies, the currents flowing from one to the other threatening to blister his skin. Arcs of lightning snapped and crackled, the blinding threads of light stabbing all the way to his soul. He couldn't breathe as the monstrous black shadow leaned toward him enveloping him with a stench of death. It wrapped itself around him like a blanket woven of thorns and whispered into his mind.

Insignificant mortal! You have nothing with which to challenge me. Perhaps I will not need to wait for the third circle of light after all.

Emhella retreated, the barbs purposefully raked across his frozen body. Taman prayed for this moment to end. He shivered in the cold yet even his icy surroundings were preferable to Emhella's malevolent hatred. The in-between world dissolved into red and orange flames and he was suddenly, mercifully, back with his companions.

"Taman?" Elena leaned forward and touched his cheek.

Taman fell into Tarz' arms. The Rock Lord lay him down and covered his frozen form with their light summer cloaks. They exchanged worried looks, the trepidation deeply etched on their faces.

They awoke at daybreak, ate a quick meal then collected their few belongings. They searched the area then cautiously walked down the main street, watching out for anything unusual. Whistler led the way, Elena and the others a few steps behind. Tarz brought up the rear leading the horses. The group rounded the last house and stepped out onto the dusty plains heading northwestward. The watery sun broke over the horizon behind them casting a pale shade of sickly yellow onto the land. They picked up their pace, shifting to the west to avoid a clump of skeletal trees when a figure detached itself from the stunted growth. They halted as one and stared at Emhella.

Taman fingered the urn stuffed inside his tunic. Mercator had commanded them to secure the powers before Emhella did, but the Vox hybrid had already found and confined them in these flasks. The dragon knew all along that the Vox had control of the magic. Why would Mercator bother sending the companions out to retrieve the powers if they were already under the Vox' influence? Emhella was going to succeed in destroying everyone in less than a day and a half. The companions could do nothing to stop him. The demon's confidence spilled over into arrogance.

Emhella was poised on the brink of victory, managing to achieve the goal that had eluded Mahn more than two hundred and fifty years ago. Mahn had stood at the forefront of his army, the Source of Darkness at his fingertips while he taunted the allies. Emhella had no use for an army. He relied on his evil power and the element of surprise. If Sara hadn't inadvertently recruited this odd collection of individuals no one would have even known what he was doing. *Perhaps I will not need to wait for the third circle after all.*

No, perhaps you won't.

He removed the flask and flipped it behind Emhella, not caring if it broke on a rock.

"Taman! No!" shouted Elena.

The dull thud as it landed in the dirt disappointed but did not surprise him.

"Well done, elf," Emhella's voice resonated with menace. He studied the group for several long moments, the apathy melting into mild astonishment.

August's jaw dropped as he gazed upon the legendary Allad. The swarthy skin, hawk-like nose and lean yet well-muscled body had been the bane of demon and human alike. No greater warrior had ever walked the land. August understood that what dwelled within Allad's body now had corrupted that once proud spirit but it was difficult not to look upon the form without being in awe.

The sun rose higher into a crystal blue sky.

"I will christen my citadel with the blood of kings and queens, gracious gifts from my long dead adversaries." Emhella offered them a mock bow. He casually flipped bottle in his hand a few times before tucking into his pocket.

A low growling rose from behind the companions. As one they turned around, the blood draining from their faces as the demons emerged and formed a circle around them and Emhella. The companions scrutinized their surroundings but all they saw were dozens of squat shapes bristling with fangs and talons. The ring of demons took several steps toward them then stopped, their high-pitched whines sounding shrill in the near silence. One of the fiends lunged at Clay, a quick burst of black immediately vaporizing the demon as the elf brought up his sword to ward it off. The smell of burnt hair hung heavily in the humid air. Flight was no longer an option.

"Where is Sara?" August's voice sounded stronger than he had thought it would.

"I no longer needed her."

August glared at the demon, the sick feeling in the pit of his stomach beginning to creep up into his throat.

"How long before we become expendable?" asked Whistler, his patience, even in the face of this grave danger, wearing thin.

"Soon, dwarf, soon."

Emhella closed his eyes and breathed deeply. His shoulders began to relax, then his arms, torso and finally his legs. He swayed back and forth, the tic beneath his eye keeping time with the voiceless words escaping his moving lips. He never acknowledged the mortals, not even when Tarz charged at the demon. The fiends quickly advanced forcing the Rock Lord back to his companions.

Their shadows collected in shapeless pools at their feet then gradually lengthened behind them. Elena leaned against Whistler; Clay and August shifted from one leg to the other and Tarz bent over and rested his hands on his knees. The sun baked their exposed skin; a dry wind stole the moisture from their bodies. The mortals drank sparingly from their canteens, the few sips of water doing very little to slake their thirst.

Emhella finally opened his eyes and gazed at the ragtag group, the ruthless black orbs terrifying to behold. They appeared as soulless as a snake and none of the humans would have been surprised if a forked tongue flicked out of the demon's mouth. The Vox dispassionately watched the mortals back up a step.

Emhella ignored the companions and focused on his cupped hands that he held out in front of him. His eyes blazed as he rubbed the palms together, the glittering black specks escaping through his fingers crackling with energy. He spread his hands apart revealing a thin strip the color of polished coal beginning to form between them. The sliver of darkness continued to elongate until it was nearly twice his height. He took a step backward, his gaze never leaving the morphing rod. The staff twirled languidly, the ends tapering to fine points. The glossy surface was devoid of any blemishes except for a series of odd runes etched in the middle. Emhella reached out and snatched the spinning shaft, his sudden and unexpected movement startling the companions back into reality.

"What in the four corners of the land does he intend to do with that?" muttered Tarz taking a step backward.

Emhella lifted the staff high into the air then jammed it with all his might into the earth burying the rod up to the peculiar markings. For a brief moment nothing happened then a cold wind began to blow. It gusted across the plains dragging along a tattered gray fog from the west. Clouds formed from within the vapor, rolling upward, their bulging underbellies blotting out the blue sky and warm sun.

PATRICIA PERRY

* * *

A woman picked through a bin of small, bright yellow fruit along the pier in Windstorm Harbor. She selected a handful, placed them on the scale beneath the weather-beaten awning, and waited for the vendor to weigh them. It was an unusually balmy day, one that even smoothed away her sour frown. She stared at the sea. It was rapidly losing its radiant turquoise hues, replaced by an unappealing gray shade. The wind tugged on her faded dress and churned up the water in the harbor. She wrinkled her nose and hastily paid for the fruit hoping she'd be back home before this deluge soaked the region. No sooner had the woman stepped onto the rocky mainland when the earth began to quake. The sea blasted huge columns of water into the air drenching everything along the wharf. The quay buckled and split, spilling carts, people and goods into the agitated harbor. She ran up to the first set of buildings; her fingers white around the handle of her basket, and turned around. She placed her hand in front of her mouth, her eyes unable to look away.

The wooden pier had withstood countless storms but it could not bear up against this eerie onslaught of darkness from the sky and from the ocean. The frightening tempest hurled boats against the rocks crushing anyone or anything in their way. The water continued to rise, the foamy liquid flung skyward hissing dangerously. The woman dropped her basket and ran for her life.

* * *

The ground began to shudder from deep beneath the surface of the earth, so violently no one above could stand erect. They swerved from side to side, clutching at anything to try to keep themselves from falling down. Garadan fell to all fours, his hands disappearing beneath the dirt bouncing wildly off the ground. He fought unsuccessfully to stand on the unstable earth, finally deciding it was easier to remain on his hands and knees. His companions soon joined him.

The ground began to crack then huge holes opened up all along the plain. Geysers of stones and sand erupted all over the place. The mortals curled up into fetal positions protecting their faces and as much of their uncovered skin as they could from the violent cascades. The torrent of dirt and rocks finally ceased, replaced by a ring of jagged boulders pushing up from the devastated plains. The companions held their hands over their ears but could not keep out the dreadful grinding and high-pitched grating sounds. They choked on the dust and stiffened every time a large rock landed near them.

* * *

Balyd, Lady Wyntyn and Hardan passed under one of the great archways supporting the domed entrance hall. Their subdued conversation caught the attention of Lord Caladan heading toward them from the opposite direction. They met near the staircase leading to the sleeping quarters. Caladan opened his mouth to speak when an unsettling rumbling rolled underneath the city. Balyd and Lady Wyntyn exchanged bewildered glances while Caladan reached out and grabbed the balustrade for support. The shaking intensified. Bits of mortar rained down from the walls; people scattered from the small chunks of rocks falling within the castle. He could hear chaotic shouting and the sound of heavy objects crashing to the floor.

The stair gave way beside them sending Balyd and Lady Wyntyn toppling backward. Balyd's arms flailed uncontrollably as he sought to grab onto anything that would break his fall. Lady Wyntyn fell down, Hardan immediately by her side. Caladan backed up until he was flush with the wall behind him. The partition to the right of the entranceway buckled, the fracture too great to continue to support the weight of the stones. It collapsed inward, one of the guards launching himself on top of Balyd a split second before the wall crumpled toward the First Advisor.

Balyd stared out through the breach in the wall at the churning clouds racing eastward. Their pitted underbellies roiled violently as they sped over Bystyn. This was not the normal precursor to a storm. Balyd's face paled as Taman's warnings blared like some bizarre alarm in his mind. Balyd had no idea in which direction Taman and Garadan had trekked but given their mission, they were most certainly in the midst of whatever was happening in the east. Then, without warning, the land ceased shaking as abruptly as it began.

-16-

Elena felt Whistler jerk as a sizable stone dropped on his shoulder, the snapping sound audible even amid all the noise. He lay across her body to shield her, refusing to relinquish his protection even when several more rocks hit him.

The earth continued to convulse, vomiting up more and more of its innards. Then suddenly silence descended upon the plains. The companions looked around.

"Sweet mercy!" exhaled Elena. She coughed several times and wiped the dust from her face, blinking for several minutes before the grit ceased to irritate her eyes.

A towering rock wall, its coarse surface blocking out the plains, surrounded them. There were three walkways around the interior of the edifice. An irregularly shaped tower stood within the center of a wide pit. A pale yellowish fog rose up from the depths below them, illuminated by brief bursts of white lights. Dozens of narrow rocky channels led from the walls to the structure, all crossing over each other like a giant spider web. A wet belching sound gurgled upward carrying with it a moldy stench. Flames licked the base of the tower.

* * *

Harald, the dwarves and the remaining Rock Lords watched in silence, their heads tilted back as the ominous clouds rushed toward them from the west. The closer the gloominess came, the more they huddled together. Harald swallowed hard as the shadows consumed the last of the daylight.

* * *

Taman turned his attention to his friends. Whistler, Elena and Tarz knelt on a stone bridge several feet away to his left and down from where he stood; Clay and Garadan pressed their backs together to his right, the raised section of rock they occupied only a couple of feet across. August perched precariously just above the two elves on a nearby column of stone.

Taman closed his eyes and steadied himself before taking inventory of his own position. He lowered his head and looked down. A platform no more than four feet square in diameter made up his world and he was just beyond the reach of all of his companions. No, there was one friend with him. He carefully squatted and picked up the pack, sighing with relief as May cautiously scampered out and hid inside his tunic.

Emhella pulled out the staff and faced his prisoners. Without a word, he opened the bottle containing the Red Fire. It drifted out of its confinement and hovered in the air before him. He repeated his actions with the Green Might but it was not as cooperative as the other magic. It undulated angrily, striking out at the demon like an angry cobra. It dodged his black shaft in its attempt to take flight but the demon's command was too strong. The companions' hopes melted away as the elven magic was finally brought under control. Next came the Source of Darkness. It immediately surged toward the Green Might, the diminished essences of those who once housed them still perceptible within the glittering mists. The two powers sought to intertwine. Emhella repeatedly blasted them with his energy, punishing them until they reluctantly took their place beside the Red Fire.

Emhella rotated his staff, the eddy of air drawing the powers in at a lethargic pace. He directed the magic to gyrate around his form, the satisfaction on his face transforming into elation as the ancient powers brushed against him. He slowly released his black energy into the whirling vortex creating a momentary swelling of the colors. A deep tone pulsed forth from the whirlpool of power and vibrated off the walls and the onlookers. Emhella closed his eyes.

August glanced up. The top edge of the wall was within climbing distance but the sharp rocky barrier offered no discernible handholds. He remembered the vision of the ruins that Mercator had shown them and wished he could recall something, anything that might help them. *Mercator knew all along we would fail,* he thought bitterly. *Why did he bother to send us out on this fool's quest?* He took a deep breath and exhaled.

Whistler's shoulder ached, the makeshift sling doing nothing to ease the pain. He pulled Elena close with his other arm. He wanted to place himself between her and Tarz but there was no room to maneuver. He tried to catch Taman's attention but the elf's focus was on his own dire predicament.

"How is he going to get off that strange pillar?" asked Whistler to no one in particular.

"We aren't exactly in any better position, dwarf."

"We wouldn't be here at all if you hadn't enslaved us!" Whistler's throbbing injury trumped his anger. He propped himself up against Elena, taking shallow breaths but that only amplified the agony.

"Please don't respond, Tarz, we're in enough trouble as it is."

The Rock Lord glared at them both for a moment then crossed his arms over his chest.

Perhaps I will not need to wait for the third circle after all. The phrase ran through Taman's mind yet again. Taman absently stuck his hand in his shirt and stroked the spider. He kept bracing himself for the rude thrust into the in-between world but that did not happen. Taman watched the powers blur together. He could just make out Emhella's grainy form holding the staff within the swirling mass. Taman stared at the gyrating column without blinking, the miniature bolts of lightning pulsating to an irregular rhythm. Emhella's confidence prompted him to complete the transformation tonight, one day shy of the third circle. Taman realized Emhella had all of the magic except for one so why wouldn't he feel self-assured? How hard could it be to coax the final power out into the open?

Taman looked up at the dark sky, the dreary clouds blocking out everything. All the information he had gathered studying the texts, maps, tomes and histories were useless in their present predicament. They needed ropes and ladders to escape this place, not words and paper. He pushed aside a dirty section of hair from his face then checked on his friends one more time. They had each started on their own particular quests but now stood together in their final hours, waiting as nervously as he did for Emhella's next move. What was it the monster had said? *'I will christen my citadel with the blood of kings and queens, gracious gifts from my long dead adversaries.'* Kings and queens indeed! Taman's mouth twisted into a bitter smile as he surveyed the ragtag group struggling to remain alive.

May climbed out of his tunic and onto his shoulder. She watched Emhella for a brief moment, her multi-faceted eyes reflecting the sparks flying out of the whirlwind. She turned to the companions, subtly nodding her head at each one then gazed down into the haze, her imperceptible whine lost within the chaos. May nuzzled Taman's neck and stroked his cheek with her leg, then lifted her head up. Two tiny fangs dripping with silver liquid gently bit into his jugular vein.

* * *

The Lady of the Sands inhaled deeply, nervously plucking at the edge of her bodice as she gazed eastward. Whatever transpired from this point forward was beyond her assistance. Helplessness overwhelmed her as she waited.

Mercator's motionless form waited on the other side of the mountain range in the north, his half-lidded eyes unreadable beneath the overcast sky. The Wraiths hovered nearby. The days of the old order were dwindling and would soon be gone. He sighed and spread his wings, pumping them once in the direction of the phantom dragons floating over the compass. The Essences of the Elements flared once then sped away.

"Go," he commanded the Kaiyeths.

The wraiths looked at him for a brief moment then headed for the mountains to the south, the four stones visible within their ethereal mist. Their features fluctuated, changing from tight-lipped frowns as they raced up the cliffs to uncertainty as they descended on the other side of the range. Fear crept into their faces as they hovered above the open space, their wide eyes no longer filled with the wrath and disapproval they had imposed upon the mortals. They surged into the forest at the base of the mountains, and disappeared into a copse of hazelnut and pine trees at the northern edge of the plains.

* * *

Taman's eyes widened but he was unable to lift his hands to remove the spider from his shoulder. Her venom seeped into his bloodstream, spreading rapidly outward to the rest of his body. It leached up into his head and blurred his vision with a pale, silver film

Taman's mouth was dry; his gaze darting in every direction. His body felt cold yet refreshed. He knew this sensation. It reminded him of walking outside in the middle of the night after a snowfall. Stars would glitter overhead in an inky sky and he could see the silhouettes of leafless trees. He'd inhale the invigorating frozen air and exhale, his breath condensing in front of his face. There would be silence, but not the kind that made him uneasy, but one that enveloped him with peacefulness. The pleasant sensation lasted for a moment only.

A relieved sigh whistled past Clay's lips as he spotted May clambering up Taman's shoulder. They had almost lost her after the expulsion from Mercator's realm then she had appeared ill and listless near the compound. Clay was ecstatic she hadn't plunged down into the noisome abyss, which they all still faced.

"We're all accounted for, Garadan." Clay pointed to Taman and the spider.

"Yes, but for how..." Garadan's face paled as he watched the spider bite into Taman's neck. Taman's body jerked once then became rigid seconds later.

"She bit him!"

The dwarves and Tarz also witnessed the bizarre event. Elena tilted her head to the side, her confused features mirroring her mates' expression. Tarz glared at the spectacle with disgust, and then glanced back to the movement going on in the center of the pit.

"It's changing," he said pointing to the demon.

August couldn't believe what he was seeing and shook his head as if to dislodge the image from his mind. He stared at the spider, her abdomen shrinking while her fangs remained buried in the elf's throat. She finally relinquished her hold on Taman, her leg weakly touching his skin once more before she tumbled off his shoulder, bounced once on the rock then perished into the void. A movement below caught his attention but he could not quite make out what it was.

Elena brought her hands to her face, terror pulsing from her eyes as she watched the powers stop spinning around Emhella. His stature hadn't changed yet he seemed to loom over them all. He still held the staff in his grip, tongues of fire crackling from one end. The flames reflected off his black eyes, the whites no longer visible. He glanced upward at the two circles around the full moon and smiled. Elena's fingers could not muffle her pitiable whimpers.

She could feel Tarz press his stiff body against the unyielding rock and Whistler's arm pulling her closer. She dared to look over at Clay and Garadan then at August. Sweat glistened on their skin; their stares filled with terrified expressions. They were at the mercy of this monster. Her attention shifted to Emhella.

Emhella wedged the staff into the rock between his feet, the abrupt release of power from the top of the rod casting ghostly shadows across his dark countenance. His cheeks, nose and eyes stood out starkly in the light while his forehead and sides of his face disappeared into darkness. For a brief second anguish replaced the triumphant expression on his face.

"Long have I waited for this moment." Emhella's voice boomed across the chasm, its deep timbre vibrating strongly enough to dislodge bits of dirt and pebbles from the edges. "Now I will prevail where Mahn failed. I do so in the presence of the descendants of those who challenged me centuries ago. You!" He pointed the end of the staff at the dwarves and Tarz, as a burst of shiny black power exploded onto the ledge beneath their feet.

Tarz swore as his fingers grasped at the uneven wall surface while the rock shelf he was standing on crumbled to within a foot of the wall. Elena suddenly stood on air and began to slip down into the nothingness, Whistler grabbing onto her tunic as she slid into the mist below. The dwarf's face twisted in agony as he tried to retain his balance while holding on to Elena, whose body dangled at an odd angle beside him.

"My revenge on you and your people is twofold," the demon bellowed waving the tip of his shaft menacingly at them. "I killed your king and his family and opened the way for that fool's dim-witted kin to enslave you," he glared at Tarz, who ignored the spiteful grin slowly distorting Emhella's features.

Tarz had no illusions about what Emhella had in store for them but he certainly wasn't going to make it easy for him. Quite the contrary. He leaned a little farther toward Elena, his back never losing contact with the rock wall behind them, and seized a handful of her tunic's material. His heavily muscled arm not only kept her from plummeting into the chasm below but also gave Whistler some respite.

"Still using the dwarves, I see," Emhella's words reverberated off the rock walls.

"Vas-ket," Tarz spat at the demon.

Emhella turned to August.

"Your ancestor has served me well, Herkah. It was well worth the price to inhabit his body. You shall witness Allad's terrible end and then follow him to the very bowels of the earth."

August narrowed his eyes at Emhella but remained silent.

"*And you*," Emhella could not keep the loathing out of his voice as his dead eyes turned to Clay. "You I detest most of all."

Clay started at Emhella's vehemence not just out of fear but also because of incomprehension. What in the four corners of the land could he have possibly done to the demon? He glanced over at Garadan; the captain's expression was also one of disbelief.

"Give me the Riannian," commanded Emhella.

"The what? I don't know what..."

Clay and Garadan twisted away from the sizzling bolt of energy zooming past them.

"*I sense it—give it to me!*"

"I don't have it!"

Emhella's menacing gaze shifted to Taman.

The world around Taman ceased to exist. The fog shifted, exposing fragments of images that seemed vaguely familiar yet he could not quite identify them. He swallowed hard as the haze dispersed leaving him standing in the very center of a swiftly flowing river. He could see his reflection in the clean waters. Droplets of water splashed across slate blue rocks protruding from the surface, the melodic sound eliciting a slight smile on his surprised features. He looked up into a beautiful turquoise sky then out across the waterway toward the unseen riverbanks.

What is this place?

A movement to his left caught Taman's attention. He turned to see what it was and cocked his head, his brows arched expectantly. The water began to swirl, forming an eddy moving so fast it pulled itself downward. Three more whirlpools took shape, each spiraling at a rapid rate. Taman leaned over as far as he dared trying to see the bottom of the vortexes but there was too much distance between them. A bubbling sound reached his ears then jets of water erupted from the swirling hollows, each one curving high into the brilliant blue sky before disappearing beyond his sight.

Taman stared after them long after they had vanished, their glistening magnificence etched into his memory. He replayed their graceful departure repeatedly in his mind until a faint booming broke his spell. He squinted at a burst of pale green gushing up from the waters, which was immediately followed by a pinkish and a light lavender spout moments later. A dim gray blast countered the beautiful arcs.

The explosions continued, the hues deepening with every outburst. Where there once was a pastel pink there now glowed a deep red. The soft green took on a hard emerald tinge while the delicate lavender glittered with an intense amethyst color. The gray transformed into an ominous black shade that threatened to steal all light. Taman watched the drama unfolding before him, the upheavals of dazzling colors keeping him from blinking lest he miss one amazing instant. Entranced by the vivid display, he lost himself in the sparkles sending tingles of excitement throughout his form. Then, the eruptions died away leaving him poised in an eerie silence. He stood still, his wide eyes searching for more when he gazed up into the murky sky then down at the water by his feet. It was thick and oily, lapping against the now coated rocks sticking up from the surface.

I know this place.

The contaminated water washed over his feet, the rivulets trickling back into the river clean and clear. Taman watched as the liquid flowing over his boots continued to transform from foul to fresh. The Riannian coursed through him urging him to cleanse what had taken countless centuries to sully. He needed to acquiesce to the demand or perish with the rest of the mortals.

Taman gave himself to the river's current, cringing as the filthy waters flowed into his core. Globs of waste and the ashes of used magic clogged his soul. He filtered the red sparks, too, the barbed existences of the demons mercilessly gouging his spirit as they passed through. The elf's vitality began to diminish, his body sagging as the force of the river poured through him. He was tiring, his bloated essence reeking of death and the muck of corruption.

Tarz looked down, the faint screeching sound drifting up through the haze. Movement caught his eye but it was too indistinct to identify. The commotion lasted for a few moments then ceased. He continued to stare, jumping as a bloody hand reached up and grabbed Elena's foot.

The dwarf looked down at the unexpected touch, flinching in fear at what was trying to yank her down into the ghostly fog. Her face lost all color as another hand seized her other foot and pulled harder this time.

"What the…?" Whistler said as both he and Tarz began to lose their grip on Elena. "Hold on, Tarz! Don't let her go."

It was too late. Elena was rudely wrenched from their hands. Whistler fell to his knees, frantically reaching into the mist for her when he, too, dropped out of sight. Tarz bonded with the rocky barrier, his hands raw from clutching the uneven surface. He did not intend to follow the dwarves to their certain death.

* * *

Sara awoke with a start. She coughed, the need to breathe taking precedence over the pain exploding from her neck. She rolled over onto her hands and knees, strings of saliva swinging from her mouth as she gasped for air. Pine needles, dirt and pebbles fell off her as she inhaled huge draughts of air, her brows squeezing together from within her crimson hued face. Her heartbeat and breathing returned to normal after many long minutes yet she could not find the strength to stand. She lifted her head and looked around, a few loose strands of hair stirred to life by some unseen wind.

She staggered to her feet, one hand tentatively touching her bruised neck as she left the confines of a small fissure. She took a step forward then stopped and looked down into an abyss expelling noxious vapors. The fog floated upward concealing a myriad of walkways. Sara cleared her throat, her eyes filling with tears as reality seeped into her soul. Emhella had built Varek-Tor.

Sara kept to the shadows as she crept around the structure ever mindful of what might be lurking in the darkness. She had traveled about a quarter of the way when the ground began to shake. She ducked and brought her arms over her head to protect herself from the debris raining down. She watched as two columns rose up from the chasm, the grating sound deafening from this position. She covered her ears, her teeth nearly jarred loose by the vibration. The tall sections of rock groaned and cracked beneath the force driving them up into the air. The mist parted for them and it was then that she saw her companions hanging onto their precarious perches. Her relief and the sudden appearance of demons from in between the fractures on the other side gave her the strength to move on.

Sara advanced toward the far section of the stony hollow, following the haphazard paths. She traveled forward for several yards then jumped onto an adjoining ridge heading ever onward. She kept track of the vague black bodies spreading out all around her, the mist obscuring the actual distance between them.

Red, green and lavender lights materialized above, the swirling mass of colors beginning to merge. She took a sharp intake of breath then scrambled up one stone bridge after another. The tips of her fingers became raw and her muscles protested but stopping to rest was out of the question. She picked up her pace then jumped back as something fell in front of her and disappeared beyond her sight. Urgency propelled Sara on.

Sara reached the rough barrier near where a pair of short boots swayed just beneath the mist's surface. She felt along the coarse wall. Perspiration beaded up on her face as she traced the length of the stone with her fingers. She gritted her teeth then bit her lip as precious time ticked by. She began to breathe more heavily as frustrated tears filled her eyes. A breeze ruffled the few strands of hair not plastered to her forehead. A half smile lifted the corners of her mouth, which faded away when a low growling arose from behind. Sara slowly turned around and slid out her knives.

The demons instantly attacked, the first two cut to shreds and kicked over the path before the remaining three covered half the distance to her. They whined and shrieked in fury, their fangs gnashing and claws slicing at the air in front of her. She chanced a quick glance toward Emhella. Her heart skipped a beat as she espied his form through the gauzy fog. The power transfer was complete. Sara struck hard and fast, eliminating the demons but not before one managed to rake his razor sharp nails across her left shoulder and chest. She winced with pain then drove her blade up its abdomen until it reached its robust jaw. Its innards spilled out, the rank stench nearly making her heave. More squat shadows filled the walkway, inching their way forward.

She stared at her wounds, the sickly light making her blood appear black. She caught her breath then resumed her place against the wall. Sara pushed away from the rocks and launched herself at the boots seizing with first one hand then with both as she tugged downward. She caught Elena, the shocked dwarf backing away from the demon while Sara grappled with Whistler. He crumpled to the ground then shot up to face his attacker, relief and suspicion fluctuating across his features as he recognized Sara. He gripped Elena's hand, glaring at Sara while the demon girl tried to convince Tarz to join them.

"I'm supposed to trust you?" he hissed at her.

"Come down or stay there and die, Rock Lord. The choice is yours."

Tarz looked over at Emhella brandishing his staff then at Clay and Garadan, their stone perch diminishing with every bolt of magic. Demons lined the walkway. The ledge he stood upon began to crumble beneath his feet. Tarz snorted once and slithered toward Sara.

August watched with trepidation as his friends vanished into the soupy mix. He frowned, concentrating and listening for screaming but no sound floated up to his ears. He glanced at Emhella, wanting desperately to help Clay and Garadan but he was too far away to be of any assistance. He began to move down the rough wall, cursing under his breath as the barrier claimed skin and blood. He huffed as his foot slipped on a brittle outcropping, his cheek burning as it scraped against stone. He glimpsed the ledge Whistler had occupied, deciding he would chance skidding down the last few feet. He tried to control his descent, his boot slipping off the shelf the second it made contact. August closed his eyes as debris filtered down on him and prayed there was something solid below him. Hands grabbed on and stabilized him as he fell into the haze; relieved faces steadied his composure.

"You have to leave that way," Sara whispered hoarsely pointing into the cavern. "Where's May? Which one of you has her?"

Tears welled up in her eyes as she watched August slowly shake his head, the loss in his expression telling her all she needed to know.

"What about Taman, Clay and Garadan?" demanded Whistler breaking through her grief, distrust clouding his features.

"Why aren't you coming with us? Are you trying to feed us to those fiends?" Tarz snarled.

"You can't do anything for them," she croaked regaining her composure while urging them into the cave with a wave of her hands. "Please do not waste any time arguing with me."

"We all go together," August intervened, his eyes searching her face.

"Some of us won't be leaving at all," she murmured looking away.

Tarz and the dwarves shifted nervously, watching August and Sara.

"Explain," August ordered.

"I'd like to know, too, August, but we have company," Tarz stated as he backed into the opening and away from a swarm of demons materializing out of the fog.

"Keep veering to the right," Sara's voice was barely audible, "there are steps leading up onto the plains."

August reached out and touched her face, the brief contact feeling like a lifetime. She pushed him into the darkness and braced herself for the onslaught. The hoard advanced, roused by the impending feast. Drool hung in long strands from their maws; claws clicked and scratched against the rocky walkway. She listened to the companions' retreating footsteps then froze as they became louder. *Why are they coming back?* They skidded to a halt behind her, Tarz' murderous gaze firmly affixed on Sara as the whining sounds echoed in the cavern behind them.

"They aren't supposed to be there!"

"Well they are!" Tarz roared at her, his face bright red.

Taman cringed as his soul purified the red flashes, each light extinguished once it passed through him. There were so many of them. He slumped over, the weight of straining the filth overwhelming him. His head flopped forward until his chin rested on his chest. *I...can't go...on.* Taman didn't see Emhella's interest shift to him nor did he notice that his friends, except for Clay and Garadan, were no longer visible.

Emhella ignored the elves, his ultimate prize there for the taking. He planted his staff into the rock and leaned against it, studying the overcome mortal housing the purest of all magic. He waved his hand across the abyss, scattering the noxious fog and exposing the group below.

The elves peered down and gasped. Hundreds of demons advanced on the group from the center of the chasm. Clay and Garadan's faces were frozen in horror as their friends glanced up at them, the resigned looks on their faces tearing at the elves' hearts. They were powerless to help them.

Emhella raised his rod and pointed it at Taman, the flare of liquid black jolting the elf upright. The demon grinned.

The Riannian's sense of urgency tore through Taman's exhaustion. She cooled his heated body and refreshed his flagging spirit, offering him support to complete the unenviable task of decontaminating the ancient stream.

Taman stirred from within his weariness and peered through half-closed eyes. The river was devoid of clutter, and bits of blue peeked through in the sky. He opened himself up to the stream once more, dreading the thorny lights progressing toward him. They entered him and scoured every corner of his being. The agony was unbearable.

Taman's companions watched in shock as he writhed from some unseen torture. They turned to Emhella but the demon's confused countenance offered them no clue. Sara slipped her hand into August's while Whistler wrapped his arm around Elena.

Tarz tapped Whistler on his hurt shoulder, the dwarf spinning around to confront him, but the look on the Rock Lord's face stilled his tongue. He followed Tarz' stunned gaze back toward the demons on the pathway, astounded as dozens of demons dissolved into thin air. The packs coming at them from within the cavern suffered the same fate. All of the fiends were gone within moments. The way out was unobstructed. Tarz pulled on Augusts' arm but the Herkah waved him off. The Rock Lord glanced longingly at the cavern then bolted into it.

Taman opened his eyes and squinted. The turquoise sky glowed protectively overhead; the river gurgled and splashed past his feet. A splotch of darkness in front of him marred the newness.

Clay and Garadan half slid, half clambered down the shaft, disregarding the trails of blood they left behind. Their friends frantically signaled to them, encouraging them to hurry. Clay glanced over at Taman as he ran and immediately regretted doing so. His foot caught the edge of the path and twisted outward forcing his body to teeter over the chasm. Garadan grabbed his garment and battled gravity for Clay's life. Clay regained control and, with a tug from Garadan, was soon dashing toward the others again. They stood huddled together watching the confrontation with dread.

Emhella raised his staff, the final piece there for the taking.

"Give me the Riannian."

Everything shimmered then faded away leaving Taman alone on an immense ice sheet, the watery sky devoid of sun and clouds. He slowly turned around, his apprehension increasing as the same vista extended outward in every direction. Nothing moved anywhere, not even a puff of wind. Taman absently touched the bite marks on his neck. He swallowed but could not dislodge the lump in his throat. A movement far in the distance caught his attention. He watched as four tiny black specks materialized in the sky, growing larger by the minute. He stared in fascination as they approached, their vague shapes composed of something he could not quite identify. They swelled in stature, transported toward him by large wings that beat the air without making a single sound. He blinked several times then took a step backward as they hovered in the air in front of him. Taman gaped at each of the four dragon-like outlines as they alit on the ground.

The closest dragon sported flames, which hugged its ethereal frame like undulating feathers; its companion wore plumes of grass and leaf filled branches. The third otherworldly beast raised its liquid wings, the foamy white edges hanging like frayed lace. The final creature fascinated Taman the most, its opaque form shifting and churning as if spurred on by some unseen wind. None of them had any discernable features.

Ancient is the blood flowing through your veins, mortal.

They spoke to him in unison, their voices neither male nor female. The words reverberating within his mind sounded like someone speaking while breathing in. Taman looked from one to the other, apprehension beginning to seep into his soul.

Who...who are you?
The Essences of the Elements, mortal.

Taman's stomach tightened.

Why am I here?
For purification.

The flaming dragon blazed brightly. Its head snaked toward him, its forked tongue of fire probing his face. Taman recoiled from the blistering heat, watching with mixed emotions as the others snapped at it to keep it at bay. Fear radiated outward from Taman's very core. It numbed his extremities and stole his voice.

Fire unexpectedly filled his vision then poured into his very being. He shuddered violently as the excruciating pain ripped through his body, the energy searing his flesh and bone. He sought shelter deep within himself, grabbing his memories to keep them safe from annihilation. The flames followed on his heels, his recollections quickly burnt to ash. His years in

Bystyn and the quest to find the heir vanished in a puff of smoke. He desperately tried to attach himself to the bits and pieces of his life but the fire razed everything without mercy. No, not everything. There, in the furthest recesses of his being was all the knowledge he had accumulated. Taman surged toward it, wrapping himself around the last vestiges of his existence as his world disappeared behind a blazing curtain of red and orange.

The wind dragon moved forward. It opened its indistinct jaws and exhaled on the immobile mortal, its breath lifting the powdery residue off Taman's motionless body.

Taman's soul skittered about like a dried out leaf on a cold winter's day, brushing up against the desiccated walls of his being. He stared without blinking at the parched landscape around him, fervently wishing for death to remove him from this horrible inferno.

He heard a far-off dripping sound then something cool trickled up against his withered spirit. It soothed away some of the pain and offered him a fleeting respite from the intense heat. Taman began to respond when great torrents of water suddenly rushed in and spread into every corner of his being. The liquid beat down on him, softening his desiccated inner world until it oozed like mud. He floated within the silt and sludge, desperately clutching the soggy remnants of his past life. The waters finally receded leaving a thick layer of fertile soil behind.

Taman lay partially buried in the dirt, his soul prodded by things pushing up from beneath him. The poking continued followed by the aroma of newly sprouted grass. Taman forced his crusted eyes to open. Clumps of bright green grasses and saplings clustered at the base of red-hued trunks, their blades and leaves heavy with dew. Dark green moss supported his head. He shifted his gaze until it focused on the white, smoky rays of light falling at an angle into the center of the glade.

Taman sat up and dispassionately surveyed his surroundings. The redolent boughs of the giant trees formed a canopy over his head; the seedlings blocked out everything beyond the clearing. Taman glanced down, cocking his head at the singed bits firmly clasped in his hands. He held them up then looked beyond them toward a hooded and cloaked figure approaching from the other side of the hollow. It drew near, its glittering silver mantle blending with the shafts of light. Taman lowered his arms then placed the fragments beneath a bush with waxy leaves and white berries. He rose to his feet and waited.

The shape crossed over to him, its graceful movements almost hypnotic. It stopped in front of Taman; a slender hand reached out and pushed back the hood. He gazed into a triangular face, a pair of multi-faceted black eyes reflecting his indifferent expression. Then, without warning, it lunged at him with fangs the length of his fingers…

"I *am* the Riannian." Taman vomited the vileness into the chasm far below, the greasy blackness soon lost in the murky void.

Bewilderment reigned on Emhella's face, the truth too slow to manifest itself within his mind. He unleashed a barrage of might from his rod, the impacts bouncing harmlessly off the elf. The demon hurled flames of red, green and amethyst at Taman with such force they enveloped him in a thick, acrid smoke. The haze cleared, revealing an unscathed elf. Emhella sent barrage after barrage at him with the same result. He leaned heavily on his staff, wondering what he had to do to obtain the magic Taman housed.

The elf raised his arms high in the air and closed his eyes. The gloomy sky began to brighten. The ominous clouds became ragged, their tattered borders fading away revealing a brilliant blue sky. A silvery mist formed around Taman's feet and spread outward, the air heavy with moisture. The vapor morphed into water, which flowed in a clockwise motion. Gray rocks jutted up from the surface, as did the two columns on which the demon and the elf stood.

Clay cringed, memories of a long ago dream tugging at his mind: a vast ocean, a giant monster and rows of sharp, serrated teeth.

Emhella recoiled from the clear water. He rammed the tip of the staff into the rock and, with a turn created a vortex that kept the river from touching him. The stream continued to rise, the water forming a liquid cocoon around him. It ascended past his shoulders and up beyond his head. The demon glared at the water, increasing the height of the whirlpool with another flick of his wrist. The column of water and the river raced upward, first one then the other taking the lead.

"This could go on for eternity," muttered Garadan.

"It could, but it won't. Look," August said pointing at the demon.

Emhella glowered at the staff, daring it not to keep up with his command. The knuckles on his hands glowed whitely, the veins and tendons bulging from beneath the stretched skin. He ceased paying attention to the mortals and to anything else outside of his bubble of safety.

A tic twitched the corner of his mouth then his head struggled to remain in position. A curious look radiated out of his eyes before understanding then apprehension replaced it. His body quivered; his hands shaking with more and more urgency as the minutes passed. Emhella exerted more pressure on the rod yet his fingers lost their grip. The staff spun wildly within his loose grasp, fragments of flesh and skin flung into the river. Emhella's head bobbed up and down then to the side, his mouth and eyes opening and closing in slow motion. His body soon followed suit, squirming and thrashing about as if he were a snake shedding its skin. The panic erupting in his eyes was swiftly replaced with another emotion: triumph.

The body stood up straight and proud as a black, grainy haze poured out and cowered near the feet. Black eyes glittered dangerously as they absorbed everything around them. They bored into each of the members, scrutinizing their worth.

August stared at the proud face of Allad. The evil within had distorted the features over the centuries but it could never erase the dignity that had entwined itself with the man's essence. August moved onto the walkway, made a fist with his right hand and brought it to his chest. He bowed deeply to Allad. Tarz joined him as did all the others, the homage they paid to the Herkah warrior transcending time and Race.

Allad inclined his head to them then smashed his arms into the whirlpool encasing him and Emhella's remnants. The entire eddy collapsed with a whoosh.

"You should have waited for the third circle," Sara whispered to the disintegrating vestiges of what once was their foe.

The in-between place shone brilliantly for a few seconds then slowly faded from view taking Taman with it. The elf scrutinized the mortals one last time before vanishing within the otherworldly panorama.

THE FORTRESS OF DARKNESS

The members of the quest stood rooted in place, staring at the empty space before them. A low rumbling deep beneath their feet shook them out of their trance. Dirt and stones vibrated crazily on the rupturing ground. They turned as one and rushed into the cavern, their arms and legs pumping faster and faster as the booming explosions behind them liberated the loose rocks in the cave.

Clay vaulted over a fissure on the floor, his sore ankle unable to bear his weight as he landed on the other side. He grimaced and lost his balance, tumbling awkwardly amongst the debris. Garadan grabbed him by his collar and yanked him to his feet, draping one of Clay's arms over his shoulder as he helped him toward the staircase barely visible through the dust. They coughed and gagged, squinting as they labored to reach safety. The others began their ascent, looking back to see how the companions were faring. Sara started to head back to assist them but Garadan waved her on. She hesitated, the collapsing ceiling seconds away from engulfing the pair. Heedless of the disintegrating structure, she sprinted toward them and slung Clay's other arm over her shoulder, the three of them rapidly reaching the steps just as the edifice caved in on itself. Tarz and the dwarves heaved Clay out of the chaos while Garadan tossed Sara out onto the plains. The group frantically tried to get a hold of Garadan's hands but were forced back to watch in horror as tons of rock came crashing down on the captain.

The immediate area shuddered intermittently prompting the companions to move to a safer distance. They stopped near the first line of buildings by the compound and stared at the pile of rubble smoldering on the plains. A streak of red burst out from the ruins arching eastward; an amethyst streak flashed as it headed west. Then, the Green Might exploded up from the wreckage. It hovered for an instant in the early evening sky then plunged toward the companions. Frightened, they scattered in every direction desperately avoiding obliteration by the elven magic. The power cast an eerie glow on everything, the sea green hue deepening the closer the magic drew near. It whistled shrilly as it descended, tongues of electrical energy lifting the hair on their bodies and irritating their skin. It pulsed brightly then slammed into the ground, sending the companions tumbling to the hard earth.

Quiet ensued, the group climbing to their feet to check on each other. All rose except for Clay, the elf lying motionless on the ground.

Clay felt the Green Might's intensity blaze through him, the prickly sensations spreading into every corner of his being. His lids slowly opened, his gaze drawn to a silhouette standing within the swirling steam. Eyes filled with roiling clouds punctuated the swarthy countenance while a hint of unearthly power radiated from his entire being. He wore a long, dark cloak, the frayed hem branching out like roots from a tree.

Taman? Are you hurt?

The shade shook his head.

Am I dead?

The apparition bowed low to him.

What are you doing?

Acknowledging the King of the Elves.

King…no, I'm just a…

The Green Might does not choose just anyone, Clay.

Clay's longing to find his family took an unexpected turn. He would have laughed at anyone who might have made this claim to him prior to undertaking this quest. He glanced around the eerie gloom seeking a reason or an excuse to extract himself from the awesome responsibility Taman placed on his shoulders. All he could find were his own doubts.

I know nothing of courts or ruling a city or if they'll even accept me as an elf let alone a king!

Place your trust in Lord Balyd and Lady Wyntyn.

You would have made a good king, Taman.

I was not meant to reign in the land of the living.

What do you mean?

I am the Keeper of the Fortress of Darkness. My realm is not for those composed of flesh and blood.

Taman gazed beyond Clay for a moment then he melted away into the darkness.

Clay watched the mist close in front of him, concealing his briefly known friend. The vapor dissipated revealing the moonlit plains, his companions kneeling beside him. He raised himself up on his elbows and studied their frightened faces. Bits of dirt fell out of their hair and off their ragged clothing whenever they moved. He looked at Tarz, the arrogance and hatred replaced with uncertainty. August and Sara knelt together beside him, their bodies touching, their journey marked by the perceptible bond between them. Clay was destined to rule the elves; Whistler and Elena the dwarves. At least he had allies outside of Bystyn's walls.

Soft white lights unexpectedly materialized near where Garadan lay beneath Varek-Tor's edges. They shifted, forming three nebulous shapes, a fourth one disentangling itself from the rubble soon joining them. They faced one another, the solitary ghost's shoulders hunched forward. Garadan's men bowed their heads to him, their fists against their opaque chests. They reached out to him, embracing their leader and friend. Garadan held them close, his soul peaceful at last. A southwest breeze blew over the plains. It gently picked up and carried the spirits home.

Sara rested her head on August's shoulder, her tears falling on his worn tunic. Whistler held Elena tightly. Tarz' hands were on his hips, his drawn features pensive. Clay stared at the retreating image with sadness.

-17-

They sat clustered within the storage shed sharing a meal they did not taste. Elena hung Whistler's arm in a sling made of shredded cloth and bound Clay's swollen ankle. She cleansed their scratches with clean water then took a seat beside her mate. There was nothing she could do for Sara's neck.

"What befell May?" Sara asked in a soft voice.

She listened while Clay revealed the spider's end. August gently wrapped his arm around her and pulled her close, resting his cheek against the top of her head.

"The Riannian," muttered the demon girl, her tone laced with awe and sorrow. "May housed a portion of the magic from which all other energies were derived."

"But why bite Taman?" inquired Elena.

"Because it was his lot to cleanse all the evil that had polluted that enigmatic place," Clay leaned against the wall, Taman's shrouded image filling his vision.

I am the Keeper of Darkness, echoed in Clay's mind.

"I'm sorry I sank my teeth into your throat, Clay."

"Don't forget about handing over the Green Might," grumbled Tarz, ignoring Whistler who was defiantly shifting his position and glaring at him. "Did you enjoy the taste of his blood?"

Elena raised her hand as Whistler got to his feet, daring the Rock Lord to continue insulting the demon girl.

"He has the right to ask those questions, Whistler. Emhella would have destroyed whoever refused to hand over the magic and, yes and no, about Clay's blood. It is not, however, something I'll do ever again."

"What will you and Elena do now?" August's voice broke the silence.

"We'll remain in the compound until next year then send a group of dwarves to Evan's Peak and see what we need to do to make it livable again. And you three?"

"We're going to Bystyn," replied Clay, the determination in his speech matching the focus in his eyes.

They stood in a loose circle, the sun shining from a dazzling blue sky. No one spoke for the longest time, each lost in their own thoughts as they waited to say their farewells. The odd collection of individuals had begun their separate missions, only to be thrust together to save the land. Hugs and handshakes firmly cemented the bonds that had grown over the course of many weeks of danger and sorrow. Sara kissed Whistler on the cheek eliciting a great deal of laughter as the dwarfs face burned crimson. Even Tarz managed a half smile.

"We'll be in touch," Clay promised them then he, Sara and August mounted two horses donated by Tarz and headed west.

Whistler and Elena watched them ride away, a pensive Tarz standing a few feet to one side. She rested her head against his shoulder and sighed deeply.

"Do you think we'll ever see them again?"

"Without a doubt, Elena."

The trio studied the pile of rubble as they galloped past it. Thick bands of smoke curled up into the clear morning; the stench of sulfur adhered to their clothing. The heap appeared lower than the previous night, the ground forced to consume its own waste. In time, nothing but an ugly scar would remain.

They made good time, reaching the edge of the woodlands by late afternoon. August suddenly smiled as two black shapes emerged from the tree line.

"Essa! Tauth!" he called to them.

The horses reared, raising their front legs up high then flew like the wind toward them.

"Where were you two when we needed you?" scolded Clay dismounting his stocky horse. He stroked Essa's silken mane then patted her graceful neck.

"We should let Tarz' animals return," suggested August.

They released the borrowed mounts to gallop back the way they had come, then they climbed on top of Essa and Tauth, Sara sitting behind August, and rode on.

I don't want to be king of the elves. Clay silently chewed over the vast responsibility that could very well be thrust his way. All he wanted was to find his family and go on wandering the land with August. He glanced over at the pair riding beside him. A bittersweet smile touched his lips. August would forever be his friend but their days of roaming together were over. The demon girl now made up August's world. He sighed and silently wished them well, hoping that they would find the peace they so deserved. A jolt of energy yanked Clay back to reality. The brief bursts had flared up ever since the Green Might had poured into him. The magic reminded him that, like it or not, he had a duty to fulfill. Clay hung his head in resignation.

* * *

They halted about a mile outside the city gates, waiting for the patrol to approach them nearly a week after leaving the compound. The companions watched one of the sentries peel away and hasten back to Bystyn. The leader of the unit, much to their dismay, was the same unfriendly elf who had demanded they leave elven lands weeks ago.

Sara shivered as she looked at a cluster of dilapidated buildings at the edge of the orchard, especially the ramshackle farmhouse. An air of disquiet emanated from within its collapsed shell. She pressed herself closer against August's body but even his hand placed reassuringly on hers did nothing to appease her trepidation. Sara glanced northward toward a dense stand of hazel and pine trees. A peculiar sensation washed over her, one that connected with something deep inside of her. She narrowed her eyes as an image began to develop in her mind…

An old woman with long white hair and pale skin gently dabbed a cloth across an aged elf's forehead as he lay in bed beneath a mountain of quilts. She held a handkerchief against his lips while he coughed then helped him drink from a mug. He struggled to lift a gnarled hand up to her face, his stiff fingers brushing against her cheek. She smiled at him and kissed his hand then tucked the blankets up under his chin. She blew out all of the lamps save one, which she turned down low and carried it to her nightstand. She removed her robe and eased her thin body into bed beside him; her head nestled on his shoulder and her hand on his chest. The old woman did not sleep. She watched as the elf's breathing changed from steady to labored. He awoke and called to her. She soothed away his anxiety and whispered something into his ear. He smiled and turned his head. Their lips met and for a brief moment they were young again. Her red-gold hair spilled across his body; his emerald green eyes sparkled with life and love. The fleeting instant passed. The woman's tears dripped onto the blue and green quilt as she lovingly stroked his cheek. She slowly faced Sara, the heart wrenching grief in her eyes overwhelming Sara...

Sara wiped away the vision as she brushed away the tears, a sudden sense of loss flooding through her being. She wanted to ride into the thicket to find out what secret lay hidden within the aromatic boughs, but August's voice broke the spell it had on her. Their present predicament chased away her need to investigate. For now, anyway.

"This does not bode well," muttered August.

The riders stopped a short distance away, the hard-faced guard analyzing all three of them, especially Clay. August and Sara shifted nervously in the saddle but Clay met his gaze unflinchingly.

"I am Captain Ansar. Lord Balyd and Lady Wyntyn await your arrival."

Taman's words echoed through his mind, *Place your trust in Lord Balyd and Lady Wyntyn.* Clay nodded in response, unaware of his friends exchanging perplexed glances.

They rode up the main avenue, the companions trying hard not to gawk at everything they passed. Crowds of elves stood upon stoops or tilted out of windows, the sound of the horses' hooves speeding up the avenue drawing them away from their daily chores. Two-story homes constructed of stone and timber huddled up against swept walkways; bright red geraniums, yellow button-like flowers and herbs spilled from window boxes and planters. A cat groomed its pure white fur on a windowsill paying no attention to the commotion out in the street. A little girl clutched a yarn doll; a boy with cowlicks eyed the strangers with curiosity. The older folk stood with crossed arms, watchful and wary; the younger elves rested their hands on their hips wondering who these injured outsiders were.

Sara clung to August, the sight of so many people at once unfamiliar to her. She felt August's hand rest on hers but that did nothing to alleviate her anxiety. She missed May's reassuring presence, her playful tugging and nuzzling forever stored in her heart. The townspeople stared at her openly, their apprehension palpable in the warm morning air.

Captain Ansar rode in the forefront, his back ramrod straight, and his expression serious but for a subtle upturn of the corner of his mouth. Caladan's accusation had stripped the lord of any influence allowing Ansar to emerge from seclusion. He had planned to return to his station in the west but opted to remain in the city to aid Balyd in his search for an heir. He was glad he had remained. The procession passed by the damaged front entry, heading toward the functional side door instead. They dismounted and followed Ansar into the very soul of the elven kingdom.

The huge oaken doors to the conference hall opened without a single creak revealing a vast chamber filled with the members of the court. They milled amongst each other talking in quiet tones about the unscheduled meeting. When Ansar entered with the unfamiliar people, they took their seats lining the room. Ansar bowed to Lord Balyd and Lady Wyntyn; Clay, August and Sara spread out behind him. The trio offered the elves a respectful nod.

"What are your names?" Balyd asked, moving closer.

"I am Clay and these are my friends, August of the Herkahs and Sara."

Heads swiveled back and forth as the court members whispered to each other, some of the lords and ladies gesturing to the group standing before them.

Balyd glanced over at August, the storied Herkahs long absent and nearly forgotten. It wouldn't have been so had the elven rulers since

Alyssa's time not ignored their stalwart allies. With any luck that would change. Sara's timidity and delicate features were in sharp contrast to the talon-like fingers she balled up into fists. And to the purple bruising around her neck. "And you are from?"

"I am part demon, elven Lord," she replied hoarsely stroking her throat.

The crowd's murmuring increased, the unfriendly sound echoing in the hall.

"What is the other part?" he gently persisted, more confused than shocked at her confession.

"Elven."

His brow shot toward his hairline. Part demon *and* part elf? He raised his hand to silence the thunderous crowd. It took several minutes for them to calm down.

"Lord Balyd," Clay's anxiety slowly subsided, "Taman assured me you could be trusted."

Balyd's face brightened. "Where are Taman and Garadan?" Clay's subdued grief elicited a sharp pang in his chest.

"Garadan gave his life for us and Taman..." How was he supposed to explain about Taman? That he now guarded the wickedness that nearly obliterated everything in the land? "Taman stands between the living and the evil."

"That will have to be more fully clarified later on, won't it?"

"Yes, Lord Balyd."

"Ansar? Would you care to enlighten the members of the court as to why these three strangers are here today?"

Ansar stood in the center of the chamber, inhaled deeply and revealed what he knew.

"Many years ago a woman came to the city seeking an audience with Queen Tryssa," he began in a clear voice devoid of doubt. "She was heavy with child and claimed that she was descended from Prince Danyl and Lady Ramira. I passed the information on to Queen Tryssa who ordered me to eliminate the challenger to the throne."

The lords and ladies suddenly gasped and an immediate roar of disapproval and calls of 'liar' filled the hall. Caladan smirked, his chagrin morphing into justification. He popped up out of his seat, his mouth opening and his long, lean finger pointing at Balyd.

"Sit down, Caladan!" Lady Wyntyn's voice ripped his bravado away. He plopped back down glowering at her reprimand and waited in the sudden quiet for Ansar to go on.

"The woman died while giving birth to two children, one boy and the other one unknown. I gave both newborns to Altac, my second in command, who took them I know not where. Altac took that secret to his grave. Years passed and I never heard anything about them again until, one day earlier this summer, I came across these three. I stared at Clay and, without fully understanding at that moment, realized I was looking at one of the newborns."

I have a sibling? Clay furrowed his brows, his stomach fluttering with a sense of excitement at the prospect of finding a member of his family.

"A king? Is he telling us that Clay is supposed to be the next ruler of Bystyn?" August whispered into Sara's ear. She shrugged her shoulders as baffled by what was transpiring as everyone else.

"We know of Aryanda's cousins' lineage, Lord Balyd," stated one of the lords glancing questionably over at Clay, "his is unknown."

"That's a very good point," conceded Balyd. "Ansar, did this woman give you anything linking her claim to the throne?"

"No, Lord Balyd."

Shouts of disapproval filled the air like a flock of birds taking flight. Dalk may not have been the best choice to sit on the throne but at least royal blood flowed through his veins. The dissensions continued no matter how often or how high Balyd held his hands for quiet. The elves were simply not going to allow a total stranger access to the imperial seat.

"How can he be considered a candidate to become king without proper credentials?" shouted more than one voice.

"Whose interests does he have in mind?" bellowed someone from the gallery.

"How do we even know his lineage?"

"How will his ascension benefit you, Balyd?" demanded Caladan standing a few feet away from the First Advisor.

Balyd glared at Caladan, the pent up frustrations accumulated over the decades surging to the forefront. The First Advisor's eyes bored into Caladan, the bile rising into his throat.

Clay's vision blurred as an emerald mist stirred to life and seeped outward. A cool, tingling sensation caressed him inwardly as it rose from the depths of his soul. The elven magic leached out from his form enveloping him in a glittering green haze. Clay could not see the dumbfounded faces or hear the sharp intakes of breath of those gathered. The power cocooned him from the collective disbelief. The magic frightened him, stealing his confidence and convictions. It began to burn into his spirit, searing into his very self. Then, a figure emerged from the surreal fog, one whose face could have been his own.

Cast aside your doubts, Clay, or the magic will reduce you to ashes.

The shape placed a hand on his shoulder and gazed deep into Clay's soul. Clay flinched from the contact, its command unrelenting as it probed the very places he had sought desperately to conceal. He coaxed out Clay's loneliness, doubt and despondency and exposed his senseless need to cling to them.

A king must never house these demons or they will destroy you and your people.

Clay did not know his name but felt the thread of kinship beginning to interlace with his essence. A woman appeared before him; her long, chestnut brown hair tied with a green ribbon, her dark gray eyes radiating compassion. She smiled at Clay, her slender golden arm reaching out toward him. She caressed his face, the touch stimulating an innate sensation from deep within Clay. He leaned his head into her embrace, her touch eliciting tears of joy and sorrow. She began to dissolve and not even his hand desperately groping at the thinning air could keep her from disappearing. He absorbed her lingering emotions and drew strength from the brief encounter. He cast away his doubts and ceased fighting the power allowing it to take over him.

August and Sara staggered backward as Clay's body emitted pulses of green light. The aura spun first in lazy circles around the elf then picked up speed. Bursts of energy shook loose, scattering the mortals as they sought cover from the might. Arms lifted up to shield their eyes from the blinding radiance until a resounding *boom* knocked everyone to the floor. August dared to glance over at Clay, his form sheathed in an emerald glow. It pulsed for several moments then faded away leaving a different Clay behind. Confidence held his back erect; clarity emanated from his eyes.

"I think," Lord Balyd stood up on shaking legs, staring wide-eyed at Clay, "he needs no other claim to the throne. Are there any dissenters?" Balyd looked around the chamber at the awestruck faces. "I thought not. Lady Wyntyn?"

Caladan watched as Lady Wyntyn walked over to Clay, the visceral need to possess power overcoming his astonishment at what he had just witnessed. The Green Might may have chosen to reside in this stranger but the power itself couldn't transform this elf into a king. Experience, knowledge and insight were vital in elevating this outsider to that status. That and support from the court. He casually glanced around at the members of the court. They wore a number of different emotions on their faces but the one they all shared was skepticism. Caladan smiled inwardly.

The woman with the regal bearing approached Clay and bowed low to him. Balyd and every other member of the court moved forward to pay their respects to their new king. A reddish tinge crept into Clay's cheeks as he gazed upon a sea of unfamiliar faces. *Orphaned, abandoned then kicked off elven lands like some drunkard out of a tavern. Now I will be king of all who sought to rid themselves of me. Life takes some interesting turns sometimes.*

Last to honor Clay were August and Sara.

"A king, eh? No wonder I did all the chores," August stated good-naturedly.

"This is all very strange to me, too, Augie."

"I guess we all got what we wanted," Sara's soft voice drifted over to Clay and August, "You are finally home and August and I are about to set up our own household."

"Will you two stay?"

"For a little while," replied August, his fingers intertwining with Sara's cool ones.

August felt the unseen winds of the desert on his face and the yielding sands beneath his body. He and Clay had traveled many miles together and shared in adventures few could have imagined. They had been the closest of friends for years, a bond that would remain strong forever. Their roads, however, would now take different paths.

* * *

The Lady of the Sands watched the cloaked specter as it espied a figure waiting on the crest of a silver dune. It descended without disturbing a single grain and hurried toward the ghost rushing forward to meet it.

Welcome home, my love.

The faint outlines embraced, their ethereal faces blending for that long awaited kiss. Allad picked Zada up in his arms, the two of them savoring their reunion. Too long had she wept; too long had he endured the wrath of the demon. Their essences spiraled together, merging as one until they formed a brilliant mist of silver that surged high into the star-speckled night before falling back and vanishing into the sands.

The Lady of the Sands stared out across the endless land, her gaze fixed on the undulating horizon. She crossed her arms, resting her hands on her shoulders. Creases marred the areas around her tired eyes and across her forehead. She sighed heavily and dissolved into a silvery cloud, the sparkles comprising the thickest part of the mass no longer as bright as before.